The clouds parted and the black surface of the Arctic Ocean came into view.

Before the plane stretched the long corridor of water opened by the vessels, flanked on either side by fractured pieces of floating ice.

"What the hell is *that*?" one of the flight engineers suddenly said. He pointed toward the sea roughly half the distance to the horizon.

Then the others saw it: a distortion in the surface. Seconds later, the sea itself rose up, flicking along its length like a carpet being shaken. The ocean rolled and exploded upward, flinging huge chunks of ice aside. For a moment, the water seemed suddenly to be speeding up at them, then just as suddenly it passed below, streaking to the east and falling away behind the bombers.

The captain thought he knew what he had seen but could not fully comprehend it. Then he thought of the ships below them and wondered if they could see the massive wall of water rising up from the ocean.

In the time it took him to reach for his radio, the damage was already done. . . .

"Outstanding ... terrifying ... all-too-real."
—Abilene Reporter-News (Tex.)

MELTDOWN

James Powlik

A DELL BOOK

Published by
Dell Publishing
a division of
Random House, Inc.
1540 Broadway
New York, New York 10036

ISBN: 0-440-23509-X

Manufactured in the United States of America

Published simultaneously in Canada

March 2002

10 9 8 7 6 5 4 3 2 1

OPM

DISCLAIMER

The setting and locations in this story are real. The organisms and biogeography of the organisms described are also real, with the exception of *Thiobacillus univerra ferrooxidans* and *Ulva morina,* which are based on real-world equivalents. The scientific and military programs, methods, data, and theory presented are authentic to the extent that they complement this dramatization. "Global Oil" and "Pegasus Chemicals" are fictional corporations in this context.

All events and persons depicted are fictitious. Any similarity to actual events or persons either living or dead is coincidental and unintended.

For Carl

MELTDOWN

We do not believe, we fear.

—FROM THE INUIT RELIGION

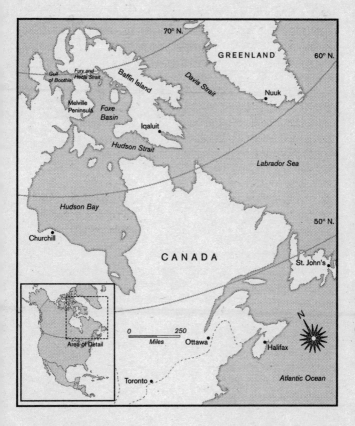

PROLOGUE

Late spring
Melville Peninsula, Nunavut, Canada

The tooth came out easily in Victor Tablinivik's hand, a mature incisor nearly an inch long and intact to the root. It was yellowed from infrequent cleaning, worn and chipped from its occasional use as a tool, but looked otherwise healthy—just like all the others. Victor took a moment to count: three in the past month alone. He knew by now that it did no good to simply jab the teeth back into their fleshy sockets and hope that they would root again. His gums, it seemed, were growing tired of them. They didn't even bleed in sorrow as much as they could have; a minute daub of blood, another, then only a small crater remained to prove that the tooth had ever been a part of him.

At a relatively young age, Victor found it commonplace to find pieces of himself coming off. He supposed such things came with age and so did not know if that distressed him; he had never before grown old. Certainly it was very unlike the aging of his parents and his parents' parents before them.

In Victor's memory, it seemed that one day his father and mother were there, the next they had been claimed by the bad spirit with the queer-sounding name: *lewkeemeeah*. Victor was raised to adulthood by his grandparents before the government *qablunaq*—white men, or "heavy eyebrows" in the Inuktitut language— came through the territory, held meetings in all the settlements, and talked about this new problem the Inuit had known of for years. Few Inuit really listened to the lectures. For this generation and the one before it, the heavy eyebrows furrowed about *lewkeemeeah*. When Victor's grandparents were still children, missionaries and doctors had come to the Arctic and told the Inuit they had *tooburqlosus,* or *small-pocks.* They had once talked about the *meesuls,* too, and how nine out of every ten men could die in an "unprepared population" like the settlement where Victor was born. The *qablunaq* admitted they weren't exactly sure what to do about this *lewkeemeeah* because it could kill quickly or very slowly or not kill at all. Victor had to laugh at that. Just being Inuit meant being killed very slowly—what did *lewkeemeeah* have to do with anything? Until the *qablunaq* brought their diseases to the Arctic, the Inuit had been prepared just fine. So what, in the perspective of the horizon that all Inuit adopt, did one more orphan or a handful of teeth matter anyhow?

The Arctic is as fluid as the sea ice itself. For as long as Victor had been old enough to notice such things, this territory was re-created differently each season. In a matter of days or weeks, entire camps were displaced miles by the moving ice or were lost to the sudden opening of new crevasses. Landfast ice broke free to become new islands while the great slabs of sea ice crunched together to form bridges or thrust up new hummocks too large to traverse.

Nunavut—"Our Land" in the Inuktitut language— represented the first major change in Canada's geography since 1949, when Newfoundland became a province. After parliamentary debate lasting nearly three decades, Nunavut had officially come into existence on April 1, 1999. Encompassing nearly 1.4 million square miles of the former Northwest Territories, one-fifth of Canada's land area, this new land was now home to some twenty-four thousand northern natives, more than 80 percent of them Inuit. Stretching from Ellesmere Island to Hudson Bay, from Baffin Island nearly to Great Bear Lake, it did look impressive on the freshly inked *qablunaq* maps. But to Inuit who knew about April Fool's Day, the transfer date seemed bitterly appropriate. During an early referendum to decide the name of this new land, dozens of Inuit had voted for BOB as a write-in candidate on their ballots; for generations, the people of Canada's north had referred to themselves as "bob," or "bottom of the barrel" in terms of recognition or support from the federal legislature in Ottawa. New land, old problems—the government had never understood this. What the diseases didn't take, or the sea swallow up, the complicated land claims now engulfed no matter how nonpartisan they tried to be. To try to place such boundaries on the slippery arctic ice was like trying to chew seal meat without teeth.

Victor looked again at the tooth in the broad palm of his polar bear–skin mitt. It was a fine mitt his wife had sewn with waterproof stitches, forsaking nylon thread to use caribou sinew in the traditional way. "In the traditional way" was an expression the *qablunaq* used to describe what they took to be the sad, quaintly primitive condition of Victor's people. By now, the Inuit had had generations of experience with the condescension of the *qablunaq*. Ironically, with their books and cameras and exhibits, it now seemed as though the *qablunaq* were more interested than were Victor's own people in keeping alive the Inuit traditions. There was

much irony in this, since the first *qablunaq* had mocked
the Inuit ways, calling them primitive and barbaric. It
was the *qablunaq* who had brought more unnatural
change than the Inuit had ever known and so began—as
Victor's grandmother called it—the fraying of the village threads.

Victor's grandmother had been one of the finest Inuit
seamstresses of her generation. Her designs with seal-
skin and caribou hides had been reproduced all across
the Arctic, were often worn at festivals and dances, and
were highly valued by museums and souvenir collec-
tors. Victor's grandfather had been one of the last true
shamans in the Central Arctic, a proud *angatkuk* who
had filled his grandson with the oral history of their culture from a very early age. It was Victor's charge to
learn of the spirits, the traditions, and the responsibili-
ties of his people.

To fully understand the Inuit is to know that the people are not distinct from their culture, their environment,
or the wildlife around them. In the distant—but not too
distant—past, to be an Inuit was to know hunger, or at
least to know *of* hunger and fear it greatly. In the hunt, as
in the community, avoiding hunger was a priority above
nearly all else. Victor remembered a winter of his childhood when the famine came especially hard and his
mother had willingly suffocated her own daughter in
order to spare food for the hunters in the village.
Historically, in times of famine, the hunters were always
the last to go hungry, for they were the only possible salvation for the village. For nomads traveling far with limited sustenance, acts such as cannibalism, infanticide, or
sacrificing sled dogs for their meat were not debated;
they were essential for survival. Girls were considered
expendable to the village, since they were often married
off by the time they were old enough to contribute useful
work. There was no retribution to be paid, no talk of the
dead as the baby girls disappeared one by one or the eld-

ers were left behind. The outposts had to move as the animals moved, and all had to move with the ice.

Victor did not cry when he learned of his sister's death, in part because he feared his father's rebuke and in part because he understood the significance of his own life being spared. In the traditional way, there is no beginning or end to the existence of the soul. A life is lived not to prepare for some hoped-for afterlife, but simply to survive, to acquire the basic needs of life in order to continue living, and to live that life in a manner that does not offend the spirits. The modern Inuit seemed to forget this a little more with each generation, and as a result, Victor feared the end of the Inuit soul. This fear and the personal sadness of his grandparents' last years haunted Victor and pushed him onward in his hunting every single day. Even if his catch did not reward this resolute dedication, the spirits would see Victor's efforts and, if he was fortunate, smile upon his family. At a minimum, they would let him catch enough food to feed his wife, Anika, and his young son, Annu. Having enough to eat was the best blessing for which an Inuk could ever ask.

Victor put the tooth into the pocket of his pullover jacket with the other pieces of himself—the ones he'd managed to find, anyway. He still liked the feel of caribou skin against his own and had Anika make his inner layers of clothing in the traditional manner. On the other hand, his outer jacket had been made by *qablunaq* of something called Gore-Tex. It was a little garish, but it was warm and did not retain moisture like the caribou pelts. On his head he wore a tuque made of synthetic black wool with the spirit of ADIDAS carefully embroidered on it in white cotton thread; on his feet, a pair of winter boots and thick wool socks from the outpost store. Victor had never found any gloves to be as warm and durable as those of polar-bear hide, so these his wife made for him, replacing each pair as they wore thin. Polar bears, too, were less abundant, and those that remained were protected by the *qablunaq* and their laws. Others—the poachers and the tourists—didn't always follow the *qablunaq* laws, and so, sometimes, neither did Victor. He carried his flaying knife, his fishing hooks, harpoons, ropes, and rifle, and he took whatever the spirits let him catch.

Always there were the spirits of his ancestors with him, so Victor never felt he was alone. And always, always, he had his dog. Victor had found the dog—a Siberian husky, weak from a skirmish with another carnivore and nearly starved to death—in the wilderness north of Pelly Bay. The dog had a snow-white mask and a thick, peppered coat worn ragged in places, but a strong chest and a healthy, upturned curl in her tail. Her sharp, unwavering eyes were subtly but uniquely mismatched in color, one blue and the other a curious gray. Victor saw hunting potential in the stray and had taken home his valuable find. His kindness had been rewarded. The dog was a truly excellent hunter, and she had stayed with him for the past five years. She could be lazy, but with her feral instincts she could sniff out seal breathing holes better than almost any dog Victor had ever seen, all the more amazing when one considered the art of ice fishing for seal hadn't been practiced much in at least a generation.

The husky was obedient and never begged for more food or rest than the hunter allowed her. Victor let his dog eat well on this trip. Sharing the bounty of the hunt was of paramount importance among the Inuit, but hunter and dog shared the spoils first, often alone and always before anyone else in the village—even Anika, who prepared Victor's food for distribution to their neighbors in the village as was done in ages past. Summer would be a difficult time for the dog, with little food for either of them and much carrying of Victor's packed tools and other gear.

The dog had become Victor's closest friend, and eventually he gave her a name: Janey. His sister's name. If there had only been enough food to go around, Victor believed his sister would have made a fine hunter someday.

The days of walking were long, punctuated only by prolonged waits at uncovered seal holes in the ice. When a seal nosed up to the surface, Victor followed the dog's lead and lunged at his prey with a handmade harpoon. As the harpoon struck the seal, its toggled point would turn perpendicular to the shaft and lodge the harpoon inside the seal's skin. With the harpoon set on the end of its braided line, Victor then had to chip away at the ice around the hole until the fat, slippery seal could be landed.

A seal in the water is cunning and quick, and an injured seal is very strong. If the seal darts when the line is wrapped too tightly around the hunter's hand, there is the chance he could lose his fingers. Victor even bragged to young Annu that fighting a monstrous bearded seal was how he lost the last two digits on his left hand. In fact, Victor had lost those pieces of himself to frostbite after losing a mitt to the sea. In the Arctic, loss perpetuated itself in this way and tempered Victor's half-truth. The water spirits had probably taken the mitt as a gift to the seals, so, indirectly, it was as though the seals had taken Victor's fingers.

Victor's insistence on hunting in the traditional way was viewed almost derisively by many of his fellow Inuit. The rest glowered with envy at the sharpness of his skills. His critics had stopped thinking about the hunt as a lifestyle and now considered it an unending series of struggles against the ice and snow for very little return. Hunting had become a job for someone else, or at least someone with a snowmobile or a pickup truck.

But Victor did not really mind hunting alone. He could set his own pace across the pack and was never concerned about crossing too much or too little terrain in a given day. He pulled his grandfather's *komatik*, an antique wooden sled about twelve feet long, supported on two runners fashioned from caribou antlers and coated with ice, lichen, and moss. Dogs, too, were no longer the possession of most Inuit because they ate too much and crapped too much for what they contributed to the settlement. The hearty, rambunctious animals of *qablunaq* lore, dogs that willingly took a sledge harness or a saddle pack were a chimera. In truth, Janey often shrugged off her packs and preferred to nip playfully at Victor's feet while he pulled his own sled.

Victor could pull or push his *komatik* loaded with nearly three hundred pounds of gear or animal meat up to twelve miles in a single day—twice or three times that if the floe was moving well with the current. If the spirits granted him a larger catch, he stashed his kills in well-hidden hutches he built along the way, for retrieval on the way home or on a later trip. Theft by other Inuit hunters was almost unheard of, but polar bears and foxes were shameless opportunists, so Victor built his stores far out on the sea ice. Very soon the ice would begin its spring movement and he would be forced to turn back, but not just yet. He had waited too long for the winter seal hunt to let it slip away.

The solitude of this kind of hunting was appealing to him. Sometimes he walked for days at a time, building temporary camps, small snowhouses, or lean-tos for shelter. When he slept it was only for minutes at a time. When he dreamed, it was of hunting. He enjoyed the art of stalking with his dog, silently finding his way across the ice, looking for quarry. When the sun turned the ice to a spongy mush during the day, he napped, then walked on the refrozen pack at evening twilight.

Victor's upbringing, with its emphasis on tradition,

now seemed little more than an anachronism, an optimistic dream to which he often referred for moral guidance or technique. He remembered his grandfather conducting ceremonies for the entire village to appease the spirits for the hunt. He remembered helping to build snowhouses and the taste of warm seal blubber and *akutuq*—Inuit ice cream—during the dance festivals. He remembered having a full set of teeth. Victor sensed that the growing disregard for the old ways—especially among the young Inuit men now expected to be leaders of the village—had annoyed the spirits of both land and sea. That was why their harvests continued to dwindle. *Kannakapfaluk,* the mother of all animals and a tremendously powerful spirit, was angry with them. And what was to be done if *Kannakapfaluk* was angry? The traditional Inuit sought only to appease the spirits. If there was no afterlife in which to believe or anticipate, in life one sought only to avoid provoking the malevolence of the spirits. The modern Inuit seemed to do nothing. However justified, it was simply easier to blame the white man and his government for the end of the past.

But Victor prayed anyway. He prayed to all the spirits, and when he prayed he asked for their forgiveness. Once angered, the spirits became monsters and they feasted on the flesh of the living.

Some say the earth will end in fire,
Some say in ice.

—ROBERT FROST

1

Below her, the ice was breathing.

Carol Harmon pulled her snow goggles down around her throat, adjusted the hood of her jacket, and tried to hold the syringe steady against the bite of the wind. Her fingers trembled not from cold, fear, or the ungainly size of the syringe, but from the awe of her magnificent trespass. The forty-gauge needle in her hand was as thick as a pencil and the plunger could draw nearly a pint of blood.

Carol shut her eyes for a moment, balancing, relaxing. She could hear the thin rasp of her own breath sliding through her throat in a shallow, steady rhythm, then see the vapor whisked away in air that was not quite twenty degrees Fahrenheit. In, out. In, out. A moment later, as if performing a gigantic mimic of this gesture, the ice moved with the gentle respiration of the whale beneath her.

She felt like a flea on the back of some immense dog, which she very nearly was. The trapped whale had been

discovered only hours earlier during an acoustical survey conducted by the U.S. research vessel *Phoenix* a
stone's throw inside the Arctic Circle. The ice, a floe the
size of two football fields, obscured the exact size of this
whale, its species, or even its sex. So far, the crew had
exposed only four square feet of the animal's thick,
blubbery hide.

Chipping down through more than three feet of solid
ice, Carol and one of her technicians eventually managed to extend the opening forward, clearing a larger
area around the whale's blowhole. Then, moving back
and following some trial-and-error searching, other
members of the research team opened another hole to
expose the smallish dorsal fin at the base of the tail. An
elongated ridge along the animal's spine gave the first
indication that it might be a *Balaenoptera musculus*, a
blue whale, the largest animal the earth has ever
known. The prospect made Carol's heart race. From the
distance between the two openings, Carol could estimate that the magnificent animal was also among the
largest ever viewed in such suspended animation.

The impromptu landing party had been so preoccupied by the discovery that they had not even thought to
look more closely at their surroundings. Then a radio
call from the *Phoenix*—moored to the edge of the ice
and nearly eighty feet above it at bridge level—reported
more animals trapped by the same floe. Four more
whales were discovered over the next hour, all of them
Balaenoptera. Unbelievable for many species, but especially so for the non-gregarious *Balaenoptera,* a pod of
five animals had been assembled here, all adhered to the
same piece of drifting ice. Individually or frozen together to form enormous accretions, such floating ice
masses provided ephemeral islands and bridges for polar bears and foxes, and temporary rookeries for seals
and walruses. To a whale, bound by bulk to remain in
the water yet requiring unobstructed access to the air in

order to breathe, a large, continuous floe was nothing but a nuisance.

As the floe slowly rose and buckled beneath them, Carol and the crew of the *Phoenix* were somewhat reassured that these whales still had plenty of energy left in them. But for these specimens to be so far north this early in the year, they must be struggling to sustain themselves, even with the ample reserves of blubber that comprised as much as half their body weight. Growing to over a hundred feet in length, *Balaenoptera* subsist on a diet of krill—shrimplike crustaceans high in fatty-acid content—using their baleen plates to filter up to five tons of sustenance per day from the plankton in the water. Frozen onto the bottom surface of the ice sheet, the whales couldn't possibly be feeding properly, much less sufficiently, and that was what concerned Carol most of all.

Soon the floe was alive with human activity. Carol's voice crackled over the walkie-talkies every few minutes, coordinating teams of technicians to examine each animal and report its condition. The remaining technicians and all available deck crew used portable heaters and set up bucket brigades of seawater to the openings in the ice, pouring as much warmed water into the holes as possible. This would perhaps lessen the adhesion and would certainly keep the animals' skin from chafing in the dry arctic air.

Such an extensive assemblage of animals was virtually unheard of, inspiring someone to dub this temporary landfall "the *Balaenoptera* floe." There was easily a career's worth of research here for someone, if only the whales could somehow be held this way and studied over time. Eventually the ice floe would break up, and the scientists knew their only reasonable course of action was to assist that process if these gentle giants were to survive. Any real studies would be incidental to their attempt to free the whales.

The most likely cause of the whales' entrapment was a late-season freeze with extremely cold temperatures. Carol knew that there hadn't been a storm in the area for more than two weeks, which meant that these animals would have been on starvation rations for some time, even after reducing their metabolic requirements. Another possibility was that the animals had simply become lost or disoriented—a phenomenon observed in whales for a number of reasons, ranging from magnetic disturbances to viral infections. In warmer climates, such maladies could cause entire pods to run themselves aground; in polar waters, the whales instead floundered in air spaces captured under the ice. Finding a breathing hole large enough, the animals might have to wait there for the floe to break up. By the time that happened, their warm-blooded bulk could become frozen to the ice the way one's tongue stuck to a piece of metal on a cold day. Without a breakup of the floe, many such animals died within a few days, their carcasses left to saturate and sink into the ocean's depths.

Whatever had put them here, Carol still had difficulty imagining their bittersweet windfall. Five whales. Over a million pounds of marine mammal, directly beneath her.

In, out. In . . . out. Breathe.

Such a discovery would be awe-inspiring to anyone; it was particularly entrancing to a professional whale biologist. Carol's interest in marine mammals of every description had followed her since childhood. The family had obediently followed the career of her father, Dr. Charles Harmon, from his graduate work at Yale to positions on three continents before settling on the west coast of Canada. There, Carol and her stepbrother, Mark, would comb the rocky beaches of British Columbia and the Pacific Northwest, looking for sea-lion rookeries. As they grew older, Carol and Mark would borrow small boats from the marine station and venture offshore to see gray whales on their annual migration to the Gulf of Alaska.

After an honors degree at Oregon State, Carol completed her master's at Stanford. Before venturing to Stanford himself, Mark had enjoyed a hitch in the U.S. Navy, working on ocean acoustics at a NAVFAC at Coos Bay, Oregon, then later, up the road at Newport, where the private sector caught his eye. It was in Oregon that Mark had introduced Carol to her first husband. Together, the three of them had worked in vaguely related areas of underwater sound propagation and had shared a nearly unbalanced passion for the sea. It had seemed the most natural thing in the world when Carol decided to specialize in bioacoustics and the study of whale vocalizations.

Carol's marriage, on the other hand, seemed like the least natural thing in the world. The eventual divorce left her deflated and without much professional motivation for the first time in her career. Eventually, she left her comfortable technicianship in California and went back to the intellectual womb of academe, this time for a doctorate at the University of Hawaii. Her work with humpback whales off the coast of Maui—a database of the complexities of whale vocalizations that she hoped to translate into a system of whale-to-human communication—was described as revolutionary and had earned her international recognition. For a brief time, it seemed as though everything in the Harmon family had found a balanced keel.

Now, more than a decade after leaving Stanford, Carol Harmon had tracked whales through every ocean and off the shores of every continent. She was doing an environmental-impact assessment in Prince William Sound, Alaska, when she met her second husband, Bob Nolan. Nolan was an environmental lawyer by training, with remarkable drive and business acumen that had helped him to develop a multimillion-dollar consortium of consulting agencies collectively known as the

Nolan Group. Nolan was motivated by banner head-lines, not quality—which generally used up more re-sources and held a lower profit margin—and he showed no remorse for that pursuit. In hindsight, Carol realized that she had known these things from the first time she met Nolan, but something had made her overlook them. Perhaps, as she foolishly blamed herself for the world's deficiencies, she had been unable to face "aban-doning" another marriage. She chose instead to let her research consume her.

Then, like some divine punishment for ignoring her family and her personal life, Carol had lost both her stepbrother and her husband within a matter of weeks. It was tragically ironic that Mark had died as a result of exposure to a highly toxic marine organism discovered less than a mile from their father's retirement home. Soon after, her husband, Bob, had been killed by the same menace. Charles Harmon had never liked either of his daughter's husbands, so his attitude toward Bob's death was unsurprising, but he had remained so clinical and dispassionate following her stepbrother's death that he might as well have been mourning a complete stranger. That had been not quite three years ago, and Carol still found it difficult to resolve the resentment she held toward her father.

Following Bob's death, the Nolan Group's board of directors had voted, surprisingly and unanimously, to install Carol as their CEO. In hindsight, she realized that their strategy had probably been to let her inexpe-rience drive the company into a nosedive, from which it would be easier to auction off its various constituents. But Carol proved them wrong. She had managed to re-tain most of the contracts and investors who had doubted the Group's ability to function without Bob Nolan. In the current fiscal year she had even been able to generate an increase in the company's earnings per share. Even so, she rarely made it to her well-appointed office at the Group's headquarters in Seattle, preferring to delegate operational matters to her cadre of buttoned-down vice presidents and financial advisors. She kept herself abreast of the Group's activities, offered opinions, and provided signatures when required, but remained heavily involved in her fieldwork for most of the year.

The *Phoenix*'s principal assigned task was to track and monitor the belugas, bowheads, orcas, narwhals, and gray whales of the Canadian Arctic. The team would also use Carol's vocalization program to determine what effect shipping traffic had on the larger animals. Underwater, the noise from a single oil tanker's engines could travel fifty miles on either side of the cruise track—to say nothing of the noise generated by the fracturing ice itself. The combined effect of this disturbance was believed to be disruptive to whale migration, breeding, and communication, a speculation that the Nolan Group had now been contracted to quantify.

Though *Balaenoptera* had been added to the endangered species list and were protected by international treaties, their numbers continued to dwindle under the influence of poaching and black-market whaling. What commercial fishing hadn't culled, global development did. Around the world, marine mammals were washing up on beaches in unprecedented numbers, killed by viruses, distemper, or a dozen other inexplicable causes. The tissues of beluga and other arctic whales routinely showed cancerous tumors, ulcers in the digestive tract, respiratory infections, and alarmingly high levels of mercury and PCBs. Then there was noise pollution. Before the onset of the industrial age, *Balaenoptera* could send their vocalizations across entire oceans. Now the cacophony of thousands of ships was slowly diminishing their watery playground.

And if not whalers, if not pathogens or noise, the ubiquitous but wholly natural threat of ice could still kill them.

Carol pressed the needle into the whale's thick hide once more. Twice her disposable needles had been bent closed by the thick, muscular flesh at the base of the tail, where the animal's blood vessels were closest to the surface. The third time the penetration was clean, and as she drew back the plunger of the syringe, the chamber filled with dark red blood. Carol carefully twisted the sample from the base of the needle, labeled it, and placed it on ice in a small box containing a dozen others. Though blood sampling was technically outside the team's investigation, the serum would provide an insight into the animal's health. She could think of two or three other researchers who would give anything for a sample of "blue blood."

"Easy," she murmured to the whale, patting its skin as she filled another syringe, then withdrew the needle. "All done, girl . . . or boy."

Carol heard snow crunching behind her and turned to see a figure in a bright orange parka suit approaching her. Jeff Dexter, her senior technician, flashed her a broad smile from behind his thick, frost-tinged beard.

"What's this I hear?" he asked. "The infamous Dr. Harmon can't even sex a whale?"

"Not without a better look," she said.

"I guess if all we can see are the blowhole and the dorsal fin, we're a little like the blind men in a herd of elephants," Dexter said. He kneeled down beside her, brushed back her hair, and gave her a warm kiss.

"I've heard of elephants too," she said, playing into the old comedy routine.

"No, no, an elephant *herd*," Dexter said. The warmth of his breath against her face was soothing and arousing all at once.

"What do I care what an elephant heard?" Carol whispered. "I've got nothing to hide."

"Then why are we whispering?"

"Because I think this is the single most exciting discovery of my life," she said. Dexter could admit the same thing, and their shared excitement left both of them yearning for a more private location in which to celebrate. But for now, duty called.

"I've got Ramsey prepping some scuba tanks and drysuits." A mischievous twinkle lit his eyes. "We're going swimming."

"You're serious?"

"You bet," Dexter grinned again. "We're going to drill another ice hole between this whale and the next one over and do a dive around two of them, at least."

"And do you have permission to do this?" Carol asked.

Dexter kissed her again. "I dunno. Do I, boss?"

"Take your camera," she said. "Matter of fact, take two."

"You're not coming with us?" he asked.

"We'll see," she said in the tone of voice that implied *probably not, work to do.*

"All work and no play . . ." Dexter warned her. For him, "all work" was rarely a problem. He was the consummate Southern California surfer boy, perpetually tanned, with a megawatt smile and a shock of blond hair that caught the sun like yellow chrome. A master's graduate fifteen years Carol's junior, Dexter had called the Nolan Group every single day, looking for a job. As she recalled, there had been a kind of well-meaning desperation in his approach that reminded Carol a little of the used-car salesman in Bob Nolan and a little of the Boy Scout integrity of her first husband.

Dexter proved himself to be a loyal and dedicated employee from the start, taking on the tasks of senior technician on many assignments, arriving early, staying late, and giving up more than a few evenings and weekends to support Carol's various contracts and expeditions. When everyone else had gone home for the night, there was Dex. When no one else wanted to log any more overtime, he was ready to go, claiming that his "charmed and indulgent childhood" was responsible for his utter disregard for time clocks and large paychecks.

In short, he was always there for her, no matter what the task. In time, after enough weekends and budget meetings over Chinese take-out, the question of whether Carol would see this young man socially had become a nonissue. The distinction between employee, friend, and confidant had blurred irrevocably, and the technician and the CEO became an item.

For his age, Dex was masterful at lovemaking, driving their encounters to sweaty extremes, but always remaining considerate of her need for tenderness, for closeness. It was the wide-eyed, unjaded youth in him who made Carol feel as though she might even fall in love again, given enough time. Ironically, this time *she* was the one who was jaded and distracted, and a part of her still needed to resolve that. Dexter carried his consideration for her into their work in a kind but professional manner, and she appreciated this most of all. It was good to know that as she forged ahead with her discoveries and adventures, someone like Dex would be there with her, as grateful for the experience they would share as for her company.

She had no way of knowing that that would all change very fast.

"Awesome!" Dexter said into the microphone of his full-face scuba mask. His exclamations were interrupted by the gurgling of his regulator as he described the scene around him. Carol and the others saw what he saw through a small camera carried by Dexter's diving partner, Tony Ramsey. Clad in their polar-weight drysuits, the two divers were dwarfed against the massive backdrop of the first animal. The water clarity was exceptional, and the crew on the *Phoenix* could even see the vast yellowish growths of diatoms on the whale's gray-white belly. It was a *Balaenoptera,* a large female. A smaller female and three males made up the rest of the stranded pod.

"See if you can find the eye," said one of the technicians into the comm link. It was a common request for first-time whale watchers. The sheer size of the animal seemed to detach it from any definite point of reference; the eye was needed to identify the massive form as an actual creature and really see it for what it was.

Ramsey panned his handheld camera left, then began gliding toward the head of the whale. Dexter's flippers could just be seen, moving ahead of his partner. From time to time, the length of polypropylene line tethering the divers to the surface drifted into view.

"There it is!" the technician called out, pointing to the monitor. And so it was, nearly buried in the gnarled folds of scarred flesh. The eye had a mildly clouded appearance, perhaps a cataract, but was otherwise alert. It stared back at the camera with neither fear nor aggression. The humans trailing along its formidable length were only the latest, and least, of its recent inconveniences.

"Poor old girl," Carol muttered. "We'll get you out of here. Damned if I know how, but we will."

From the warmth inside the *Phoenix,* the group of scientists watched the divers cross the open water beneath the ice and explore the second whale. All remained entranced for the next fifteen minutes, until the excitement of the venture and the numbing cold of the water conspired to cut short the divers' supply of air.

Reluctantly, Dexter and Ramsey swam back to their entry hole chipped in the ice.

"Okay, folks, let's get back to work," Carol said. The others reluctantly obliged as she made her way aft to the *Phoenix*'s main lab. Two small coolers filled with blood samples waited there on the bench. She pulled on a pair of latex gloves and prepared the first sample for a cell count. While a relief crew continued to chip away at the floe, she could at least run some preliminary serum tests. What she had seen of the whales deeply troubled her; they looked more malnourished than she had wanted to believe.

Dexter appeared half an hour later, his face still flushed with exertion and excitement from the dive. "You've *got* to go down there," he said after relaying a first-person account of his experience, as if Carol herself hadn't seen much of the same thing via Ramsey's camera. "I can't believe you don't want to go down there. I mean, this is *it*. This is your *thing*." Dexter's age was showing, as it often did when he was excited.

"I will," Carol said, but her eyes remained focused on the eyepieces of her microscope. "But when I do, I want to be sure of what we're looking for. What we can do to help these big fellas besides letting them loose."

As Carol heard herself speaking, she sounded so . . . maternal. Worse—she sounded old. At Dex's age—hell, even ten years ago—the Carol she thought she knew wouldn't sit right down at the lab bench. She wouldn't be concerned about the danger or the frigid water temperature. She would dive with the whales, then dive again, then screw Dex's brains out for hours more until her excitement finally abated into deep-seated happiness. Carol the scientist, Carol the CEO, Carol the expedition leader and contract officer was guiding this exchange, and Carol the woman found she didn't like it.

To her continued amazement and appreciation, Dex understood. Instead of being put out, he came to her and embraced her. Instead of ridiculing her meticulous dedication, he *thanked* her for the opportunity of being with her, moored to this particular piece of ice in all the Arctic Ocean.

Come to think of it, they still had time for a shower.

"You read my mind," Dexter said in response to her offer. Carol promised him that she would look at just one more sample, then meet him in their cabin.

As it happened, it was several samples and nearly three hours later when she finally looked up from the microscope. She saw the time and gasped, letting out a guilty moan. As a partial peace offering, she stopped in the *Phoenix*'s galley to pour two large mugs of hot chocolate. Pausing at the door of their cabin, she unbuttoned her shirt suggestively, licked her lips, and stepped inside.

Dexter was not in their bunk or on the cabin's small settee. For a moment, Carol thought he must have given up waiting and gone back out to look at the whales. Then she heard the sound of his coughing from the cabin's private head.

She tapped tentatively at the door. "Dex?" she asked. "Sweetie? What's wrong?"

Carol pushed through the door and saw Dexter, clad only in his underwear, sitting on the floor. He was hunched forward, his legs wrapped around the stainless steel base of the toilet. The bowl was filled with bright red blood, which was also splattered onto the rim and turned-up lid.

"Oh my God!" Carol exclaimed, her voice rising to nearly a shriek. The two mugs of cocoa dropped from her hand, ceramic exploding on the tiled deck. "What's the matter! What happened?"

Dexter appeared only vaguely aware of her presence, and nearly incapable of responding. "Sick," he mumbled. He coughed again, another spurt of blood erupting from his trembling lips. "Ohhhh . . . shit."

Carol snatched a blanket from the bunk and wrapped it around Dexter's stooped shoulders. She bolted into the corridor and nearly collided with Susan Conant, the ship's industrial first-aid officer and the closest they had to a medic on station. Susan was just twenty-seven years old, and her inexperience and potential for incompetence had never seemed greater to Carol.

"Carol, I need you to come—" Susan began.

"No," Carol said. "I need you to have a look at this." She pulled Susan back into her cabin and into the head.

"I know," Susan said. "Tony's got it too."

Carol shook her head in disbelief. "What? Ramsey too?"

"He collapsed on the deck a few minutes ago, and when we brought him to his cabin he started vomiting blood."

"Why didn't you report it!"

"I *am*. This is the first chance I've had."

"Well, what is it?" Carol demanded.

"I don't know. I don't think it's food poisoning. As far as I know, no one else on board has it. But Jeff and Tony were the only ones—"

"—in the water," Carol finished, her eyes growing wide. "*Help* him," she said, pointing to Dexter in frustration. "Do whatever you can."

Carol sprinted off down the corridor to the bridge. She told the *Phoenix*'s captain to radio to the Canadian Coast Guard, then recall all personnel from the ice outside. Two crewmen were down and they would need immediate medevac transport to Churchill or Cape Dorset. Anywhere but here.

If the sudden severity of Dexter's affliction was shocking, Ramsey's reaction was utterly terrifying. By the time Carol made it to the ship's infirmary, Ramsey was already in an advanced state of shock. His skin was flushed an angry red; he had long ago voided the various fluids from his stomach and bowels, and both were now replaced with intermittent splutters of blood. Two of the *Phoenix*'s technicians had wrapped him in blankets and now held him tightly against the bunk as his body quaked and shivered uncontrollably. A small tensor bandage had been hastily jammed between Ramsey's teeth to keep him from biting through his own tongue, and nothing in his wide, glassy eyes suggested that he heard a word of their attempted comfort.

"*I can't see!*" Ramsey shrieked. "Oh, Christ, my eyes are burning up!"

A technician pressed a cold compress to Ramsey's eyes. Within minutes the violent seizures lessened and his body went limp with exhaustion. Seeing the robust man suddenly shivering helplessly on the bunk almost made Carol wish for a return of his frantic struggling.

Dexter was brought in on a makeshift stretcher, trembling and unable to walk under his own power. Carol sat next to him on the bed and stroked his hair. Like Ramsey, Dex's skin had taken on an angry red pallor; like Ramsey, he was unresponsive to any queries.

A desperate list of explanations for these symptoms ran through Carol's mind. Both men were in prime health, with no history of epilepsy or other serious maladies. Whatever it was had happened too quickly to be viral and not quickly enough to be some kind of inorganic toxin. They weren't hypothermic and they hadn't been in the water long enough to get the bends, though their affliction seemed to be just as pervasive. Yet it was as if every system in their bodies was shutting down by convulsive degrees. However quickly the medevac helicopter arrived, it might not be fast enough.

It was the strange, abraded burns on the victims'

skin that led Susan to speculate that what they were witnessing could be the acute stage of severe radiation poisoning.

"Radiation poisoning!" The words buzzed in Carol's mind even as she spat them back at Susan. "That can't be it."

"I hope it isn't," Susan said. "I hope to God I'm wrong." They both knew that if Susan's speculation proved to be even remotely correct, the two divers could potentially have exposed the ship to even more mysterious horrors. "But nothing else fits."

"This *fits*?" Carol almost shouted. For the effects to be this severe, this fast, the level of exposure would have to be huge. "What did they do? Walk through a goddamn reactor?

"Hang on, Dex," Carol whispered to Dexter, holding his face in her trembling hands. "Hang on, honey." His eyes slowly blinked once, indicating that at least he could see her.

"How long until the helicopter gets here?" Carol barked at the crowd of gawkers standing in the corridor. She knew, as they did, it was an unanswerable question. In the Arctic, even emergencies progressed only as fast as the weather allowed.

Carol made a series of frantic calls over the next several hours. Soon—soon enough, she hoped—the search-and-rescue helicopter came and left, taking Dexter and Ramsey back to the mainland. It was only the beginning of a tag-team evacuation to the nearest appropriate medical facility, which now looked to be seventeen hundred miles away, in Toronto.

By nightfall, the vast remoteness of the Arctic suddenly seemed to drown Carol. Despite the *Phoenix* and its able crew, Carol felt utterly alone and she was very frightened. Even if she hadn't anticipated the roadblocks and dead ends produced by her calls to the various government, emergency, medical, and defense agencies, a part of her knew whom she would eventually need to contact. She realized this with a mixture of regret and comfort. Regret because he always seemed to be her last resort; comfort because she knew he would find a solution to this problem. He always did. Somehow and in some way, that was an assurance she needed very badly at the moment.

The only problem would be finding him.

2

The bow of the research vessel *Alfred Lansing* pushed over the crest of another thirty-foot wave, then led the ship down into the succeeding trough. The ballast water inside her 270-foot hull slammed forward with a thunderous boom as the stern rose toward the thick overcast sky, then heeled over and crashed back down toward the icy gray water of the Weddell Sea. The cables and guide wires that ran from the afterdeck to the instruments towed behind the ship slackened, then pulled taut as the *Lansing* nosed over the next crest. The ship had been rocked by the autumn storm for the past four days.

Clad in thick cold-weather suits clipped to the ends of safety tethers, the two men far out on the *Lansing*'s transom held on to anything bolted down.

"I think the weather's letting up." Brock Garner unzipped his jacket collar and grinned at the man gripping the rail beside him, his research assistant and technician, Sergei Zubov.

"Yeah, but now it's letting down," Zubov shouted back, then adjusted his footing as the angle of the *Lansing*'s deck reversed again. "Now it's letting up again."

"See? It's all in how you look at things."

In this world of permanent wind and ice, arguably the birthplace for weather patterns all over the globe, the *Lansing* provided a work platform for three dozen people for up to seven weeks. Stowed in virtually every available space was the equipment and personnel for no fewer than six distinct research studies, each with its own need for access to the ship's full-time crew. The pecking order for sampling time on station was only occasionally a democratic process. Often, several wholly unrelated experiments were tossed together on the same manifest, selected as much for their ability to fit with the other pieces on board as for their scientific merit, political clout, or supposed urgency. The complement of principal investigators on this cruise included an ozone specialist, two ocean physicists, a polar geologist, a chemist, and Garner, the only biologist.

Early on, the *Lansing*'s full-time crew had known that this would be a cruise for sick bags and, so far, their temporary charges—the researchers and science crew—had borne out that expectation. All except Garner, the last to get his sampling gear out of the water and the first to get it wet again the next day. Everything about the way he tackled his sampling protocol suggested that he'd seen far worse conditions than this.

Despite outward appearances, Garner himself felt as though he hadn't slept in days. His sharp gray eyes remained clear and focused above a week's growth of beard, but he had been dressed in his cold-weather suit for so long that it had come to feel like an extension of his skin. The muscles throughout his lean, six-foot-two-inch frame ached and more than once he had felt his knees begin to tremble from sheer exhaustion. Nonetheless, he drove his data collection forward as if it were some kind of vendetta, which in a way it was.

Zubov's assignment was to assist that vendetta. A husky Ukrainian who exceeded Garner's own height by two inches and outweighed him by a hundred pounds, Zubov had a thick beard and a head of curly black hair that, taken with his massive frame, made him look more like a lumberjack or professional wrestler than an electronics technician.

The radio in his hand crackled. "Fifty meters and rising. One minute," said Donny Clark, the winch operator and the only other crewman obligated to be on deck in these conditions.

Zubov relayed the tow status to Garner, who took the radio and spoke into it. "I need my baby brought in fast, Donny," he said. "Fast as you can as soon as she hits the surface. I'll give you the word."

Zubov took the radio back. "He means as fast as *we* can, not as fast as *you* can," he said to Clark. Their intent was to retrieve their sampling instruments from the water and get them onto the deck before they could be damaged by the waves, bounced off the hull, or lost to the sea below. But Zubov knew from experience that if the cable were taken in faster than he and Garner could accommodate the slack, one of them could suddenly and violently end up on the wrong side of the railing.

The object of Garner's professional passion—currently being hauled back to the ship from a depth of one hundred meters—was a five-foot-diameter sphere crafted from titanium, glass, and PVC packed with electronics, cameras, sensors, and various bottle-sampling devices. The water-intake ports on the front of the device distinctly resembled eyes, nostrils, and a mouth, and in conjunction with the ungainly array of electronics sprouting from the top of the sphere, the device was given an obvious nickname: the Medusa sphere. It was the latest in an unattractive but innovative series of machines designed by Garner himself to sample and record communities of plankton—microscopic plant and animal life—as they subsisted below the surface of the storm-tossed Southern Ocean.

As Garner and Zubov peered into the wake-washed sea behind the *Lansing,* Medusa emerged from the murky depths and came into view just beneath the surface. Medusa's depth here was immaterial; as each wave heaved the *Lansing* up, then down, the "depth" of the fifty-thousand-dollar sampler could vary by as much as a five-story building.

The deck was suddenly alive with motion and the sound of mechanical adjustment. The winches holding Medusa's cables whined to life, acting in concert with the large A-frame that angled back over the *Lansing*'s stern.

Garner made eye contact with the winch operator: *Get ready.*

The *Lansing*'s bow tilted sharply down into another wave trough and the wire connected to Medusa pulled in sharply, along the hull.

"Now!" Garner shouted, spun his arm in the air to signal Clark, then lunged across the deck to join Zubov as Medusa broke the surface. The timing was perfect: as the wire angled back down, away from the hull, the gleaming sphere shot from the water. It dangled in midair and away from any obstacles, suspended from the *Lansing*'s A-frame boom.

The bow crashed down again and Medusa angled inboard as Clark paid out enough line to lower the device toward Zubov's outstretched arms. Garner swung around his friend and slammed the stern rail closed to prevent Medusa from sliding back overboard. Momentarily distracted, Garner didn't see Zubov lose his tenuous grasp on the sampler as it wheeled danger-ously away from him. The mundane operational ballet they had practiced countless times suddenly went dan-gerously awry.

"I'm losing her!" Zubov shouted, drawing Garner's attention. By the time Garner whirled around, Medusa was already out over the railing and Zubov was strain-ing after it. A length of the sampler's thick communica-tions cable had snagged around Zubov's waist and threatened to snap his spine if the device were to sud-denly drop from its present position.

"Hang on!" Garner shouted, trying to wrestle the ca-ble away from his friend. Zubov still leaned perilously out over the rail, one hand gripping one of Medusa's wings to prevent the device from swinging any further.

Now the increased tension in the cable wrenched Garner to the deck as he lost his footing. Zubov let out a gasp as Medusa's full weight pulled him out over the water. Clark was frozen at the winch controls, unable to assist the men without allowing Medusa to swing freely. Zubov grimaced again as the cable pinned him tighter, threatening to rip him through the bars of the railing or topple him over it.

"Let go of it!" Garner shouted again. "I'll cut it loose."

"Not a chance!" Zubov yelled back.

Though the five-hundred-meter cable was sheathed in Kevlar, Garner had engineered a breakaway chink every few feet on the cable to allow for maintenance and repair—and potential emergencies like this. In sec-onds he had the cable's armor stripped away and drew a knife to slice through the electronics inside.

Before the knife went to work, the Lansing finally pitched forward again and Medusa came back over the deck. Clark let out more slack and Medusa came quickly to the deck. Still prone, Garner pulled himself across the pitching deck and clipped Medusa to the deck with a pair of safety lines.

As suddenly as it had started, the peril abated.

"That's why we don't deploy instruments in thirty-foot seas." Zubov glared at Garner. "*We* being those of us with less-ambitious sampling requirements. *Us* being everyone but you." His complaint was only semi-serious. At twenty thousand dollars a day, the researchers aboard the *Lansing* couldn't afford to wait for more agreeable weather. As winter set in, four days of stormy weather would begin to look relatively attractive when weighed against the next four months. Very soon the waters through Drake Passage would be whipped into conditions fully deserving of their reputation as the most dangerous in the world. Bounded on three sides by land, the Weddell Sea is a convenient repository for wind, waves, and ice. These elements roll and recirculate in a permanent maelstrom, a meteorological testament to the bitterness of the Antarctic. More than in any other body of water, sanctuary in the Southern Ocean is far away and sparsely distributed.

"Were you really going to let Medusa pull you off the ship?" Garner asked.

"I didn't have a choice," Zubov replied. "She's the only reason I'm on this tub. I didn't even bring a deck of cards. And I wasn't going to spend the next week repairing that umbilical. I can't believe you were going to cut it."

"Are you kidding?" Garner replied, clapping him on the back. "That's a twelve-thousand-dollar cable. The knife was for your legs."

The black humor broke the tension as Medusa was properly secured and clamped in place until her next use. Given the amount of data that the umbilical provided on every tow and the value of the station time already compromised by the storm, more than a few researchers might consider one technician's life a regrettable but necessary trade.

With the last A-frame tow of the day completed and the twilight becoming full night, the *Lansing*'s deck was secured and the running lights switched on. Garner and Zubov peeled away their cold-weather suits and hung them in the ship's aft laboratory.

"See you in the morning?" Zubov asked. Except for the second watch, most of those on board had retired for the day. The scientists slept off recurring seasickness in their bunks, read thumb-worn paperbacks, or sat through their two hundredth screening of *The Empire Strikes Back* on videotape in the officers' lounge. Zubov himself was overdue for the nightly poker game with the *Lansing*'s off-duty crew.

"See you. Get some rest," Garner confirmed. He himself had to wade through a day's worth of data from Medusa before dawn, then prepare the sampler for its next tow, at 4:00 A.M.

Garner's path to the decks of the *Lansing* had been a long and convoluted one since his upbringing on an Iowa farm. Retiring early but respectably decorated from the U.S. Navy at the rank of lieutenant commander, Garner had excelled in several valuable areas of military intelligence. Ultimately, however, Garner's well-developed acrophobia limited his advancement up the military's career ladder. In truth, on the infrequent occasions Garner mentioned that chapter of his life, he would say that he remained intrigued with the practice of intelligence gathering but had grown disillusioned at how that intelligence might later be used—about the only thing he shared with his former father-in-law, Charles Harmon.

Military targets and perceived enemies of the state gradually became less interesting to him than broader, more academic pursuits. Garner exchanged a background in ocean acoustics and electrical engineering for the pursuit of a doctorate in biological oceanography. For one of the very few times in his life, professional skill and personal interest had come together. Most days, this incidental confluence of fate, aptitude, and pleasure provided him with enough stability to weather most of life's storms, even those in the Southern Ocean.

Garner had started his thesis—use of an automated sampler to describe plankton population structures—as an attempt to design a better mousetrap. As Medusa's mechanical problems accumulated and diversified, Garner suddenly found his research taking on the premise of an engineering project. Then, to justify the expense and frustration of the sampler's design and give credibility to its results, he found he needed to extend Medusa's sampling to other oceans and other seasons. These more ambitious plans to test Medusa, in turn, led to further complications and disappointments with the device's design. It was becoming clear to more people than Sergei Zubov that if Medusa wasn't Garner's ultimate undoing, his own meticulousness would be.

Zubov's reputation for being cantankerous and bellicose where Medusa was concerned was exceeded only by his expertise and resourcefulness. After a dozen cruises as Garner's assistant, Zubov had reached the tenuous but manageable compromise with Medusa that expert mechanics and complex machines sometimes do, and Garner could no longer imagine completing his work without one or the other. When it came time to sample the Southern Ocean, Garner had recruited Zubov from his usual assignment—boatswain on the research vessel *Exeter*—to accompany him on the *Lansing* for this third and possibly last excursion to Antarctica. Now, while the *Lansing* was laboring toward Drake Passage, the *Exeter* was on a research cruise to Palau as part of the World Ocean Circulation Experiment, or WOCE. In his contempt for this geographical juxtaposition, Zubov made a daily point of reminding Garner that he should really be basking in the tropical Pacific.

For all her ingenuity, it wasn't long ago that Medusa had seemed destined for some high-tech scrap heap. Then she had proven instrumental in identifying and tracking a monstrous red tide that had swept ashore from the northeast Pacific Ocean. In recognition of his ongoing service in a reserve commission, Garner had received a promotion to full commander and the Legion of Merit from the U.S. Navy. To Garner's initial chagrin, this sidetrack had pushed his dissertation back at least six months, but the dramatic applied demonstration of the device had been enough to keep research grants coming in.

Now, at just thirty-eight years of age, William Brock Garner found himself to be a reluctant Navy commander twice retired, a flawed husband once divorced, an inventor of international repute, and a local hero to the citizens of the Pacific Northwest. But still not yet, not quite, a Ph.D. *Mr.* Garner still needed these data from the Southern Ocean before he could aspire to being *Dr.* Garner. It seemed too frivolous to admit aloud in light of his academic accomplishments to date, but he needed the credibility of a Ph.D. to feel he had achieved at least a modicum of professional acceptance. He needed his committee back at the University of Washington to sign off on his dissertation before he could begin to let loose the sense of struggle and self-defense that had gripped him for far too long.

To an equal degree, Garner's work was also driven by a passion to collect, to describe, to translate, and, finally, to resolve what—in his estimation—were among the most important dilemmas facing the planet. In the case of the Southern Ocean, this necessarily included the condition of the plankton, especially the incalculably immense populations of krill that sustained the world's largest planktivores, the baleen whales.

Gradually, Medusa was defining the parameters of these minute but vitally important organisms. Most significantly, Garner's invention was finding a diversity of species—notably their larval life stages—more than ten times higher than had ever been described. With the thinning of the ozone layer over the South Pole, the amount of ultraviolet radiation striking the sea surface had significantly increased. Exposed to increased irradiation, the reproductive cells of many plankton species, up to six times more susceptible to destruction by ultraviolet light, were gradually being destroyed. It was not the sort of thing making front-page headlines—yet—but slowly, almost imperceptibly, the ocean's plankton community was becoming sterile. Some estimates of plankton population decline now reached 15 percent, with entire generations being killed off long before reaching adulthood.

Any credible description of ocean conditions needed round-the-clock observations and multiple replicates. Plankton biologists often work through the night, when the zooplankton come up to the surface waters under the cover of darkness to feed on phytoplankton satiated by the day's sunlight. Dawn had just broken on the eastern horizon when Garner and Zubov finished Medusa's 4:00 A.M. tow, without incident. Zubov, a little wealthier from his night's poker winnings, shuffled off to his bunk to get some sleep.

Alone on the afterdeck, Garner tilted his head back and stretched, gazing appreciatively at the weak sunrise. Below his feet, he felt the *Lansing*'s powerful engines gently vibrating the deck as the ship plowed toward the next sampling station. Such moments were too precious not to enjoy, if only temporarily.

Clark poked his head out of the aft lab. "Garner— call for you on the bridge."

Garner followed the winch operator forward and made his way to the bridge, a twinge of concern building in his gut. Who would be calling him out here? Most of those who knew where he was wouldn't know how to reach him on the *Lansing*. Indeed, the ability to be out of touch with the civilized world and its cellular phones, fax machines, pagers, and electronic mail was a side effect of Garner's career choice that he considered a professional perk.

The radio operator said the caller was a Dr. Carol Harmon.

"Where are you?" Garner asked, a trace of a smile coming to his lips. Knowing his ex-wife's affinity for adventurous locales, she could literally be anywhere.

Carol gave him the specifics of their recent acoustic survey and how the *Balaenoptera* south of Baffin Island had waylaid them. "More importantly," Carol's voice came back over the static-laden connection, "where are *you*?"

Garner recounted the events of the past few days. Although Medusa was working marvelously, he and Zubov would be hard-pressed to get all their sampling done within the next week, even if the weather held up, which seemed unlikely. To fail in that, as it now appeared they might, would cost them the entire season and add at least another year to his data collection effort.

Their get-acquainted chatter had taken less than a minute, but Garner could already detect a nervous edge in Carol's voice. This wasn't just a social call.

"What's up, Doc?" he asked. "It sounds like you're up to your neck in more than just whales."

Carol hesitated before replying, uncertain how to begin or continue. "It's not just the ice that's got them," she finally said. "I think there's something in the water up here."

Something in the water. The purposefully nondescript statement suggested something more foreboding than vague. The last time Carol and Garner had discovered "something in the water," in the Pacific Northwest, a devastatingly lethal biological menace was already on the rampage.

Carol detailed their last two days on the ice with the whales, the dive taken by Dexter and Ramsey, and the terrifying symptoms that seemed to come from nowhere. "When Susan called it radiation poisoning, I thought she was nuts," Carol added, still incredulous at what the crew of the *Phoenix* had seen. "Then we got out a dosimeter—the only one we have, of course—and the samples confirmed it: the whales are cooked, the water is cooked, and for all I know, *we're* cooked."

"Cooked with *what*?" Garner pressed. "As a guess." He knew Carol's guesses were better than most thorough analyses.

The background radiation levels Carol relayed to him were incredible—easily a hundred times higher than anything occurring naturally in the environment. What mattered as much as the level or duration of exposure was the exact kinds of radionuclides—nuclear fission products—they had found.

"Enriched uranium," she replied. "At least, too much U-235 to be natural. Strontium, maybe. Cesium. Beryllium. A whole cocktail of minor elements, but of course it's the long-lived bastards that caught my attention."

"What about plutonium? Radium?"

"We don't know yet."

"Have you dredged any of the sediment for higher levels?"

"*Not yet*. We've got one dosimeter and it doesn't come with a recipe book for the stew we're finding up here."

"All right," Garner soothed her. "Back up. How can you be certain it's a local source of contamination?" Whales and other arctic mammals, by virtue of their size and position at the top of the food chain, were known to accumulate toxins, chemicals, and other pollutants in their tissues. Blue whales, traveling the world in their migration, had a tremendous opportunity to accrue things like long half-life radionuclides.

"As near as we can guess, this pod has been frozen in the ice for at least a week. But if the radioactivity in their flesh is accrued, it's a hundred—a *thousand*—times more concentrated than anything I've ever heard of." She listed the various governmental bodies she had contacted so far and the thoroughly blind-ended suggestions each had given her. "Even the nuclear regulatory agencies refuse to consider this as a potential military or industrial radiation source," she finished.

"And natural radiation sources aren't under anyone's formal jurisdiction," Garner added. "A hot potato, literally."

"What we've found can't be natural," Carol said. Garner could envision the set of her jaw, hands on her hips. Determination wasn't lacking in his ex-wife, something he had admired and at times resented during the directionless days of his early career. "And if it *isn't* natural, then . . ."

"Then you've got a big problem," Garner said.

"My biggest problem is that you're in the wrong bloody ocean," Carol said. She knew Garner already knew the reason for her call, and that the result of it would have an immediate effect on his own research. For as much as she had struggled with those reservations, she had made the call nonetheless. "I need you," she finally said, and with that admission the rest of her words followed in a rush. "I need you to come up here and help us figure out what's going on."

"If what you've just told me is correct, I'd have to agree," Garner said.

"I knew you would. I'm sorry. I should've taken a hint when I found out you couldn't possibly be any farther away from me and still be on the same planet. But once spring sets in, the melting ice could make any kind of contamination a lot worse. This floe is going to break up in a few *days*. If there's any chance of us identifying and containing the problem, we need you, we need Sergei, and we need Medusa up here. The sooner the better."

Garner didn't dispute the urgency of the request. He knew that Carol would have considered every plausible theory and official avenue before raising the alarm; if she was calling him, she had exhausted all more straightforward channels. Never mind that he needed at least another week in the Weddell Sea to get all the data he'd hoped to get. Never mind that the *Lansing* wasn't due back in the States until the end of the month. Never mind any of it. Carol needed him.

Garner relayed the *Lansing*'s present position. "What can the Nolan Group do to help us out?" he asked.

"How long will it take you to get to the Falkland Islands? I can have a Nolan jet waiting for you at Stanley. You can fly up, transfer to a helicopter at Cape Dorset or Hall Beach, and be here by the weekend." She made it sound like a junket to Cape Cod.

Garner was less optimistic as he worked out the itinerary in his mind. "I guess it depends," he said.

"On what?"

"On what the in-flight movie will be."

Relief rushed into Carol's voice. "Anything you want. *Everything* you want; it'll be a two-day trip." She paused again, overwhelmed by gratitude. "Thank you, Brock. Thank you so much."

Garner finalized the travel arrangements and confirmed them with the *Lansing*'s captain. "We can make the Falklands by Thursday," said the captain, a soft-spoken, experienced man named Mike Hahn. He was used to fielding cockeyed requests from agitated researchers and had a placid, evenhanded temperament to accommodate them. Hahn saw no point in getting into pissing matches over egos or priorities; the *Lansing*'s fee was the same regardless of what her ports of call were. "But yours is only one vote in six. The rest of the principal investigators will have your head on a platter if we lose any more station time."

In the weather officer's estimation, a side trip to the Falklands might help the *Lansing* avoid another approaching storm front, which would doubtless help to deflect the perceived inconvenience to the other principal investigators, or PIs. An added incentive for those who had been seasick for most of the past week was the prospect of at least twelve hours on solid ground once they got to the Falklands.

"Looks like you're in luck, Mr. Garner," Hahn said, then called for the revised course.

"Really?" Garner mused. "Somehow it doesn't feel like it."

Garner entered Zubov's cabin with a sharp knock and relayed the content of his discussion with Carol. His friend, already in his bunk, listened with half-closed eyes.

"They're gonna have to stop charging you full price on these little junkets," Zubov said. It wasn't the first time that Garner's cruise time had been interrupted by urgent news, calling him off the ship prematurely and suspending his planned sampling regime. "You want me to finish up here with Medusa?"

"No, I need you both to come with me. Pack Medusa for travel, then gather up your stuff. We won't be back on the *Lansing* this year."

Zubov still could not believe what he was hearing. An impromptu journey nearly pole to pole with half a ton of gear and a maverick researcher with severe acrophobia. Still more incredible, it wouldn't be their first inconvenient detour to result from such an invitation.

"You're gonna have to stop taking calls from that woman," Zubov said. Both men knew that the odds of Garner ignoring a distress call from his ex-wife were as remote as a long, balmy spell in the Southern Ocean in May.

As Zubov pulled on some clothes, Garner switched on the lamp above the desk and paced the small cabin from end to end. He recited items from a mental list of on-hand materials or substitutes they could arrange to pick up along the way. Over more than nine thousand air miles, they would be passing any number of possible depots.

As Garner finally finished, Zubov looked at his friend.

"Anything else?" Zubov asked sarcastically. He knew Garner well enough to know that there was always something else to be added to the manifest.

"Geiger counters," Garner said. Zubov saw the familiar look of theoretical distraction settle over his friend's face. He hated that look; it invariably resulted in tasks of unreasonable proportions. "Radiometers. Dosimeters for handheld use on dry land and waterproofed gamma spectrometers that Medusa could be modified to carry."

"Right," Zubov said, shaking his head dumbly. "Dry land equipment for use on top of the world's largest slush puddle and some custom-designed, waterproofed gamma specs. On two days' notice." This time his tone was acerbic. "And exactly how many of those will we be needing?"

"A lot," Garner replied. He was deadly serious.

3

As agreed, Carol dispatched a Nolan Group jet to the Falkland Islands to retrieve Garner and Zubov. The pilot, Ed Dunning, a gruff, heavyset man in his mid-fifties with a slight paunch, had retooled his career after being laid off by Delta. For his younger and more congenial copilot, Jim Lawrence, the job with the Nolan Group was one of his first in private industry. The two men arrived on the island only hours before the *Lansing*, rented a flatbed truck from a local sheep farmer, then met the ship at the government dock in Port Stanley. Zubov supervised the loading of Medusa onto the truck using a walkie-talkie and hand motions—some required, some unnecessarily obscene—to direct the crew operating the vessel's deck-mounted crane. Watching the intricate and convoluted procedure, the Nolan Group pilots could only shake their heads in disbelief and growing annoyance. It was still hard for them to comprehend that the purpose of their two-day trip was to retrieve an ungainly crate and its two unshaven but jocular keepers. For their part, the rest of the *Lansing*'s researchers and deck crew were happy to watch the proceedings from one of Stanley's British-style pubs. Given the alternative—another two days of violent rocking on the Weddell Sea—most gladly made this concession to Garner.

The cab of the farmer's truck was small and fitted with two seats scavenged from a pair of tractors long ago petrified by age and rust. Garner and Zubov rode in the back with the five-cubic-foot crate housing Medusa and smaller boxes filled with the rest of their gear.

"Are there many potholes in the road?" Garner asked. He thought of Medusa's more delicate instrumentation and wondered if they should take any exceptional packing precautions. He also anticipated the pilot's answer.

"Potholes? So many you'll hardly notice," the pilot answered. During the entire journey back to the reserve airport, one or another of the truck's wheels was continually lower than the rest as the vehicle jounced from one drop-out to the next. To the two pilots, still rattled from their landing at the small airfield, packing the two passengers onto the back of a sheep farmer's truck along with their temperamental luggage to personally share in the discomfort of this pole-to-pole trek was immensely satisfying.

As the truck waggled and wrestled with the road, its straining diesel engine managing little more than fifteen miles per hour, Zubov uncapped a Coca-Cola he had purchased from a vending machine at the government dock. He tried to put the glass neck of the bottle to his lips without bashing himself in the teeth. "We definitely need more stability in our lives," he said.

"I think I'd prefer storm waves to this," Garner said. "At least they're more rhythmic."

"And they don't smell like sheep."

The refueled, gleaming-white Lockheed Jetstar III waited for them at the reserve airport with all the misplaced elegance of a swan in a garbage dump. The jet was custom-built as a "combi," in pilot parlance, with a horizontally hinged door for large cargo while retaining a reduced number of seats in a comfortable passenger cabin. The Jetstar was probably the most advanced technology the airfield had seen since the British-Argentine conflict of 1982.

The airport wasn't the only one serving the Falklands' highly elastic population of about two thousand citizens, but it was the closest facility for the *Lansing* among the collection of nearly two hundred *Islas Malvinas,* as the Argentines knew them. With the approach of winter, the seasonal facility had been almost entirely shut down, with most of the field equipment stored in half a dozen dilapidated cargo hangars. The smell of spilled fuel and grease and the aroma from an exposed landfill wafted over the pitted tarmac from an adjoining field.

"You guys landed on *this*?" Zubov said, impressed.

"Yes, we did," Dunning replied, in a tone suggesting that he expected an apology from his charges.

"We thought about putting it down in the ocean and rowing ashore," Lawrence joked. "That might've been a bit smoother." It was remarkable that the jet had been able to land at all on the rutted, pockmarked strip of broken asphalt posing as a runway.

"Frost heaving," Dunning grumbled. "The frozen water in the pavement—pretty shitty pavement to begin with—opens up potholes and sinks. From the looks of this place, I don't think they're too used to routine maintenance." Only three other aircraft could be seen on the airfield, and none of them looked recently used.

The westerly winds had abated, but the thick overcast persisted and the amount of sunlight had been di-

minishing with each passing day. The sea was dull and
humorless, too shallow and broken by weathered boul-
ders to permit a landing by the *Lansing* or any large
vessel. Ten miles to the north and just visible around the
point were two offshore drilling platforms—a sign of
the not-too-distant future as foreign-owned oil companies began plundering the oil and gas reserves of the
South Atlantic. Garner couldn't help but uneasily muse
that, if the rigs were successful in their exploration,
there would be cause and money enough to build a
proper airport here. The local population could triple in
size and the ripple effects of this economic boon would
only have to traverse Drake Passage to reach Antarctica
and its unsuspecting population of three million fur
seals and 180 million Adélie penguins.

"You ready?" Zubov asked as the last of Medusa's
gear was securely stowed in the Jetstar.

"Wind's picking up," Lawrence said. "Better to go
now than risk it later."

"Let's go," Garner said.

The flight range of the modified Jetstar was twenty-five
hundred miles, meaning that they would have to make
at least four, and probably five, refueling stops—the last
of these likely being Churchill, Manitoba, on the western edge of Hudson Bay, or Cape Dorset, on Baffin
Island. There, Garner and Zubov would transfer to a
chartered helicopter for the trip to the rendezvous point
with the crew of the *Phoenix*. Until then, Garner and
Zubov were free to rest, sleep, or eat and the plane's
AirFones would be available for calls to arrange the
shipment of more equipment to the *Phoenix*.

With the cargo stowed and the flight plan set, Garner
and Zubov settled into two of the four leather seats in
the truncated passenger compartment. Garner hated

takeoffs, second only to landings. The sounds of the aircraft's cargo compartment thudding shut and the clanking from below as Lawrence pulled the chocks away from the wheels and climbed aboard were unnerving. The increase in the noise from the jet engines as the aircraft began to taxi, shuddering and halting as it passed over the potholes and fractured pavement beneath its wheels, was even more unnerving. A final hesitation, then the Jetstar began to pick up speed, the jolts from the landing gear coming faster and faster. Outside, the flat gray line of the sea rolled past the window, broken only by the fractured bedrock that lined the edge of the runway. To Garner, the cold, bleak water seemed to lurk out there, like a hungry shark waiting for the Jetstar to overshoot the end of the runway and topple into the ocean. The airplane's fuselage shook as though it were beginning to come apart, and Garner focused on his hands as they gripped the armrests of his seat.

"What the hell?" Zubov muttered from across the aisle. "Are we gonna *drive* there?"

With a final crescendo of thumps, the Jetstar lifted from the primitive runway, then banked toward their first refueling point, nineteen hundred miles north on the eastern coast of Brazil.

Zubov called forward to the pilots. "I hope São Paulo has something better than that."

"Until we get back to the States, the stops ahead of us will make 'Stanley International' look like LAX," Dunning called back. He was still looking for an apology.

Zubov gave Garner a mock look of terror. "Oh . . . my . . . God," he said, his eyes wide. He knew that joking about Garner's aversion to heights was more therapeutic than dwelling seriously on it. Garner himself wasn't entirely without a sense of humor about his affliction; he had even christened his live-aboard sailboat in Friday Harbor, Washington, the *Albatross*.

Before they had even reached cruising altitude, Zubov unbuckled his seat belt, stretched his bulky form with a dramatic yawn, then moved back to the plane's modest galley to plunder the well-stocked refrigerator. He returned and plopped heavily into the seat beside Garner, his arms piled high with snacks and miniature liquor bottles.

"Want something?" Zubov asked, nodding his head at the cornucopia of junk food in his arms. "Chee·tos? Snickers? Tanqueray?" A pair of bread sticks stuck out of his bearded mouth like walrus tusks.

Garner glanced at the offering, then shook his head and turned back to the window. His face had grown noticeably paler since he strapped himself into his seat and that seat had become airborne.

Zubov laughed at his friend's expression. "Man, the trouble you won't go through to satisfy that woman."

"It's not the flying—" Garner began his familiar mantra.

"I know, I know," Zubov said. " 'It's not the flying, it's the altitude.' But the two go together so damn well. Like Oreos and milk. Like beer and pretzels." He puffed out his chest and changed his voice to a dramatic baritone. "Like Brock Garner—and *danger*!"

Garner shot his friend a sharp look, then turned back to the window.

Zubov burst out laughing at his own joke, then pushed most of a chocolate bar into his mouth.

"It's *funny,* man," he said. "Sure, a phobia is a phobia. I'm scared of women with hairy legs. But you? Charles Lindbergh would give up flying after some of the shit you've flown through." Small planes, jetliners, helicopters—Zubov knew that circumstance had forced his friend reluctantly onto all of them, only to let fate deal him an unflagging assortment of mechanical failures, bad weather, and ill-timed circumstance intent upon trying to produce a crash. "Hell, if the Wright Brothers had you for a passenger, we'd still be riding bicycles."

"I know, Serg," Garner said. "I'm trying not to think about it."

"But you *should*," Zubov continued. "Because you've walked away every time. You're like a cat with seven lives."

"Nine lives," Garner said automatically.

"For you, I'd say seven," Zubov said.

"Shut up, Serg."

For the next hour, the two men sketched out a list of materials and contacts to be called as soon as the AirFones were in range of North American airspace. They speculated on the logistics of getting all this gear to the *Phoenix* in two days or less, then worked out a series of compromises and contingencies. At the moment, neither of them knew what to expect; anything they could scrounge would be better than nothing at all.

Zubov yawned again and stretched out across a bench seat along the rear of the cabin. Despite the mild turbulence that rocked the plane and the constant, muffled roar of the engines mounted aft on the fuselage, he was asleep within minutes, adding his own nasal drone to the overall dissonance.

Seeing the sea slip by far below was only one source of Garner's current displeasure. He hated sitting there, hated being strapped bolt upright into the narrow seat with almost nothing to do for the next day and a half. He didn't want to sleep, or eat, or read—not just yet, anyway. Without Zubov's animated distraction, Garner realized he was stuck there, alone with his thoughts. It was a place he generally tried to avoid.

Auftrieb was Johannes Müller's Germanic term for plankton, known into the 1800s only as nuisance material that clogged fishing and sampling nets. Viktor Hensen later coined the term *plankton* from the Greek for "tending to wander," which was an apt description of Garner's lifestyle during his research career. His initial lack of discernible direction had cost him his marriage to Carol. There had been women since Carol, of course, the last being an extended affair with Ellie Bridges, an emergency-room physician he had met during the cleanup operation in Puget Sound. Ellie attributed her eventual departure to Garner's unending travel, the long weeks at sea and ports of call without so much as a telephone, much less the comforts of home. Even their home—the *Albatross*—didn't have the comforts of home. Global oceanography is not a pursuit to be carried out in an attic apartment or a corner of the garage, and Garner's absences, though regrettable, were many. Ellie claimed to feel like an anchor in the decidedly fluid sphere of Garner's life, though such thoughts had never once occurred to Garner himself. After a brief sabbatical, Ellie had regained her passion for medicine and returned to practice in Canada.

In the wake of the affair, Garner immersed himself even deeper in his work. It was a too-familiar reaction. If his career was going to come at someone's personal expense, then he'd better make it the best possible career he could. Though still only a master's graduate, Garner had earned international recognition and support for Medusa and its applications. Medusa's detractors and critics grew fewer—or at least, less outspoken—as each new research paper was published in outlets ranging from *Science* and *Nature* to more specialized tomes like *Crustaceana*. Eventually, even the National Science Foundation and the National Oceanic and Atmospheric Administration had had to concede substantial long-term funding for Garner's fantastically promising work. The fact that Garner did not yet have his doctorate seemed irrelevant to everyone but himself.

The work might speak for itself, but Garner's life offered it little competition. He *was* his research. His curriculum vitae had become his list of family values. His publications were his progeny. Research cruises were vacations, and society conferences, cocktail parties. Now with a firm hold on a research career, Garner surmised that it must be some other personal failing that continued to interfere with his personal life. After all, no journey to the remotest corners on earth comes without the traveler running away from something. Past regrets began to cloud his concentration and remind him that he was growing old, or at least growing up. That process never got any easier or less time consuming.

Garner rolled over in the seat and tried to sleep. As he dozed off, he recalled the sound of Carol's voice, asking for his help once again. She was as close as Garner knew to a constant influence in his life. Maybe that was why he had never quite gotten over her.

Garner made certain he was awake for each of the fueling stops in South America, including Caracas, where Dunning and Lawrence were replaced by a fresh crew for the next two legs of the marathon journey. The majority of Garner's time was spent on the phone, trying to secure borrowed gear. It was the next day when Garner awoke from the latest in a series of brief, restless naps, one of the airplane's flannel blankets drawn up under his chin. Zubov was snoring on a seat across the aisle, a pile of candy wrappers on the seat beside him. He looked like an overgrown child sleeping off a Halloween binge.

Garner unbuckled his seat belt and moved forward, slightly stooped in the low-slung cabin, and poked his head into the cockpit. The copilot held the controls while the pilot dozed in his seat.

"Welcome back to the States," the copilot said. "You can tell from the smog."

"Where's our next fueling stop?" Garner asked.

"Somewhere in Jersey. Either Trenton or Newark. Depends on the traffic ahead of us. Why?"

"If we have to stop anyway, let's make it someplace useful," Garner said.

The pilot stirred beneath his down-turned cap and smiled for the first time. "Hey now. Jersey's plenty useful—for certain things."

"Where did you have in mind?" the copilot asked Garner.

"How about the center of Western civilization?" Garner replied.

The marble vistas and nonstop activity of Washington, D.C., were a jarring change from the trappings aboard the *Lansing*, not to mention the more pastoral surroundings of Stanley, São Paulo, or Caracas. Both Garner and Zubov appreciated the chance to stand fully upright as they walked across the tarmac to the main terminal of Reagan National Airport, but the air felt thick with the grit and odor of an urban Friday afternoon.

After a brief stop at the National Science Foundation's headquarters in Arlington, Virginia, and the seventh-floor offices of the Division of Polar Research, Garner and Zubov crossed Randolph Street to the Office of Naval Research, or ONR. They were given security badges at the front desk, then escorted upstairs and through a set of doors marked

BUREAU OF THE NAVY/
NAVAL ORDNANCE LABORATORY
RESTRICTED ACCESS

Two doors from the end of the hall, Garner recognized a familiar nameplate, as well as the man in its corresponding office.

Scott Krail was lean and handsome in a boyish way, with a compact physique that didn't look as though it had altered the fit of his uniform since his graduation from Annapolis. Just a handful of years older than Garner, Krail was one of the Navy's youngest commanders—a distinction that Garner would doubtless have shared with him sooner were it not for life's Auftrieb. In addition to being a master tactical analyst, Krail was one of the Navy's best-educated officers, with a depth and breadth of knowledge that ranged from nuclear engineering to seamanship to the odds-on favorite for the week's Monday Night Football game. When Garner left the Navy, Krail had just been assigned to special projects for NOL. God only knew what he was up to these days.

"Great to see you, buddy!" Krail said. He jumped to his feet as the two men strode into his office and greeted them both with a vigorous handshake. "What's it been? Four years? Five?" He snapped his fingers as he remembered. "Yeah, five. We met for a drink down at the Old Ebbitt Grill just before I transferred down to this backwater from Nav Intell." Without pausing for breath or waiting for a reply, Krail stood back to look at his guests. "Even Lewis and Clark had better fashion sense than you two," he said with a laugh.

With the exception of their cold-weather jackets, grossly unsuited to Washington in late spring, Garner and Zubov were still wearing the same clothes they had worn when they departed the *Lansing*. Neither man had showered or shaved in nearly a week and both still had the gaunt, vaguely haunted look of the wilderness. To complete their accoutrements, both now carried an armload of U.S. Geological Survey maps and Coast Guard navigation charts borrowed from another friend of Garner's at NSF.

"We've been on the road again," Zubov admitted. "Don't mind the smell."

"Pole to pole in two days." Krail shook his head. "Sounds like some kind of publicity stunt for the

Explorer Channel—you sure that woman of yours is worth it?"

"She's not mine anymore, but yeah, she's worth it," Garner said. "You know that." Krail had known Carol and her stepbrother, Mark, when Garner was still in the service. Krail had, in fact, been among the first to suggest that Garner consider academe as a civilian outlet for his obvious affinity for the sea.

"I do," Krail said. He motioned for his guests to take a seat, then poured three mugs of coffee from the carafe on his credenza. "And now Carol Harmon, the levelest of academic heads, CEO of a top-five ecoconglomerate, has turned Chicken Little over some kind of rad spill south of Baffin Island. She called me too."

"With good reason, it sounds like," Garner said, accepting the coffee. "She can't test it completely, but she says she's detected radioactive cesium, strontium, maybe some uranium. At the least, concentrations of uranium 233-to-238, too high to be natural. Maybe some plutonium? Beryllium too? Beryllium's used to trigger nukes. That sounds like weapons waste to me, Scott. And it sounds like there's a lot of it in the water up there."

Krail wrinkled his nose in disagreement. "Uranium in the Arctic isn't a problem. There have been some reports around Great Bear Lake—the Sahtugot'ine Inuit around Déline come to mind. They're talking about lung cancer from a uranium mine that operated up there fifty years ago." The casualness with which Krail seemed to dismiss local health effects did not go unnoticed by either Garner or Zubov. Perhaps Krail had spent too much time behind his desk in the Restricted Access wing. "And then there's the airborne crap that settles out of the atmosphere. Mild radiation. PCBs. Maybe some natural sources, but nothing on the scale that she described on the phone. The thing most people forget when it comes to things like 'spilled uranium' is that it gets taken up in the environment pretty quickly."

" 'The environment' includes wildlife," Garner countered.

"Sure, yeah," Krail conceded. "But the concentrations just aren't high enough to be suspect, much less lethal."

Garner wasn't nearly as diffident. Very little was known about the movement of uranium through an ecosystem. Iodine 131, with a very high specific activity, had a half-life of about a week, but its cousin I-129 had a half-life of seventeen million years. Plutonium didn't travel well in the environment, and would likely settle out in the sediment—far worse than the publicly perceived threat of "radiation leaks" from plutonium was the out-and-out loss of stored material from poorly guarded nuclear waste facilities around the world. Uranium, for its part, was still a bit of a mystery. No one really knew how it moved through the environment. Given all of these considerations, Garner found Krail's cavalier attitude slightly annoying—at the very least, their friendship should have been above the usual Navy PR rhetoric.

"What about live weapons?" Garner asked.

Krail almost scoffed. "You mean lost or leaking nukes—something like that?" Garner nodded. "Not a chance," Krail said. "Hollywood paints a different picture of it, of course, but just *losing* a U.S. nuke is a virtual impossibility. As you might expect, our most destructive toys are also the most locked down." He indicated the computer terminal on his desk. "You give me a weapon type and I can tell you *exactly* how many we have and *exactly* where they are. And for fifty bucks," he added, whispering behind his hand in feigned confidentiality, "I'll even tell you who they're pointed at."

"What about someone else's weapons, like the Russians?" Zubov asked.

"Ah, the Russians," Krail said with a somewhat sentimental resonance. Given the stumbling of the Great Bear in recent years, discussion of the once-fervent Cold War and the threat of the Soviet Menace had almost been reduced to charming anecdotes. Far from eliminating or even reducing the threat of nuclear attack, the ebb of the superpower had probably done just as much to destabilize the world's nuclear arsenal. With weapons, parts, facilities, and even scientists now bartered internationally as frankly as coffee or grain, those charged with providing the common defense could admit only to losing track of many pieces on the global chessboard. Krail reiterated these sentiments as he briefly discussed the latest nuclear developments of the Russians, the French, and the Iraqis. India and Pakistan had recently put on more nuclear fireworks shows for the sake of national pride, but it was generally agreed that the threat of those arsenals was vastly overestimated. To hear Krail's evaluation, America was almost ready to place a classified ad to recruit a new Evil Empire against which to fortify its national defense budget, but—"China's shaping up to be a good *faux* foe to build Cold War II around. I see from the newspapers that the Pentagon's spin doctors are off to a good start."

A lack of obvious culprits wasn't what Garner wanted to hear. "Carol says the radiation seems to be mainly in the water column, not suspended as atmospheric fallout," Garner said. "I thought it might be debris from an underwater weapons test."

"Either way, we would have heard about it," Krail said.

"What about a waste dump?" Garner suggested. "The Soviets used to dump their nuclear garbage straight into the Atlantic—I'd guess they still do."

"Sure they do, but nothing like this has come across my desk." *Trust me*, said the look on Krail's face. Garner only wished he could. The lack of specific details about Carol's findings was beginning to bother him. In Krail he had a friendly, learned ear for this discussion, but Garner was left grasping at straws.

Garner unrolled a Coast Guard chart on Krail's table and pointed out, as precisely as he could, where the *Phoenix* had encountered the blue whales and where, given the seasonal wind and current patterns, the floe might have drifted in the past few weeks.

"It's a long shot," Garner said. "But as soon as I confirmed the location on the chart, I thought of *Scorpion*."

"Which one?" Krail chuckled. It was somewhat of an inside joke around ONR. During World War II, the *Scorpion*, a diesel-powered U.S. submarine, had been lost without a trace. Years later, the Americans and the Soviets had each lost a nuclear submarine named *Scorpion*. The Americans' sub had been a Skipjack-class vessel apparently sunk by a battery explosion after patrolling the Mediterranean Sea in mid-1968.

Krail provided the story of the Russian *Scorpion* for Zubov's benefit. "We first heard about the sub via our Arctic SOSUS arm," he began. "A major avalanche of sediment in a submarine canyon system in the Gulf of Boothia. The seismic disturbance we detected might have been written off as an earthquake, except that the smart little bugger doing the analysis filtered out another disturbance *before* the landslide signatures began."

"What kind of disturbance?" Zubov asked.

"We still don't know," Krail replied. "Some kind of detonation, but definitely man-made. It was either a delayed weapon, like a mine, or an accidental explosion aboard the vessel. Whatever it was, the brass thought it suspicious enough to suggest we go have a look. What we found under four hundred feet of water and half a mountain of rock was a nuclear sub so advanced it made the *Red October* look like *Chitty Chitty Bang Bang.*"

"What year was this?"

"Eighty-five. At the height of Reaganomics and paranoia about the Soviet Menace. Until then we thought our Los Angeles–class subs were the sweetest boats in the ocean. Then we find this huge motherfucking Ivan with technology we were years from implementing. She was a reengineered Soviet Typhoon–class with a triple hull of honeycombed titanium, anechoic plating, shaft shielding, and cavitation damping we couldn't even get to work on a chalkboard. All new weapons and new sonar arrays. Fifty thousand horses produced by two transmutation reactors cooled by liquid lead." Twenty years later, transmutation reactors—power plants that used neutron bombardment to generate power from the waste products of other reactors—were just beginning to be evaluated by the private sector. "After reverse engineering her, we figured she could have done thirty-five knots as quiet as an ant's fart. There's still a lot of head scratching as to how they managed to get past our watchdogs on the Kola Peninsula." Krail paused for a moment, apparently remembering those days, then his eyes turned to Zubov. "Ingenious motherfuckers, those comrades of yours."

Zubov was used to U.S. military types referring to his heritage as though it were some kind of pestilence. "Then why tell me?" he asked. "How do you know I won't go skipping back to 'Ivan'?"

Krail lifted an index finger toward Garner. "Because you're with him. And what hasn't already been leaked to the international intelligence community by now isn't worth knowing."

"So what was *Scorpion* doing in the Canadian Arctic?" Zubov asked.

"Probably looking to embarrass us," Krail admitted.

"And she succeeded. Our detection network missed her completely and we still don't know if her captain was intentionally trying to leave us a calling card, or whether someone on board screwed up while navigating the canyon."

"Hell of a tight spot to try and park a boat that big," Garner said.

"Like I said," Krail replied, "maybe her captain was just trying to flip us the bird." Krail's casual tone suggested to Garner that his friend wasn't telling the whole story—but perhaps the story was really just as trivial as Krail was suggesting.

"Anyhow," Krail continued, "now we've got this seven-thousand-ton piece of Jules Verne in the middle of the Canadian Arctic—too far from home for the Soviets to do anything about it. The fact that we *could* recover *Scorpion* was probably the only thing that deterred the Russians from building dozens more. Whatever sunk her did more for the national defense than any two hundred intelligence operations."

"You salvaged a *Soviet* warship?" Zubov asked skeptically. "I bet they had something to say about that."

"They should have," Krail said. "But they were just as red-faced about the whole thing as we were. Neither side wanted to admit the boat had ever existed. We called it the tomato standoff."

"What about the Canadians?" Garner asked. "The site is inside their territorial waters and they're a nuke-free country."

"Nuke ninnies only protest what they know about," Krail said with a wave of his hand. "I suppose someone high up on their defense ladder questioned our operation, but we convinced them it was in their best interests." He laughed. "What the hell were the *Canadians* gonna use to salvage it? Canoes?"

Krail then told the men to wait as he checked the reference number on Garner's chart, dialed an extension on the telephone, and relayed the information to the answering party. A few minutes later, an ensign knocked at the door, holding what appeared to be a rolled-up transparent plotting sheet.

"Technically I'm not supposed to show this to civilians," Krail said as he took the chart and unrolled it over the chart Garner had provided. "So you'll have to look at this with one eye closed. You too, Ivan," he said to Zubov, with a good-natured wink.

As the two charts were aligned, it was obvious that the transparent chart was a complete rendering of the Coast Guard chart, only with currents, landforms, and bottom contours shown in far more precise detail.

"Obviously, the Navy gets to use a much more recent and more detailed version of the bathymetry," Krail said. "These plots outresolve even our best SASS plots. The data they're plotted from is still classified. There are things out there we don't want just anyone picking up in a marine shop or ordering over the Internet, and the Gulf of Boothia is hardly a place where we need to regularly post updated hazards to pleasure boats."

Garner was impressed at the level of detail rendered on Krail's chart. The transparent sheeting not only provided a multicolor depiction of far more chart elements, but also a holographic depiction of the seafloor itself. "Speaking of Jules Verne," he said. "I didn't know you guys had these."

"Then someone's still doing their job," Krail said.

Garner studied the enhanced chart before them. At the approximate coordinates of *Scorpion*'s demise, Krail's chart showed a narrow, elongated chasm on the seafloor. The depth profile showed a nearly constant 280 meters bounded on either side by walls that topped out at 100 meters. Squared type set along the middle of the heavily branched formation declared the name of the canyon: THEBES DEEP.

"Ominous name," Garner observed. "As in 'the plague of Thebes'? Famine and death of the youngest until Oedipus returned and solved the riddle of the Sphinx?"

"Man, you read way too much." Zubov shook his head, impressed.

"Everyone can use a little Sophocles now and then," Garner replied with a shrug.

"It's nothing that erudite, I'm afraid," Krail said. "I think the geologist who found it was named Thebes. Albert Thebes."

Garner shot Krail a stung look and Zubov let out a bellowing laugh. "Oh, but *your* version is good too," Zubov said, nudging his friend.

"Whatever it's called, that's where Ivan took his dive," Krail said, indicating the position on the chart.

"If she was trying to hide, *Scorpion* couldn't have picked a better place," Garner noted. "Deep and noisy as hell, with the ice grinding above and the branches of the canyon below."

"A good place to make repairs too," Krail agreed. "Maybe she was damaged and that led to her taking the low road—low enough that she'd never be recovered. She almost made it."

"And you still say there's no chance the wreck could be part of the current problem?" Garner asked again.

"None," Krail assured him. "That case is closed. Even if it weren't, you and Carol aren't equipped to attempt a look-see at that depth. Hell, half the Arctic fleet barely pulled it off. *Scorpion* had two reactors. One we recovered intact, the other we believe was buried in a submarine earthquake. Transmutation reactors are very clean, so even if her cores were cracked open, it's highly doubtful we'd see this much contamination this long after the fact." Krail pointed to the chart again, indicating the narrow channel between Melville Peninsula and

Baffin Island. "Besides, look at the tight bathymetry here. Show me where contaminated bottom water could find its way through all of that into Foxe Basin?"

"No one's talking about bottom water yet," Garner corrected him. "What Carol's found so far is on the surface, probably carried along by the ice."

"Over hundreds of miles? Through that logjam? From *one* inoperative sub's reactor *decades* after the fact?" Krail insisted. "You might as well blame the mine at Déline. Or the *Lenin*."

The *Lenin,* the world's first nuclear-powered ice-breaker, reportedly had a major reactor accident while on an arctic cruise. Then there was Kosmos 954, a nuclear-powered spy satellite that had crashed in Canada's Northwest Territories in 1979, scattering radioactive debris over miles of tundra. Other weapons operations had used Canada's northern territory as a friendly approximate to Siberia for years. Certainly none of these incidents could be considered a massive radiation source on an individual basis, but Garner found it troubling that there were so many minor culprits in a place as supposedly remote and untouched.

"C'mon, buddy, use a little common sense," Krail urged him. "Believe me on this one."

"I believe you," Garner said. *I believe you, but you're trying a bit too hard to sell me on the point,* he thought. "It's just that I've come across 'highly implausible' scenarios before, and—"

"And they tend to be the messiest," Zubov added.

"Agreed," Krail said. "Which makes it either very honorable or very stupid that you'd even bother to go look."

"She's worth it," Garner said again.

"Worth the honor or the stupidity?" Krail asked.

"Both. But thanks for your help."

"You know what they say about free advice," Krail

said. "You get what you pay for. But let me know what you find." Krail fixed them with his studious eyes. "If there's anything up there we don't already know about, I'd be interested. Very surprised, but interested."

"You, me, and a few others," Garner said.

4

From Churchill, Manitoba, a chartered De Havilland Twin Otter carried Garner and Zubov to Cape Dorset on Baffin Island, though Medusa had to be freed from her packing crate to fit inside the smaller aircraft's narrow fuselage. At Cape Dorset, the travelers were transferred to a Canadian Helicopters Sikorsky S-61 for the last leg of their nine-thousand-mile journey.

Compared to the luxurious accommodations aboard the Nolan Group jet or the rugged functionality of the Twin Otter, the Sikorsky felt like the offspring of a garden shed and a paint shaker. Built to be an offshore transport, the helicopter had been modified for long-distance shuttling of cargo and personnel to support the oil industry. Its current home range was the vast eastern expanse of Canada's Northwest Territories, now Nunavut, including the waters of Hudson Bay, Hudson Strait, and Foxe Basin.

The cost to the Nolan Group of delivering Garner and his unique device was already enormous, and with that consideration, Garner's uneasiness returned. Carol was far from frivolous when it came to such expenses, and there was more to her request than personal efficiency. She really did believe that the cost of importing him and Zubov was justified compared to the eventual cost of leaving them to do their work in the Antarctic.

As aboard the Jetstar and the shepherd's truck, Garner and Zubov were relegated to a makeshift space behind the pilots—this time room for them had been created within a cavernous cabin once intended to carry up to three dozen troops but now used almost exclusively for cargo. Strapped into a pair of jump seats facing aft, Garner and Zubov had a clear view of Medusa, now seated on a borrowed mattress and strapped to the floor over the helicopter's center of gravity. The vibration through the Sikorsky's airframe was still uncomfortably intense, varying only slightly as a gusting headwind caused the helicopter to jump in altitude, then drop down sharply as it made its way out over the southern edge of Foxe Basin. Above them, the rotors were hammered through the cold arctic air by two turboshaft engines, the thudding blades flickering past the pale sunlight like a strobe. The stench of kerosene and other hot fluids was thick and cloying. Garner turned his attention away from his growing nausea and the anxious tingling in his chest and focused instead on a forgotten lock washer that vibrated and bounced on the floor of the helicopter.

"Where do you suppose this came from?" Garner asked, nudging the small galvanized ring between his boots.

Zubov shrugged. "Hell, in a rattletrap like this it could've come out of anything—the seat, the hatch, the hoist, the main rotor—"

"Thanks. You're a big help."

Garner turned his attention back to the window and

gazed out over the majestic landscape slipping past them some three hundred feet below. If one could endure the bitter cold of winter and stay on top of the ice, in summer the Arctic was truly one of the most stunning environs on earth. Seen from the air, the nearly unimaginable stillness resembled a lake or an inland sea more than the savage ocean it was reputed to be. It was only the first of many deceptions this place had in store for visitors.

Along the treeless horizon, snow-encrusted vistas rose up from the sea and distant islands loomed like sounding whales. Ice jutted from the water as much as fifty feet before dropping off sharply or tapering to elongated shapes that bridged the naturally formed crevasses. Wind had sculpted many of the taller icebergs with almost artistic skill, rounding edges and bridging sharp peaks to create stunning profiles.

Unlike the churning slate gray of the Weddell Sea, the ocean here is a deep cobalt blue—nearly black—held in a placid stillness. Garner could see that the spring melt had clearly begun in earnest; massive fissures fractured the sea ice into rafts of every description. Soon the resident plankton populations would respond to the increased daylight here and return in abundance to the surface waters of the Arctic Ocean. With this florescence would come the Arctic birds—eider ducks, guillemots, gyrfalcons, and gulls—for a few weeks of feeding and breeding. The seals, walrus, and whales would exploit an ocean surface free of the ice that not only interfered with breathing but also provided a firm foundation for predators. On land, the herds of caribou would be returning from the south, ragged and hungry from their long winter, but food enough for equally hungry polar bears along the coast or for the ravenous Greenland sharks that patrolled the shallow channels between islands. Come summer, the

Arctic would open its ice-locked doors and welcome one of the most plentiful but most delicate food webs ever studied. With less than 2 percent of the species diversity found in the tropics, the Arctic was far less resilient to disturbances, human or otherwise. It was this landscape, this slumbering horn of plenty, which now beckoned to Garner, inviting him closer.

Closer. Each time the helicopter lost altitude and the ground suddenly rose up beneath them, Garner was convinced it had nothing to do with turbulence, but rather, that they had used up the last of their fuel and were about to plunge into Foxe Basin. The stark but beautiful wasteland below only made these daydreams more credible: this place of extremes and superlatives, of desolation and simplicity, lent itself easily to thoughts of sudden demise.

"There it is," the pilot's voice suddenly came over their headsets.

Garner twisted around in his seat, straining to look forward. He could just make out the dull red shape of the *Phoenix*'s hull, a gunshot wound against the expansive white background. Since the Nolan Group lost the *Kaiku* in Puget Sound, the four-hundred-foot *Phoenix* had become its research flagship. This was the first time Garner had glimpsed the ship since the refitting Carol had requisitioned. Even from a distance, the improvements to the renovated vessel were impressive. The entire bridge had been enlarged and raised two full decks to accommodate a larger superstructure. The expansive antenna array suggested the latest in radio and satellite communication equipment, and heavy-duty winches had been added to manage the variety of scientific gear to be coordinated by the ship's boatswain.

Zubov shared Garner's appraisal of the ship. "The Nolan Group never does anything on a small scale, do they? The thing looks like a cruise ship." The obvious envy in Zubov's voice was strictly professional. Except for dedicated military ships, most government research vessels could not come close to having such comfort and technology, nor could they justify the budget required to build one. They also did not pay their crews nearly as well.

Surrounding the vessel on three sides was a variety of equipment and personnel offloaded to the ice in a kind of makeshift base camp. Garner could see the holes broken in the ice and at least one of the whales still trapped beneath the floe. It appeared as though a large piece of the ice had calved into the sea, and Garner wondered if this had anything to do with one or more of the whales being released.

As the helicopter lowered toward the *Phoenix,* a figure in a bright blue exposure suit stepped down from the bridge, a radio gripped in the hand he waved above his head. From the man's beard and longish, sandy blond hair, Garner correctly guessed that this was Patrick Byrnes, the ship's operations officer and Zubov's counterpart on the *Phoenix.* Byrnes had, in fact, been the boatswain assigned to the final voyage of the *Kaiku,* and it was good to see that Carol had reassigned him to an equally impressive post.

Byrnes pulled down his scarf and drew the radio to his mouth. A moment later his voice came over the helicopter's radio.

"Welcome, gentlemen," Byrnes said. "We just put out the red carpet for you."

Garner could hear the pilots talking, first to each other, then to Byrnes: "I hope you don't expect us to land on your deck," the pilot said. Although the *Phoenix* was equipped with a small helipad, a landing with the ship's communications array fully deployed, as it now was, would be impossible.

"Negative," came the reply. "We wanted to build some kind of landing pad next to the main camp, but the ice there is probably too thin. What's your loaded weight?"

The pilots relayed this information. "That's about what I thought," Byrnes confirmed. "You're too heavy."

"Not for long, if we keep using up our fuel chitchatting with this guy," the copilot muttered.

Byrnes pointed out a large "X" that had recently been sprayed on the ice in fluorescent green paint about a hundred yards from the ship. Someone had added a happy face to the design and topped it off with a mane of long, tangled "hair" that stood nearly on end—a humorous caricature of Medusa.

"Set down over there," Byrnes said. "We'll meet you with the SnoCats."

The pilots had the helicopter on the ground within minutes, its tricycle landing gear biting into the snow. If the ice buckled or groaned in protest, the sound was lost beneath the whine of the engines as they were powered down. Garner and Zubov bailed out of their jump seats and began unfastening Medusa even before the rotor blades had stopped.

"Don't worry, fellas," Garner said. "We'll leave you time enough to get home for dinner." As always happened when he stepped down from an aircraft, Garner felt a hollow sense of relief spread through him. With the arduous flight now over and the task of a rapid unloading before them, Garner felt his fatigue begin to ebb for the first time in forty-eight hours.

As the cacophony of the rotor blades died away, Garner could appreciate the sounds of the Arctic. He held his breath, closed his eyes, and listened for a moment. Even from a hundred yards away, he could faintly hear the grumble of the *Phoenix*'s generators and the thin chirping of metal pitons being hammered into the snow to accommodate any variety of activities. Closer, ubiquitously, the sloshing and sucking of the sea and the gentle bobbing of the floe were a reminder that this was not solid land they had breached. Otherwise, the air was utterly silent.

They had already unloaded the smaller crates by the time the first SnoCat arrived. The *Phoenix* apparently operated a small fleet of the oversized snowmobiles with steel treads and a generous, three-walled cab for the driver. The ugly but functional machines looked like bulldozers that had been run over by an eighteen-wheeler. Byrnes was driving and Carol sat beside him on the bench seat, her hands braced on the walls of the cab for support. As she saw Garner and Zubov, her face broke into a wide grin behind her tinted goggles.

"Welcome to *Balaenoptera* beach," she called, hopping off the SnoCat and giving Garner a warm embrace.

"The natives seem friendly enough," Garner said, as he kissed her.

"Only for you southerners," Carol said.

"Lady, from here *everyone* is a southerner," Zubov said, stepping over to them and wrapping Carol in a bear hug.

"As you can see, we have all the comforts of home—mass transit, sport diving, gourmet dining," Carol said, sweeping her arm behind her.

"And wildlife," Garner said. "Don't forget the wildlife."

"Oh yeah, we've got wildlife," Byrnes agreed. "By the truckload."

"And contamination by the Sievert," Carol added gravely. A Sievert was a unit of equivalent biological dose—tissue exposure to radiation. Typical exposures were given in *milli*Sieverts, or one-thousandths of a unit, which made Carol's remark all the more chilling. "All five of the whales seem to be carrying horrific levels of uranium and cesium, as well as a laundry list of other radionuclides we couldn't even begin to measure clearly. So far there aren't many culprits we *haven't* found."

"That's my first concern," Garner said. "This whole station must be hot, yet I don't see anyone in radiation suits."

"There are some things even the Nolan Group can't arrange on short notice," Carol said. "I'm beginning to find out how unprepared everyone is when it comes to the possibility of a nuclear leak. Suits are coming—a lot of things are coming—so for now we've got these whales and a whole lot of questions."

"You're not concerned about exposure?" Zubov asked.

"Of course I am, Serg," Carol said. The grim set of her jaw showed every ounce of her vested leadership in this expedition and its crew. "But at this point we still have no idea where to go. Any given direction could be out of danger or farther into it. I guess I'd rather keep a foothold in the area than risk losing track of it completely."

"The atmospheric rad levels—as best we can measure them right now—seem to be nominal," Byrnes added. "The greatest accumulation is in the flesh of the whales, with the water column not far behind."

Garner asked Carol about the status of the two divers. "We had them airlifted out," she said. "Helicoptered to Cape Dorset, then onto a Canadian Forces Medevac Hercules to an ICU in Toronto. The doctors there confirmed exposure to at least six Sieverts of radiation, though with the effects of immersion it's hard to tell for sure." Carol didn't have to elaborate further—in a few minutes of diving, the men had been exposed to more than three thousand times the usual *yearly* dose of radiation, and a level twice as great as that received by the first emergency teams to arrive at the Chernobyl nuclear accident. Many of those men had collapsed within hours of returning from their missions. Most had died, painfully, within days, after experiencing blindness, lesions and sloughing of their flesh, and a nearly complete collapse of their circulatory, nervous, and excretory systems.

Now, reflecting on how Dexter had looked in his cabin and how much his health had worsened by the time the SAR helicopter arrived at the *Phoenix,* Carol's voice wavered. "I don't think I want to know how they're doing now. Not really," she said. "But they're in good hands. Let's hope for an improvement and pray we'll see them again soon."

If Garner and Zubov had been impressed by a glimpse of the *Phoenix* from the air, Carol's personal tour of the vessel was stunning. The original hull had been sliced open and lengthened, reinforced with frame struts sixteen inches apart—instead of the usual thirty-six inches—and an additional inch of iron plating, then stitched back together. The vessel's twin diesel engines had been overhauled and the screws shielded from ice damage by more plating. The superstructure had been nearly doubled in size to accommodate a larger research lab and a battery of new onboard computers, including state-of-the-art sonar, communications, and a global positioning system rig. Belowdecks, the holds had been improved to better suit the reinforced hull, and twenty crew cabins had been added to the enlarged super-structure. The bridge had been fitted with ceiling-to-deck polarized windows that offered a sweeping view of the surrounding sea. An environmental-monitoring station had been added to the quarterdeck, assisted by a new A-frame and assorted cargo cranes along both gun-wales.

Carol finished the tour with obvious pride. "I think it's the best privately held icebreaker in the world," she said.

"It might've been cheaper to build a new boat from scratch," Zubov said, only half joking.

"Sure," Carol said. "We thought about it, but then we'd have to decommission the old vessel and I hate wasting anything." It was a typical Carol Harmon understatement: while most people spoke of "not wasting" something, they usually meant paper bags or leftover food, not a twelve-thousand-ton ship.

As they completed their tour, Carol apologized again for the expedition's lack of radiation-monitoring equipment. The single dosimeter they had aboard was barely adequate for testing the air and the lab samples they had collected from the whales, and she berated herself for not foreseeing the need for it.

"Carol, you can't be serious," Garner said. "From what I can see, you're prepared for every possible contingency *except* this, and no one could have predicted what you've found. There's a limit to what a ship can carry."

"Even this tub," Zubov joked.

Carol chewed her lip, unconvinced. "Still—"

"Yes," Zubov agreed, straight-faced. "You should have brought a still. I could use a drink." He caught Garner's sharp look and sighed. "All right, I'm going." He shrugged back into his exposure suit and returned outside to assist Byrnes's crew in bringing Medusa aboard.

Left alone in the main lab, Carol briefed Garner on everything they had learned since discovering the whales. "The floe is already beginning to break up," Carol said. "One of the whales finally struggled free yesterday and we could lose another one in the next day or so." Given the serious nature of what they had found in the whales' tissue, the notion of freeing them from their attachment to the floe had become secondary to learning as much as possible about the animals and their condition. The focus of the *Phoenix*'s crew had become, first, to keep the behemoths alive and, second, to keep them readily accessible for as long as possible. Even with unobstructed passage through the ice, any vessel would find it impossible to follow the whales for any period of time once they made a break for open water. "As you might expect," Carol added, "a hundred-ton blue whale doesn't ask permission. Except for being stuck to this damn ice, it pretty much does whatever it wants."

"You've got them fitted with tracking devices?" Garner asked.

"Of course," Carol said. "Probe transmitters threaded through their back muscles." The harmless, practically disposable devices were routinely employed to track the migration of large aquatic animals like whales, seals, and sharks in the open sea. "We'll have a running record of their movement, speed, depth, and basic metabolism, but only from this point forward. We still have no way of knowing how they got here."

They returned to the *Phoenix*'s bridge and pored over the large chart table there. The latest estimation of the floe's movement was marked on the charts, and Garner compared this with the known ocean currents through the area. The charts were standard mariner issue from the Canadian Hydrographic Office, and Garner mentioned the high-resolution versions he had borrowed from Krail. "I think we'll need as much information as we can get."

"So far that's not much," Carol said. "In the past three days, I've called the U.S. Nuclear Regulatory Commission, the EPA, the Sierra Club, the Canadian Energy Commission—even the native legislators in Iqaluit and Igloolik. When I start asking if they know of any radiation spills in this area, they act as though I'm putting out an APB on Godzilla."

"That bad?"

"If they know anything, they're not talking," Carol

said. "Only Nuuk, in Greenland, reacted with any sort of concern. They said they had a Japanese scientist working there who knew something about radiation and they would have her contact me. I've got a great technician on board with some medical training—Susan Conant. She was the first to give us a diagnosis, but even she admits she's out of her depth on this. We all are."

"Are there any observers who could help you?" Garner asked. Research vessels working in foreign waters often invited a representative of the host country on board to act as a liaison, a watchdog for any impropriety, and occasionally even as a navigator or pilot. For the current expedition, Canada had provided one such observer to ride along with the *Phoenix*.

"The kid's name is Seaborg," Carol said. "A summer intern. The Canadian government took some flak when they awarded this contract to an American company, so Seaborg was thrown in as a kind of peace offering. If this isn't his first job, I'd like to know what was. I think he's asleep more than he's awake, and when he's awake he's playing golf on the computer."

"A nubby," Garner ventured. Nonuseful body, in naval terms.

"He takes care of table scraps pretty well," Carol said.

"In any event, I doubt the lack of information is a conspiracy against you," Garner said. "That would suggest they know about it in the first place. If it's a spill, chances are the only people who know about it are the ones who spilled it, and they likely won't be stepping forward voluntarily."

"Do you think there's been some kind of illegal dumping?"

"From what you've shown me, the high-level elements are too concentrated to be from a natural source and they're too impure to be from weapons." He could see Carol's disappointment. "I know, it doesn't answer the big question."

"That's why you're here," Carol said. "To have Medusa tell us where."

Garner looked at the chart again, using his fingers as a pair of makeshift calipers to approximate distance and direction.

"I'd say we need to let the whales go on their way. Then we get Medusa in the water as soon as Serg can get radiometers attached to her and working in conjunction with the bottle samplers. Once the field equipment, rad suits, and your Japanese expert get here, we can head north against the prevailing current. If we can get some reliable radiation levels from inside the current, we should be able to follow the concentrations upstream to the source along the coast of Baffin Island." He saw the dubious look in Carol's eyes. "Simple, right?"

"Only to you," Carol said in resignation. She looked again at the samples they had already collected, still wrapped and enclosed within the plastic "safe" boxes they had jury-rigged. "You know," she continued, "if this is a large-scale radiation source, Medusa will become permanently contaminated."

"I know," Garner said. He also knew that sacrificing his only operating sampler would mean losing even more time before he could return to his own research, maybe even scrapping his entire thesis project. "Looks like I didn't plan for this contingency either."

The uncrated Medusa sphere was lowered onto the *Phoenix*'s afterdeck and her support equipment stored in the main lab. Zubov continued to be impressed by the ship's onboard resources, including a compact, six-seat hovercraft that was packed in its own hangar in the aft cargo hold.

"*Essential* equipment up here, let me tell you," Byrnes said, patting the hovercraft's shiny fiberglass hull.

"Essential, huh?" Zubov said. He was skeptical, but looked at the machine with envy.

"Oh sure. We need some way to get across the ice when it begins to break up. Something *practical* in addition to the helos, Zodiacs, the SnoCats, snowmobiles, snowshoes, and our own two feet." Byrnes flashed Zubov a grin. "Ah, what the hell. There was room for it in the budget and it is *sooo* cool to drive."

As two overworked boatswains with a host of professional complaints in common, Zubov and Byrnes took a natural liking to each other. Whatever was broken or lost, whatever the erratically ingenious mind of a scientist could imagine or request, it was the job of the boatswain to provide. However, where Zubov liked to take an active hand in the work he assisted, it was enough for Byrnes to have a steady job and reliable income from the Nolan Group, something he had never had as a commercial fisherman.

Finished for the moment, Zubov followed Byrnes forward for a cup of coffee. "I can't believe you turned down a WOCE cruise to Palau just to help Garner," Byrnes said, shivering slightly as he pulled off his parka. His smaller and much leaner physique made it more difficult for him to shake off the cold. "*Palau?* I'd give my left nut to go there."

"I'd rather work with Brock than catch a tan," Zubov said, though he would probably never admit it to Garner himself. For all his overly elegant sampling plans and uncompromising perfectionism, Garner was hardly the typical career academic. It was more than his background in the Navy or the unending struggle for funding that made him different. Garner had common sense, a necessary but surprisingly rare commodity at sea. What Garner considered important to note in the broad scheme of things usually was. He had a natural leadership quality and Zubov was drawn to follow it.

Byrnes chuckled. "You and him must have some kind of history for you to follow him to both poles in the same week."

"I hadn't thought of it like that, but I guess we do," Zubov considered. "Brock's a good egg, as eggheads go. He needs me, and I know that his needs are legitimate, unlike a lot of uses of my time. And when *Carol* needs me, I know the shit has really hit the fan, so I come along for the ride. It's like that Spanish proverb—'it's good to have friends, even in hell.'"

"Is that what you think this is going to be? Hell?"

"Radiation is always hell," Zubov said. "My father was a nuclear engineer. He was the first in our family to go to college and that was enough to alienate him from his friends and neighbors. Until then, we had been farmers, working the land. No one understood the allure of higher education, much less the need for it. My dad didn't agree. He had a single-minded purpose to improve himself, to improve the welfare of his family."

"But you didn't follow in his footsteps?" Byrnes asked.

"I tried," Zubov said. "As a kid I read books on Bikini Atoll and the Manhattan Project and Hiroshima. I actually had pictures of mushroom clouds tacked up in my room. At night my father would tell me about this detonation or that one, how many kilotons it was, where the blast was or what the test hoped to prove. I think that the only time I could get him to talk to me— really talk to me—was when I was asking him about bombs. Later on I took college courses and I read my father's notes and his engineering books. I don't think I had any real interest in the science of it all, but I wanted to understand what my father did for a living. I wanted to see what could make him go so far against the grain, to put up with being thought of as such an odd-ball." He shrugged. "Once I figured out my dad, there was no need to go to school."

"Me too," Byrnes said. "But my options were simpler. My old man was a longshoreman in Baltimore. He told me I could work the ships or I could move out of his house. Eventually I got my ABH degree—Anywhere But Here."

"My dad said if I ever moved out, I might as well move as far away as I could and be the best I could be at whatever I chose to do," Zubov said. "The States seemed pretty far to an eighteen-year-old."

"Immigrant?"

"Actually, I greased the wheels by calling myself an orphan and a refugee and ended up living with friends of the family. The first job I got was on a trawler in the North Atlantic. When I was finally naturalized, the first thing I did was apply to NOAA. I guess you could say the sea bit me and I bit back.

"If I learned anything about my father's work, it was a respect for nuclear elements," Zubov continued. "That's why I said 'hell.' He used to call radiation the Middle East of environmental problems—all the discussion, all the government programs, all the best intentions in the world won't fix the problem if the hatred is allowed to boil over. It kills, and it keeps killing for longer than any of us can ever know because that is all *it* has ever known."

Byrnes blinked, not certain how seriously to take the Ukrainian's strangely passionate anecdote. "You sound a little bitter," he said.

"Have you ever heard of Pripyat?" Zubov suddenly asked.

"What?" Byrnes asked. Zubov repeated the word. "No. What is it?"

"Pripyat is my hometown," Zubov said. "Population about fifty thousand, north of Kiev on the Pripyat River. Factory workers, mostly, and farmers. They picked rocks from the fields to grow potatoes, they raised livestock to put food on the dinner table. 'Work the soil and the soil will work for you,' they said."

"There's something to be said for the simple life, all right," Byrnes agreed. "Cling to your roots and you'll never get blown around by the wind."

"Funny you should say it like that," Zubov said. "As a boy, I remember the wind in Pripyat always coming from the north. Always. It was cold because it came down from Finland and the Barents Sea, bringing the feel of winter with it no matter what the month." He paused, struggling slightly at the prospect of continuing. "But in the spring of 1986, the wind changed direction. My relatives wrote me letters saying it was suddenly coming from the south. The crops were confused, they said. The cows were confused. The farmers were confused because they didn't know what this new wind would bring—these were very superstitious people. In 1986, no one knew what the change in wind would bring, but few of them thought it would be good. They complained, but they didn't know why—at the time."

"So what was it?" asked Byrnes.

"You don't know?" Zubov asked, as if it should be common knowledge. Resolution smoldered in his eyes. Despite Byrnes's obvious interest, Zubov struggled for a moment before he could continue.

"To the south of Pripyat, about ten miles and up-wind only in 1986, are the four reactors of the Chernobyl nuclear power plant. On the morning of April twenty-sixth, some arrogant bastard decided to see if he could run Reactor Number Four without any cooling water. Minutes later, the reactor turned into a nuclear volcano and my parents, my brothers, and six hundred thousand others got a close-up look at hell."

5

With a violent crack, the floe split almost in half, a huge chasm spreading quickly across its equator like horizontal lightning. The sudden fracture caught a team of technicians from the *Phoenix* off guard; they had to scramble back from the sudden precipice and scoop their field gear away from the edge. Even so, their SnoCat and two boxes of field samples were caught above the rift and toppled into the ocean below. The SnoCat plunged immediately into the depths, while the sample cases reeled on the churning surface for a moment before rolling over and following the heavy machine to the bottom.

For the first few moments there was nothing but sea foam visible at the bottom of the crevasse. Then the first of two whales glided past the break in their former prison, the enormous animals weakened and scarred by the ice but freed to the ocean once more. As if in salute to its well-intentioned captors, the flukes of the second animal broke the surface of the water, then glided along for a moment before disappearing into the swash. The parted halves of the floe, each relieved of its obligation to the other, bobbed and twisted on the sea as their new mass found equilibrium.

Stunned and mildly shaken, the trio of researchers gazed over the lip of the new canyon in time to see their morning's work sink beneath the waves. Some of the lighter gear still floated on the surface, and they pawed at it using the long poles they had for probing the ice. As each piece was gingerly retrieved, it was set aside on a large, disposable tarpaulin. Like all gear that touched the water, it would have to be safely contained until the incoming radiation detection equipment could confirm its degree of contamination.

From their position overlooking the ice, those aboard the *Phoenix* couldn't help but see—and hear—the massive break. "Wichita? Wichita, come in . . . !" The team's surviving walkie-talkie crackled to life with Byrnes's voice from the bridge of the ship. "Wichita" was the expedition's code name for this particular site on the floe. Rather than remembering coordinates or absolute positions, each site was named after a U.S. city in relative direction and distance from where the *Phoenix* was moored. "What the hell just happened?" Byrnes asked.

"Stress fracture," the lead technician reported back. "It was bound to happen eventually." The new canyon had split the floe in almost a direct line connecting four holes recently drilled in the ice. The weight of the floe was divided across this man-made fault line, and the struggling of the whales below had been enough to finally split the formation in two. As the two halves of the ice continued to drift, the contrived grouping of cities was separated in a line extending from San Francisco to Detroit, with a slight dogleg directly through Wichita. To relieve some of the gravity of the situation, someone offered a well-known geological saw: "The earth has moved, but it's not San Andreas's fault."

"How are the whales?" This time it was Carol's voice on the radio, unmoved by the attempt at levity.

"We lost the two trapped between here and Denver," the technician replied. "Mom and calf seemed very happy to say good-bye, but we also lost two sample cases and a SnoCat. Dammit, Carol, I'm sorry."

Carol's hesitation in answering was enough to tell them she wasn't pleased with the team's carelessness, but she didn't for a second doubt the sincerity of the apology. "Shift happens," she said. "Pack up whatever you have left and head over to Miami. The male over there looks like he'll be the next to break loose. See if you can double-up the sampling regime there to make up for the lost material."

The team confirmed this arrangement. "Um, could you send us another SnoCat too?" the technician asked tentatively.

"Roger that." It was Byrnes's voice again. "Though I should make you walk. SnoCats aren't disposable. Technicians are. *Phoenix* out."

On the *Phoenix,* Byrnes signed off and caught Carol's sharp look. "Oh Christ, Carol, I didn't mean anything by that." It had been exactly a week since Ramsey and Dexter were taken off the ship.

"That's right, you didn't," she said coolly. She noted the breakup of the floe in her log while Garner checked the updated weather conditions with the meteorologists. As the days warmed further, more fractures could be anticipated. The ice would soon relinquish its grip on the two remaining whales, which would be good for the whales but bad for those on the *Phoenix* trying to determine the source of the animals' illness.

"I don't like this," Carol admitted to Garner. "With the melting, the drift, and the stress on the floe, it's only going to get more dangerous out there. We've been chopping away at that formation out there for a week now." After discussing the available options, they agreed to halt all drilling and digging until the conditions stabilized or there was another good freeze.

"From the ice cores you showed me, it was old ice to begin with," Garner said. "It survived last summer, maybe the one before that. It's been frozen and refrozen over the winters, compacted in warmer weather, then cemented together again. It isn't going to break up in the usual way, assuming there is such a thing as 'usual.'"

"I can't risk losing anyone else or any more gear," Carol said. She turned back to Byrnes. "Is it practical to pull everyone except Miami back to the ship by tomorrow noon?"

"The geologists never like breaking camp," Byrnes said. "But I'm sure we can convince them to finish their coring."

"Right—finish up, but no new holes," Carol agreed. "Not until the last of the whales is gone. If they want to keep coring, they can take boats out to the smaller, broken pieces."

"Gotcha, boss. Safety first."

Again Carol's thoughts strayed to Dex and Ramsey, lingering for only a moment before she pushed them away for the sake of the matters at hand. She retrieved the radiofax she had received that morning from Dr. Junko Kokura, the nuclear researcher visiting western Greenland. The authorities there had told Kokura of the *Phoenix*'s request for help and she had agreed to interrupt her work with the Inuit populations there to come and take a look.

Carol reviewed Kokura's résumé a third time. She was a rare hyphenate in the field of nuclear research, possessing experience both as a nuclear engineer and a field physician studying the effects of radiation on human biology. First at the University of Tokyo, then

Georgia Tech, and finally at Johns Hopkins University, Kokura's research had focused on the effects of industrial radioactive fallout on remote populations. Along the way she had helped to upgrade the Environmental Measurement Laboratory for the U.S. Department of Energy and conducted extensive field research on environmental radiation surveillance. Her extensive list of publications included studies of radiation-induced cancer, biological effects of radiation, risk assessment and protection standards, health physics, radiation emergency response, and environmental exposure.

"This is unbelievable," Carol said, handing the fax to Garner. "Not only is our only respondent an unquestionable expert on these kinds of things, but she happens to be in the neighborhood."

The next twenty-four hours were filled with near-constant activity. The first of two scheduled equipment airdrops brought to the *Phoenix* a small complement of silvered radiation suits, dosimeters, and gamma spectrometry devices; containment boxes; and other basic field equipment for working in irradiated areas. Carol, Byrnes, and Zubov took an inventory of the new arrivals and began dispensing them to the *Phoenix*'s crew. The next order of business was to determine whether the ship itself was becoming too contaminated, then to perform an extensive remeasurement of radiation levels all over the site, including levels of specific isotopes whenever possible. Finally, the two remaining *Balaenoptera* were freed from their attachment to the ice near Miami station only minutes after the *Phoenix*'s technicians implanted the long-range tracking devices into both whales.

In the main lab aboard the *Phoenix,* Carol and Garner watched a small display as the final two tracking devices were activated. The pair of blips representing the Miami whales began sending back information about the animals' movement. The whales slowly left the floe, broke the surface momentarily, then dived to a depth of forty feet. Within an hour they had joined their three former inmates. Initially, all five animals stayed within ten miles of the *Phoenix*.

"Amazing," Carol said. "I've never known blues to exhibit such social behavior."

"I guess spending a little time in lockup together makes close friends," Garner said with a smile. "The question is, where are they going to go now?"

"You think they might lead us back to wherever they encountered the contamination?" Carol asked.

"Possibly," Garner said. "Or maybe they'll just continue south—out Hudson Strait and into the North Atlantic. In that case, I say we backtrack to the north and sniff around with Medusa."

"An area like that wouldn't leave much room for them to move, or breathe. Some areas of North Foxe Basin have complete ice cover for nine months of the year. And Fury and Hecla is only two hundred miles up." Fury and Hecla Strait, a narrow waterway separating Melville Peninsula from the western end of Baffin Island, averaged less than four hundred feet in depth and, excluding seasonal ice cover, was just ten miles wide. In this formidable bottleneck for floating ice and the ocean circulation of the Central Arctic, it was easy to imagine the *Balaenoptera* being similarly inconvenienced.

"My thinking exactly," Garner said. "If they hit a dead end just north of here, there's less area for us to search." In this case, "less area" still left over thirty thousand square miles of Foxe Basin itself, and Garner knew it. It was, at least, a less daunting search area than anything to the south.

"So we're really hoping that they ran into this radiation source locally."

"At the end of a dead-end street, so they've been soaking in it," Garner agreed.

"Then so have we." Carol looked extremely nervous at such speculation.

"Maybe," Garner said. "But the truth is, we may never know where the whales have been." Even though blue whales were known to revisit the same oceans on a regular basis, no one knew how well defined their migration routes were, or if they truly "migrated" at all. Their "home" range could extend from pole to equator. The vastness of Foxe Basin might look like a teacup in comparison to the area they might have to search.

Looking at the lab samples again, the recently delivered dosimeters provided some more specific and encouraging news, though hardly less disturbing: the younger *Balaenoptera* possessed the highest levels of contamination, arguing in favor of contamination via recent food intake. That meant that the plankton themselves were irradiated, a speculation that Medusa would soon attempt to resolve with greater clarity.

Junko Kokura arrived that afternoon as the sole passenger of another Canadian Helicopters Sikorsky. Given the recent fracturing of the ice, the helicopter didn't try to set down on the floe. It descended to within inches of the *Phoenix*'s helipad, then the doctor scrambled out of the passenger cabin, pulling a large backpack with her. Byrnes had the doctor in the *Phoenix*'s lab before the sound of the helicopter had even faded into the stillness of the Arctic twilight.

Carol joined them minutes later. "Welcome, Dr. Kokura," she said.

"Thank you—and please, call me Junko. This place is too cold to be tripping over titles and surnames."

Carol liked the woman immediately. She was petite, standing just over five feet tall, with a slight build but obviously in good physical health. Her black hair was pulled back from her face and unabashedly streaked with gray. Her eyes were flat and dark, but twinkled with a warmth that suggested a hint of good-natured conspiracy. Her handshake reflected that good nature, as did the way she dipped her head and angled closer, genuinely listening to anyone who spoke to her. Her calm, matter-of-fact manner contained not a trace of impatience; she persistently but politely asked Carol and her technicians questions about what they had seen on the ice. It was indeed a shame that the *Balaenoptera* had broken free only hours before the doctor's arrival, but a quick inventory of the blood and tissue samples collected by the *Phoenix*'s technicians provided much assurance that no empirical stone had been left unturned.

When Junko felt that she had heard enough, she set to work.

"First things first," she said. "What have you done to keep the outside from getting inside?"

"We've closed off all but four hatches," Byrnes said. "Inside those, like the one you saw, we've hung two layers of heavy-gauge plastic sheeting to make a kind of airlock. Inside that, we cleared an area for people to hang their outside clothing." He added that any hatches leading from the holds into the lower decks of the ship were also temporarily sealed and opened only when absolutely necessary. They had greatly reduced the amount of "threshold activity" by leaving as much regularly used equipment on deck as was possible, even if it meant taking chances with clutter and freezing.

"Excellent," the doctor replied, "now let's see if we can rig a second chamber for showering and a place for changes into inside clothing. A regular emergency lab rinse station would be fine, if people don't mind the chilly water. And we'll put sentry dosimeters in high-traffic areas and inside each 'airlock' for people going in or out to check themselves for exposure. Although the air seems pretty clean, I don't want to take any chances of radioactive dust being tracked into the ship. The food and water should be checked at least twice a day. And no one goes outside without a respirator or a dust mask. Seventy percent of what we can expect will be due to internal exposure to the radioactive material. The external contamination can usually be washed away."

"*Usually?*" Byrnes repeated, cocking an eyebrow. "Pardon my French, Doc, but it sounds like you think we may be up to our ears in a good deal of shit here."

"That's not exactly my choice of words." The doctor smiled politely. "But, yes, correct. Until we know more, the level could be higher than our ears."

"You're not inspiring us here, Doc," Byrnes said.

"With radiation it is best not to think in terms of absolute solutions," Junko countered. "First we have to stem the source and then worry about containing the spill. When it comes to exposure—to us, to the environment, or to your equipment—we will do everything we can under the field radiologist's mantra of ALARA—as low as reasonably achievable."

Byrnes seemed rooted to the deck with this news. He was used to managing compromise in any shipboard operation, but "ALARA" seemed disappointingly inconclusive.

Zubov, on the other hand, could not have been more inspired by the doctor's warning and her matter-of-fact appraisal of the task before them. Given the chance, he'd gladly listen to Dr. Junko Kokura all night.

As the available hours of sunlight slowly increased toward a single, continuous glow, the regularly scheduled meals were the primary means by which the crew of the *Phoenix* marked the time of day. Food on polar survey vessels, oil rigs, and research cruises is unexpectedly gourmet in its preparation and necessarily ample in its portions. The food not only provides comfort and warmth against the elements, but keeps the crew burning calories. Cooks are often selected from among the more adventurous hotel and restaurant chefs, and the *Phoenix* was no exception: Carol had personally hired her chefs from the kitchens of Galileo and Lion D'Or in Washington, D.C., favorite restaurants of hers while she was working as an environmental lobbyist for the Nolan Group.

In an attempt to ease the growing tension and welcome Junko, the galley crew declared this Monday "Hawaiian Night" and dressed in appropriately garish serving attire. The walls of the mess were decorated with coconuts and conch shells, and fresh fruit slices and paper umbrellas were inserted into the drinks, including the coffee. Given the exquisite feast and the frenetic pace of the previous week, Junko's first meal aboard the *Phoenix* took on an air of optimism and casual camaraderie. The small group of scientists and deck crew occupied a corner table in the former officers' mess and quickly became friends.

"The Arctic is a collector," Junko related as dessert was served, "a deep-frozen museum and crystal ball for all the world's problems. The Inuit in Greenland are no different than countless other native peoples, from Borneo to Africa to India. Everything about their culture is intertwined with the environment. Everything they know is inexorably tied to their ancestry as well as their descendants: what's to follow is based on what has come before."

"A fair analogy for science as well," Garner observed.

"Yes," Junko agreed. "And the Inuit are attracted to modern technology, or at least goaded into using it. After being displaced from the traditional ways, they are often asked to either step aside or lead the charge in exploiting their environment."

"How bad are the areas you've been working in?" Carol asked.

"The Eastern Arctic is a good indicator of where the Inuit territory as a whole is going eventually. Alaska has its tourism and the Western Arctic has exploited natural reserves ranging from uranium to, recently, diamonds and oil. Where we are now, the change in native peoples has been more gradual, but the widening poverty gap is changing all that. The promising oil speculation studies of the 1970s haven't produced many takers in today's market. The Central Arctic can keep up with the white man or they can watch themselves drop from the thread of history."

"What attracted you to the radiation biz?" Byrnes began. "Was it—?" He stopped short, realizing his mouth had once again spoken before discretion engaged his brain.

"Hiroshima?" Junko nodded. "As a matter of fact it was." At first, the others at the table didn't know whether to believe her, because, "I wasn't even born when the bomb was dropped," Junko continued. "In the months leading up to it, the Allies had been dropping one hundred thousand tons of bombs on Tokyo every month, so it seemed unlikely that any act of war could catch the Japanese off guard. The atomic bomb did. Three quarters of the city's buildings were immediately destroyed. Seven thousand people were incinerated by the blast itself, and one hundred forty thousand dead from radiation sickness by the end of the year. After five years, two hundred thousand people, 54 percent of the population, were dead."

"Were any of your family among them?" Zubov asked cautiously.

"My brothers," Junko nodded. "Five of them in all.

They were in school when it happened. Ours was a big family, and bigger all the time because my mother wanted a daughter but kept having sons. Eventually my parents couldn't afford any more children. But after the bomb, my parents left Hiroshima and moved to Kyoto to start rebuilding their lives. Did you know that Kyoto had been the planned target for the first A-bomb? But as a former capital city and a center of culture and intellect, it was spared. War has such queer morality."

"And in Kyoto your mother finally got her little girl," Carol said. There were almost tears in her eyes.

"Yes," Junko admitted. "So you see, were it not for the bomb and all the death it brought, I would not be here. And that, Mr. Byrnes, is what attracted me to the 'radiation biz.' "

The soft-spoken, almost maternal tone of Junko's reply showed no trace of admonition, but it had a sobering effect around the table.

"Beautiful story," Zubov said. It was the orphan in him talking, longing for his own happy ending.

Garner noticed the unexpected but palpable chemistry between his friend and the Japanese doctor and glanced at Carol. From the sly look she returned, she was as surprised as he.

"So here we are," Junko concluded. "Each of us on this ice for different reasons, now embarking on a journey for the same reason. Discovery."

"To discovery then," Zubov said, raising his glass in a toast, paper umbrella and all. His eyes had not left Junko's face in half an hour.

The second airdrop of field equipment came just after dawn the next day. The single large container contained another batch of radiation suits as well as more shielded cases and radiation detectors. The suits resembled a lightweight version of industrial fire-fighting gear—one-piece, silvered suits with cylinder-shaped helmets and self-contained, battery-operated respirators. Boots and gloves locked into place on gaskets attached to the suit's cuffs and a single, squarish window allowed the wearer to see his or her surroundings, albeit with little peripheral vision. Carol thought it was like looking at the world from the bottom of a coffee can.

Junko gathered everyone together in the infirmary and gave them a quick tutorial in nuclear field medicine. She pulled a box of plastic swabs out of one of the delivery cases. "These are nasal swabs," she explained, demonstrating their use. "Run them around the nostril, then check them for radionuclides. For the time being, inhalation is our worst enemy and the nose is the easiest way to be exposed. We'll start with one swab per day per person, moving to two or more if we start getting higher exposure levels."

Next, she took out several bottles of potassium iodide. "Radioiodine has a short half-life and chances are it will evaporate before it affects us. But if it doesn't, it will lodge in the thyroid gland. Supplements of regular iodine every day will offset that possibility." Next came several bottles of calcium supplements and antacids. "Similarly, radioactive strontium and radium soak into the bones in place of calcium. And potassium supplements counteract the uptake of radioactive cesium. So we'll start taking these—not the best solution, but a cheap and convenient stopgap. From what we know of the isotopes out there, anything is possible. These are specific preventatives, but there are a lot of general habits you have to pick up, irrespective of the kind of radioactivity."

She then regarded the assembled group with an expression as serious as anyone had yet seen. "Until we know more about this, those airlocks *must* be used. Change clothes each time you pass through them and wear the space suits anytime you're outside, over your cold-weather gear. Back inside, shower and change into fresh clothing. Drink plenty of water and report any symptoms to me. Between examinations, wear these." She handed out plastic film badges to everyone. The three-square-inch indicators could be clipped to the belt or lapel. "These are our best hedge against incidental exposure. If you are exposed to any radiation, they'll begin to fog up. Watch for fogging on your badges and those of your crewmates."

"What about the hardware?" Byrnes asked. *My* hardware, his protective tone suggested.

"Following proper decontamination procedures, you should be hosing down every external surface with water," Junko replied. "Ordinarily I suppose you could draw a hose directly from the water, but that isn't an option for us, so we'll just have to wait and see. It will depend on how much radiation is in the water passing over or through it."

"ALARA," Byrnes grumbled.

"ALARA. Yes."

Junko then gave a quick but thorough examination to all the technicians and engineers aboard the ship. Not surprisingly, those who had spent the most time on the ice—Carol and Byrnes among them—had received the highest doses of radiation, but even these still hardly approached levels for health concerns: less than two hundred milliSieverts. After more than a week alongside the whales, only the two divers had experienced anything close to radiation sickness; for the time being it seemed that simply staying out of the water was sufficient to avoid dangerous levels of exposure.

Next, at Byrnes's persistent request, came a thorough examination of all the sampling equipment that had been immersed in the water. The cables and winch spools, used for all equipment, were the hottest, but were still below hazardous levels. The syringes and field packs used to contain the whale samples also showed elevated levels, but Junko didn't believe there was any immediate danger to those who had worked in and around the ice holes.

Garner and Junko continued their inspection. While no one aboard was in any immediate danger, the dosimeters' revelation of the silent, invisible contamination of the ship was stunning. Every item of deck equipment, every yard of the outside surface, and all the cabins immediately inside hatches and doorways were checked, and all revealed at least some level of cesium, radium, or uranium contamination. As the investigation moved systematically along the vessel from bow to stern, the contamination teams tagged every hatch, horizontal surface, and piece of deck equipment with one of a series of color-coded tags ranging from SAFE to HIGHLY CONTAMINATED. The color of the tags helped to establish an initial estimate of the ship's contamination. If the crew could indeed locate the source of the contamination and cruised upstream to find it, eventually everything that went outside might merit a "highly contaminated" tag.

Despite the vehement protestations of the two geologists on board, Carol gave the order to pull up the equipment at all stations and return to the ship for departure. She knew this was only the beginning of the inconveniences and broken promises for which she would be responsible. If this, the largest and highest-profile excursion of her directorship, were to become a laughingstock, the board could call for her resignation. She doubted that she could count on the Nolan Group's legal advisors to back up a claim that she was taking the safest recourse to avoid future lawsuits from her passengers and employees. In the short term, the loss of station time was expensive enough; in the days and weeks that followed, the prospect that they would all be exposed to a major environmental health hazard was inestimable.

Before the contracted funds even reached the bank,

the *Phoenix* would have to be completely refitted if it were ever to be useful again. Oh yes, the Nolan Group's trustees were going to *love* hearing all about the *Phoenix*'s maiden voyage.

Given all the arrangements Carol had made to bring people to this place, it was the least she could do to transport those who wanted to leave back to safety with no loss of wages. She circulated word for the others to provide her with a list of everything and everyone they wanted taken off the ship. A helicopter would be called back the next day or the day after that, then the *Phoenix* would continue its grim sojourn in the north. It was reassuring that Byrnes and the rest of the Nolan Group employees volunteered, each and all, to stay with the *Phoenix*. Within the hour she received a call from Don Szilard of the True North program, the major sponsor of the Nolan Group study on the acoustic disturbance of marine mammals.

Szilard seemed utterly disinterested in the *Phoenix*'s exciting side trip to the *Balaenoptera* floe, except for the costly loss of the SnoCat and the samples at Wichita. As the money behind the expedition, Szilard was much more concerned with speculation that the entire study might have to be abandoned, or at least postponed. To do so was an explicit breach of contract, and refunding the payroll of the returning personnel was a significant compromise to the budget.

"Why the hell are you sending people back?" Szilard asked for the third time in the past ten minutes.

"Because I think we could be in some real danger here, Don. My people mean more to me than any contract."

"I'm sorry to hear that," Szilard said, not clarifying whether it was the danger or the dropped contract that struck him most. "If you think the danger is that great, why isn't *everyone* coming home? Why aren't you notifying the proper authorities?"

"And just who would be the 'proper authorities'?" Carol snapped back. "I've called every radiation watchdog from the EPA to the Coppertone girl and no one seems to give a damn."

"Then maybe you shouldn't either," Szilard pressed. "That's not why you're there—True North is."

Carol was struck by the condescension in Szilard's voice. She could almost see the sweaty, misinformed, and grossly overweight Szilard admonishing her from behind his desk overlooking Ottawa's Sparks Street Mall, and the thought made her flush with anger. "I didn't expect this either," Carol said tightly, "but whatever it is, we're awash in it now. It's not like we'll charge you any more for the study—the program will just have to be delayed. Until we can find out whether or not there's a need to panic, we're the only ones willing and able to check it out." She didn't dare tell him that the ship had already been severely exposed to the radiation and could even have to be quarantined before long. Eventually the *Phoenix* could be too hot to continue work—for True North or anyone. Given the recent turn of events, it would be a shorter journey to keep pressing forward until the radiation source could be stemmed.

"What does your onboard observer say?" Szilard asked. That he would confer any sort of jurisdiction on Seaborg, the Canadian kid, was annoying enough; that he might actually value Seaborg's opinion over Carol's was beyond insulting.

"He says he misses his Nintendo," Carol said curtly. "He says he misses his mom's cookies and milk."

"Hold on." Szilard took a long moment to respond, as if he were writing notes or trying some revised calculations. For a moment, Carol wondered if he was also considering some future legal or financial recourse. They both knew the first-year funds for the project had yet to be deposited; in Carol's exuberance to win the contract she had offered to deficit-finance the first two cruises. Any breach of contract could mean losing the entire project.

Szilard was clearly considering the same point. "If we lose the season over this action," Szilard said, "it will be my recommendation that we lose the Nolan Group as well. I will be putting a hold on your funding for this quarter until I see at least a preliminary report from this cruise."

"You can't do that!" Carol said. She knew she had let too much panic creep into her voice. Such administrative wrangling was unheard of—usually.

"I can and I will," Szilard said.

"Dammit, Don! You *know* how much I wanted this work," Carol said. "You *know* that no one can do it as well as the Nolan Group, and if you reassign the contract you'll lose a lot more than one season. If we ignore these rad levels, leave them for someone else like God-knows-how-many people already have, then we could all be in a lot of trouble. Even True North isn't worth my people getting sick or the loss of one human life. That's why I'm not even on the clock. If you were *here* you'd see that. But you're not. *I* am and *I'm* in charge and I say *the acoustic study will have to wait.*" The ship's radio operator, Stuart Frisch, returned from his break, still munching from a bag of Doritos. Hearing the timbre of his employer's voice, he quietly turned on his heel and left.

"I appreciate the bind you're in," Szilard said, sounding only slightly less patronizing. "But we have to keep focused on the contracted statement of work. I'll give you until the end of the week to revive the agreed-upon sampling schedule, but after that I'll have to forward my recommendation to cancel your funding. That's not a threat, it's a promise."

"Then I'll go over your head. I'll call Rutherford,"

Carol said, dragging Szilard's boss into the fracas. The floodgates of her desperation had sprung fully open.

"I'm not the one in over my head on this, Dr. Harmon," Szilard said coldly. "It's your decision how to proceed from here. You can do what we've agreed you're to do, or you can go off on some wild goose chase far outside your jurisdiction. In the meantime, I'll assume I can look forward to some data we can use and at least a draft of your report. Soon."

Carol found Garner, Zubov, and Junko on the afterdeck. All three were dressed in radiation suits and were checking the latest modifications to Medusa.

The eerie similarity to the experience in Puget Sound was too strong to ignore. "Déjà vu," she said.

"You can say that again," Zubov said.

"I think she just did," Garner agreed and gave Carol a wink. "There's something about giving you a hand—I just know I'll end up needing full-body protection."

"I think I'm the one who needs protection," Carol said. She was still bristling from the exchange with Szilard. "At least, I think I'll pull the plug on our phone line. Frisch better start screening my calls or we're going to end up with no money and a mutiny on our hands."

"Sounds like working conditions you're familiar with," Junko said. "Sergei told me about what happened in Puget Sound."

"Yes, these two do fine work," Carol said. "If you don't mind explosions, sunken vessels, and excessive collateral damage."

"Surgical precision is overrated," Zubov said, grinning sheepishly at Junko.

"Not among surgeons," the doctor bantered back.

Garner shot Carol another knowing look—the

notion of a May-December attraction between Zubov and Junko was undeniably growing. Such a prospect, however improbable, reminded Carol of her own affair with Dex and she silently reprimanded herself for not contacting the hospital for an updated status report. Tomorrow for sure, with Junko listening in on the patients' treatment and progress.

Garner turned his attention back to Medusa. An orderly design was no longer an issue for his marvelous but temperamental plankton sampler. In order to add the extra weight and resistance of the gamma spectrometers and still have the device fly properly underwater, he and Zubov had to devise and install yet another ungainly collar and harness apparatus.

"There's got to be a better way," Garner complained. "My baby is getting uglier by the minute." Part of him knew there was no better way to track the contamination, that was why Carol had called them; part of him knew that towing Medusa through a spill of hot water would mean rebuilding another prototype from scratch. "Give us tonight to run another set of tests on the electronics," he said to Carol. "If your crew is ready, we can load Medusa onto the A-frame and be ready for a fresh start at first light."

"I'm ready to get going before that," Carol said. "I'm getting sick of just sitting here, so I've asked the captain to take us off station tonight. If we've got two hundred miles to cover to the north, we can cross half of that by midmorning. You can deploy Medusa then, if it's ready, or we can set up another temporary camp."

The intercom next to the winch controls buzzed, making Carol jump. It was Frisch, the radio operator. "Carol? Call for you," he said.

Assuming that it was Szilard calling to either retract his threat or add to his list of demands, Carol said impatiently, "Not now. We're a little busy here."

"I think you should take it," Frisch replied. His voice unnaturally even and calm.

She turned to look at the tiny intercom. "Who is it?"

"It's the ICU at Toronto General," Frisch said. "Dexter and Ramsey both died this afternoon."

After confirming the details of the deaths with the hospital, Carol Harmon called Dexter's parents in Portland, Oregon, and Tony Ramsey's wife in Tacoma, Washington. Carol was told by Ramsey's sister-in-law that Joanna Ramsey wasn't taking any calls from the Nolan Group. Dexter's parents simply referred to Carol as "you bitch" and told her to expect a call from the family's legal counsel.

Garner caught up to Carol an hour later. He came down the narrow corridor below the *Phoenix*'s bridge and knocked on the door of her cabin. Carol mumbled a semblance of invitation and Garner entered to see her sitting at the cabin's small desk. She was trying hard to put on a neutral face for any visitors, but her eyes were rimmed red and her hands clutched a shredded tissue. When she saw Garner, her tears welled up again and her entire body began to tremble.

"Oh, shit," she whispered as Garner knelt beside her at the desk. "What have I done?"

"All you *could* do," Garner said. "The best you can with the information you've got."

"That's not true," Carol said. "I should have stopped them from diving. *I* was the one who was so adamant that we examine the blues."

"No one comes on a venture like this with a stand-back attitude," Garner said. "Everyone is on this ship because they want to be. Because they want to help you, regardless of the consequences. We all know what we're in for. We've read the fine print. With this crew, I bet you could have charged admission to see those whales up close."

"It should have been me on that dive," Carol said in a small voice. *"It should have been me."*

Garner wrapped his arms around Carol and guided her over to the cabin's modest bunk. "Since when did you start blaming yourself for every calamity?" he asked.

"Since I became the boss," Carol said, staring at the tissue in her knitted fingers. "Since my name started going on the contracts and statements of work."

"None of which include a massive spill of radioactive material," Garner said.

For a moment, Carol seemed to warm to this showing of faith. But thinking of the events of the last few days, she lapsed into silence once more. "Tell that to Don Szilard," she said.

"Maybe you should," Garner said. "Fly down to Toronto, do what you can at the hospital, then pay True North a visit in Ottawa."

Carol shook her head. "I can't do that. I can't just abandon the ship for some personal junket."

"A highly *necessary* personal junket," Garner corrected her. "Call it damage control. Call it peace of mind. Whatever it takes to get yourself back on track." Carol remained unconvinced as Garner pressed the issue. "Junko's our new resident expert. And Patrick and Sergei could run this ship without a wheelhouse if they had to. There's an airlift coming for the others anyway—what's one more passenger?"

"You make us sound like a bunch of deserting rats," Carol said, then fell silent.

For a moment Garner hoped he had gotten through to Carol. It was a lie that she could simply leave the ship without compromising the expedition, but at the moment, her peace of mind mattered more to the success of their venture. If there was a time she could be absent, it was in the next few days while Medusa was playing bloodhound.

"Come on," Garner pressed. "You know I'm right."

"No," Carol said finally. "The Nolan Group VPs can smooth things over with True North and with the next of kin. Two of my crew are dead. The only way I can make amends for that is to find out what's responsible for it."

The commitment in her eyes was daunting; she had declared war on the invisible, unknown killer.

"We don't even know if there *is* a possible source around here, let alone one we can stem," Garner said. "Why don't you let us take an uncolored look for it and then decide whose heads should roll because of it?"

Despite Garner's attempts to comfort Carol and partially relieve her of her duties, his rationale did little to placate her. She felt threatened by even a temporary loss of command and Garner's objectivity only turned her resistance against him, a give-and-take scenario they had played out often enough in the years that they were married.

"I'm staying here," she said. "And you're staying here. Sergei's staying. Junko's staying and the *Phoenix* is staying, even if I have to end up selling Girl Scout cookies to pay for it all. We're going to find out what killed my crew and poisoned those whales. The rest of the world can just go to hell until we find out exactly what's going on up here."

6

Victor Tablinivik awoke to the sound of rain, a series of wet dripping noises on the snow outside, interspersed with dull taps that vibrated the canvas roof of his lean-to.

Janey didn't like the weather, and had crawled into the other end of the shelter while Victor slept. Now she lay staring mournfully outside, her muzzle on her paws, mismatched eyes glowering at the apparent inconvenience.

Another thump on the roof, this one far too large to be a raindrop. Victor sat up. Now he could hear something outside that sounded like running water. His first thought was that the sea ice on which he had camped had broken free from the shore—it wouldn't be the first time the floe had made him a castaway.

But no, not that . . .

Victor brought his aching body to its knees and peered out of the lean-to. On the ice before him was a small bird, an arctic sandpiper. As it lay on its back, struggling to move, its wings fluttered wildly against the ice, making the noises Victor had thought were raindrops. Sandpipers were usually summer shorebirds—the warm weather must have tricked this one into coming back. Then Victor saw another sandpiper lying nearby, this one clearly dead and making no sound at all. Then another. And another. Yet another sandpiper glanced off Victor's hood and fell, lifeless, to the ice between his hands. Peering around the edge of the canvas, Victor saw another bird bounce off the canvas of his lean-to and struggle momentarily before lying still. Janey wanted no part of this apparently easy meal.

Standing, Victor now looked beyond his *komatik*. Hundreds of birds dotted the unending whiteness, dozens of them falling from the sky with those dripping sounds, the rest flailing weakly on the crusted ice, making the thin rasping Victor had thought was running water.

As Victor listened a moment longer, the sound quieted, then stopped. Silence returned. The sky had emptied and Victor stood amid a thousand or more dead shorebirds, each no larger than his clenched fist.

Victor broke camp and moved on. There was nothing for a hunter to do in the face of such a bad omen but relocate and hope *Kannakapfaluk* only wanted him to move to a more bountiful place.

Two hours later he found the carcass of the bear.

The polar bear is a wise hunter and is as much a role model as an adversary to the Inuit hunter, which made its discovery even more disturbing than that of the hapless birds. It was supposed to be a good omen to encounter this majestic sovereign while hunting—at least it meant another preeminent predator was on the same track—but Victor didn't know what to make of finding a dead one. The bear was a large male, as long as Victor's sledge and perhaps half a ton in weight. On closer inspection, Victor knew that the bear had not starved, nor did it appear to be injured. In the cold, the carcass had not begun to decompose, although it had evidently lain here for some time. The bear's muzzle was frozen to the ice, twisted into a pained snarl, its gums caked with dried blood—Victor had recently taken especial note of such things—though not from a recent meal or any apparent struggle.

Even when inexplicably fallen, all animals were treated with respect in the Inuit culture. By tradition, it was offensive to consume the flesh of land animals while on sea ice, or sea animals while on the land. The animal's spirit must be kept with its natural order. The carcass is fully consumed or otherwise used; no portion is ever wasted. The *qablunaq* name for this land was *Arktos,* from the Greek for bear; the Inuktitut word for the animal, *nanuk,* meant "sea bear," because the great hunter appeared most at home in the water. Polar bears are excellent swimmers, sometimes seen in the ocean tens of miles from the nearest landfall, confidently bear-paddling with their massive, webbed front paws. For this reason, the Inuit consider the polar bear a sea mammal in the same way that river fish are considered part of the land.

Victor took this rare opportunity to look at the animal up close, to touch its fur and stoop to examine the carcass. The bear's hide had worn ragged in several places; the fur had tufted and shed in large divots, exposing the skin below. Beneath its fur a polar bear's skin is black—all the better to absorb the Arctic's limited solar heat. The fur itself, though appearing white, is translucent hair, thickly layered, and hollow—all the better to channel heat toward the animal's skin. Guard hairs on the outermost layer of the hide stick together whenever they become wet, providing a water-resistant coating and preventing heat loss as the bear swims or dives—one reason the hide made excellent boots and mittens.

Victor searched around for any sign of disturbance in the snow. Had the bear been taken by another hunter, the Inuk surely would have claimed his prize, or prepared the carcass before returning with a larger sled. Scientists or government rangers would have marked the carcass with their radio collars or plastic tags. But there were no marks on the animal and no tracks surrounding it. Not even the arctic foxes had come to dine on the once-mighty hunter. Janey herself, though always respectful of Victor's kills, seemed to keep an extra distance from the bear. The mound of once-proud animal lay unwanted and utterly alone in the middle of the late-spring melt.

Victor did not usually allow himself to dwell upon his own mortality, for no good could possibly come of it. But he knew he was sick, perhaps very sick. Possibly even on his way to dying alone on the ice, frozen solid in a twisted and snarling pose. Most of Victor's symptoms—like his persistent headache or the traces of dark blood in his urine—were unknown to anyone else, even his wife, Anika. Other signs were more obvious, like the gaps in his smile where once-healthy, unbroken teeth continued to fall out. To be toothless in one's dreams was a bad omen because it represented famine and death—something the Inuit, with their paltry selection of natural prey, knew far too well. To be toothless when awake was simply bad.

On his head, a little more hair pulled loose each time Victor drew back the hood on his parka. Hairs also shed onto the woolly blanket he used as a pillow. His black hair still grew thick and unruly, but like the bear, sizable bald patches were developing underneath. His scalp, normally pale and almost translucent, was now nearly as brown as his flat, roundish face, though the newly uncovered skin was less weathered and tended to burn. Less noticeably, his skin was gradually getting thinner, and with that came a loss in his natural insulation. The rest of him just *ached,* bone deep. Victor told his wife he was simply getting old, but Anika never looked as though she believed him.

Victor and Janey camped near the bear that night, but still no scavengers came. The next morning they walked on, the ice growing slushy as the sun rose higher in the sky. The floe seemed to protest every one of his footsteps, every sporadic lurch of his *komatik.* He knew it was too late in the year to be hunting on the sea ice. At any moment the ground could open up and swallow both of them. By now, Victor knew, he should have moved inland to hunt the returning caribou, but the winter catch of seals had been poor and he had seen almost no walrus on this hunt. Unless Victor could catch a few more seals this spring, there was the risk of running short of food before fall. Besides that, he knew the fishing inland had been poor last spring. And the spring before that. The char in the streams had looked undernourished and their flesh tasted sour even before it was allowed to ferment. The springtime caribou still looked too gaunt and tough to warrant the attention of any serious hunter.

While Victor and Janey trudged ten or fifteen miles each day between hours spent stooped and waiting at the seal holes in the ice, Anika was at home. She cared for young Annu, preparing the meat from Victor's last hunting trip for storage and gnawing on the news the DIAND doctor had given her: she had the *lewkeemeeah.* There was every possibility that Victor had it too—he certainly had *something*—if he would only sit still long enough to be examined. Anika knew only that her husband had lost a lot of weight over the winter. Like most Inuit, Victor suffered no apparent health effects from a diet high in energy-rich fats and oils. It was another *qablunaq* myth that Inuit were fat; more often than not, the rigorous lifestyle and naturally elevated metabolism kept the Inuit hunters' bodies lean and hard under the bulky, layered clothing that gave them such apparent girth. It was also untrue that the Inuit were somehow indifferent to the cold—fifty degrees below zero knew no genetic defense—but unlike the *qablunaq,* the Inuit knew there was no point in becoming distressed by it. Cold was a constant, like ice and snow and losing teeth.

As the Inuit also knew well, next to the cold, the utter dryness of the polar environment posed the largest threat to survival. Less than eight inches of precipitation fell here each year. Despite the constant presence of snow and ice, most of it is tainted with brine, even without the pollution. Meltwater must be captured before it can be defiled and, for the sake of expediency, it is rarely boiled, except for soup. The Inuit know well that seals, caribou, and fish may provide necessary sustenance, but this means nothing if there is no good meltwater. Victor could taste grit, oil, or spoor in a meltwater source, but no one knew the taste of mercury, lead, PCBs, or any number of invisible pollutants that distilled out of the atmosphere into the *apun,* the fallen snow. He only knew that, both literally and figuratively, the meltwater had not tasted the way it should for far too long.

Victor could ignore his own health, but he could not ignore the hunt. *Kannakapfaluk,* the mother of animals, was not pleased. The seals were missing. The fish were sick. The bears were dying, or moving hundreds of miles south to plunder the garbage dumps and trash cans in places like Churchill and Arviat.

Victor tossed a fresh piece of seal blubber to Janey, then tugged his *komatik* around another hummock. From the appearance of landmarks on the shore, he estimated he could be as much as ten miles out onto the frozen edge of Foxe Basin—a long way to swim back if he underestimated the pack or the weather. But even this far out and this late in the year, the upthrust ice was more than four feet thick, so he could easily attach a pulling line and climb around the rise with both his hands free. Victor hauled the sledge after him, then took a moment to adjust his stowed equipment. He built a small fire with the remains of a cardboard box he had found, then beat the frost out of his wet clothing before laying it out to dry. To survive the Arctic means always to have a dry change of clothes, for wetness steals heat and rots garments made from animal hides.

Victor quickly changed into his spare clothing, then sat down on the ice to have his breakfast. As he chewed, wincing whenever the plugs of food found a fresh crater in his gums, he became aware of a new noise. It was not the breathing of the ice. It was not *tariuq*, the sea, or *hilak*, the sky. It sounded mechanical.

Victor carried an encyclopedic knowledge of this area, so much so that *qablunaq* like the RCMP and the Army often enlisted his help as a paramilitary ranger. Rather than being lost in the absence of any discernible landmarks, without even the regular punctuation of day and night, Victor knew exactly where he was, which made his discovery all the more surprising. He should have been miles from anything human, much less mechanical. He crawled up the face of a large hummock and peered south, into the low sun.

Against the whiteness of the landscape, the ship stood out like a scar on the snout of a seal. It was surrounded by ice, moored to a large floe in fact, but drifting along with the rest of the pack.

Victor squinted against the glare and moved around the ridge of ice for a better look. It was an icebreaker. A large one, with many *qablunaq* and their equipment spilled out onto the ice. Many of them were clustered around holes chipped through the ice and were stooped over the openings as if they were hunting for seal. If they were, they would be greatly disappointed—seals were smart enough to stay well away from a noisy production like that. If, instead, the *qablunaq* were broken down out here, well, good luck to them.

Now a snowmobile came toward him, at least as far as the continuous plateau of ice permitted. Both riders were wearing fancy orange and silver suits. The one on the back of the machine, a woman, was waving one arm above her head as if to say, "Come closer," or, at least, "Don't run away." She would be waving a lot more frantically if that snowmobile decided to break through the ice.

As the snowmobile drew nearer, Victor could see that the driver was *qablunaq*, but the woman was not. Not *qablunaq*, not Inuit. Something in between.

The machine stopped as close to him as was possible on the ice and its riders hailed him to approach them closer.

Victor waved back. Now what did these *qablunaq* noisemakers want?

7

Even after the longest of journeys in the harshest of conditions, an Inuk remains considerate of his personal appearance and that of his possessions. This persona must especially be maintained among *qablunaq*. The Inuit knew how they had been ridiculed by the white man since the arrival of the first trappers and explorers, and so when given the opportunity to say nothing, they willingly accepted it. Following after Junko, Victor climbed the landing ramp with almost imperious dignity. As the crew of the *Phoenix* greeted him, his broken smile was reserved at first. But once the bond of several handshakes had been established, Victor's natural grin crept across his weathered, suntanned face with little resistance. To them, he was an anachronistic statesman of the entire Inuit nation; to him, the *Phoenix* was an astounding and convenient oasis after two straight weeks of traversing the ice on foot.

Victor took a particular liking to Sergei Zubov. As Junko explained, many Inuit were rabid fans of professional wrestling—as were a surprising number of native peoples around the world. Victor thought the big Ukrainian bore a striking resemblance to Angelo Mosca, the legendary Canadian wrestler and football player of the 1970s. Now that satellite dishes and VCRs had invaded the Arctic settlements, the popular icons of other cultures were woven into the native cloth.

"Big man! Good man!" Victor said, breaking his imperious facade and patting Zubov on the arm, visibly impressed. "I want my son to grow up big and strong like you."

Zubov flushed, uncertain how to respond. "I hope he does, Victor. But tell him that the NFL and the WWF pay a lot more per pound than NOAA ever will."

For her part, Janey was immediately at home on the ship. Unlike her owner, the sled dog was beyond nobility and incapable of pretension; any opportunity to be unsaddled from her pack was a welcome reprieve. She willingly accepted the petting and good-natured roughing-up offered her, then nuzzled the crew for handouts. She began wolfing down the gourmet table scraps provided by the galley before the dish was even set on the deck.

Junko took the opportunity to pass a dosimeter over the dog. Despite the thickness of the husky's hair, it showed remarkably little sign of contamination.

"She seems clean, but I don't want her inside the airlocks until we can examine her more thoroughly," Junko said, then regarded Victor. "*You*, on the other hand, are coming with us." She urged the Inuk out of his outerwear and into a change of clothes for use inside the ship. He obliged her, for Anika's sake if nothing else, but refused a shower—the loss of his accumulated sweat and skin oils would significantly lessen his insulation to the cold. Instead, Junko found him a plastic cap to keep his unkempt hair from carrying radioactive particles farther inside the ship.

After lunch, Junko brought Victor down to the ship's

infirmary, which under the doctor's direction had been expanded to encompass three adjoining cabins. Garner took a seat and watched the examination without saying a word.

Junko accurately anticipated Victor's reluctance to be examined by a stranger. It was a response common among the Inuit and nearly every native group she had ever seen. Humor was a good enticement. So was candy, though tobacco or alcohol would have been more effective. Like many Inuit, Victor did not seem to place an intrinsic value on material goods—an item was as valuable as the degree to which it was needed; a *qablunaq* was as trustworthy as her closest association to the Inuit. So she told him she had examined many, many Inuit in Greenland, including the elders and legislators of their largest towns. This experience combined, as Junko also knew, with her appearance (after all, the Asian and the Inuit people were separated only by a land bridge and about seventeen thousand years) finally persuaded Victor to strip to the waist and climb onto the examination table.

"You're not feeling very well, are you?" Junko said quietly as she began her cursory inspection. It was more of a statement than a question. Even to a casual observer, Victor's face showed more than fatigue and windburn. His complexion was mottled beyond the effects of regular harsh freezes or the constant glare of the ice pack for half the year. "Tired?"

Victor shrugged. "Inuk's always tired."

"Headaches?"

Another shrug. "Inuk's always aching."

"Coughing up blood?" Victor looked at her blankly. What was a cough without a little bloodied phlegm?

Next Junko noted the staples of Victor's diet in a new file. "Do you eat *muktuk*?" she asked.

"Oh yes!" Victor said enthusiastically. "*Muktuk* is

the best, when you can get it." Made from the blubber of beluga whales, Junko also knew *muktuk,* via bioaccumulation, was increasingly found to contain alarming levels of PCBs and lead.

The doctor tilted Victor's head back slightly and shined a penlight over his inflamed gums. "I see you've lost some teeth recently." Over lunch, it was impossible for her not to notice Victor's missing teeth and the obviously sensitive stragglers. Inuit used their teeth like an extra appendage, so it wasn't uncommon for them to be cracked or missing; in Victor's case it was something else. The teeth looked healthy enough, but they had started falling out. Healthy teeth, particularly those that were continually stressed, did not fall out; they grew stronger—chipped perhaps, and worn blunt, but strong as any bone. In addition, the gums had recessed and many of Victor's remaining teeth were exposed to the root.

"You look like a hockey player I once knew." She gave him a wink. "How big was the other guy? Or was it a polar bear?"

The humor seemed to disarm Victor and he smiled his broken smile. "Nah, I wasn't fightin'. And the bear was already dead when I found 'im."

In the brief time Victor had been sitting there, several strands of his coarse black hair had slipped down to the table from under his plastic cap. On closer examination, Junko noted the irregular bald spots that had begun to open up on his scalp. More evidence of exposure to radiation, slight but indisputable.

At least Victor's eyesight was razor sharp and his balance was good. A nasal smear for inhaled radionuclides was high but not alarmingly so. Junko moved her stethoscope over Victor's chest and back and listened to his respiration. In years past, Inuit could develop respiratory problems as severe as those of coal miners. The condition was typically more pronounced in women, who spent more time indoors around the smoky seal-oil lamps that centered the snowhouses and created their hospitable charm. Hardly any Inuit lived in such a manner anymore; phlegmatic, raspy breathing these days was more often the result of cigarettes. Victor's breathing sounded surprisingly clear, but his skin was sallow, blotchy, and pallid wherever it had not been exposed to the sun. His torso looked almost bruised, and his hands, thick with calluses and not-quite-healed frostbite, retained many nicks and scratches that seemed reluctant to mend. Decorative tattoos depicting the hunt or Inuit spirits covered much of his upper body, carefully applied by himself or others in his clan.

Junko paused to scribble in her notebook. "How long has it been since you've seen a doctor?"

"Not since Anika started living with that *lewkee-meeah*," Victor said.

It took a moment for the comment to register, then Junko realized what her patient had said in his blunt accent.

"Your wife has leukemia?" she asked. "She was diagnosed with it?"

"Oh sure," Victor said. It was as if she had asked him about hunting seals; the words came easily and matter-of-factly. Yes, he knew about leukemia. He didn't like it, but in his village he heard it mentioned nearly every day. In terms of conceptualizing it, however, understanding it in a manner beyond the taste of the air or the texture of the snow, *leukemia,* to Victor, remained an intangible in his life—a bad spirit.

Junko gently plied Victor for more information about what the doctors had said about Anika. Shrugs this time. He was not inclined to follow Anika to the doctor's—even if they came by while he was at home between hunts—and was less inclined to listen to their talk of disease. He let Junko draw some blood from his arm; she said they didn't have the proper equipment on board to do a detailed series of tests, but they could get started. "Before I let you go, I want to look at your white cell count, okay?" she asked. "I'm going to give you some iodine and some calcium tablets. *Take* them, understand? I also want the name of Anika's doctor and the number of the DIAND clinic."

Victor seemed to think this woman's sudden interest in Anika and the village was amusing. He chuckled and flashed her his blighted smile. "Sure, Dr. Junko. I'll show you where the *lewkeemeeah* lives. Soon there's gonna be more *lewkeemeeah* than Inuit. Soon we'll all fall down like that bear."

Soon we'll all fall down. The words taunted Junko as she swabbed Victor's arm and drew a syringe of his blood. "There's a place west of here, Victor," she said as she worked. "A town far inland, called Déline. Ever hear of it?"

Victor shook his head.

"It's a Sahtugot'ine town, on Great Bear Lake," Junko added.

"Ohhh," Victor said with a smile of recognition. "I know Sahtugot'ine. I heard them bastards play tough hockey."

"Near Déline," Garner said. It was the first time he had spoken during the entire exam.

Junko glanced at him, mildly surprised. "That's right—you've heard of it?"

"A friend in Washington mentioned it," Garner said. "Uranium, was it?"

Junko nodded. "Uranium and radium from the Eldorado mine. They used it for the Manhattan Project in the forties, then left nearly two million tons of radioactive mine tailings at the bottom of the lake. Déline is on the opposite shore and many of the men there worked the mines for years, carrying the radium and uranium dust home to their wives and children."

"What about long-term effects?" Garner asked.

"That depends who you ask," Junko said. "Until

recently, the Sahtugot'ine kept an oral history of their people, so much of 'what was' was lost. In the past ten years, they have been investigating a reduction in the average life span and various incidents of cancer—lung cancer is almost a certainty with chronic exposure to radon 222, a daughter of radium 226."

"Lung cancer didn't hurt their bastard hockey players none," Victor offered, then laughed until he saw that neither Garner nor Junko was.

"If the tailings are in the lake, the radiation is in the groundwater," Junko said as she revised the comments in her book. "And if it's in the groundwater, it's in everything"—she looked at Victor—"even the ice on their bastard hockey rink."

Garner considered this information, then mentally compared the geography Krail had shown him with their current position. Déline and the Eldorado mine were easily nine hundred miles away and could safely be ruled out as a source of the current contamination. But there were other abandoned mines and other ore deposits. There were many lakes and watersheds connecting them over vast areas.

They waited as Victor pulled his borrowed sweatshirt back on, then asked for another to wear over it.

"Not quite as warm as your own clothes, are they?" Junko said with a smile. "Your wife's tailoring is very beautiful." She turned to Garner. "Did you see his mitts? Polar-bear skin with waterproof stitching."

Victor smiled proudly at the compliment, which prompted in Garner another thought.

"Victor?" he asked. "What did you mean when you said, 'the bear was already dead when I found him'?"

At Carol's insistence, the *Phoenix* left their temporary station southeast of Igloolik that afternoon, half an hour after the departure of the helicopter carrying those who wanted to leave the ship. Victor's sled and the landing ramps were the last items to be brought aboard, then the decks rumbled as the massive diesel engines were throttled up. A quartet of propellers thrashed the water, shattering the grease ice knitted to the hull and releasing the floe's frosty grasp on the ship. The icebreaker reversed slightly, then turned into the westerly wind.

Though he rarely used maps for his hunting, Victor was well familiar with the nautical charts used by the *Phoenix*'s crew. The Inuk said he could follow the landmarks well enough to guide the *Phoenix* back in the direction he had come, at least over the last twenty miles of his trek, and to the location where he had discovered the polar bear. Picking out familiar landforms along the coast, Victor showed Garner and Carol his approximate path over the past month: a series of elongated loops outward from his settlement like the leaves on a clover. Each loop approached a hundred miles roundtrip, and Carol was impressed that a single hunter and his dog could cover that much ground.

"That much *ground* I could never cross," Victor corrected her. "The drifts and valleys would make it impossible to walk or pull my sled. The sea ice has ridges but it's a lot flatter."

"Still, I can't imagine crossing that much distance on foot with that immense sled, especially out here," Carol said. The near loss of her technicians at Wichita was still a sharp memory.

Victor considered her perspective. "Inuit don't talk about distance for the same reason they don't talk about the cold or the snow—there is too much of it and no amount of worry will make it go away. If you need to get somewhere, you just go."

"You get there because of the snow, not in spite of it," Garner observed. "Good advice for all of us."

Victor had been impressed by much of the ship, but

especially the bridge. The greenish, polarized windows drew his attention immediately and he looked out over the *Phoenix*'s bow with wide-eyed amazement. Ahead, the massive hull easily cleaved through the broken pack as the ship completed its wide arc to the north. The view offered by the five-story superstructure was commanding.

"Now *this*," Victor said, still grinning, "is how to travel on the sea."

Garner went below, donned a radiation suit, and stepped outside to assist Zubov with Medusa. The spherical sampler was attached and readied on the ship's A-frame. Then, on Garner's order, the device was tilted out over the stern.

"Last chance to leave her uncooked," Zubov said. "Sure you don't want to reconsider?"

"I'd say we no longer have a choice," Garner said.

As Zubov passed commands to the winch operator, the Kevlar-coated fiber-optic cable was paid out. The deployment was accelerated as Medusa approached the surface of the water, shortening as much as possible the time the device would be jostled in the wave wash. The turbulence quickly passed as the sphere dipped to five meters, then ten—thirty-three feet or one atmosphere of pressure. Garner called up to the bridge and had the *Phoenix*'s helmsman hold the ship on its present course.

Retreating inside to the ship's main lab, Garner faced the small bank of electronics used to monitor Medusa's "eyes," "nose," and "mouth." For recording purposes, the incoming data were divided into organic and inorganic fractions, the former recording the biological activity in the water and the latter recording the physical and chemical properties of the water itself. A third set of instrumentation had been patched in to the existing controls to remotely record the findings of the new radiation equipment added to the sphere.

Garner performed a series of system tests, flipping

through all the recording channels and each of the macro- and microfocus cameras. If there had been any error in the way the device was primed, these preliminary tests would find it. "Nitrate and phosphate are registering," he relayed to both Zubov and the winch operator after inspecting the data from a cluster of probes designed to measure the nutrient content of the water. "Light meter on. T-S profiling on." While marine biologists usually specialized in the macroscopic world—invertebrates, fish, or marine mammals large enough to move easily through the water—oceanographers concerned themselves with the measured or predicted properties of the water supporting ocean life, and in the case of microscopic organisms, some fundamental parameters were essential. The T-S— or temperature-salinity—curve, which showed a plot of the heat and salt content of the water with depth, was a time-honored indicator in ocean science. These physical properties could not only be used to define parcels of water, but also to predict water motion and the potential for habitation by marine organisms.

Garner now turned his attention to Medusa's organic data. "Bottles one and two primed for firing," he called out to Zubov. "Firing," he confirmed a moment later. The readout confirmed that the first two of Medusa's water samplers had snapped shut, capturing a small parcel of water from a depth of about fifty meters or five atmospheres of pressure. These samples would later be used as a backup confirmation of what Medusa's particle counters, probes, and cameras recorded or estimated electronically.

"No shortage of zooplankton," Garner observed. "Lots of copepods . . . euphausiids . . . jellies." Indeed, at first glance, the densities of the most common microscopic animal plankton appeared to be on a par with expected values for the Arctic Ocean at this time of year. Although precise species identification was something typically left for later work in the lab, Garner readily recognized several forms and these also appeared normal and intact. "The adults are alive and kicking," he said. "No obvious signs of damage or mutation."

"Thank God for that," Zubov's voice came back over the radio. "I don't think I could handle an encounter with Frankenshrimp at this hour."

"Just mind the wire angle and the tow speed, smartass," Garner said.

He turned his attention to the new devices hooked onto the rig and confirmed that the initial settings were correct. "Starting gamma specs," he said. The display came alive, with the needles on three of the radiation meters jumping once, then remaining pegged at maximum scale. Puzzled, Garner adjusted the scale on the devices, increasing the range they measured by a factor of ten, then a factor of one hundred, then one thousand.

The needles responded in unison, settling back toward the left side of each scale.

From his position on the afterdeck, Zubov could see nothing of the readouts from the various instruments Medusa carried. "How's it looking?" he asked.

Garner's silence was enough to bring Zubov back inside. He ducked through the hatchway into the airlock and looked through the plastic sheeting at the readings on the instruments.

The three gamma spectrometers showed radiation levels nearly twenty-five hundred times their initial setting, which Garner had conservatively set at ten times the expected natural level.

"We've got a spike at twenty-five thousand times normal," he said, still not believing his eyes.

Guided by Medusa's scrolling numbers, the *Phoenix* continued on a northward course. The radiation-detection instruments trailing below the ship continued to show alarmingly high levels, rising slightly along an unusually strong temperature anomaly measured at a depth of approximately ten meters. Watching Medusa's readouts carefully, Garner directed the ship from the main lab, calling for a doubling-back each time the track of the radiation was lost.

That the direction Medusa was telling them to follow was almost identical to the path Victor had taken south was an unfortunate coincidence. There was no question that the Inuk had walked over some of the highest levels of contamination as he traversed the ice. On the other hand, the whales had continued south since their release, and if their present course suggested anything to Garner and Carol, it was that the whales were probably moving away from the spot where they had been contaminated. Whether this movement was an aversion response or just a natural segment of their seasonal migration could not be determined. At least the *Phoenix* remained on the right track.

Carol knew that as their path continued to diverge from that of the whales, they would lose the radio signal of the *Balaenoptera*. Reluctantly, she called the Nolan Group's headquarters and arranged for another vessel to search for the corresponding tracking signals as the whales entered the North Atlantic.

"The find of a lifetime slipping away," Garner remarked, sharing her disappointment.

"Don't worry, it gets easier each time it happens," she sighed.

With its battery of sensing equipment and sampling devices deployed, the *Phoenix* was a floating archivist, cartographer, and geophysicist of Foxe Basin. Seismographs plotted the contours of the sea-floor beneath the ship, while sonar and radar described the location and thickness of the surrounding ice, immediately comparing these data to a database of comparative information downloaded from recent polar research studies. Medusa's electronics described the chemical, physical, and biological nature of the water itself, and at least half a dozen deckhands watched the horizon with high-powered binoculars. But only Victor could know exactly where he had seen the fallen polar bear, and it was he alone who spotted the correct position on the floating ice.

The carcass of the bear was no longer there. Only a crescent-shaped fracture gave any indication of what had happened. Given the unseasonably warm weather, the weight of the bear had been enough to eventually break through the pack, causing the carcass to roll over and sink to the bottom. Victor could see a remnant of blue ice that might have once been part of the larger floe, but there was no sign of the bear. Neither were there fresh tracks leading up to the dead bear; the foxes and other scavengers had stayed away.

"Just them fish here now," Victor commented off-handedly to Byrnes.

"What fish?" Byrnes asked, following Victor's gaze toward the broken floe.

"There—under the ice," Victor said and gestured with his mitt. "But they're dead too."

Eventually, Garner and the others saw what Victor had indicated. Trapped beneath a small area of thin, nearly translucent ice, a floating accumulation of tapered, whitish bodies came into view. Victor said that the fish had drifted there only recently, otherwise he would have seen them when he had passed by before.

A landing plank was lowered, and Garner, Carol, Byrnes, and Victor ventured down to the pack. Using ice axes, they eventually cleaved an opening in the ice large enough to allow a closer inspection of the fish.

"There must be an entire school here," Byrnes said.

"Not a school," Garner corrected. "Just a big assemblage of different kinds." Looking over the dead fish, Garner pointed out a half dozen different species—tom-

cod, grayling, char, for instance—that would not naturally be found together. The thinness of the ice and its
slight upward bulge suggested that air trapped beneath
it, combined with local current action, had gradually
accumulated the dozens of fish from the water column.
The four slowly spread out over the expanse of the floe
and confirmed Garner's speculation: wherever the contours on the underside of the ice permitted it, dozens—
now hundreds—of fish had collected at the surface.

"If we took a dive under the thicker parts of the
floe," Garner said, "I'm sure we'd find a lot more."

"No diving, please," Carol said, slightly flushed.
"We've had enough of that for a while." Instead, she
agreed to have Medusa's cameras brought around for a
closer look. As the lenses were refocused to show the
underside of the ice, an eerie spectacle was revealed.
Hundreds upon hundreds of fish of nearly every description floated dead along the ice. Countless more had
no doubt sunk to the bottom or were carried off by the
currents.

"The tomcod and char are saltwater fish, but the
grayling and some of the others are freshwater," Garner
explained. "If both kinds are being killed, a huge area—
coastline and open water—might be affected." This was
an even more troubling possibility, for it could mean
that one or more river systems were the source of the
problem.

Victor was the first to see the small hooks lodged in
the mouths of the grayling. "Those river fish were already caught," he said. "I recognize those hooks—a
buddy of mine uses them all the time."

"Then how did they get out here?" Carol asked. The
Phoenix was nearly ten miles from shore.

"Looks like the ice opened up on my buddy," Victor
said quietly. "Since he ain't here, I guess them fish is all
that floated on his sled."

Junko couldn't help but notice Victor wasn't the least

surprised his friend had apparently fallen through the melting ice and drowned. To the Inuk hunter, such a fate seemed almost predestined. The sea provided bounty for only so long before reclaiming its debt.

Medusa confirmed that the highest levels of contamination were flowing along a subsurface current from the west. Junko and Zubov joined the group and, working quickly with a pair of dosimeters, determined that the detectable radiation in the atmosphere was not much worse than it had been at the *Balaenoptera* floe. The levels in the water, however, continued to increase.

Externally, the fish looked healthy. There were no obvious injuries, bruising, or lesions. Garner suggested that a number of each species be retained for dissection and examination in the *Phoenix*'s lab. The group remained on the ice only long enough to cut a few holes, collect a few bushels of fish, place the specimens into shielded coolers, and cart them back to the ship.

As they completed their inspection of the area, Garner noticed Victor kneeling alone at the edge of one of the ice holes. "Come on, Victor," he said. He saw the pain in the Inuk's expression and so tried to keep his tone cheerful. "Ship's leaving, with or without you."

"I think it should leave without me then," Victor said. The loss of the regal bear combined with the discovery of so many dead fish was a disappointment even a traditional hunter found hard to withstand. "Thank you for showing me your wonderful boat, but I think I should head back to my village. It's time to go home." *Kannakapfaluk* would agree. Anika too.

Victor would not elaborate further on his need to leave the *qablunaq* ship, though the others could hardly insist that he stay. Byrnes and two of his crew helped to offload Victor's sledge from the *Phoenix*'s deck, and Janey accepted a final round of petting from the scientists and deckhands before taking up Victor's pack.

"You're sure about this?" Byrnes asked. "It's a long way to the nearest gas station."

"Not as long as it used to be," Victor said solemnly. He was still numbed by the possible death of his friend. "But closer to my home."

"I will call those doctors you told me about," Junko promised Victor, giving him a parting hug. "We're going to find an answer to your problem as soon as possible, okay?"

"Okay," Victor said. He'd heard such things from *qablunaq* scientists before. So far, that answer had gone the way of his smile.

Garner was the last to approach Victor. He dug in the pocket of his suit and pulled out a small stone. "This is a piece of the earth near Antarctica," Garner explained. "A place called Elephant Island." He explained where Elephant Island was—a tiny scrub of rock in the Weddell Sea nearly at the *South* Pole. Victor's eyes grew wide as he understood this, and he accepted the gift with all the reverence of a religious icon, vigorously nodding his appreciation. The stone was carefully deposited in the pocket of his jacket, next to his renegade teeth.

Victor moved off at once, hauling his sled by its towrope and beckoning Janey to come along. His odd collection of traditional hides and store-bought goods might be practical, but they would hardly protect him from the unseen contamination of the ice he now traversed.

Good luck to you, Victor, thought Garner.

Zubov and Byrnes took advantage of the momentary lack of activity to retrieve Medusa from the water, recalibrate her sensors, and refit the device with a clean set of sampling bottles. Carol told the deck crew to shower and steal some sleep while the scientific crew tried to determine how they could analyze the fish. Over the next two hours, Garner, Junko, and Carol worked with a handful of technicians to subject the samples to radiation testing, then carefully prepare blood, skin, and tissue slides from a number of specimens.

"The radiation levels are very high, but not nearly what was contained in the whales," Junko said. "The fish are lower on the food chain—with less fatty tissue—so we might expect that. Cold-blooded animals are also less susceptible to radiation uptake."

"Then again, maybe it wasn't the radiation that killed them in the first place," Garner said. His gaze was firmly fixed on the eyepieces of a stereo microscope, looking at a blood sample from one of the grayling.

"What else could it be?" Junko asked.

"I think these fish were killed by heat shock," Garner said.

"*Heat* shock?" Carol and Junko replied, nearly in unison.

"Some freshwater arctic fish are known to have glycoproteins in their blood," Garner explained. "A kind of antifreeze that allows them to live in very cold water without having to expend a lot of metabolic energy." He indicated the results of the tests performed on the fish blood. "These fish have extremely low levels of glycoproteins, and a lot of the skin tissue shows signs of sudden or prolonged exposure to temperatures beyond what they can handle."

"Where would there be that kind of heat source here?" Junko asked. Even as she uttered the question, the answer came to her. "Of course. The fission reactions of both plutonium and uranium 235 produce a lot of heat."

Garner retrieved the temperature and salinity data from Medusa's computers. He downloaded the information to a computer in the *Phoenix*'s lab and soon the monitor was showing a detailed temperature plot of that morning's survey.

"Right here," he said, pointing to a clearly defined spike in the temperature profile. Medusa had shown the anomaly all along, but even a well-trained eye sees only what it's looking for. "Looks like we've got a temperature anomaly along the same depth as the increased rad levels."

"Or a temperature anomaly *because* of the increased radiation levels," Junko speculated. "But that would mean—"

"—That would mean we're dealing with a massive source of contamination somewhere up the line," Carol finished.

Garner studied the temperature plot again. "If we can reset Medusa's onboard computers to chart and follow the increase in temperature over distance, we can try to locate the source."

"And that source has to be larger than anything natural," Junko said. "Possibly even larger than any industrial or military sources ever catalogued."

Garner agreed. "As I said, let's hope it's just one source."

The lab's intercom buzzed. It was Frisch, in the radio room. "Call for you, Carol," he said.

The radio operator's page was becoming all too familiar to Carol. "Stuart, you're becoming one of my least favorite people around here, you know?"

"Sorry," came Frisch's reply.

It's Szilard, she thought. *Or that little creep Seaborg. Or the lawyers. They're shutting us down as the world's most ineffective emergency response team.* "Unless it's Publishers Clearing House with a big, fat check, tell them I'll call them back."

"You better take it, Carol," Frisch said. "It's the Canadian Coast Guard."

"What do *they* want?" she asked.

"Our help," Frisch said. "They want us to respond to a possible emergency."

I thought we were in an emergency already, Carol said to herself. *What the hell does the Coast Guard want?*

"It's a distress beacon," Frisch explained as Carol arrived at the radio room. "They want us to check it out."

Carol took the microphone and waited as the call was patched through. The caller identified himself as Captain Neil Parsons of the Canadian Coast Guard, somewhere out of Iqaluit.

"After nearly two months of enforced radio silence, we've picked up an emergency beacon from the *Sverdrup Explorer* coming out of Fury and Hecla Strait," Parsons explained. "The ship is frozen into some ice, but there isn't enough of a platform for a helo to set down, even if we had the range to reach her. So far we've only been able to do an aircraft flyby of the vessel under low overcast, and that hasn't told us much. No one's answered our hailing and no one is visible on deck, but the ship appears to be seaworthy."

"What do you think it is then?" Carol asked.

"I suspect it's something trivial—either their radio's out or their batteries are run down in the cold and the captain is too proud to admit it. As you probably know, the *Explorer* made an explicit request for privacy. If it wasn't for the beacon, we wouldn't even be bothering you."

"What about *your* ships?" Carol asked Parsons tersely. The Coast Guard had flatly rejected her request for a routine flyby to check out the possible radiation source; now they wanted the *Phoenix*'s assistance. "What exactly do you guys get paid for?"

"Obviously we are short on other options or I

wouldn't be deputizing you," Parsons said. "The *Bernier* is the closest Coast Guard vessel to the *Explorer*'s location and she broke a propeller shaft about an hour after we registered the beacon. There's a fishing vessel in the Hudson Strait that might assist too, but she says she's blocked by the ice."

"How convenient for them," Carol said. "I don't suppose the ice is blocking their nets."

"Maritime law requires that you provide search-and-rescue support if necessary. I wouldn't be asking if it wasn't at least temporarily necessary. Common sense and common courtesy dictate it."

"There's no need to lecture me, Captain Parsons," Carol said. "Send us the latest coordinates and I'll have my captain respond to that location ASAP."

"Thank you, Dr. Harmon," Parsons said. "If it turns out there's some type of emergency up there you'll have all the assistance you need. Just let me know." The connection was broken and Carol stuck out her tongue at the dead microphone.

"Where was that intrepid spirit and generosity a week ago?" Carol asked Frisch. She muttered a profane remark under her breath, handed the radio back to her crewman, and marched out of the room, nearly colliding with Garner in the corridor.

"As if we don't have enough to keep us busy, now we've got to go play Lassie for a group of yachtsmen," Carol said. She said *yachtsmen* as though there were some sort of obstruction in her throat.

Garner was impressed when he heard the name of the vessel in distress. "You mean THE *Sverdrup Explorer*?"

"One and the same," Carol said. "Norway's backward little time machine."

Garner couldn't help but notice Carol's resistance to providing a mandatory check of a vessel in distress.

"I know I'm being terrible, but *really*," Carol said.

"It's like stopping to check out a car alarm—when's the last time anyone did that?" She looked at Garner then and the stability in his eyes brought her down to earth. It felt good. "I know, I know. I guess it could just as easily be us someday."

"Someday? Like tomorrow?"

"Yeah, like tomorrow."

8

The *Sverdrup Explorer* had been built as part of a meticulous, modern-day re-creation of the *Fram* expedition. The *Fram*—Norwegian for "forward" and symbolic of the days when explorers steadfastly believed they had free license to choose their own direction—set out to sail the waters of the high Arctic. Fridtjof Nansen, the expedition's leader, wanted to use the drift of the ship to prove the existence of a cross-polar current that ran northwest from Siberia to the North Pole, then south past Greenland in the Davis Strait. A durable, four-hundred-ton wooden vessel was designed specifically to be frozen into the ice. Once there, the vessel and its crew followed the drift of the ice for nearly two years, learning more about polar oceanography than any expedition in history. The three-masted ship was hewn from solid wood more than two feet thick, its triple hull reinforced with sheet metal and given well-rounded sides to allow the vessel to pop up onto converging ice rather than being crushed by it. A retractable propeller and rudder also reduced potential ice damage, while a 220-horsepower steam engine and a windmill provided virtually all of the vessel's power.

Under the command of Captain Otto Sverdrup, the ship had sailed from Larvik, Norway, in 1893 with twelve men and a five-year supply of provisions. It was frozen into the ice near the Siberian Islands and drifted for nearly two years before breaking free of the ice at Svalbard. The expedition and its successor (from 1898 to 1902, also under Sverdrup's command) were considered triumphs. In all, Sverdrup managed to log more than seven hundred days in the Arctic, crossing nearly twelve thousand miles, surveying more than ten thousand square miles of shoreline and contributing unprecedented knowledge about the general circulation of the Arctic Ocean. To the present day, oceanographers routinely used "Nansen" bottles to sample parcels of water or spoke of the "Sverdrup"—a unit of volume transport equal to one million cubic meters per second—when discussing ocean currents. The original *Fram* was eventually memorialized in 1935 and put ashore at Bygdeynes, Norway, where it was heralded as a national treasure.

The idea to re-create the *Fram* expedition was that of a man named Malcolm Neddermeyer. Neddermeyer was a burly, unabashedly chauvinistic Norwegian mountaineer, explorer, and businessman who had accrued his modest millions selling water purification filters. The *Sverdrup Explorer,* an exact reproduction of the *Fram,* became his passion and unbridled promotion. Over the next decade, Neddermeyer's infectious enthusiasm convinced private-sector sponsors in both Norway and Canada to subscribe to the vision. Neddermeyer used his effusive charisma and considerable wealth to generate widespread public awareness of the event, particularly how exactly the *Fram* had been re-created and how Neddermeyer's crew would forgo "any and all modern conveniences" to duplicate more precisely the original expedition.

With all eyes turned his way, Neddermeyer then set out to do what most vessels in the Arctic specifically avoid: to be frozen into the ice. His crew would then follow the movement of the pack as it drifted—this time past Ellesmere and Baffin Islands, including Fury and Hecla Strait—for up to two years. But unlike other vagabonds who used press agents, satellite phones, and laptop computers, Neddermeyer insisted he would not contact the outside world until the *Sverdrup Explorer* sailed back into Oslo Harbor, as the original *Fram* had done more than a century before. Though the expedition's sponsors initially complained, the mystique and uncertainty of the *Explorer*'s success eventually added a kind of collector's fervor to merchandise created for the event and a serial adventure quality to the infrequent news of the ship's progress around the pole. Not since Thor Heyerdahl's 1947 South Pacific voyage in the *Kon-Tiki* had the public been so forcefully engaged by such an event, which amounted more to a high-priced gimmick than to any research experiment.

Now, some twenty months after the *Sverdrup Explorer* had sailed into the known-but-unknown, its emergency beacon had broken the prolonged silence.

The *Sverdrup Explorer* appeared on the *Phoenix*'s radar screen just after midnight. Over the next hour, the Nolan Group vessel approached to within half a mile of the *Explorer* before anchoring. Although the *Phoenix*'s sensor array could provide a detailed description of the surrounding obstructions even in complete darkness, Carol wanted her crew to have nothing to do with the vessel until 5:00 A.M. That would give them at least twelve hours of solid daylight before the sun once again began to slip below the horizon.

Frisch had tried to hail the *Explorer* for the first hour after they came into range, then again before he retired for the night, to no avail. If the crew of the *Explorer* had seen the *Phoenix*'s approach, they had no interest in communication, even if it meant avoiding a possible collision with another vessel. Until full dawn, the glow of the *Phoenix* would have to serve as a night-light for both vessels.

Garner studied the *Explorer* from his position on the bridge of the *Phoenix*. Though there was little moonlight, the distinctive silhouette of the *Explorer* could easily be seen against the silvery cast of the floating ice. Garner had heard how Neddermeyer, ever the megalomaniac, had waged a jurisdictional war to build his ship exactly to the original specifications. As construction progressed, some unexpected concessions had to be made—for example, the sturdy oak and greenheart timbers used to construct the original *Fram* had been virtually logged out of Europe and so were imported. But the belligerent captain remained steadfast in his goal, even disputing the twentieth century's more rigorous requirements for lifesaving, navigation, and communication equipment for the sake of historical consistency. Garner didn't know the official outcome of that dispute, but the *Explorer* now floated on the ice as silent and dark as a ghost ship. Only the persistent beeping of the vessel's distress beacon let them know she contained any electronics at all.

"What do you make of it?" Zubov asked him.

"There's no way they couldn't have heard or seen us approach," Garner replied. "They may be living in a floating log cabin, but *we're* lit up like a parade float. If they really were in some kind of distress, they would have sent up a flare by now." Zubov wondered if the *Explorer*'s crew was foolish enough to leave even their flares behind.

Daybreak revealed a carpet of broken ice floating between the two ships. As Captain Parsons had relayed, it was too small an ice formation to permit any sort of helicopter landing, but the *Explorer* itself looked in good condition. The sails on all three of her masts had been secured, her sturdy windmill stood silent, and the gear on the deck was lashed in place. There was still no sign of any activity on the boat and all hailings were ignored.

"Okay, *now* I'm worried," Byrnes said, as Garner, Zubov, and Junko joined him on the deck of the *Phoenix*. "What are the odds those Norwegian bastards froze to death out here? Or starved?"

"If you believe the press on Neddermeyer, he wouldn't ask for a glass of water if his beard was on fire," Garner said. "It wouldn't surprise me if he abandoned ship rather than face the humiliation of failing in the face of his promises—or to add drama to his tale."

"Maybe they set out for the pole on foot and forgot to set the parking brake," Byrnes said. In 1895, Nansen had made a similar attempt, leaving the *Fram* and trekking on foot for several weeks.

To Zubov, the silent vessel brought back too many eerie memories of the *Sato Maru,* a freighter that he and Garner had found adrift and whose crew had all succumbed to a then-unknown plague. "You thinking what I'm thinking?" Zubov asked his friend.

"I'm trying not to," Garner admitted.

Carol joined them last. All were dressed in their cold-weather gear, full radiation field suits pulled over that. Looking every bit like astronauts from some 1950s science-fiction movie, the team gathered together some rudimentary emergency and first-aid equipment, then waited as one of the deck cranes lowered a Zodiac inflatable boat into the water.

"How are the rad levels?" Garner asked.

"Actually, much lower than where we were yesterday," Junko answered. "Still high, but the main contamination seems to be localized behind us—for now."

"Let's hope it stays that way," Carol said testily. She hated the claustrophobic sensation produced by the radiation suits, the binding of the locking collars at her neck, wrists, and ankles, and the ridiculously small plastic window that served as her viewport to her surroundings. The knowledge that she was breathing recirculated air only increased the feeling of being wrapped in a dry-cleaning bag. "Come on, troops," she said, stepping into the Zodiac. "Let's go see what's what."

Garner, Zubov, Junko, and Byrnes followed her into the boat and Byrnes started the outboard motor. A straight-line route to the *Explorer* was not possible through the floating ice, so they circled around the other vessel until it was between them and the *Phoenix*.

As Byrnes nosed the Zodiac into the ice, Zubov leaned his bulk over the gunwale, testing the floe for strength. "If it'll hold me, it'll hold you," he announced to the others and climbed out of the boat.

"This is really strange," Byrnes muttered as he climbed after him. They were no more than fifteen yards from the side of the *Explorer,* yet no one aboard had come on deck. The sound of the Zodiac's outboard motor alone should have been enough to draw the attention of all hands. "No lifeboats?" he asked, nodding at the *Explorer*.

"Longboats and sledges," Garner replied. "True to the original." The longboats, at least, appeared to be in place. Why?

"Stick close and watch your footing," Carol cautioned. She dropped down several inches as she stepped into a patch of soft pack, then regained her stride.

"Ahoy!" Garner called out as they neared the ship. "Hel-lo?"

Garner led them aboard. Of course he had seen pictures of the *Explorer* in the news—all of them had—but this was the first time any of them had seen it in person.

Only Garner had seen the original *Fram* enshrined in its museum in Bygdeynes. The two vessels were, as reported, identical, but seeing the *Explorer* here in the Arctic brought history to life in a way that no landlocked memorial ever could. Garner could see how Neddermeyer had been so persuasive in convincing anyone with the slightest nautical bent to follow his dream.

"Here's your answer about the boats," Zubov said, examining one of the smaller, overturned hulls. Two planks had been chopped from the hull of each one, rendering them unable to float without major repairs. The sledges were missing from their racks, either taken off the ship on foot or thrown overboard by a saboteur. "Looks like someone didn't want the party to break up before the ice did."

Garner gazed up at the masts and rigging of the carefully reconstructed schooner, a brand-new vessel from the distant past. As Junko had observed at dinner, the polar regions of the earth were natural archives of those who had tried, and failed, to conquer her. Provisions and animal carcasses left on the ice froze solid, remaining edible for years. Ships were effortlessly crushed to the verge of sinking, then held suspended between the surface and the bottom for decades. Explorers who conquered this territory never fully lost the chill from their bones, while those who failed were perfectly preserved by the cold, frozen into the ice to provide a warning for those foolish enough to follow. As if the timelessness of the landscape itself weren't obvious enough, with the discovery of Victor and now the *Explorer* it seemed as though the ghosts of the past had gained more of a foothold.

"*Hel-lo?*" Zubov yelled, stamping his boots on the wooden deck to clear his feet of snow.

"We are from the American research vessel *Phoenix*," Carol called out. "The Coast Guard asked that we board you." She couldn't shake the feeling that they were walking through the crosshairs of a sniper's rifle scope, a hidden observer who might mistake the landing party for high-tech pirates.

Junko crouched near the deck with a dosimeter probe in her hand. "Forget what I said about lower levels," she said, examining the device's readout. "This ship is *cooked*. The contamination in this metal sheeting is as high as anything we've seen yet."

"But still safe for these suits, right?" Carol asked automatically. "I mean, if we have to wear these damn things, they're doing us some good, right?"

"As far as we can know," Junko said, still studying the instrument. "Though without any shielding, I can't say the same thing won't happen to the *Phoenix*, eventually."

"I thought you said the rad levels were *lower* here," Byrnes said.

"Yes. Around here—now—the water isn't as contaminated," Junko started to explain.

"But this ship's adrift," Garner finished. "It passed through or along the radioactive slick somewhere upstream and retained its contamination."

Junko agreed. "And we have no way of knowing the duration of exposure."

"I doubt the crew would know it, either," Garner said. "They'd have no reason to carry radiation equipment with them." The statement was obvious from a historical perspective, but Garner thought he would say it aloud to reassure Carol about her self-punishing shortsightedness. Carol's glance told him she saw right through the attempt, but appreciated it nonetheless.

"All the equipment in the world might not have helped," Junko said. "With these levels, it's hard to imagine anyone . . ." Her voice trailed off, not uttering the word the others each guessed: *surviving*.

"Hello!" Carol yelled, turning as she moved toward the *Explorer*'s main hatch. "Last chance for you men to get decent before we come in." She did not want to admit the obvious reasons why no one aboard the *Explorer* had responded to the commotion on deck. She did not want to think about why Dex and Ramsey weren't sharing this mysterious discovery with them.

Stepping down into the small cockpit, she grasped the handle of the main cabin door and pulled it open.

Inside there was only dusty silence.

Garner moved past her with a large lantern flashlight and stepped down into the main cabin. The sensation of stepping into the past returned. *Primitive* did not begin to describe the living conditions of the vessel, which resembled an oak-lined root cellar more than any kind of research vessel, past or present. The room had no windows and the oil lamps that hung from the wall showed no sign of recent use. Scraps of food dotted the preparation area, but the main eating table looked unused. Garner recalled Sir John Franklin's ill-fated expedition of 1845. Lost in the frozen expanse west of Melville Peninsula, many of the 128 men were likely poisoned by the lead solder used in canning their food supply. There was no sound, save for the gentle sploshing of the sea against the ice, the creaking of the thick wooden hull, and the thin hiss of the regulators on the radiation suits.

Moving forward, Garner stepped down a narrow corridor between the crew cabins. Personal effects were strewn on the floor, the bunks were unmade, but there were no occupants in any of them. True to the last detail, there was no nylon or Gore-Tex here, only nineteenth-century textiles, wool, cotton, leather, and oilskin. It looked as though many of the crew's boots and warmest clothing were also on board, which suggested that no one had left the vessel on foot.

Now the ship was filled with noise as Byrnes and Zubov made their way aft, banging doors and lockers and bellowing greetings, to no avail. Closer behind him, Garner could hear Carol and Junko taking rad levels from every available surface, the dutiful electronic chirp of the dosimeter, and the comparison of these to the levels measured outside.

Garner stepped forward farther still, outside once again onto the forward deck. The space was divided roughly into thirds, with crude pens built along the gunwales with planking and chicken wire. The kennels, where Neddermeyer's crew would have stowed the sled dogs they had brought along—sled dogs! But not flares!—for no other purpose than consistency with the *Fram* expedition.

It was then that Garner stepped around a small pile of wooden casks and found the dogs.

Six huskies, dead on their leashes, lay atop each other on the floor of the pen, painfully posed with their legs curled beneath them, muzzles angled back as if in some last, baleful howl. Both the water and food bowls had been licked clean and the area was wired shut, holding them back within a few yards of the crew's food stores. From the wounds on two of the animals, Garner surmised that the dogs had resorted to cannibalism before succumbing to death. The blood from their wounds had long ago congealed, while the temperatures aboard the vessel kept the carcasses below the freezing point. Garner counted twenty-seven dogs in the twin racks of holding pens before the inhumanity of the scene stopped his census.

"Back here!" someone shouted. It was Zubov's voice, not panicked—never panicked—but loud and concerned. Garner wheeled away from the kennel and ran aft, ducking his head as he navigated the low beams inside the cabin. He came up quickly behind Carol and Junko in the aft passageway.

In the rear of the vessel was another large room that could possibly have been intended for storage of dry goods but had instead been converted into a rudimentary infirmary. At a glance, Garner counted eleven human bodies lying on the floor in grim mimicry of the spectacle he had just seen. Like the dogs, the men were frozen where they sat. Many were under thin blankets or lay curled up in the fetal position. It was obvious that many had experienced vomiting or diarrhea before death, but none had ventured back to their bunks only a few feet away. Their skin was locked in a grayish pallor marbled with the angry pink and ominous black of frostbite. Among those whose eyes remained open, the eyeballs were sunken and showed signs of residual bleeding. Many of the faces were recognizable from the publicity photos of the expedition on CNN, ESPN, and the Explorer Channel, but none resembled Neddermeyer.

The positions of the bodies in the room seemed odd. Zubov explained that he and Byrnes had actually had to push their way through the door, only to find the men seated around the perimeter.

"It looks like they took precautions to keep anyone from getting in here," Byrnes said. "But I don't get it. If they were sick, why did they all retreat in here, not to the galley or their bunks?"

"And why didn't they call for help?" Carol asked. She was becoming enraged, though whether from the demonstrated foolishness of these men's ridiculous machismo or the terrifying reminder of Dex's and Ramsey's deaths she did not know.

Garner stepped around the bodies closest to the door and looked at them from another angle. In a morning of ghosts, the sight of the men now lying dead before him was chillingly reminiscent of past accounts of early polar expeditions, successful or not. Amundsen. Peary. Scott. Franklin. Shackleton. Neddermeyer had stubbornly added himself to this list a century too late. The men, some of Scandinavia's best—or at least wealthi-est—yachtsmen, had died weak, cold, and hungry, but they had died with resolve.

Examining the scene, Garner tried to make sense of it all. "They weren't retreating. They were advancing. They set up a blockade to keep anyone from getting out of here, even while they slept or after they were too weak to move. With their food only a few feet away."

"Getting out from where?" Byrnes asked. Nearly in unison, the five of them turned to look aft, at a second door leading into the room.

"Whatever they wanted stopped was in there," Garner said. "And I think I know what—or who—it is."

The small enclosure, built into the hull nearly as an afterthought, was the most heavily fortified cabin on the ship. The timbers in the walls and door were part of a bulkhead and easily too thick for any of the knives or hatchets the landing party could see on board. Garner and Zubov retreated to the afterdeck, where Zubov lowered his friend off the *Explorer*'s crowded transom.

"Hurry up," Zubov grunted. "The meals on the *Phoenix* haven't made you any lighter, buddy."

Garner moved across the ornate transom of the ves-sel only a few feet above the icy water, in search of a chink in the *Explorer*'s wooden armor. Moments later, he found what he was looking for: a small porthole that looked into the curious room. The opening was far too small for a man to climb through, but large enough to allow a good view of the horizon and, if necessary, the firing of a flare pistol from inside, had there been one. Garner found the recklessness of Neddermeyer's histor-ical dream more chilling each time he reconsidered it.

Garner's light flicked over something shiny. Through the gloom he could see it was the ship's transmitter. Beyond it, next to the heavily barricaded door leading to the fortress, lay the frozen body of the twelfth and final member of the *Explorer*'s crew.

"What do you see?" Zubov called down.

"The two things between these men and survival," Garner called back. "The radio and the captain."

Garner and Zubov eventually got into the radio room with the assistance of a chainsaw borrowed from the *Phoenix*'s tool stores. Examining the clues left before them, it became apparent that Neddermeyer had fended off a possible mutiny by barricading himself in the small cabin along with the ship's logs, charts, and radio. The rest of the crew, like Neddermeyer, probably already sick and weakened by radiation poisoning, had battened-down the ship and staged a mutiny outside the radio room. Neddermeyer's log mentioned their "urging" him to call off the expedition for health reasons, but he continued to ignore them "for the greater good."

True to his delusions, Neddermeyer kept records with an antique quill pen, taking bearings from the stars and marking these on his charts. Entry after entry in his log spoke of the coming of spring and the breakup of the ice that would, mercifully, mark the successful end of their odyssey. Facing the prospect not only of abandoning the expedition but of losing several men, Neddermeyer had tried simply to outlive the unknown, invisible killer.

Garner found that the *Explorer*'s emergency beacon was the same make and model as the one he carried aboard his own *Albatross*. The device could be set so that it had to be manually reset every twelve or twenty-four hours and would begin beeping if this reset failed to occur. Figuring back to the time when the Coast Guard first noted the beacon, Neddermeyer had been dead less than two days.

The final entry in the log concluded with: *All but three of us dead. With the end of this quill, weakness begs me to surrender. Passage through Fury and Hecla was hellishly slow, exhausting what little hope I have left. God have mercy on me for what I have done. To their families, my shame. To those who succeeded where I have so obviously failed, my admiration.* Notwithstanding the stoic melodrama and the antiquated use of words, it was indeed tragic that Neddermeyer believed his vessel to be so far from safety. He had chosen death for twelve sailors rather than face defeat by Sverdrup's Arctic.

Even if the facilities had been available, there was no need for an autopsy on any of the men. The dosimeter indicated absorbed doses of seven grays in the fortress, and even higher on the blankets the men had used to stay warm in their last hours. Other than the whales, these were the highest environmental levels they had yet recorded; Junko speculated that the boat's wood construction had amplified the level of saturation.

"Killed by starvation, cold, and radiation," Junko mused. "In that order, if they were lucky."

"It was arrogance and stupidity that killed these men, in that order," Carol said bitterly. "The best we can do is try not to join them."

Carol returned to the *Phoenix* within the hour to radio her findings back to Parsons. The stunned silence on the other end of the line in response to her description left little to the imagination; Parsons was only beginning to appreciate the horror they all now faced.

"I'll notify the Norwegian authorities so that they can tell the next of kin," he said. "Right after I get a nuclear emergency response team up to your location. The NORAD radar post at Hall Beach and the Canadian Forces at Iqaluit and Resolute have already been placed on alert."

"Alert? To do what?" Carol said, her anger finally

boiling over. "To expose more people to this radiation? To soak more vessels in this stuff and send them back to God-knows-how-many ports around the Arctic?"

"Then what would you like?" Parsons asked evenly.

Carol hesitated—what *would* she like? The question posed was the sudden answer to the demands she had been making for nearly two weeks. Now that she was in a position to have someone listen to her and *respond*, she found herself hesitating. It was too late. What she had just witnessed aboard the *Explorer* went beyond a mere call for help. The *Phoenix* was alone at ground zero of some invisible, slow-motion nuclear detonation. For as far as they needed to go along this toxic trail, to invite assistance at this point could mean countless more deaths.

"I'd like to be allowed to continue our investigation without interruption," Carol said. "I'd like to use the people I have with me to determine the extent of this problem. Then, once we know exactly what's going on, I'd like your unconditional support to clean up this mess."

"How can you be certain you'll find the source?" Parsons asked. "I need some assurance." There was more concern than doubt in his voice.

"I have to be certain," Carol said. "So do you. Right now, we're all you've got."

9

Junko worked tirelessly to examine the fallen crewmen of the *Explorer*, drawing blood and taking as many notes as possible on the condition of the bodies without further disturbing the scene. Carol reminded Junko of this before she returned to the *Phoenix* to report their finding to the Coast Guard: learn whatever you can, but don't touch anything else—maybe the Nolan Group could avoid a lawsuit for a change. It was now a matter for the maritime authorities, the expedition's insurers, and the sailors' next of kin to determine and address what had gone wrong.

Though the equipment Junko was using wasn't sophisticated enough to define the specific ratios of the various isotopes and their daughters, the signatures she derived suggested a toxic stew steeped in cesium, strontium, highly enriched uranium, and plutonium. In everyday terms, this was high-level reprocessed waste, most likely left over from weapons manufacturing. No wonder no one wanted to admit ownership.

As a physician, far more disconcerting to her was the suffering the men had obviously endured in the hours and days before their death. The frozen bodily fluids on every deck of the ship testified to the painful spasms and seizures they must have experienced as the radiation took hold of their internal organs. Their skin was mottled and blistered to the consistency of runny oatmeal from the combined effects of desiccation and degeneration. So great was the apparent level of their exposure that conditions that took months to become evident in Hiroshima and Belarus had manifested themselves in these men within days.

The sight was beyond ghastly, beyond comprehension. Inside her suit, Junko resisted the urge to vomit—or shriek. What could it possibly be like to die in such a manner? How large a dose was required to weaken these healthy, young men so severely that the prospect of wresting control of the radio, of even feeding themselves, became insurmountable tasks? In her travels to the incidental or accidental hot spots of the globe, Junko had grown accustomed to seeing horrors of the flesh. She had seen birth defects in the young and rampant, lethal cancers in the elderly. She had seen blindness, scorched flesh, and sterility stretched over entire populations. Homelessness in places where entire communities had stood, famine and drought in the midst of luscious crops and abundant water, all stripped of their utility by tasteless, odorless, inescapably fatal contamination. She thought she had witnessed the fallout of the worst aspects of the human condition, but she had never seen anything like what had been found in a single cabin aboard this simple wooden ship.

She heard Zubov approaching behind her and turned around, nearly stepping into his arms.

"You okay?" he asked her. In that moment there seemed to be no room for awkwardness.

"I really don't know," Junko said. "I guess I wasn't ready for this today."

"You mean there have been days when you expected this?" Zubov asked.

"Yes," she admitted. "There are days when I've had to." She could see the sallow look on Zubov's face as he looked upon the men of the *Explorer*. He was standing among ghosts of his own. Somehow that knowledge was enough to ease her fear.

"It's good to have company this time," she said.

It seemed the most natural thing in the world to close his arms and embrace her then. "I was just about to say the same thing," he said.

Forward, Garner spread Neddermeyer's notes and charts on the main dining table. He glanced up as Carol and Byrnes returned from the *Phoenix*.

"What's the good word?" Garner asked.

"We've got the cavalry's interest," Carol said. "And when news of Neddermeyer's conduct gets out to the media, I'm sure the circus will be coming to town in droves."

"Do you think that's wise?" Garner asked. "I mean, the ship—the whole area—is hardly secured from investigators or souvenir hunters at this point."

"Parsons promised me a news blackout on what we've found, including the exact location of the ship," Carol said. "I told him that I didn't even want a response team here, at least until we can suggest some safe limits and procedures for dealing with the area. Fortunately, Canadian law protects the scene of marine and aircraft disasters for just this reason. Besides, if anyone else *could* get to the *Explorer* right away, we wouldn't have been recruited in the first place."

"Not to mention that the *Phoenix* has already commandeered every piece of field radiation equipment in the Northern Hemisphere," Byrnes added, shaking his head. "So they're inclined to let us take the lead on this."

"Canaries in a coal mine," Zubov mused as he and Junko joined them.

"I thought you'd be used to that by now," Carol said. "Especially working with Brock."

"I am," Zubov replied. "It's the size of the cage that's beginning to get uncomfortable."

The news blackout was a good thing. Junko could vividly imagine the response of the international media to the news of a major, inexplicable radiation leak in the Arctic Ocean. The remote location and relatively low population density of the area might initially keep the story off the front page, but the merest mention of the *Explorer*'s fate would change that soon enough. As Three Mile Island, Sellafield, and Chernobyl had shown, the reaction of a misinformed public to reports of "accidental" radiation leaks was invariably far too hysterical in the short term and far too complacent over the long term. The public seemed to think that radiation, like a brushfire or a train wreck, required only a dedicated cleanup effort to make it go away. Contamination like this would never go away, not in fifty thousand human generations.

First things first: identify the vector. Stem the source. ALARA.

"All the same," Junko continued, "we can't just leave these men here. Besides, won't the ship just continue to drift?"

"Yes, and no," Byrnes said. "We obviously can't tow the *Explorer* with us, so I told Parsons we'd put the ship in a storm anchorage, leave the beacon on with a portable backup, and let them know when we figure out the best approach."

"I can't see the next of kin, much less the Norwegian government, agreeing to that arrangement for very long," Junko said dubiously.

"Then we'll have to hurry," Garner said. "Short of wrapping the *Explorer* in a big, lead-lined Baggie and pushing it back to Oslo, there isn't much more we can do about this mess—we have to get back to our own mess."

Carol checked her watch. "I'm worried about your respirator units," she said, nodding to Garner, Zubov, and Junko, who had remained aboard the *Explorer* almost the entire day. The devices ran on rechargeable batteries and were only intended to operate for six to eight hours at a time. "The filter cartridges are putting in overtime as it is and we've still got to lock down the ship before we can leave."

"Then we'll go back for fresh batteries," Garner said. "These notes are the best source of information we've got so far and I don't want to leave them behind just yet." The charts from the *Explorer* would also be invaluable to them, but those would have to be left behind for investigators of the tragic expedition. Additionally, the weathered paper showed radiation levels far too high to risk bringing it aboard the *Phoenix*.

Byrnes indicated the *Explorer*'s charts. "How are we doing with those?"

By comparing Neddermeyer's notes with his celestial observations and the crude notations on the charts, Garner and Zubov were able to reconstruct the track of the ship's drift over the last several weeks of the expedition. "If Neddermeyer was intending to duplicate Sverdrup's original course," said Zubov, "he failed miserably."

"The *Explorer* came too far north before it froze into the ice," Garner estimated. "Once it did, the floating ice was so large it moved not only with the currents, but was turned and held back by the pack ice on all sides of it. By December, Neddermeyer surmised the same thing in his diary, but it was too late to change his mind. The deviation from his hoped-for route into Davis Strait continued to increase until only the means and accommodations were similar to the original *Fram* expedition."

"Sounds like grounds for a mutiny to me," Byrnes said.

"Could be," Garner agreed. "There was no reason to continue the voyage, especially when the crew started getting sick."

"No reason except ego," Carol said.

"A hundred years ago it was known as bravery," Byrnes parried.

Carol started to retort, but her words stalled. For a moment, the ghosts returned to the galley of the *Explorer,* sitting down at the table next to the landing party from the *Phoenix.*

"They were drinking contaminated meltwater," Junko said. "Catching contaminated seals and fish to supplement their provisions. Everything was reused or recycled."

"If anyone out on this ice was going to feel the effects of the radiation, it would be these men," Garner said.

"And the Inuit," Junko said. "Victor and his family and many others. I didn't think I'd ever say this, but the rest are probably better off getting canned goods at the government store."

"I doubt any of them could even imagine what was happening until it was too late," Byrnes said. He meant the men aboard the *Explorer,* but the encounter with the Inuk and his *lewkeemeeah* certainly applied as well. "If it wasn't for the *Balaenoptera,* the same thing might have happened to us."

"The same thing *did* happen to us—two of us," Carol reminded them. "And we don't know if the rest of us will get out of the woods." She looked at Garner. "That's up to you."

For a moment there was no one in the room but Garner and his ex-wife. It could not be more obvious how much faith she was placing in his ability to get the *Phoenix* to the source of this nightmare. Whatever past differences there had been, Carol needed Garner's experience, she needed his confidence and objectivity. More than that, she needed *him*.

I know, came the reply in his eyes, *I need you too.*

"The *Explorer* was designed to drift, like a drogue on top of the ice, and she seems to have done that extremely well," Garner said. "Her track not only lets us know how the floes have been moving, but where she's been. That's the direction we should head next—back up the surface currents to wherever the *Explorer* first encountered the radiation."

Garner showed the others a series of bearings marked in pencil on Neddermeyer's chart. The points began nearly one hundred miles northwest of their present position. "If the *Explorer* had followed its intended route," Garner continued, "she probably would have drifted too far north to be exposed to the radiation at all. Instead they came around the end of Baffin Island, through the Gulf of Boothia and Fury and Hecla Strait. The bottleneck in the strait slowed them down enough to exhaust their supplies and their energy. I hate to say it, but their bad luck might be just what we need to narrow our search area."

Nearly nineteen thousand square miles of ocean and broken coastlines were represented on the charts before them. Even a glance at the sheer scale and desolation surrounding them was enough to cause doubt about the massive problem that they now faced.

"We'll move north—to the end of Foxe Basin, at

least—and keep sniffing the currents with Medusa until we find a possible source," Garner said. "Given the levels we're seeing here, I can't imagine we're too far from it."

Carol studied Garner's face as he continued to study the map. His expression was nearly ashen, hardly convinced by his own spoken confidence. "See anything?" she asked him.

Garner thought a moment longer, then said, "What Sverdrup and Nansen found in the 1890s, Neddermeyer was in the process of repeating when he drifted through the radiation: there is a strong surface current in the eastern Arctic, coursing up the coast of Greenland." He indicated the region on the chart. "Along the way to Baffin Island, it curls off to the west, then flows back to the south as the Baffin Land Current."

"Then where does it go?" Junko asked.

"Eventually it becomes the Labrador Current and divides, either dovetailing into the Grand Banks or flowing clockwise, east across the North Atlantic. A cold, dense, highly nutrified front is formed there by the convergence of these two or three water masses."

That jibed with what Carol knew about baleen whales. "Whales end up there, because that's where the plankton accumulates."

"Yep," Garner agreed. "Fishermen too, because that's where the whales and the fish are." He indicated the position where the *Explorer* and the *Phoenix* were currently reconnoitered. "Where we're sitting now is really the beginning of a cold-water wellspring that eventually flows into most of the Northwest Atlantic. From there, it will eventually hit what's left of the fishing grounds off the Grand Banks and the shipping lanes of the North Atlantic. Less likely, but possibly, it could also contaminate the subsurface currents and bottom water."

"And where does *that* go?" Junko asked again, intrigued by the interconnectedness of it all.

"The bottom currents go into the general circulation of the Atlantic, flowing south and west before being upwelled onto the shores of the northeastern United States," Garner replied.

"In other words, unless we can stem the source," he finished, "the debris passing us right now could become radioactive surf on a shoreline of thirty million people."

The following morning, those aboard the *Phoenix* held a brief memorial service for the crew of the *Sverdrup Explorer*. After anchoring the vessel against the current and retrieving the last of the landing equipment, Carol gathered everyone in the *Phoenix*'s main clean room. She included a few words about Dexter and Ramsey, and reiterated her previous offer: anyone who wanted to be airlifted from the vessel could still do so, but this would be their last chance until the source of the radiation was discovered.

Twenty-five pairs of eyes looked back at her, then at one another. It had become second nature when passing or regarding a fellow passenger on the *Phoenix* to drop one's gaze to the radiation film badges each of them wore around their neck or clipped to their collar. It was a silent means of checking the health of one's colleagues, of looking in on them, as if the individuals didn't themselves consult the colored film on their own badges a dozen times an hour. It was also a sign of camaraderie, a necessary nuisance they each shared. "I wonder if this is how a pod of tagged whales feels," someone remarked. For now, every one of them was immersed in the same tragic situation, and all—at least as far as their badges were concerned—remained in good health with minimal exposure.

In the end, every one of them resolved to stay with the ship to the end of the cruise and returned immediately to duty.

Garner and Zubov replaced the sampling bottles on Medusa and recalibrated her thermometers, salinometers, and light meters. Once again, Medusa was hoisted high on the A-frame, then swung back and down into the wake of the *Phoenix* as the ship's diesel engines grumbled to life. The sphere disappeared beneath the waves and was guided back on its tow wire to a depth of twenty meters. The onboard radiation meters responded almost immediately, rising to indicate the highly elevated radiation levels the crew had come to expect in the surface current.

"This isn't going to last for long," Zubov said. "There's so much radiation in the water, it's frying the probes in the gamma specs." The probes' manufacturer had not anticipated—had never even imagined—the need to measure such intense levels of radiation.

"Then we'll order more," Garner said.

Zubov looked at him dubiously. "Would that be a catalog order or the Internet, sir? Priority Mail or FedEx?"

Silently, a hundred questions roiled inside Garner. "We'll burn that bridge when we come to it" was all he said.

"All right, but believe me, we're gonna come to it," Zubov said.

The *Phoenix* headed west, following the current upstream. As Medusa dutifully relayed information from the water column below, Garner called minor course corrections up to the bridge. In this manner, the *Phoenix* managed to track the hot water like an iron-hulled bloodhound with its sensitive, very expensive nose trailing behind on an electronic leash. The temperature anomaly in the water column persisted and the radiation levels continued to rise. Twice the sampler had to be retrieved so that Garner could recalibrate or replace the spectrometers, which continued to respond erratically to the intense bombardment of radiation.

By the time Medusa had been retrieved for a third time that afternoon, the patience of Zubov and the deck crew was beginning to wear. Each retrieval, they knew, wasted valuable time and forced the *Phoenix* to slow her progress, at least temporarily. They had run out of clean sampling bottles and were beginning to reuse some of the less contaminated ones. More significantly, the absorbed radiation levels—which now approached a whopping twenty grays in spots—were interfering with the electronics of Medusa's cameras. Unless the optics on the sampler were overhauled soon, there was a chance she would have to fly blind. After a further inspection of the problem, Zubov estimated that it would be hours before the sphere was ready to be deployed again.

"Goddammit," Zubov said. "I hate it when I'm right." *Which is most of the time, if anyone'd bother to listen,* he thought.

"Do what you can," Garner said. He was just as annoyed, but knew there was no point in exacerbating the situation. "We're falling behind on the wet samples anyway." By Zubov's most optimistic estimate, Garner would have at least the rest of the day to work in the lab, so he and Byrnes set up a series of processing stations and put the *Phoenix*'s technicians to work.

"Wet samples" referred to the water sampled directly by Medusa's automated Nansen bottles. Even with modern technology, bottles were the principal means by which oceanographers sampled and determined the chemical and biological properties of the sea. Modern methods and instrumentation had greatly streamlined and foreshortened this process—Medusa, for instance, could determine more about "the state of the sea" in a single tow than a small army of laboratory technicians could in a week's time. Still, the wet samples collected in Medusa's gullet required analysis, if only to confirm what the various probes, particle counters, and cameras were describing digitally.

Over the next several hours, as the samples were processed and identified, Garner gradually developed a catalog of plankton species and a rough map of population densities for several of the main zooplankton groups. Encouragingly, the radiation appeared to be doing little to reduce the plankton's density or the species' apparent vitality. The lack of effect on these entry-level members of the marine food web, however, could not be assumed of the higher-order organisms that fed on them. As the *Balaenoptera,* the arctic fisheries, and even the men of the *Explorer* had shown, the lethal effects of the radiation could silently accumulate in the tissues of higher organisms, with devastating consequences.

Garner switched from counting and sorting Medusa's zooplankton samples and set up the *Phoenix*'s fluorescent microscope. Housed inside a small black tent to block outside light, the ingenious instrument revealed microscopic organisms—bacteria, virus particles, and other cell constituents—when they were treated with specialized dyes that glowed brilliantly under ultraviolet light. This particular scope could reveal the presence of organisms less than one ten-thousandth of an inch in diameter, far too small to be caught by any net or tracked by submersible cameras.

For the next two hours, Garner moved quickly through a dozen or so samples decanted from Medusa's water bottles. Once again, the bacterial levels Garner found were not at all inconsistent with "clean" samples from outside the water heated by the reaction of the radionuclides. What caught his eye was a particular bacterium he had never seen before.

Garner racked the microscope to its maximum magnification and focused on a single group of the mysterious cells. What first called it to his attention was the unusual way in which it had taken up the bright acridine orange, a staining compound of zinc chloride that targeted the fats of bacterial cells and made them glow orange under the fluorescent light. The unusual-looking cells easily constituted the majority of the bacteria in the last case of samples. Backtracking over all the samples he had processed so far, Garner saw that the abundance of the bacterium corresponded to the highest levels of radionuclides in solution. The strange visitor not only tolerated the radiation in which it was forced to live, but apparently thrived in it.

Garner was not on a first-name basis with the bacteria of the polar oceans—hardly anyone was. Except among marine microbiologists, bacteria were typically an assumed-but-ignored constant in water samples, as even the best instruments remained myopic to much of the submicroscopic world. Further, while most researchers were aware of bacteria's ubiquitous presence, few possessed the patience or interest to decant the cells from the larger samples, rear them in some growth medium in the laboratory, then identify the resulting homogenous cultures. No, the presence of some unknown bacterium in Medusa's sample bottles was not surprising—that there was suddenly *so much* of it was.

Garner stooped and looked again into the microscope. What the hell could it be?

"Thiobacillus ferrooxidans," Junko said confidently. The species name slipped from the doctor's tongue as though it had been well practiced. She studied the plated culture under the fluorescent microscope a moment longer. "But it's a long way from home," she said. "It could be a sister species too, but I'll bet you it's from the genus *Thiobacillus.*"

"How can you be so sure?" Carol asked Junko.

"When I was in India, working with the United Nations, the ore samples we were assigned to inspect were loaded with this bacterium. *Thiobacillus* speeds up the oxidation of iron and sulfide minerals," Junko continued. "In other words, it loves radioisotopes and helps break down sulfur, which explains why it helps to control the acidic wastewater of uranium mines. The exact effect of radiation on the bacterium's metabolism isn't known. But in uranium and radium mines with a low-to-marginal lode yield, *Thiobacillus* is being used with increasing regularity. The bacterium is fed metal sulfides and sprayed on ores with a concentration of less than 1 percent uranate, the insoluble form of natural uranium. The bacteria then convert the uranate to soluble products that are concentrated and purified."

"Sounds like a tedious investment," Carol said.

"The net effect on the overall yield of most mines is slight," Junko agreed. "But in regions such as India where natural supplies are low, it can make the difference between loss and profitability. *Thiobacillus* was also used here in Canada to revitalize the Stanrock mine."

"But as you said," Garner pointed out, "it's a long way from home."

"Natural, abundant growths of this bacterium aren't impossible," Junko said. "Obviously it can survive somewhere in nature, even without mine tailings. I just wouldn't expect it to occur anywhere radiation levels are low."

"Then I'll bet it's putting on the feed bag here," Carol said.

Junko nodded. "The culture will grow exponentially with an appropriate food source. Like most bacteria, the other factors to consider are heat and moisture."

"It has plenty of that too," Garner said. "Probably why it's made a profitable living inside the temperature anomaly."

"But the heat source hasn't always been here," Carol replied. "A better question might be, where did it come from in the first place?"

"It's hard to imagine anywhere in the Arctic that could support it for any length of time," Junko agreed.

"Which means that the source of this contamination is either highly enriched or recently created," Garner said.

"Most likely both," Junko added. "Either way, it's got to be a man-made source."

As dusk approached, they gathered in a conference room off the main lab of the *Phoenix*. Zubov and Byrnes slumped in chairs, nearly catatonic with fatigue. Conversely, Junko furiously scribbled in the spiral notebook she was using to maintain detailed medical files for everyone on board. Wearing thick cotton sweatpants, her hair pulled back in a ponytail, Carol had not been without a strong cup of coffee or a radio in her hand for the past six hours.

"How's Medusa holding out?" Carol asked Zubov.

"The rad sensors are royally screwed," Zubov said.

"Then God save the queen," Carol said.

"I could use both their help," Zubov grumbled. "It's bad enough that we're trying to estimate actual rad levels in solution. Add to that the magnitude of those levels and it's pretty much a lost cause trying to get any sort of direction from the data. The water's hot, Medusa's hot—even the casing on the goddamn probes is hot. There's no way we can rely on readings from any of the gear once it's been cooked."

"Then forget about using Medusa to track the radiation," Garner said. "The levels will probably be off the scale anyway. We can use the dosimeters on deck every hour, or every half hour, if we need to." They had been keeping a running log of the atmospheric radiation. While it was hardly an exact correlation with the contamination in the water, it was far less demanding on the instruments.

"What do you want to track instead?" Zubov asked.

"We'll use the DOM channels to monitor the bacterial levels," Garner replied. DOM—dissolved organic matter—was a common indicator of living material too small or indistinct to be captured with nets or seen with the naked eye. "And keep an eye on the temperature and salinity on the inorganic channels." Garner was gambling that both the bacteria and the radionuclides coincided within a single, dilute, and clearly heated water parcel. The presence of *Thiobacillus ferrooxidans* and temperatures of a specific range would indirectly tell them which body of water should be followed upstream.

"What would be the ideal culture temperature of this bacterium?" Garner asked Junko. Even among arctic species, it was typically only increased temperatures that promoted such wholesale growth of microbe populations.

"I don't know," Junko said. "But I could make some calls if you'd like." She thought for a moment, revisiting the extent of her experience with the organism in India. "Perhaps as little as forty-five degrees Fahrenheit."

Forty-five degrees. Low for a lot of microbes, but still significantly warmer than the thirty-three degrees more typical of water around Baffin Island. For *Thiobacillus* to be this plentiful in natural samples of seawater at thirty-three degrees suggested a much warmer incubation temperature farther upstream. Despite conditions that should be significantly lethal to the organism, there were still plenty of cells left in the heated water below.

Garner ran a quick calculation through a computer model based on the volume of heated water and the activity of the *Thiobacillus ferrooxidans* they had recorded. The temperatures of the hypothetical heat source predicted were improbably high—nine hundred degrees Celsius or higher—the kind of temperatures produced by boiling fission products. If these numbers could be believed, what they were searching for was not simply a leak of radioactive material, but an undersea nuclear fission reaction.

He nodded at the computer and its display of thermal exchange calculations. "If this is right, there's enough heat upstream to cause significant melting if we can't find the source."

"How significant?" Carol asked.

"Significant enough to make a little radioactive contamination an incidental consideration," Garner said.

"*Incidental?*" Byrnes asked.

Garner adjusted the model and ran another series of speculative numbers through it. He scratched at his chin as the results were calculated. "I wish I'd paid more attention to heat budget equations in school," he admitted, "but these numbers look right. Left unchecked, there's enough heat upstream to eventually dump a very large amount of warm, fresh water through the Hudson Strait and Labrador Sea into the North Atlantic."

"So the North Atlantic gets warmer," Byrnes said.

"Yes," Garner said. "According to this, warm enough to hold back the normal flow of warm water flowing up from the equator."

"So then the Arctic would get colder," Byrnes followed.

"Right," Garner said. "There's enough heat being generated by the fission reactions to melt a lot of ice, to disrupt the flow of heat coming in, but not enough to replace the normal amount of incoming warm water."

"So eventually the entire Arctic would begin to refreeze," Carol said, "which would negate the flow of heat from the equator even further."

"And the polar cap would continue to grow, maybe even creating a global disruption of weather patterns," Garner said. "What we're seeing here is a repeat of the climate conditions we think existed twelve thousand years ago."

"The last ice age," Carol said quietly.

"That's right." Garner nodded. "Unless we can stop the heat coming from this radioactive debris, we're sitting on top of the *next* ice age. And this one will be our fault."

10

After a late dinner, Junko and Zubov retired to the doctor's cabin and shared a pot of green tea. The level of intimacy in their discussion might have disappointed Garner and Carol.

"The Aral Sea is nearly extinct," Junko said. Unlike Zubov, she had been to eastern Europe many times since the accident at Chernobyl—significantly, she was *allowed* to tour these areas—and was well abreast of the latest reclamation projects going on there. The Aral Sea, once part of one of the largest lakes in the world, now practically a desert, was a recent destination. "Virtually all of it is gone, drained off to Central Asia to provide irrigation for the drought-starved crops," she said. "What remains is a sludge of toxic sediment, pesticides, and heavy metals. Kidney disease, liver cancer, arthritis, bronchitis, all of them up more than 2,000 percent in the past decade."

"There must be a million people on the Aral in Karakalpakia alone," Zubov considered grimly. He remembered the Aral from childhood summer vacations. "I had no idea it was so bad," he said, almost apologetically. For his entire adult life, he had found that the best way not to miss his homeland was not to think about it. Talking to Junko, he realized just how much he still yearned to know.

"It's not the land you once left," Junko said. "In another twenty years it might become the land *everyone* has left. Now the gold-mining industry there is responsible for spilling hundreds of tons of cyanide as waste by-product."

"How is Belarus?" Zubov asked. Belarus, in what was now an independent territory, had been less than a hundred miles north of the reactor at Chernobyl and directly in the path of the immediate fallout.

"That depends on whose numbers you want to believe," Junko said. "The Soviet statistics still list thirty-one fatalities from the explosion itself and as many as seven thousand—eventually—from the radiation. Those are only immediate estimates—as many as seventeen million people could have received at least some exposure. The World Health Organization released a study that showed no significant increase in leukemia or other cancers in the decade after the disaster. An exception was thyroid cancer, of which more than one thousand new cases have been reported in adults."

"In adults," Zubov repeated.

"Yes, but congenital malformations in children, by some reports, are up more than 30 percent. In the areas worst hit, 80 percent." Junko tried to push away the vision of precious, cherubic faces horribly skewed by deformations of bone and cartilage, hands and feet twisted into indistinct, fleshy clubs. Down syndrome. Cleft palate. Blindness. Stillbirths. The list of horrors went on and on. "As usual, once the hysteria of the moment died down, the far graver problem of *long-term* exposure to the radioactive fallout was almost completely ignored." There would forever be detractors who claimed that the alarming increase in cancers and birth defects was merely a statistical anomaly, the result of better reporting and closer global scrutiny that had brought the worst fringes of the problem to the verge of public outrage. But statistical anomalies would not help the children of Belarus and Pripyat.

Zubov asked about his hometown, where fifty thousand people had been evacuated days after the explosion. The evacuation should have begun within *hours* if public safety were the true issue, but the government had reacted too slowly. Even then, many of the local villagers, ignorant of the invisible killer and mistrustful of any effort to displace them from their land, refused to evacuate. Eventually relieved of the 135,000 human "obstacles," Soviet chemical troops excavated six inches of topsoil from hundreds of acres of land, asphalt was laid down over hundreds of acres more, and thousands of buildings were washed with chemicals designed to bind radioactive particles. Entire forests were leveled and marshes plowed under in an attempt to cover over the radioactive cloak that coated everything.

In the areas tens or hundreds of miles north of Chernobyl, rain deposited the radioactive fallout on an unsuspecting populace. Entire farms were forever contaminated, and fresh food and water had to be brought in from far-distant places. For those closest to the explosion, most of the immediate health risk was believed to be from inhalation or other incidental consumption of radioactive iodine isotopes. "A lot of those cancers could have been prevented if emergency crews had known enough to treat people with simple iodine," Junko explained. "That's why it was one of the first preventatives I asked Carol to get up here."

"What about lowering safe-exposure thresholds?" Zubov suggested, struggling to find any resolution to such permanent destruction.

"How low is low enough when you're talking about radiation, Sergei? Plutonium, cesium, radium—unstable isotopes cause cancer. They will destroy genetic material. They will kill. Now or later, but eventually they will kill."

"We haven't learned much, have we?" Zubov said. "In the thirties and forties the United States introduced a generation of kids to cancers by exposing them to X rays. Hell, the nuclear tests in Nevada exposed *everyone* to some degree of fallout. If Eastman Kodak hadn't noticed the radiation spoiling their film stock in Rochester—Rochester, New York! Twenty-five hundred miles away, right down the jet stream—just think of what the public wouldn't have known."

"Or still wouldn't know," Junko agreed. "Like the accident at Rocky Flats." Beginning in 1951, the facility at Rocky Flats, Colorado, had been responsible for building and storing the cores for virtually all U.S. nuclear weapons for nearly forty years. In May of 1969, a fire in a building that contained thirty-five hundred kilograms of plutonium nearly sent up a volcanic eruption of deadly plutonium oxide.

Their conversation eventually returned to the Arctic and Junko's growing concern that the Inuit were about to face an environmental calamity they were incapable of preparing for. "After Chernobyl, there was a massive survey by the Scandinavian countries to look at the degree of exposure over their own populations. Eventually they found entire herds of reindeer contaminated at levels well above the acceptable limits. But just as the Inuit rely on caribou, the Lapps rely on reindeer for sustenance, so what was the government to do? Allow the Lapps to eat meat known to be dangerous, or keep them away from the herds and effectively destroy their entire culture? A slow death, whichever you choose."

"What about Victor's situation?"

"I've called both of the clinics he mentioned and asked them to track specific case histories on Melville Peninsula," Junko said. "Obviously they wouldn't tell me much over the radio, but they did say they'd welcome a visit anytime."

"That sounds encouraging."

"Oh, they wouldn't try to *hide* anything," she said. "No one is covering up cases like Victor's, it's just that no one is looking into them. Community doctors in the Arctic are spread far too thin as it is. Even if you can get supplies and equipment, even if you can get women and men like Victor on the examination table, this is hardly the climate—social or otherwise—to develop and promote proper health-care programs. It's enough of an effort to give out condoms and antibiotics, let alone setting out to discover hidden sources of radiation." She looked at him staring back at her with rapt attention. "But I *will* contact Victor's clinic," she assured him. "Just as soon as we get out of here."

"I know," Zubov said.

Despite their grim discussion, Zubov could not help but be entranced by the doctor's knowledge and passion for her work. The warren of regulatory agencies, panel reports, field clinics, advisory boards, and governmental programs in which she operated would easily have numbed many researchers into hapless submission. The Arctic itself might have discouraged the rest. This woman, however, seemed to gain strength from massive, convoluted bureaucracy and use that strength to fight. If any individual was capable of breaching those administrative barriers, Zubov was certain it was Dr. Junko Kokura. He admired that about her most of all.

Junko shivered, recalling the vivid memory of what they had discovered aboard the *Explorer*. Zubov took her delicate hands in his own massive palms and held them there, sharing their warmth but not knowing how to proceed. Despite his popular, outgoing disposition

and his exotic ports of call, Zubov was not experienced
with meaningful companionship. Touching another
human being, much less seducing a most engaging
woman, had not been part of his daily routine. He
rarely approached women—his last intimate relationship was a distant memory. Yet it was not loneliness,
isolation, or sexual attraction that had inspired his interest in Junko. It was the woman, the whole woman, in
all her beauty, wisdom, compassion, and humor. These
things radiated from her eyes, her words, and the gentle
touch of her hands.

It was simply, preeminently, her.

"Well, Sergei," Junko said, slipping her hands out of
his grasp and sliding them softly over the outside of his
hands and wrists, her nails lightly tracing lines along his
thick forearms. "As usual, I have enjoyed our talk, but
it is getting late." Her voice held the understated allure
of a woman who had not needed to be seduced in many
years but continued to be open to the possibility, even
from a novice.

"Yes, it is," Zubov said, his heart poised on the
threshold between leaving and entering further still.

"Then what do you suggest we do now?" she asked.

Her continued caress inspired his answer.

"What is the Spanish Armada?" Carol said to no one,
then took a drink from her tumbler of Jim Beam and
water. Whiskey was considered contraband on board
the *Phoenix*, but tonight she didn't care. She leaned forward on her bunk, anticipating the next question like
a volleyball player awaiting a serve. "Who is Emily
Dickinson?" *Yes!* Another correct answer. "What is the
Black Sea?" Three for three.

So far she had amassed almost twice as many points
as the returning champion on *Jeopardy!*, the game show
playing on the small television at the foot of her bunk.

As well she should have; she had watched this particular videotape at least four times in the past month. At the moment, her ego needed a boost.

There was a knock at the door. "Go away," she growled. The door cracked open anyway and Garner ducked his head inside, one arm held behind his back.

"Are you decent?" he asked with a smile.

"For you? Always, darling," Carol said. She held up her tumbler of amber liquor. "For Mr. Beam, well, that's another story."

Garner stepped into the cabin and drew his trailing hand into view. He held a dessert tart with a single birthday candle flickering atop it. Carol only needed to glance at the topping to know it was raspberry cheesecake, her favorite.

Garner handed her the tart and leaned close to kiss her on the forehead. She caught the faintest whiff of his cologne as he murmured, "Happy birthday, sweetie."

"I was trying to avoid the issue," she said. "The day started with a funeral service and went downhill from there." Carol had never been one for birthdays, and the events of the past two weeks had hardly changed her attitude. From an early age, Carol's ability to celebrate had been impaired. Carol's father—when he was home in May and not attending spring conferences abroad—had frowned upon noisy gatherings of children and loudly made known his loathing for any kind of sweets in the house, including birthday cake.

Now that she thought of it, Carol's birthdays had been regularly marked and celebrated only since she'd known Garner. While they were married, despite his other absences, Garner never missed a birthday or an anniversary. He had an infallible memory for such occasions and never failed to send a card or flowers from wherever in the world he happened to be. Of course, the years he had managed to be home were by far the best.

"I told the crew that if anyone tried to ambush me with a party I'd make them walk the plank," Carol said.

"I figured as much when nobody else brought it up," Garner said. "But it's hard for me to overlook these things. On condition of anonymity, one of the cooks whipped this up for me and I said I'd deliver it personally. I guess that makes me a plank walker."

"A plank walker, huh?" The notion was amusing to her. "You should try using Vaseline for that."

She sat up in her bunk, propping her pillows behind her. Next to the intercom at the head of the bed, Garner noticed a stack of books and reports, each one bookmarked or dog-eared a portion of the way through. Carol had always been a voracious reader; the current selection included a number of weathered *Scientific American* magazines, coil-bound tomes of ice cover and salinity data, a biography of Nikola Tesla and the Philadelphia Experiment, and Von Clausewitz's classic text *On War*, in the original German. No fluffy bedtime reading for Dr. Harmon, Garner mused—no wonder she was so uptight.

"Good thing you didn't have to send flowers from Antarctica," Carol said. "The delivery boy would have had a hell of a time getting to me." Gradually, her pout faded into a grateful smile. She pulled him back by the collar of his turtleneck for a tender kiss on the lips. "Thank you," she said. "I don't deserve you, you know?"

"Yes," Garner agreed. "You've been saying that for a few years now." In truth, the phrase had been *I don't deserve this,* which had been regularly uttered during the months of their divorce in a much different context.

"If you keep this up, I just might have to change my mind," she said. His body was so close to hers now, his scent and his tight, lean muscles only inches away from her. And his eyes: those marvelous gray eyes that could reveal either the cold, predatory gaze of a wolf or display the most honest, loving warmth she could possibly imagine. Not at all like . . . like . . .

Like the arrogance of Bob Nolan. Like the eagerness of Jeff Dexter.

Suddenly overwhelmed, the Widow Nolan faltered, then broke.

Tears welled up in Carol's eyes as she crushed herself to Garner's chest. Sobs wracked her body as his powerful arms drew her close. "I'm crying again," she said, ashamed. "Why am I always crying around you? I *never* cry—isn't that sad? I never cry anymore. Only with you."

Garner broke a crooked grin. "Thanks. I guess there's a compliment in there . . . somewhere."

"I don't *feel* things anymore," she continued. "It's all rush, rush, rush. Wait and worry, then worry some more. Lose a friend and miss the funeral. Lose a contract and just shrug it off. Find an entire pod of blue whales and then just let them go, off to fight the next fire. Relationship? What's that? Sex, no sex, what's the difference?"

"I could show you a subtle but definite distinction there—" Garner began.

"—It's not that I don't care, of *course* I care. I *do* care." She was trying as much to convince herself as Garner of this. "I probably care too much. I just don't let go like I used to. And for every one thing I relax on, ten more things come along to juggle. First it's the whales, then the *Explorer*, now you're talking about a goddamn ice age and nobody is laughing about it."

"Tangent after tangent," Garner said.

She nodded. "Until it seems like I'm just running in circles."

"It doesn't look that way to the rest of us," Garner said. "There isn't a person on this ship who doubts who the boss is. They're here because of you, not in spite of you," he added, borrowing some of Victor's philosophy.

"Then I must be a good actress," Carol said.

"Or a good leader," Garner countered.

"Then why do I feel so out of control?" Carol said. "Why do I feel like this ship runs no differently than the *Explorer*—drifting at the mercy of the currents with a stubborn, egotistical know-it-all at the helm?" She paused, trying to collect her courage once again. "I can do this," she said. "The numbers are a little bigger, the risks are a little higher, but it's basically the same thing I used to do all the time when . . ." *When I was younger.* "Things just aren't the same as—"

As they were with you, she wanted to say, but the words were lost.

Garner took her face in his hands and looked at her. Even after all this time, his touch thrilled her. His compassion eased a world of hurt. He knew exactly what she wanted to say. He probably also knew exactly why she struggled so hard to say it. Bob, even Dex, would have pressed her to say it, if only to assuage their fragile male egos. Not Garner.

"Carol, the world isn't turning the same way it used to," he said. "If you need proof of that, think of Sergei and Junko making out two doors down."

"Can you believe that?" Carol said, the surprise lancing through her sadness, instantly adding the frivolity of a slumber party to her morbid ruminations. "There must be fifteen years between them!"

"Fifteen years and fifteen inches," Garner said.

"Hmmm," she mused. "Maybe it isn't such a bad deal for her after all." She raised her eyebrows knowingly.

That was it. They both fell into a bout of laughter.

A crackling noise drew their attention. It was the raspberry tart, forgotten on the bookshelf. The candle had burned down to the topping, which began to burn.

"You'd better blow that out or we'll set off the sprinkler system," Garner said. "Hurry up—make a wish."

Carol closed her eyes with exaggerated tightness, then blew out the nub of candle.

"Did you wish?" Garner said.

"Uh-huh," Carol said. "I said: I wish I may—"

"Shhh!" Garner scolded. "No telling."

"—I wish I might—"

"I said: no telling."

"—share this bunk with you tonight."

Garner stopped protesting. "Oh. That's a little different then."

Carol wrapped her arms around Garner's neck and stared directly back at him. "Yes, it is, isn't it?"

"Change is good."

"Change is *very* good."

"So they tell me."

They kissed again, lingering, becoming one. Garner joined Carol on the bunk and enfolded her in his arms. They held each other for the first time in longer than either of them could remember. There had been an intimate bond between them many times, before reality and inevitability intervened. There had been much time apart, but even separated across the miles, there had always been *something*. At this moment, the reasons for their parting seemed scarcely to matter.

Their lovemaking seemed so natural, so inevitable, that neither was sure who began it. Carol luxuriated in the pleasure of Garner's touch and he, in turn, accepted hers. Clothing was slowly, purposefully pulled away and they were alone in their nakedness in Carol's narrow bed. She was intoxicated with the comforting warmth radiating from Garner's body. He emitted a passion and sincerity she had not known with any other man. That was it. She berated herself for ever forgetting this feeling, then realized it had never been forgotten, simply denied. Now, however, she succumbed to him, letting her body enjoy the waves of pleasure coursing through her, strong and reassuring, building to a pinnacle then slowly released in a series of delicious orgasms.

They lay together for a long while afterward. Neither slept, neither worried about the consequences of this one moment or the crisis that continued to rage around them. There was only skin, warmth, and comfort, and a mutual desire for the moment not to end.

The intercom next to the bed squawked. Carol groaned, wishing she could ignore it. In a few seconds, the squawk repeated itself, longer this time. Then again. Carol reached her hand from its cocoon and pressed the TALK button, already dreading what the interruption meant, no matter who it was or what they wanted.

"Yes?" she said, then released the button to listen.

"Dr. Harmon?" It was Zubov's voice, overly formal. He knew he was interrupting something. "This is Sergei Zubov? Of the deck crew? We're having a bitch of a time with this Medusa sphere and we seem to have misplaced her father, Commander Garner." Oh, yes, he knew he was interrupting something and was enjoying it to the fullest. "He's not in the lab and he's not in his assigned cabin." He said *assigned cabin* with all the authority of an offended schoolmaster. "No one's seen him since dinner and we believe he may have fallen overboard with a raspberry tart."

It was Garner's turn to groan. He lifted himself up and leaned toward the intercom's speaker as Carol pushed the intercom button again. "On my way, Serg," Garner said.

"Thank you—Dr. Harmon?" Zubov said, still deadpan. "You should take something for that throat of yours. You sound positively masculine."

As Carol released the button, Garner kissed her good-bye in stages, starting at her navel, then addressing her breasts, neck, earlobes, and finally, her waiting lips. "I'm sorry," he whispered.

"Don't be," Carol said. "Duty calls." She resented the words the moment they escaped her lips. It was the selfless, blindly faithful remark of a doting mate—a role she had intentionally given up long ago. Too long ago.

Yet as she watched Garner dress, watched him pull on his jeans and tug his turtleneck down over his dark head of hair and lean defined torso, the bitterness passed and the thought of his leaving no longer seemed like a personal rejection. Duty called—it always called Garner—but for Carol, the notion of being there for him when the duty ended had taken on a newfound appeal.

Damn you, Brock Garner, she thought as she watched his silhouette slip out of the cabin and into the corridor. She scarcely believed her own distracted thoughts. In the midst of the most crucial contract in the Nolan Group's history, in the track of the most terrifying environmental disaster the world could imagine, she was falling in love with her ex-husband all over again.

11

From the base pad to the top of the flare boom, the structure was as high as a fifty-story building and three times as heavy, although barely a third of this elevation could be seen above the arctic ice. It stood defiantly in nearly three hundred feet of frigid water, balanced by the weight of nearly one million tons of subsurface ballast. The structure was designed to operate ceaselessly for twenty years. It could operate at minus eighty degrees Fahrenheit or in wind gusts of one hundred miles per hour. The ramparts along its legs were engineered to withstand the impact of six million tons of ice, an event statistically probable only once in ten thousand years. This margin of safety was neither wildly paranoid nor severely pessimistic. It was not necessarily massive waves or harsh winds that required such fortification, but the random, continual creep of the arctic pack ice. Under such conditions, a structure is built to last or it is built to be immediately disposable.

Global *B-82* was one of the most formidable and

technologically advanced oil rigs ever constructed. Standing empty, the gravity base structure, or GBS, weighed more than half a million tons. Added to this were four hundred thousand tons of iron ore ballast that had been poured into the GBS before grafting the structure to the seafloor. The combined weight of the five topsides modules and support elements was another thirty-three thousand tons, which still did not include the storage capacity for over a million barrels of crude oil in the reservoir set inside the GBS.

The comparatively fragile yet invaluable interior structures of the GBS were protected from the sea by a five-foot-thick concrete external ice wall. This included the lifeblood of the rig itself: the three cells of the oil reservoir surrounded two drill shafts, a utility shaft, and a riser shaft that carried oil to and from pipes run along the seafloor—the offshore loading system, or OLS. High-tensile concrete had been poured into an outer wall of sixteen sharply angled, outward-facing teeth designed to withstand collisions with pack ice and bergs by distributing the force of the ice impact. This design could easily withstand the impact of a million tons of ice without sustaining structural damage and as much as ten times that amount without suffering irreparable harm. As an additional measure, *B-82* also had a state-of-the-art ice-monitoring system and was fully equipped for ice wrangling and deflection if necessary.

Ice deflection was constantly necessary.

Matt Charon awoke without an alarm clock exactly on time, rinsed his head under a jet of cold water, dressed, and made his way to the galley, stopping only long enough to fill his heavy mug with black coffee. Even at fifty, Charon looked as though he could effortlessly do two hundred push-ups or single-handedly wrangle the sway collars on a drill head. In fact, he did both on a daily basis. Moving up the corridor, he strutted more than walked, with the majority of his body's mass pushed up and forward of his center of gravity like a two-legged bulldog. He wasn't tall, but he was broad. The seams of his flannel shirt threatened to burst under the strain of his ample biceps and thick forearms. He had a wide, sharply defined jaw and a broad skull covered with a receding turf of graying hair. His eyes were as black as Louisiana crude oil and his sense of humor, known only to few, was blacker and cruder still.

There was not a soul aboard B-82 who did not know Charon or note his heavy approach on the metal deck plating. As the crew chief moved through the topsides from his cabin, past the mud module to the process module, every single crewman nodded a silent good morning. Then they quickly turned and dropped their eyes in hope that their boss had no specific need to detain or reprimand them. Charon's attention to detail and his sudden, volcanic temper were legendary on the rig.

Rumor had it Charon could be a helluva nice guy— jovial even—if you could outlast the granite facade he usually presented, and if you didn't screw up your assigned job. Hardly anyone on Global B-82 really knew Charon, but they certainly knew *of* him. His demeanor was measured less in terms of personality or intelligence than degrees Fahrenheit or the number of hornets currently buzzing up his tightly wadded ass. Charon himself would have wanted it no other way. On a good day, he could count the words he had to speak on one hand without needing the thumb. What his crew thought of him was irrelevant; what he thought of them was what kept Global B-82 running.

B-82's service module, or the hotel as it was known, had room for 250 men; 210 were shift-work employees, which left forty beds for visitors to the rig. On the roof of the hotel, jutting out over the main lifeboat station, was the helideck, where someone had spray-painted the slogan OPEN FOR BUSINESS 24–7–365 below the Global

Oil logo. Someone else had added, in parentheses, DOES NOT INCLUDE OVERTIME. Charon himself was certain there was a twenty-fifth hour in every day and an eighth day in every week. Finding it was only a matter of discipline.

Charon's next stop was his office, an elevated, glass-walled enclave that overlooked the utility module, the rig's command center. From this location, he could monitor all the essential functions of the rig at a single glance. A small bank of closed-circuit television monitors allowed him to peer into any of the rig's modules. E-mail, voice mail, and radiophone kept him in touch with his employers and a compact satellite dish brought 150 channels of boredom relief to the crew in the hotel. A computer uplink to the latest GOES and HRPTN weather satellite data let him see what the weather had in store for B-82, though it hardly mattered. The rig was a world unto itself.

The encrypted message tagged as PRIVATE had come to Charon's inbox overnight via satellite. Charon read the message once, twice, then reencrypted it and flushed it through the scrambler.

There was going to be a break in the routine. *Shit.* There was going to be an interruption and a whole lot of yakking to endure.

"Dust off the welcome mat," he said to the deck supervisor, Lucas Stimson. "Ten hundred hours today."

Stimson scowled. "Three hours. D'you think they gave us enough warning this time?" he asked sarcastically. "It better not take long. I've got an air-hockey game scheduled for noon."

Charon did not comment. It was not up to them to prepare anything; they were expected to be in a state of constant preparedness. Nonetheless, he took the opportunity to reread all of B-82's progress and activity reports for the past week, then tried to anticipate the kinds of information he would be expected to distill, encapsulate, and report. It was nearly 9:30 A.M. the next time he looked, but he was ready to face whatever was coming up.

At 10:02 A.M., *B-82*'s warning Klaxon sounded, calling all hands to their ready stations. The corridors and ladders were suddenly alive with activity as crewmen hurried through their frantic but well-drilled assignments. Charon left the processing module, pulled on a parka, then followed his men down the ladders and across the topsides, which stood just fifty feet above the water. Most days the surface of the frigid ocean was as placid as a lake.

The sun had just lifted itself fully above the southern horizon, casting the scene in a pale, refrigerated light. A thick haze was drifting across the broken ice pack, a combination of airborne dust, salt, and ice that blurred the features of the landscape within sight of the rig.

Now Charon noticed that the wavelets coursing past his platform had begun to flatten, the first indication that their guests had arrived. Moments later, the 320-foot, matte-black shape of the submarine's hull rose from the depths. The magnificent machine gracefully parted the floating fragments of surface ice with its diving planes and bulbous nose, rising into view less than one hundred yards from the landing platform. The silent behemoth drifted easily into its mark, wake swirling forward over the sail and foredeck and the temporary dock *B-82*'s crew had lowered.

From his position at the foot of the topsides, Charon could make out the hull number of the submarine: SSN-666. The USS *Hawkbill,* a Sturgeon-class nuclear attack sub. First commissioned in the 1960s as one of three dozen sophisticated, ultraquiet attack submarines, the *Hawkbill* had eventually been assigned to polar patrols and defense activities. The end of the Cold War, however, had seen the data-gathering potential of SSNs used with increased frequency for public research projects. The refit of the *Hawkbill* had been a major accomplishment in this endeavor: the submarine had taken on an impressive array of sonar, seismic equipment, and a battery of other electronics intended for use by academic and governmental researchers. Once a stealthy warrior shrouded by top-level security, the *Hawkbill* had become one of the Navy's preeminent flagships for the mapping and description of the polar ice.

As the *B-82* crewmen leaned over the railings like boys on a sandlot fence, the sail of the *Hawkbill* cracked open and two crewmen stepped onto the bridge. They were followed a moment later by an officer—a commander Charon didn't recognize. The man was compact and had a lean-looking face, but the depth and evenness of his tanned skin ruled out any lengthy amount of time inside a submarine. A ride-along, Charon guessed. A fucking diplomat. A visitor who, as the morning's message had advised, felt the need to interrupt Charon's carefully crafted routine.

The officer found his footing on *B-82*'s docking platform and easily climbed the rungs to the deck. Two crewmen pointed out Charon and the man stepped quickly over to him. The tanned commander saluted first.

"Good morning, sir," he said to Charon. "I was dispatched from Arlington to see if I can lend some assistance to your situation. My name is Krail. Scott Krail."

12

ater, water everywhere, but not a drop to drink.
Junko awoke with a start. The bliss of a deep sleep
cut cruelly short left her momentarily disoriented as to
where she was, and why. The *Phoenix*. Her bunk. Some
indeterminate time between midnight, when Sergei had
left her, and dawn. Soon returned the numbing avalanche of things to do, precautions to take and hazards
to consider. First and foremost of these was a single
consideration:

Water, water everywhere,
But not a drop to drink.

The potable water supply aboard the *Phoenix* came
from a gigantic freshwater tank set deep in the hull.
Byrnes said the tank had a capacity of five thousand
gallons, or roughly enough water to be rationed—for
drinking, bathing, and sewerage—among forty people
for up to a month; slightly longer for a smaller crew.
The *Phoenix* also had the latest desalination equipment,
and under normal conditions it might purify enough

seawater for cooking and showers. But these were hardly normal conditions. The ocean could not be used at all, and even though the ship's complement had been reduced to twenty-six, the rinsing requirement for anyone passing through the *Phoenix*'s makeshift airlocks had probably maintained, if not increased, the normal levels of consumption. Although the sea ice that floated all around them had only one-tenth the salinity of the ocean, it was still too briny to drink. The permanent fast ice along the shore was thicker and less saline, but even more likely to be a repository for any number of pollutants, from dust to radioactivity.

Subtract from the tank's capacity the water already consumed by the crew since the vessel left port and the water remaining in the tank could be down to three thousand gallons or less. The amount of water left over for cooking, showering, and drinking might be approaching critical levels. Rationing was really in order, but a lack of proper rinsing—especially in the lab and the airlocks—would only increase the potential for contamination.

As Junko roused herself and dressed, she reminded herself to ask Byrnes to check the tank's volume more often. Short of finding a pristine glacier and boiling it into meltwater, Junko would have to talk to Carol about having a replenishing supply of fresh water brought up to the *Phoenix* by helicopter. The remaining crew would have to skimp on personal hygiene and limit the number of in-and-out trips through the airlocks.

Junko began her daily rounds on the bridge, attending to those crew members she encountered there. She took nasal swabs to check for possible inhaled contamination, checked their detection badges, and made certain everyone was taking iodine tablets and calcium supplements. By now she had devised a short list of questions to elucidate symptoms from general lethargy to specific aches and pains or sources of bleeding. All of the crew still appeared to be in excellent condition. The safety precautions, primitive as they were, seemed to be staving off the current environmental conditions.

Stuart Frisch was her next examinee, another one of the crew members whose youthful energy and affinity for junk food seemed to eclipse any obvious need for sleep. His usual good spirits made him one of Junko's favorites, though his overall naïveté was still distressing.

"How many people would it take to operate the *Phoenix*?" she asked him as she swabbed his arm with alcohol and drew a blood sample. "A dozen? Eighteen?"

"I suppose that'd depend on who the people were," Frisch shrugged. He meant not only which deck positions were retained but also the ability and resourcefulness of the individuals selected. "And that would depend on what you needed to do." His tone suggested that he did not consider himself on the short list of essential personnel in either category.

Byrnes was far more definitive and much less receptive to the notion of further skeletonizing the ship's crew. "No bloody way," he said. "You start cutting back on bodies, doubling up on watch time, and people get tired. People get tired and accidents start happening." The latter point was not trivial. Carelessness on the deck, a momentary lapse in attention, and someone could be swept overboard. Even an accidental fall on the frozen steel deck was enough to break a wrist or a collarbone. A poorly spooled or overstressed line could too easily snap, recoiling with enough force to cut a man cleanly in two. Byrnes had seen exactly that happen to one of his men aboard the *Kaiku*. "You start pulling more of us off the boat and those who're left won't be able to do much more than sit around and look at each other."

The comment was straightforward enough, but it reminded Junko of the spectacle she had seen aboard the *Explorer*. She shivered slightly as she made her way back to the lab, donned her Tyvek laboratory suit, gloves, and boots, and began looking at the latest batch of blood samples from the crew. The act of dressing in the disposable equipment reminded her to check the remaining supplies of suits, gloves, and respirators as well. The ship needed more respirator filters and batteries, gloves, and hoods. They needed more of *everything*, and with each passing hour the ship's engines pushed them deeper into the Arctic, farther away from any source of provisions.

Junko heard Garner and Zubov coming inside, slamming the hatch behind them and stamping the frost out of their bones like a pair of rambunctious teenagers. They waved to her through the thick polyethylene partition, then began the tedious process of stripping off their outdoor suits and scrubbing down. When this was completed, they stepped into the inside portion of the enclosure and began to re-dress. Zubov pulled on his clothes and decided to raid the galley before getting some sleep. Garner might have done the same, but the racks of samples on the lab bench held him back. Entering the lab itself, both men paused to test themselves in front of the radiation detector mounted just inside the airlock. Garner waved his hands, arms, and torso in front of the device, which produced a green light of approval. Zubov did the same, adding a waggle of his derriere to the ritual, momentarily dancing in front of the monitor like a great, oversized duck. He gave Junko a wink, knowing she was watching him, then ambled off down the corridor to his cabin.

Garner flashed her a smile. "Morning, Doc," he said. "You look like you have something on your mind."

She certainly did have something on her mind. Everything and nothing, all at once. Unlike her admirable colleagues, fatigue was beginning to make its presence felt to Junko. In the ER, they called it "running on fumes."

Water, water everywhere, but not a drop to drink.

It was time for the doctor to start heeding her own prescriptions.

In the days since the *Phoenix*'s lab had been converted to a makeshift nuclear field facility, several experiments had been run using small amounts of the radioactive water. Provided that the material was contained, there was very little risk of exposing the laboratory technicians to elevated levels of radiation. Nonetheless, an ever-larger portion of the laboratory equipment—from beakers and culture dishes to microscopes and centrifuges—had been labeled with colored tags indicating degrees of contamination. Though much of the equipment could still be used, discarding the items permanently ruined by the modest experimentation would add even more to Junko's mental shopping list.

Garner began his work in the lab exactly where he had left off: examining a culture of the marvelous bacterium known as *Thiobacillus ferrooxidans*. The previous evening he had separated the *Thiobacillus* from the rest of the samples, then decanted the cells into a series of petri dishes with a variety of food sources. The makeshift experiment was designed to determine which food sources the bacterium liked best and what effect this might have on its reproductive capacity.

As Garner peered into the fluorescent microscope, counting the cells yielded by each culture, Junko relayed her concerns about the water supply and her suggested course of action.

"We need a minimum number of hands on board to maintain safe operation, but those hands will use water," Garner concurred. "We should also have the galley lock up all the sodas, juices, and bottled water they have left and adjust their food preparation. When that's done we'll run the numbers again."

"I'm worried that still may not be enough," Junko said. The sounding Byrnes had done that morning showed approximately twenty-seven hundred gallons remaining in the tank. "And the hotter we become, the farther out we go . . ." She did not have to elaborate.

"Let's see if Byrnes is willing to pare down his estimates any further," Garner said. "If the musical chairs leaves anyone standing, we can airlift them out on the helo that brings in the water."

"Everyone seems to be devoted to Carol and the Nolan Group," Junko mused. "We may have to pry them away from their stations, or at least draw straws."

"That's better than losing any more lives," Garner said. "Beyond a certain point, we'll all be at risk no matter who stays."

As Junko turned back to her own workstation, the sleeve of her suit brushed one of Garner's petri dishes. Before she could catch it, the dish flipped up on its edge and dumped its contents onto the top of the bench. She was momentarily terrified that she had cooked the lab. "Oh dammit," she stammered. "I'm sorry, Brock. I'm tired. No excuse, I know. I should have been paying more attention."

"Relax, that one was just a control," Garner said. If the dish had contained hot water, even such a relatively minor spill would have necessitated an involved scrubbing procedure. Everyone working in the lab would have had to don hoods and respirators until the bench could be scoured and the wastewater siphoned into the ship's containment tanks. Wasted time. Wasted water. Cooked equipment. Contamination.

Even this was not enough to placate Junko: "Here I am, playing mother hen to all these kids on board, and I go and make a careless mistake that even a rookie—"

She cut herself short, picked up a sponge from the sink, and began wiping the countertop. She scooped up as much of the spill as possible with one careful swipe, then daubed the rest dry. Her chagrin was hardly warranted by the minor incident.

"Junko, it's *okay*," Garner assured her. "If you're going to spill anything, plain ol' seawater is the thing to spill. *That* we've got lots of." He waited as Junko wrung out the sponge, then waved the wand of a dosimeter over the site of the spill. The bench had not been contaminated. "There, see? No harm done."

"No excuse," Junko said again. She stepped back, the sponge in one gloved hand and the dosimeter in the other. "Do I look like the cleaning woman in a breeder reactor or what?" she asked with a chuckle.

The image was striking to Garner. "What if you and I hop the next bus back to civilization?" he asked suddenly.

Junko wasn't certain she had heard him correctly. "Us?" she asked. "You mean, leave the ship?"

"Not for long," Garner said. "Just a couple of days. Look at this," he said, indicating the microscope. He pushed back from the bench to allow her to look through the eyepieces.

She brushed the hair back from her face and complied. "What am I looking for, exactly?"

The binocular lens of the scope revealed a fluorescent galaxy no larger than a dime. Against the vibrant, ultraviolet background of the nutritive culture, the aggregation of *Thiobacillus* glowed brilliantly from their treatment with the acridine orange stain. Several of the cells also exhibited a second color, a bright, chromatic yellow that seemed to fill many of the cells to the point of bursting.

"The yellow is cesium 137," Garner explained. "Stained, radioactive cesium in soluble form, taken directly from Medusa's bottles."

"It looks as though the cells are digesting it," she observed.

"Exactly," Garner said. "*Digesting* it. Last night I inoculated the dish with radiocesium. Today, it's almost entirely absorbed by our little friends here."

"That's wonderful!" Junko said. "It means the bacteria are actually helping to clean up the hot water."

"Not exactly," Garner cautioned. "The radioactivity may be moved into the cells, but the cells are still in the water."

"I see what you mean," Junko agreed. "It doesn't matter if the radionuclides are in the water or in the cells suspended in solution, the effect on the environment is the same."

"Almost," Garner said. "And here is where I think we might get a break. The *Thiobacillus* survive only within the water heated by our radiation source, right?"

"Right. The colder, surrounding water can't support the bacteria."

"But inside the slick the cells are thriving," Garner said. "And they're slurping up radioactive debris like crazy."

"So what we've really been measuring isn't the radiation in the water, but radiation ingested by the *Thiobacillus*."

"Which means the radiation itself is being drawn into the heated water," Garner said. "Taken up by the organic matter in solution."

"But how does the *Thiobacillus* 'know' how to stay with the nuclides?"

"Bacteria act a lot like sharks in how they track a scent from a distance," Garner explained. "It's not that they know which way the source is, but when they lose the scent, they double back until they find it again."

"So it's the allure of the nuclides that's keeping the *Thiobacillus* floating along with the isotopes in solution."

"Right." Garner nodded. "So instead of trying to retrieve the radionuclides from the water, maybe we can achieve the same effect by collecting the bacteria."

"How do we do that?" she asked.

"I have no idea," Garner said, still grinning from ear to ear. "But I know a guy who might."

"Who?" Junko asked.

"His name is Roland Alvarez," Garner said. "He's a seaweed expert at Dalhousie University."

"In Nova Scotia."

"Yes," Garner said. He was practically bursting with excitement. "Halifax. Where you and I and that sponge are going as soon as the Evian truck gets here."

Garner and Junko relayed their findings to Carol and Byrnes over breakfast.

"You want to take a culture of *Thiobacillus* to Halifax and do *what*?" Carol asked again.

"I want to see if he knows of any way we can collect the bacteria from solution, cleanly and easily," Garner said.

Garner's sudden confidence had caught Carol off guard. She was certainly willing to try anything at this point, or consult anyone who might be of some assistance. That Garner was talking about going *there* instead of bringing someone to the ship was what concerned Carol. She wasn't yet sure whether she was reluctant because the plan meant further delays, further expenses and logistical complications, or the loss of Garner's guidance in the midst of this situation.

"Do you really expect to accomplish anything in just a day or two?" Carol asked.

"Probably more than in the same amount of time here," Garner said. "Serg and I were up the entire night with Medusa and she is one sick baby. Virtually all her sensors have been cooked; we're lucky we can still track temperature and dissolved organic matter. Serg still needs another day or two to replace the sensors for which we have extras and to recalibrate her cameras. I think I could give you more bang for your buck in Halifax, and I need Junko's expertise on *Thiobacillus* to let us know when we're getting close to an answer."

Carol remained unconvinced. "We haven't got *time* to start running lab experiments two thousand miles from here."

"I can radio Roland before we leave," Garner said. "He can have his cultures set up when we get there. Give us another day after that. Two at the most. If we strike out, we'll come back."

"Promise?"

"Promise," Garner assured her.

Carol turned to Byrnes. "And what do *you* want for Christmas? A pony?"

"We can get a thousand-gallon tank of potable water brought in from the NORAD radar site at Hall Beach," Byrnes said. "Set it on the helipad and strap it down, then run a feed into the showers or the sewage system, or both."

"Will that solve our water problems?" Carol asked Junko.

"It will give us some breathing room—or bathing room, as it were," Junko replied. "But it still assumes we won't need to be at sea for much longer than another week or ten days."

Byrnes wasn't completely assured. "Don't ask me what happens if we need more water after that," he said. "We can draw from the tank on the helipad first, but it'll be sitting outside and eventually it will be contaminated too. Once it's spent we can't just throw it overboard and in the meantime we'll lose our emergency landing pad. If we need more water after that, we'll have to airlift the empty tank from the deck and replace it with another full one." His glance at the others suggested that there was no way in hell that would happen, at least not in his lifetime.

"So time is working against us," Carol said. "We ration water and step up the search operation." She nodded at Garner and Junko. "And you two test your sponge theory damn fast."

"Can we take anyone else with us?" Junko asked Byrnes. She was still hoping to increase the number of nonessential personnel who could be taken off the ship.

Byrnes rubbed his eyes. "The SAR helicopters have a payload capacity of about fifteen tons, but they'll be stretching it with a thousand-gallon water tank plus enough fuel to reach us, even from Hall Beach," Byrnes said. "The water alone is going to weigh four tons. When they drop that, they should have plenty of room for six passengers and whoever goes with them can take a Canadair jet south from Hall Beach."

"Six? No more?" Junko pressed again.

"I can give up as many as four from the deck crew," Byrnes countered. "Carol, you could probably give up two officers and as many technicians."

"Maybe," Carol speculated. "But eight is too many. Say six plus these two?" She nodded at Garner and Junko.

"I don't like it, but okay," Byrnes said.

"The bill on this little vacation is getting out of hand, isn't it?" Carol said.

"We're almost done shopping," Garner said. "In a couple more days we'll have all the resources we need up here."

"That's a little pointless with no one left here to use them, isn't it, darling?" Carol feigned a smile in his direction.

"Two days," Garner said. "C'mon. *One* day."

"You'll spend almost that amount of time in the air,"

Carol said. In truth, it would be about a five-hour trip to Halifax, provided they could get a VIP jet on such short notice.

Carol looked at Junko. "You agree?" she asked the doctor.

"I'm with Brock," she said.

Carol looked to Byrnes. "You agree? Look who I'm asking—you never agree."

"I'm out of brighter ideas," Byrnes admitted. "Except the one where we all go back to Seattle, find a pool hall and a fireplace, and let the friggin' military come up here and get cooked."

"All right," Carol said. "Go. No Captain Bligh, I. No Malcolm Neddermeyer either."

"We won't return to find you barricaded in the radio room, will we?" Garner asked her.

"Of course not," she said. "On this ship, the dry storage locker is much tougher to break into."

By the time the Canadian Forces helicopter arrived the following morning, Garner had finished processing the rest of his wet samples and packed two cases with cultures of *Thiobacillus*. Junko did her rounds, inspecting the crew of the *Phoenix* one last time before packing up for the trip to Halifax.

Byrnes and Zubov donned light, laboratory-style containment suits and rendezvoused with the helicopter hovering above the bow of the ship. The downdraft from the rotors of the heavily loaded helicopter was intense, forcing both men to find handholds to prevent being blown to the deck. As the massive tank was lowered onto the helipad, the next concern was releasing it from its harness. Too little tension and the tank might slide off the pad; too much tension and the cable could snap, lashing out at those on deck or, worse, pulling the helicopter into the superstructure of the *Phoenix*.

The rotors of the helicopter savagely pounded the cold, dry air above the ship, creating a massive buildup of static electricity that crackled against the metal edges of the deck. Before the SAR crew could drop a wire to help ground the helicopter, a charge of fifty thousand volts had built up along the helipad.

"Watch the static charge until the grounding wire is set!" Zubov shouted to Byrnes above the roar.

Zubov's warning wasn't heard. Struggling just to keep his footing against the savage wind, Byrnes strayed too close to the tank's harness. A violent blue spark shot from the tank to his hand, blowing his arm back and throwing Brynes backward onto the deck. He slid nearly fifteen feet before his safety line snapped taut and stopped his fall.

"You okay?" Zubov shouted, his eyes wide.

"Yeah." Byrnes nodded, still shaken. "The amps were too low to cause any harm. Beats the hell out of a tequila buzz, though."

Once the grounding wire was set, the two men climbed onto the side of the tank and set to work releasing the tank's harness from its pendant. With a final heave on the cable, the harness was released and the vertical tornado from above subsided as the helicopter retreated to a higher altitude.

"I hope we've got the placement right on this damn thing," Byrnes shouted, stepping back to examine the ungainly structure now occupying most of the remaining open-deck space on the ship. "It's hard to tell a four-ton gorilla where it can sit."

"Just as long as it doesn't go looking for bananas," Zubov replied. He rechecked the chains fastening the tank to cleats set into the perimeter of the helipad on all sides. "It's not going anywhere." The plan was to attach a bleeder hose and a siphon pump to the tank and run the new supply of fresh water into the main lab, the showers in the airlocks, and the galley. This would shunt water use away from the *Phoenix*'s primary supply until the tank was empty and would give the vessel up to ten more days at sea.

In addition to Garner and Junko, Carol had selected seven nonessential crew members from the *Phoenix* to return to the mainland. High above them, the helicopter pilots were already beginning to raise concern about their fuel supply; the *Phoenix* had less than fifteen minutes to get her assigned emigrants up the hoist line and into the jump seats.

A basket filled with personal effects, laboratory gear, and Garner's samples of *Thiobacillus* was lifted first. Next, a SAR technician was lowered from the helicopter along with an empty harness for the passengers. Two of the *Phoenix*'s junior technicians went next, then Junko, the third-watch cook, and the second-watch helmsman, with the SAR tech assisting them one at a time into the empty horse collar and shuttling them up to the helicopter. Garner and Zubov watched as two deckhands were reeled up into the waiting helo, then the empty horse collar descended to the deck on its own. Above, they could see the SAR tech pulling at his own harness, which had apparently developed some sort of problem. The tech rolled his hand in the air, indicating that Garner should take the harness and come up alone.

The notion that he would have to take the sickening ride unassisted left a cold feeling in Garner's stomach. "How many lives did you say I have left?" he asked Zubov.

"Seven," Zubov said as he grabbed the swaying harness and helped Garner wriggle into it. "Maybe six and a half," he added, giving the line suspended from the helicopter a closer look. "Listen: don't go out of your way," he added, trying to keep Garner distracted, "but if you're passing a drive-through, bring me back a decent cheeseburger."

"Hold the pickles and onions, right?" Garner said, studying each carabiner as it was clipped shut. The harness continued to sway slightly in response to the helicopter's movement above.

"And ketchup for the fries," Zubov said. "Ketchup or forget it. And a shake."

"That stuff will kill you, you know?" Garner said.

"Sure, and this place is Club Med," Zubov replied. Then, as the harness was finally slung around Garner's shoulders, he added: "Hurry back."

"Okeydoke."

"I'm *serious*," Zubov said. He gripped the straps of the harness and looked Garner directly in the eye. "Take care of yourself and hurry back. We need you here, man."

Zubov stepped back, looked up at the hoist operator, and spun his finger in the air. The line heaved upward on Garner's chest. Garner could feel the weight of his body press heavily against the harness, then his feet lifted off the deck. The line that held him immediately swung out over the icy water, then returned on its pendulous movement as it was reeled in. In their anxiousness to return to base, the helicopter's crew had already begun moving away from the ship. Garner looked down to see the deck of the *Phoenix*, already as small as a toy, and the trio of Carol, Zubov, and Byrnes standing just forward of the new water tank. The distance between them began to increase rapidly. Far below Garner's dangling feet, dozens of pieces of broken pack ice slipped past, drifting atop the forbidding black water of the Arctic Ocean. To the east, the outline of Baffin Island—the fifth-largest island in the world—rose up out of the sea like an enormous, snowcapped whale.

"It's not the flying," Garner recited in midair. "It's the altitude. The *rapidly increasing* altitude."

The familiar knot returned to the pit of Garner's stomach as he was lifted past one hundred feet . . . one-fifty . . . two hundred feet. Then the bottom of the helicopter, as immense as a dirigible when viewed from this angle, filled his field of vision. He could see the call number of the aircraft and the two large drop tanks containing extra fuel. He could also see the seams in the aircraft's body and the rivets that held the aluminum sheeting together, several of them ringed with black and showing wear.

Garner focused on the airman leaning out of the cargo cabin, one hand on the winch head and the other lightly guiding the line. Instinctively, he grasped the end of the wire protruding from his harness. *Don't bother holding the line. It's got ahold of you a lot stronger than you could ever get ahold of it,* Garner remembered the words of a rock-climbing instructor he had consulted, briefly, unsuccessfully, to overcome his acrophobia. Gripping the wire did nothing to ensure Garner's security, but it did slow the rate at which he was spinning. Above, the airman waved his finger, *no.* The greatest threat to Garner's well-being at this point was not being dropped by the wire, but losing an ill-placed finger in the pulleys of the hoist.

Then, as suddenly as the heart-stopping lift had begun, it was over. Garner was drawn up past the landing gear of the helicopter and stopped alongside the cabin. He could see the others from the *Phoenix,* still strapping themselves into their jump seats. The wire jerked to a stop and the firm hand of the hoist operator grasped the back of the harness, rolling Garner the rest of the way into the helicopter.

Opening his eyes, the first thing Garner saw was Junko. She smiled at him and clapped her hands together. "Congratulations!" she said. "Sergei told me how much you don't like to fly."

"It's not the flying—" Garner began again.

"Nonsense," Junko said, waving him off. "Of *course* it's the flying."

A second airman helped Garner extricate himself from the harness, then Garner slumped into the last available jump seat. He looked straight ahead at an auxiliary fuel cell that took up most of the room in the cabin. *I am strapping myself into a flying fuel bomb,* Garner could not help but think. *A flying fuel bomb above a radioactive slick in the most disorienting landscape in the world. What's there to be nervous about?*

As soon as the helicopter had drawn clear of the *Phoenix* and turned back toward the mainland, Junko withdrew a dosimeter from her backpack, quickly calibrated it despite the harsh vibration of the cabin, then waved it slowly around each of her fellow passengers. Garner and the others watched her with their full attention, waiting for the instrument to announce that someone had been cooked. It was an hour's flight to the next substantial human settlement, much less a medical facility equipped to handle radiation poisoning. Last of all, Junko carefully examined the metal floor of the helicopter.

"Clean as a whistle," she finally announced. Her fellow passengers slowly let out their breath. "Evidently the atmospheric rad levels are still low. The downdraft of the rotor blades might also have helped to blow back any airborne fallout."

This, she knew, was unrealistically wishful thinking, but it seemed to set the others at ease. In point of fact, the helicopter crews dispatched to Chernobyl to dump yard after yard of sand onto the atomic inferno had received massive doses of gamma radiation, shot directly through the bottom of their aircraft. The fiery pit below them only consumed more—liberating more heat, more radiation, more misery. The facility burned so hot that water sprayed onto the flames was actually split into its explosive constituents of hydrogen and oxygen.

Eventually the pit had been sealed with a massive dome unimaginatively known as "the cover." The lives lost in the building of this sarcophagus, the ongoing flaking and cracking of the poor, hastily prepared material shielding the buried monster, were not discussed in the headlines. As one Soviet author had observed, the sarcophagus at Chernobyl would need to last longer than the Egyptian pyramids in order to survive the devil it contained. Because of the building materials used and the slipshod engineering, however, it was beginning to crumble in less than two decades—a severe thunderstorm could split it open. Meanwhile, human nature declared that the calamity was over and returned to its daily life, while the heroes were never spoken of again. All for the sake of a clean, economical way to satisfy humankind's rampant desire for electricity.

Junko shivered in her seat and stared out at the vast miles of ice. Einstein was right, she mused. Nuclear energy is a hell of a way to boil water.

13

Eleven men crowded into the small, nondescript meeting room built above the process module of Global *B-82*. The enclosure, referred to by those who knew about it as "the tank"—in homage to a more sophisticated room of similar intent in the Pentagon—measured barely three hundred square feet. Most of this meager space was occupied by a single conference table. A secured-line speakerphone sat on the table and a combination whiteboard and projection screen was mounted on one wall. A yellowed coffeemaker looked much more thoroughly used than any of the audiovisual equipment.

The tank was soundproof and structurally isolated from the rest of the rig's topsides. A self-contained computer system logged data about the rig's surveillance activities from a hidden alcove. Inside each wall was a quarter inch of lead sheeting, enough to confound the most sophisticated listening devices. Similarly, once the access hatch was closed, there was no audible evidence of the factory's worth of industrial equipment that labored endlessly just outside or the two hundred Global Oil employees carrying out their duties.

A casual glance around the table revealed two different factions. On one side sat Charon, his right-arm Stimson, and four other officers—Wigner, Rieger, Duncan, and Teller—who acted as either shift supervisors or foremen on B-82. All of them were former U.S. Navy or Marines, charged with directing both the rig's civilian and military operations. Krail's contingent had less brawn but possessed puffed-out chests sporting enough ribbons to launch a parade. Present were Ed Snow, the commander of the *Hawkbill*, and Frank Groves, his executive officer. Two others, Navy lieutenants, represented the sonar crews on the submarine. Evidently, mused Charon, they thought they were impressing someone.

Charon had handpicked every single man aboard B-82 for this assignment, just as Charon himself had been handpicked to lead them. During the entire process, Charon had not seen a single uniform or consulted one printed résumé. Now the very presence of the contingent from the *Hawkbill*, these men in their dress uniforms, implied a disdain for Charon and his crew, men of grit and substance who could actually be relied upon to conduct delicate operations. Charon was hardly intimidated by the younger officer, but Krail's constant movement annoyed him. The little pissant was too uptight for this kind of work, and the last thing Charon wanted was to set this terrier yapping any more than need be. Let him say his piece and go away, preferably sooner rather than later.

"With the introductions made all around, I guess we'll get started," Krail began. Stimson rolled his eyes, making certain that Charon caught the gesture. Krail's toastmastering made it sound as if some personal allegiance, not implicit duty, was responsible for their attendance. "I'll try to make it brief," he said.

"So far you're not trying very hard," Wigner muttered from the other end of the table. Krail shot him a sharp look, then glanced at Charon as if to say *please curb your pet*. Charon found that funny. His men had earned the right to piss wherever, and on whomever, they chose. Krail would be well out of his ballpark to challenge them on the basis of any standard-operating-procedure indiscretion, by Washington standards or otherwise.

"As you know," Krail continued, "we've been patrolling the area for the past two days, looking for radionuclide debris. In addition to her existing array, the *Hawkbill* has been fitted with submersible gamma spectrometers in order to detect the presence and location of possible leakage from the plug. In short, we've got a helluva set of ears and eyes tuned into this, but so far they're not revealing anything."

"The plug" was a man-made containment hatch that sat at the bottom of Thebes Deep, approximately three hundred meters below *B-82*'s main deck. Constructed to facilitate the passing of nuclear waste materials into a natural storage chamber in the bedrock below, the plug was actually a capped tube that extended down through the seafloor nearly an eighth of a mile before opening into a larger opening called simply "the pit." Fifty feet in diameter and constructed from steel-reinforced concrete, lead, and boron carbide, the plug was the only portal to the cavernous natural storage facility and its troublesome cache, a fortified rock sarcophagus designed to last ten thousand years.

Then, in the winter of 1985, the Russian submarine *Scorpion* had penetrated Thebes Deep and located the plug with its sonar. Soon after that, according to the Arctic segment of the SOSUS surveillance system, there was an explosion and *Scorpion* had been crushed by the resulting collapse of the canyon wall. The landslides continued for days, burying not only the submarine but the plug itself under millions of tons of basalt.

In the weeks and months following the incident, the Navy mapped the devastation at the bottom of the canyon with unmanned, remotely operated vehicles—ROVs—packed with cameras and radiometers to establish whether the waste cribs had been breached. Later, as more funds and resources were given to the operation, *Scorpion*'s debris field had been salvaged, and controlled detonations supervised by Charon himself were used to set off even more landslides to bury the evidence. A crisis had been avoided, but as the political embarrassment detonated behind closed doors in both Moscow and Washington, the possibility that foreign powers possessed the stealth technology to leave such expensive calling cards around U.S. military installations suddenly loomed large.

Global *B-82* was one outcome of such concerns. The costs associated with the operation of ongoing submarine, surface, or satellite sentries were weighed against the placement of a permanent guard post. The idea of combining a listening post with a drilling platform operating in the private sector had been proposed as almost a lark. Decades earlier, USGS surveyors had speculated on the potential for crude oil along the lip of Thebes Deep. The same geological processes that had carved large, natural vacuoles such as the pit might also have provided natural reservoirs and sand lenses thick with fossil fuel, but the technology of that era had yet to make ocean drilling in the high Arctic a cost-effective enterprise. By the late 1990s, the Hibernia project off the Canadian Maritimes and others like it in the North Sea had advanced the technology of oil drilling in harsh environments far enough to overcome such obstacles. Now the problem was finding a suitable sponsor from the private sector to justify and offset the cost of setting up such a facility. Eventually, Global Oil put up $5.2 billion in construction costs in exchange for unconditional mineral rights to the area within a hundred miles of Thebes Deep and a host of generous tax subsidies.

Global *B-82* represented a new breed of covert communications posts, completely visible but absolutely unseen by the public eye. Befitting the ravenous appetites of the military and the oil industry for computer hardware, *B-82* was both a proving ground and showcase for technological innovation. While it continued to labor tirelessly, producing 120,000 barrels of crude per day for Global Oil, the facility's surveillance activities also continued unabated, routing satellite transmissions to and from National Reconnaissance Office satellites, the National Security Agency, and U.S. military operations throughout the Arctic Circle. *B-82* had indisputably become a major component in the new era of "networked warfare."

"While we haven't yet found anything of note," Krail was saying, "that doesn't mean there isn't a problem. We are now receiving hourly reports from a polar-orbit NRO intelligence satellite and have been monitoring the communications of a civilian icebreaker—the *Phoenix*—en route to this location. What this information collectively suggests is that there is a waste spill up here. A big one. The fact that this meeting is necessary should tell you that we don't know why." If Krail had expected to shock anyone in Charon's group with this confessed ignorance, he failed. "My orders are to use you men and the facilities of the *Hawkbill* to locate the source and stem it before this matter draws any more attention."

Teller was the first to interrupt. "Excuse me, sir," he said. "But if the plug was leaking, we would be the first to know about it, not some civilian vessel or a spy bird.

Our own instruments down there are supposed to let us know if the levels go up even a trace."

"Assuming they're operating," said Groves, the *Hawkbill*'s executive officer.

"Well, if they're *not* operating, then what the hell are we all doing here?" Stimson retorted. "Pumping gas for you boys in Arlington?"

"I realize that, Lieutenant Teller," Krail said, ignoring Groves and Stimson's outburst. "Frankly, I *am* a little surprised that no one aboard this rig is showing signs of exposure to radiation. If what we think is going on *is* going on, you all should be sitting at ground zero."

"I thought that's what the shielding was for," Rieger said. "To protect us from leakage effects." The tank was not the only portion of the rig that had been fortified. The base of the entire topsides had been specially modified with reactor-grade radiation shielding. Clay and sand mixed in with the concrete of the GBS's ice-wall were intended to further absorb any radionuclides that might eventually leach their way from the pit to the seafloor and beyond.

"You may be shielded, but that doesn't account for what we're reading from the water column," Krail said. "And they're finding severe contamination downstream. But straight down, where a leak from the plug should be, the *Hawkbill*'s instruments are finding nothing."

"Then how can you say the plug is leaking?" Rieger asked again. No one from Charon's crew was about to take lightly the suggestion that they were somehow negligent in their monitoring activities.

"I can say it because nothing else between here and Oak Ridge is capable of producing the kind of debris the *Phoenix* has been reporting," Krail said. "Nothing else, known or unknown, plausible or implausible. Period."

"Is it possible that the drilling somehow damaged the

plug?" asked one of the *Hawkbill*'s lieutenants. Drilling from a platform such as *B-82* was directed not only straight down but also snaked outward and down from the GBS for thousands of meters according to the viability of the oil deposits and the accommodation of the rock.

"No," Wigner said. "We regularly conduct seismic surveys to check the integrity of the plug. Even if we missed something, which we haven't, that still doesn't explain the lack of radionuclides below us."

"The base pad of the GBS is solid," Teller agreed. "And we haven't recorded any landslide activity inside the canyon for at least a month."

"What do you want us to do?" Stimson asked.

"I want you to help us locate the leak," Krail replied. "We'll continue to survey the canyon wall with the *Hawkbill* and check any recent landslide areas for elevated levels of radiation."

"If you don't want to believe our regular status reports," Stimson said, "then what more could we possibly do for you?"

"You can give us a credible cover for the operation and the benefit of your experience," said Snow, the *Hawkbill*'s commander. "Even our sonar arrays lack the detailed resolution to check the plug itself or look for newly opened fissures. We need something more hands-on, like sending someone down to check the plug welds up close."

"We've got cameras down there already," Stimson said. "We've got seismic probes and radiometers within fifteen feet of the plug and they aren't telling us shit about a rad leak."

"I said hands-on," Krail replied.

" 'Hands-on,' " Stimson repeated. "You're talking about a depth of three hundred meters in places."

"Use your JIM suits," Krail countered. The pressurized deep-diving suits used on the rig allowed divers to work comfortably at depths of up to six hundred meters. *B-82* was equipped with two such suits for routine maintenance, but their regular use was only to the rig's base pad at one hundred meters' depth. Tripling the dive depth, while still within the suit's capacity, increased the potential for accidents and was far more psychologically taxing on the diver.

·"We also have a one-man submersible that will take an operator down to one thousand meters," said Snow, the *Hawkbill*'s commander. An eighteen-foot Sea Sprite DSV—deep-submergence vehicle—was piggybacked onto the *Hawkbill*. "It's small, it's fast, it's available, and the transit time to the surface is a lot less. It'll also give us another set of eyes down there." Snow nodded at Krail. "His."

"As far as anyone on the Global crew needs to know," Krail said, "the Navy will be helping you to conduct a structural inspection of the gravity base structure and the base pad. The *Hawkbill* is just here to loan you the DSV for a few days, then we'll be on our way. As a precaution I'd also like Mr. Charon here to oversee the offloading of all the oil in the GBS."

"You said a civilian icebreaker was 'en route'?" Wigner asked Krail.

"The *Phoenix,* a research ship out of Seattle operated by the Nolan Group," Krail said. "They picked up the trail of the radionuclides in Foxe Basin and have been following it north."

"Following it how?" asked Rieger, Charon's second-watch foreman.

"They've got radiometers in the water and are following the isotope debris upstream," Krail replied. "They've got our scent."

"*There's* your security breach, right there," Teller said.

"It gets worse," Krail continued. "They also found the *Sverdrup Explorer* with all hands dead, apparently from acute radiation poisoning. Two of the *Phoenix*'s crew also died of exposure."

"Why haven't you shut them down?" Stimson asked.

"So far, we've been lucky," Krail answered. "No one seems to believe what the *Phoenix* is reporting. The *Phoenix* doesn't seem to believe it either—without a clear-cut evaluation of the problem, they're asking for a news blackout."

"That won't last," Teller said.

"No, it won't last. But we've also got one of our own on the *Phoenix:* Commander William Garner."

"And he knows the score?"

"Not yet, but he will," Krail said. "Right now the best recourse is to let his civilian investigation proceed unobstructed. If our little look-see can't tell us where the leak is coming from, they'll be the only ones with a handle on where it's going."

"But you *will* intervene at some point, right?" Stimson pressed.

"Of course," Krail replied.

Stimson wasn't convinced. "I still can't see why we need to risk sending divers down there for no good reason," he said. "If you ask me, it's a waste of time—this seems to be the one place the leak *isn't.*"

"Your reservations are noted, Mr. Stimson," Krail said. "We have our orders, and *your* orders are to follow *my* orders." Krail glanced at Charon. "Something I'm sure Commander Charon understands fully."

Exasperated, Stimson looked to Charon for support. "What do you think of all this, Matt?" he asked.

Charon chose to maintain his stony silence. For the time being, this was Krail's circus and Krail would be the one to give himself enough rope to make a noose.

Besides, it was no one's goddamn business what Matt Charon thought of all this.

Hanging in their storage racks, the JIM suits looked like the abandoned skin of some gigantic alien insect. The carbon-fiber hulls were molded into a torso, legs, arms, and head consisting entirely of bulbous spheres attached to each other by articulating joints. The spherical form was necessary to withstand the pressures on the suit at depth, either from the crushing weight of the deep sea or the controlled, one-atmosphere internal environment that surrounded the aquanaut wearing it. Instead of gloves, which would be unmaneuverable under such pressure, the arms terminated in a pair of two-fingered hydraulic "hands" resembling an enormous set of pliers. The bulbous helmet did not rotate atop its titanium collar; rather, the diver could turn his head to look around and out through any of four, inch-thick portholes. The customized, latest-generation suits used by Global B-82 contained a rebreathing apparatus that circulated the air in the suit, scrubbing away lethal accumulations of carbon dioxide with a battery-operated filtration system. Alternatively, the suit could be powered by a fiber-optic cable running to the surface, which was also used to control the helmet's communication equipment.

The four-hundred-pound suits were too heavy for their occupants to don in the usual manner, so instead the diver had to climb down through the neck collar. Once the aquanaut was inside, the helmet was lowered onto the collar and attached. A crane was used to guide the suited JIM diver into the water, then lowered him on a guide wire to the bottom, a slow-motion elevator ride that could take up to fifteen minutes. On the bottom, JIM divers communicated with each other and the surface via the comm link. The climate-controlled conditions in the suit allowed JIM divers to work for up to six hours, though salvage divers typically succumbed to fatigue—or boredom—long before that.

Clad in B-82's two JIM suits, Stimson and Rieger were carried through the bottom of the drilling platform and lowered past the lip of Thebes Deep to the foot of the canyon. The divers' controlled fall came to an end 280 meters down and just thirty meters away from the plug. They switched on their helmet lights to reveal a world hardly more remarkable than the water column itself. The floor of the trench was covered only with fractured pieces of basalt that had tumbled to rest from the original walls of the canyon.

Krail followed the JIM divers to the bottom in the Sea Sprite. The blunt, one-man craft resembled a cigar with sawed-off wings and a transparent, dome-shaped end-cap that served as the pilot's window. Small and highly maneuverable, the Sea Sprite had been developed specifically to allow the inspection and repair of drilling platforms. It used inverted wings to "fly" underwater much like an anti-airplane, while hydraulic compression of an air chamber adjusted the buoyancy of the DSV in the same way a fish used its swim bladder. The Sea Sprite could travel nearly twice as deep as the JIM suits and could cover far more distance on the bottom, given its twin impellers and the absence of an umbilical connection to the surface; however, the vessel was more limited in its ability to pick up and manipulate objects. Krail's task was therefore to take further photographic images of the benthic debris around the plug and guide the JIM divers to newly opened fissures and other areas of interest. If the area checked out clean, they would expand their search, moving north toward the buried wreck of *Scorpion*, more than two nautical miles along the canyon from *B-82*. Anything not immediately below the rig's GBS would require that the JIM divers be dispatched from a modified hatch on the *Hawkbill*—logistically very difficult but not impossible.

From his position inside *B-82*'s surveillance command module, Charon checked on the progress of the three submerged men. Over the Sea Sprite's comm link,

Krail continued his procedural commentary as he worked his way through the film magazines of the submarine's high-resolution cameras and provided direction to the JIM divers. After three hours of searching and receiving nothing more than normal background levels of radiation, the trio returned to the surface. Wigner and Teller now donned the JIM suits and the Sea Sprite was fitted with fresh batteries and film packs. Krail remained in the submersible, returning to the bottom before either of the replacement divers had finished suiting up. By the time Wigner and Teller joined him, he had already surveyed a large portion of an elongated rise. After two more hours they had surveyed another quarter of an acre of the canyon floor, but it quickly became apparent that the second shift of divers would find nothing more substantial than the first.

"Hate to say we told you so, Commander," Stimson said to Krail through the comm link.

"No we don't," Teller corrected him. "We told you so, Commander. Whatever you're looking for isn't coming from around here."

"Could've told you that before you got your nose wet," Charon's voice broke in on the conversation from his perch high above on the topsides.

"I didn't realize you had more pressing matters on your timetable, Commander Charon," Krail said coolly.

"Congratulations," Rieger's voice came over the headset, defending Charon without hesitation. "You've reestablished the only location in the entire Arctic Circle known to be nuke free. What's next? A task force to disprove the downness of gravity?"

After nearly six hours in the tight confines of the Sea Sprite, Krail was too tired to fence with the men's sarcasm. Anyone posted to B-82 had to be a tough son of a bitch, immune to chains of command, disciplinary action, or admonishment. Charon's men responded only to Charon, and Charon himself clearly wasn't about to give an inch in this investigation, especially if it meant he had missed a major breach of the waste facility. Charon's corner of the universe was operating exactly as he wanted it to, exactly as it *should,* and Krail could go peddle his concerns elsewhere.

"Let's call it a day," Krail said into his microphone. "Tomorrow we'll load the JIM suits into the *Hawkbill* and move a little closer to the *Scorpion* site." Even as he made the suggestion, he regretted it. *Scorpion*'s wreck site was even less likely to show any results. Not only was the location under the same watchful cloak as *B-82*'s hidden sonar arrays, but the kind of radionuclides being reported by the *Phoenix* could not have come from the buried submarine. There was no other explanation except that the pit was leaking, and until they found out where, people would continue to die.

Krail shivered inside the clammy confines of the submarine. He switched off the chatter of the JIM divers returning to the surface, then toggled the joystick controls of the Sea Sprite, angling the tiny submersible upward.

As he approached the surface, the water around him began to lighten with muted daylight and the ghostly blue glow of the ice. He was exhausted, but tried to prolong his last few moments of privacy anyway. Too soon he would be back on the topsides and back in the tank, trying to convince the same belligerent audience that there was a deadly problem here, somewhere, to be addressed.

14

The *Phoenix*'s outbound personnel were ferried to the Hall Beach NORAD station, where they transferred to a Canadair CC-144 Challenger jet. The jet took the group southeast to Gander, Newfoundland, for connecting flights, then delivered Garner and Junko to Halifax, Nova Scotia—all told, nearly nineteen hundred miles. As they traveled south, the drifting white patches of ice and snow gradually gave way to cobalt blue ocean, the surf swirling endlessly against the blunt, scarred cliff faces that made up the Canadian Maritimes. Moving over Cape Breton Island and the mainland of Nova Scotia, Junko thought that the windswept, granitic plateaus of Nova Scotia seemed even less hospitable than the icy waters of the North Atlantic. The area would be among the first to suffer massive radioactive contamination if Garner's plan failed.

From the air, the city of Halifax was immediately recognizable. The port city of 150,000 was nestled into a steep hillside beneath the Citadel, a nineteenth-century stone fort. Stretching outward from a gleaming, modern downtown core, boxy wooden homes, canning factories, and assorted other buildings that had supported the once robust fishing and whaling industry had weathered and crumbled. Through the mist, row upon row of somber, black windows faced the sea, anticipating a return to prosperity as mournfully as a lover awaits the return of a sailor.

Garner was the first to climb out of the Challenger as it landed at CFB Shearwater, across the harbor from the city. "I think I've racked up enough frequent-flier miles this month for a free trip to the moon," he said, hefting his two cases of samples with him.

"Business class," Junko agreed. "Shaken, not stirred."

They were met by the duty officer, who escorted them across the rain-soaked tarmac to a waiting van. A driver took them across the harbor into Halifax, then down Oxford Street to the campus of Dalhousie University, which was nearly deserted during the annual break between the spring and summer semesters. The van deposited Garner and Junko in front of the life-sciences building and the two travelers made their way to the top-floor office and laboratory of Roland Alvarez.

Although Alvarez's phytoplankton lab was well known throughout their particular corner of academe, Garner and Alvarez had never met, except for brief nods of recognition at phycological conferences and society meetings. In part, this was because of the disparity in their respective avenues of research: Garner's Medusa sphere sought to reduce the need for hands-on identification of plankton samples, while Alvarez's work delved into the classical realms of meticulous cataloging and illustration. Each field needed the other to comprehend the whole.

Alvarez welcomed his visitors into his cluttered office,

stacked high with manila folders, student papers, and research journals. The professor's midriff sagged a bit more than Garner remembered, and his wiry hair had grown a little thinner and grayer. Alvarez's sharp, twinkling eyes, however, reflected a mind still passionately engaged in the pursuit of science. Though on the verge of retirement, the professor still wrote or coauthored a dozen research papers each year, supplementing these with numerous conference presentations and the production of a ceaseless stream of eminently qualified botany graduates from his modest laboratory. As an ever-increasing number of prospective students were wooed by high-tech careers in biochemistry and genetics, the shortage of classically trained archivists, taxonomists, and systematists—big-picture researchers—was in danger of undermining the entire foundation of biological science. Alvarez seemed to take tremendous pride in championing these nearly forgotten but essential avenues of study.

During what should have been the pastoral twilight of his career, the quality and quantity of Alvarez's work seemed to be reaching a flourish. As evidence of this, ranks of two-hundred-gallon tanks occupied every available square foot in his lab. Dozens of meticulous drawings of algae and bacterial cells were tacked up everywhere in a kind of two-dimensional museum of the unicellular world.

Garner knew that several facilities around the world had been established to catalog and archive phytoplankton species—in fact, he liberally borrowed from many of them in identifying his own samples. He knew that most stock cultures were limited to a single test tube or a flask or two of each species that could be decanted or purchased for comparison with field samples of indeterminate species composition. Alvarez's lab, however, had taken this methodology to the extreme, harboring large, beautifully homogeneous cultures of the most dominant algae in the North Atlantic. Cultured in this way, the specimens could be provided to fish farms or other researchers doing large-scale comparative studies.

"The untimely death of tenure and the attrition of the department here are unfortunate," Alvarez admitted, "but they haven't hurt me. As long as I remain willing to take on graduate students, and to keep publishing, the physical plant keeps tearing down walls from the empty laboratories around us and letting me expand my space."

Alvarez then gave Garner and Junko a brief tour, pointing out the location of necessary bench equipment and laboratory supplies. He paused several times to address one culture or another as it floated in the large seawater tanks, discussing the merits or limits of each for the task at hand. He also showed his guests a side room containing a large, broken-down sofa and a folding Army cot. "It's nothing fancy," he apologized, "but you won't waste any time commuting and you can't beat the price."

He switched topics back to Garner's task. "It occurs to me," Alvarez speculated, "that you need an alga that not only grows extremely well on ice, but also has a remarkably fast metabolism and the ability to reproduce rapidly—perhaps more rapidly than any culture we know of."

"The conditions will be light-saturated, but the species can't rely on photosynthesis alone," Garner said. "We need to create a large-scale, fast-acting uptake of the contaminated bacteria."

Garner was especially interested in ice algae, phytoplankton species that—like countless microbes—thrived in the thin liquid interface between sea ice and the water supporting it. Such species had adapted to subsist in semi-insulated areas of constant movement and very little direct sunlight—fatal conditions for most true plants. Growing in thin, fibrous strands on the underside of floe ice, certain species of algae used any firmament they could find to photosynthesize, grow, and reproduce. So tenacious was the attachment of these algae to the ice that many species could only be isolated by filtering the cells from meltwater.

"Finding such an alga might be possible," Alvarez said. "But finding one that is also capable of withstanding the temperatures in your anomaly is a far different story."

"Do you think it has to be a local species?" Garner asked.

"Unquestionably," Alvarez said. "Given the tremendous quantity of culture material you'll need, it isn't practical to import an exotic species. Even this lab doesn't have access to large, purified cultures, and growing the cells would take weeks." Alvarez scratched at his beard. "No, what you'll need to do is somehow invigorate the processes among species already out there."

In confirming the arrangements with Alvarez by radio, Garner had faxed the phycologist a list of the most prevalent algae found in Medusa's wet samples. Species, he reasoned, which were already coexisting with the *Thiobacillus*.

"Did you see any likely candidates on my list?" Garner asked.

"Three," Alvarez said. "The first is too rare in the field and too finicky to keep alive in laboratory culture, so I doubt it'll be of much use. The second is much easier to culture and grows quickly, but I don't know if the adsorption of bacteria will be high enough."

"And the third?" Garner asked.

"The third is *Ulva morina*," Alvarez said. "Not at all like its macroscopic cousin, *Ulva latuca*, which most people know as sea lettuce. *Ulva morina* is a mar-

velously tough microscopic alga found around volcanic
fissures in the North Atlantic."

"So it's tolerant of high temperatures," Garner said.

Alvarez nodded. "And it coexists with sulfur-sniffing
bacteria like your *Thiobacillus*. So your short list of
candidates may be very short indeed. I've got a couple
of calls in to the Bedford Institute of Oceanography—
just across town here—but I think *Ulva morina* will be
your best and only bet."

"Do you have a culture of it here?" Garner asked.

"A small one. One of my students, studying the
botany of extreme environments, brought back a seed
culture from her fieldwork in Iceland. It's enough material to see how *Thiobacillus* responds to it, but if it
works, I'll have to think hard about where to get the
kind of quantity you'll need."

The three academicians worked together to set up a
bench-top experiment using Garner's hot samples of
Thiobacillus and Alvarez's stock culture of *Ulva morina*. The first set of trials had just been prepared when
a delivery arrived for Junko, in care of Alvarez's laboratory.

She signed for the two smallish packing cases couri-
ered from the National Livingston Laboratory. As
Alvarez cleared some additional desk space for her,
Junko carefully unpacked a laptop computer and a processing unit from inside the cases.

"Ah, the ubiquitous magic box known as the computer," Alvarez said. "I tried one, for about six months,
back in the 1980s," he said. "The department makes
me use an e-mail account, but in general I avoid them.
Packed in boxes like this, the beasts seem harmless
enough, but I'm not so certain about the rest of the
time. I guess I still haven't found a worthwhile use for
them."

"I might not have either," Junko said as she began

setting up the machine. "We'll know more in an hour or two."

Junko tinkered with the new computer long into the evening while Garner continued his experiments using the *Ulva* culture and the *Thiobacillus* collected by Medusa. Meanwhile, Alvarez had taken a keen interest in the bacterium and occupied his time by looking at it under his fluorescent microscope, housed within a black-sheeted area in the corner of the lab. It was past dusk and the lab had grown utterly silent, save for the sound of seawater percolating through the culture tanks.

The sudden sound of Alvarez's voice made Garner and Junko look up with a start. "Eureka," Alvarez said from within the lightless enclosure. "Or 'bingo,' or 'hot damn,' or whatever we mad scientists are supposed to say. I think I've found something.

"Look at this," Alvarez said, beckoning them inside the tent. As Junko complied, Alvarez narrated what she was seeing. "On the left is one of the Medusa samples you brought in," Alvarez said. "On the right is a preserved sample of bacteria from one of my students' fieldwork."

"They look the same to a novice like me," Junko said. "Except for the effects of the preservative, maybe."

"They *are* the same," Alvarez agreed, as Garner took his turn at the scope. "Now look at this." Alvarez moved the field culture aside and set a new slide next to the sample taken from Medusa.

This time Garner carefully studied the comparison. "Not the same," he said. "The one on the right has a different membrane structure and isn't as crowded with organelles." In monitoring Medusa's camera arrays as they flipped though countless images of plankton assemblages, Garner had become expert at noting gross differences in cellular structures.

"Not bad," Alvarez said, impressed. "It took me the past hour to notice the same thing. The culture under there now, the one on the right, is a natural strain of *Thiobacillus ferrooxidans,*" Alvarez explained.

"Yet it looks different," Garner said.

"Because it *is* different," Alvarez said. "Only marginally, but as you can see, indisputably. In fact, the difference is so slight that I might even chalk it up to chance mutation or environmental factors."

"Except for the near-perfect match with the other slide," Junko said.

"That's the eureka," Alvarez continued. "Almost an exact match with a species that is not ordinary *Thiobacillus ferrooxidans,* but a precisely modified strain." He paused for a moment, enjoying the rapt attention of his small audience. "The matching bacterium is one found in the field samples collected off the coast of Iceland—the same site as our parent culture of *Ulva morina.* Eventually we identified it using a single, obscure reference in the literature to *Thiobacillus univerra ferrooxidans.* To avoid confusion we took to calling it *Thiobacillus univerra* or, simply, *Thio-uni,* since, as we discovered, it isn't really a natural species at all," Alvarez said.

"It isn't?" Junko asked.

"No, it's man-made," Alvarez said.

"*Man-made?*"

"*Thio-uni* is not a natural bacterium," Alvarez repeated. "Although based on natural *ferrooxidans,* the *univerra* variety was cultured for laboratory use in the 1940s, though that work wasn't made public until a few years ago."

"How did you find it?" Junko asked.

"We didn't," Alvarez chuckled. "It found us. As I mentioned, one of my graduate students was describing

Ulva morina and its epiphytes." Epiphytes were lower plants that, like lichens and mosses, attached to larger algae and subsisted there in symbiosis.

"And one of those epiphytes was *Thiobacillus*—" Garner began.

"—univerra *ferrooxidans*," Alvarez finished. "Cynthia had a damnable time finding anything exactly like it in the literature, which is meager enough for marine bacteria, and especially so for the polar regions. Fortunately, Cynthia had a working knowledge of Russian and found a note in the back of a Soviet botanical journal." A proud, sentimental look came over his face. "Diligent girl, Cynthia was. Most of her contemporaries would have just tagged the oddball species with some incorrect but convenient name and moved on. But not her. She kept at it until she found the right culprit."

"What was the *univerra* strain used for?" Garner asked.

"Cleaning up radionuclides with a long half-life," Alvarez said. "Specifically plutonium, cesium, and strontium."

The realization dawned on Garner and Junko in an instant. "I'd say that deserves a 'eureka,'" Garner said.

"Maybe even a 'hot damn,'" Junko agreed.

"Indeed." Alvarez nodded. "And as you know, historically, the Soviets were tight-lipped about their nuclear program. Much of their literature was sealed away for fifty years, including their work with *Thio-uni*. Even today, it might not be a matter of public record, except there seems to be a movement afoot to share the extent of their environmental problems with the rest of the world—for a price."

"They have to," Junko said. "They don't have the technology or the money to dig themselves out of the problems they've created. At least their situation provides a good model for others *not* to follow. More than one nuclear policy wonk has suggested Russia's threat to reopen Chernobyl is just a bargaining tactic to get funding from the West for new power plants."

"I hope they don't scrap the old ways entirely," Alvarez said, "because I think they were onto something with this bug. They tinkered around with a natural culture of *ferrooxidans* until it acquired a taste for radionuclides in addition to naturally occurring isotopes. The idea was to use the hearty little beast to help clean up the wastewater from their bomb factories and weapons arsenals."

"Almost like the use of *Thiobacillus ferrooxidans* in solution mining for uranium," Junko added. "In India, *Thiobacillus* was naturally present. It weaned itself on radionuclides and leached them out of the bedrock by bonding them in solution. It's a very promising area, but there's still a worry about groundwater contamination."

"Hats off to the Indians for the effort anyway," Alvarez said. "The Soviets were never able to get their experiments to work on a large scale. Of course, they were speculating with much larger amounts of nuclear material."

"So how could *Thio-uni* find its way from a Soviet lab into Icelandic coastal waters," Junko asked, "much less into the Canadian Arctic?"

"No problem at all," Alvarez said.

"Heat," Garner speculated.

"Precisely," Alvarez said. "The heat of volcanism around Iceland, and the heat of your mysterious radiogenic source up north."

Garner recalled his conversation with Scott Krail. "The Soviets reportedly ditched some of their obsolete nuclear submarines directly into the North Atlantic, not to mention those that had reactor explosions or any number of assorted accidents. It isn't far-fetched to think they tried to neutralize their accidents with something like *Thio-uni*."

"For all we know, they could have been culturing bacteria from magma-heated water," Alvarez added. "Following that, it wouldn't take much to introduce the bacterium into the environment as an exotic species. As you probably know by now, the little beast grows remarkably well under favorable conditions."

"A classic case of natural selection," Garner said. "Once introduced into nature, the *univerra* strain thrives in warmer locations because anywhere else is too cold to support it. But I still doubt *Thio-uni* could be naturally present in such abundance where we've found it, even with a good supply of sulfide minerals as food."

"Maybe not," Alvarez admitted. "But as you see, a lot of potential good could come from this strain."

Junko agreed. "The Kola Peninsula, where the Soviet nuclear fleet was based, has had countless spills and an enormous stockpile of abandoned nuclear fuel. A chemical processing facility in the Ural Mountains is attempting to recycle some of their reactor products, but in general they don't have modern equipment or the funds in place for proper disposal."

"So I understand," said Alvarez. "Millions of gallons of radioactive water and hundreds of thousands of cubic feet of solid wastes, all in need of decontamination. Even fifty years ago, they knew they would have to find natural mechanisms to clean up their dump sites. Low-tech solutions that didn't require the transport or redistribution of unstable containers. Planting aspen trees along contaminated rivers was one idea; using *Thio-uni* in digesting ponds was another. I've kept an eye out for *Thio-uni*'s triumphant return to the literature, only to be disappointed."

"This looks like the ideal facility to put their theoretical work to the test," Garner said to Alvarez. "Why haven't you taken up the cause of *univerra* yourself?"

Alvarez laughed. "If only I had the time and energy,"

he said. "The study of *Thio-uni* was, briefly, fascinating to me. Then I took a look at my desk! It seems there's always another monograph in need of revision, another class in need of an instructor, or a dozen other projects I could list."

"Sounds like you could use a computer," Junko teased.

"Perhaps. In my next career," Alvarez said with a wry smile.

"If *Thio-uni* is turning up off Baffin Island," Garner said, "we may get a crack at your proof of concept sooner than that."

"Whatever became of your student's research?" Junko asked. She noted that Alvarez referred to his student and her work in the past tense.

"Very sad case there," Alvarez chuckled again. "As she was writing up her thesis, the poor girl fell in love with a pre-med student. Despite her obvious abilities, she lost interest in science and dropped out to be a . . . a . . . *homemaker* and *mother*. Oh, she graduated, of course. Won accolades for her student research, but never bothered to publish it. Six hundred pages of meticulously identified and cataloged species—enough to fill a monograph unto itself—all practically unused. What price, love."

"I'd like to see a copy of her manuscript," Garner said.

Alvarez located the bound thesis—*Phytoplankton Assemblages of Iceland and Southern Greenland* by Cynthia Marie Grogan—amid three dozen others on a designated library shelf in the lab. As Garner thumbed through the manuscript, its potential value was immediately apparent. Although the data were nearly six years old, Grogan had carried out extensive observations over nearly three full years before that. Included among the extensive list of figures were several diagrams showing seasonal fluctuations in *Ulva* density with water temperature and current speed. The annual fluctuation in natural phytoplankton density appeared to be very slight, providing a good set of parameters to begin studying the curious interaction between *Ulva morina* and *Thio-uni*.

Garner managed to skim about half of Grogan's manuscript before nodding off to a restless sleep on Alvarez's guest sofa. He awoke with a start only three hours later. Junko was sleeping, curled up on the cot under a musty wool blanket. Alvarez himself had assisted them until 2:00 A.M. then gone home, leaving a note that he would return with a bag of bagels and fresh coffee for breakfast. As he had done aboard the *Phoenix,* Garner prepared a series of petri dishes in Alvarez's lab to replicate the uptake of the radionuclides by the *Thio-uni*. The bacterium once again managed to absorb virtually all of the plutonium, strontium, and cesium present in the seawater.

As the second step in creating his "algae sponge," Garner pipetted the contaminated bacterial cells to a larger vessel containing a culture of *Ulva* at approximately the same cell density, water temperature, and salinity described in Grogan's thesis. Then he read the last two chapters of the manuscript as he waited for the alga solution to respond, admiring the pale yellow sunrise of a new day as it dawned through the stained, dust-shrouded windows of the lab. Interrupting Garner's reverie, Alvarez arrived with breakfast and they roused Junko.

"I see what you're doing, Brock," Junko said as she munched on a bagel, "but it seems like an unduly complex design. If you've already demonstrated a high uptake rate by the *Thio-uni* in solution, then why not simply cool the solution enough to kill the bacteria?"

"Think about it, Doctor," Garner coaxed her.

"Sorry," Junko said. "It's too early in the day for my

brain to be functioning at full speed." She chewed her bagel a moment longer. "Well, for one thing, the dead cells could release the radionuclides back into solution."

"I suspect they would," Alvarez said. "Especially if the isotopes weren't first converted to an inert form."

"And if not that, there would be the risk of contaminating the sediment on the bottom," Junko said. "The source of the radiation would just be re-created somewhere else on the bottom."

"My thoughts exactly," Garner said. "Hence the *Ulva* sponge."

"So what will we use to take the *Ulva* out of solution?" Junko asked. "We can't just leave it stuck to the ice."

"For the time being, I'll be happy to show that the alga can collect the radioactive bacteria on its surface," Garner replied. "At least, it's a much larger cell than we might be able to collect with more traditional sampling devices."

"You mean nets?" Junko asked.

Garner shook his head. "The phytoplankton cells are still too small. They'd slip through the mesh almost as easily as the bacteria."

"What then?" Alvarez asked.

Garner shrugged again, uncertain of the answer. "Still working on that."

They returned their attention to the experimental dishes Garner had set up. Each dish was positioned under the fluorescent microscope, then a camera on the scope projected the activity in the dish onto a television screen. As the researchers watched, the *Ulva* cells, seeded onto an ordinary ice cube and pushed slowly through the solution, collected the *Thio-uni* cells.

Garner then inserted the dosimeter probe into the dish containing the cleaned solution. The instrument showed a reduction in radioactive content by more than 99.96 percent—the radiation had been almost completely removed from the seawater.

"Eureka," Junko said, breaking into a huge smile.

"Bingo," Alvarez agreed.

"Hot damn," Garner said, relieved but not wholly convinced. "Or whatever we mad scientists are supposed to say."

There were still six hours until their scheduled return to the *Phoenix*.

With the encouraging news from the laboratory bench, Garner and Alvarez turned their attention to Junko's borrowed computer, which she had finished calibrating.

"I'd like you two to meet PATRIC," she said, "the handy little gizmo that I hope will add a few more pieces to our jigsaw puzzle."

"PATRIC?" Alvarez asked. "I've never heard of it, though that isn't much of an admission for a Luddite like me."

"I haven't heard of it either," Garner admitted.

"Boys, boys." Junko smacked her lips. "I thought girls were the ones who found computers icky. PATRIC is computer-modeling software designed to calculate the direction and magnitude of radioactive fallout. It's kind of an advanced descendant of models like MESODIF or TRAC, only it works in real time," she explained. "Ordinarily it uses Air Force weather data to estimate radiation dispersal through the atmosphere."

"Couldn't weather or defense satellites do the same thing?" Alvarez asked.

"They could, if the source of the radiation was airborne or on the surface," Garner said. "But in this case, there is no fallout cloud. The atmosphere is comparatively clean and the radiation source is below the surface."

Junko turned back to the computer and her fingers flew rapidly over the keyboard. "With PATRIC, a fluid is a fluid—whether it's air, water, or sand. What I've done is take the density and viscosity assumptions for air currents and replace them with the data recorded for the water currents."

"Clever," Alvarez said.

"Often, the first forty-eight hours after an accident provide the only reliable data for where the fallout is going to travel," she continued. "We're way behind in this case, but we have a lot of individual field measurements we can use to hindcast the model. That's what I was doing half the night, inputting our data."

"If PATRIC is a military application," Alvarez asked, "then why isn't the military doing this kind of analysis?"

"For one thing, they refuse to admit there's a problem," Junko said. "For another, even if they modified the program as I have done, they wouldn't have any real-time data from the gamma specs, or temperature, salinity, and current information along the *Phoenix*'s cruise track."

"But you do," Alvarez said.

"Thanks to Medusa," Junko replied.

"Hmm. I always suspected there was a useful purpose for electronic gadgets in fieldwork," Alvarez said, giving Garner a mischievous wink.

"The sooner the contamination is reliably modeled, the better," Garner said. "Then we can continue to update the known variables until we get a very accurate real-time scenario."

"Then you can tinker with the computerized scenario to see the outcome of various actions before actually doing them," Alvarez concluded.

"In theory, yes," Garner replied. "But no matter how good a model is, Mother Nature inevitably manages to throw us a curve ball."

On the computer's screen, the data were translated into a three-dimensional plot of the "cloud" as it appeared beneath the surface of Foxe Basin. As Garner had predicted, the highest levels of contamination were concentrated around the temperature anomaly created by the heat-liberating reaction of the radionuclides. "It's not as contained as I'd like," Garner said, "but most of the contamination seems to be concentrated along the heat gradient."

"And in wildlife. And in humans," Junko added.

"But not in the sediment and not spread over a large, diffuse area," Garner said. "That's encouraging. At least we have a target to shoot for."

"Do you really think the *Ulva* will be enough to bring the bacteria to the surface and soak it up?" Alvarez asked.

"It won't need to," Garner said. "As long as the alga is there, in abundance, wherever the heated water reaches the surface." He studied the computer plot of the slick once more. "Right now, what I'm more concerned about is stemming the flow at its source. Can you back it up that far?" he asked Junko.

"I can try," she said. "We can factor in the radionuclides we know of—chiefly cesium, strontium, and plutonium—which have a known half-life. Using the long-lived isotopes, we can estimate the original amount of radiation and the possible distance from the source. The gamma spec is showing trace amounts of others, but they have a much shorter half-life and will probably dissipate on their own."

"We could also estimate the source of the heated water itself, right?" Garner asked.

"Right. If we know the decrease in temperature with distance, and the angle at which the heated water is rising toward the surface, we can estimate where it's originating."

Over the next several minutes, this information was added to the computer model, constructing the hypothetical origin of the slick. The PATRIC program dutifully stepped back the plot in quarter-mile increments until it hit a digital brick wall.

??? MULTIPLE POINT SOURCES WITH EQUIVALENT PROBABILITY [P<<0.001]??? the model spat out, then stopped its calculations.

"*Multiple* point sources?" Garner asked. "Can you plot them on a map?"

"I'm afraid not," Junko said. "The program doesn't have the actual maps we need in its database. The best I can do is track each possibility individually and get an approximate set of coordinates. Then we'll have to translate those to a chart."

"Do what you can," Garner said. "See what you can come up with while Roland and I try to find a few hundred acres' worth of *Ulva*."

Junko checked her watch. "How much time do we have?" she asked.

"Little to none," Garner said. "But you can keep trying calculations on the flight back, if you need to."

"Gee, thanks," she said. "Am I looking for anything in particular? I mean, besides a needle in a stack of needles?"

Garner turned back to the unrolled charts. The cruise track of the *Phoenix* over the past four days was marked on one of them. He compared this information to the PATRIC plot, then used a set of calipers to walk across the chart, moving west and north from Foxe Basin through Fury and Hecla Strait. The calipers now stood in the middle of the Gulf of Boothia.

"Here," he said finally, using a pencil to lightly trace an elongated oval on the chart and showing it to Junko. "If you get anything in this area, that's our best guess."

Junko noted the approximate coordinates of the area. "What's there?" she asked.

"A little-known hole in the seafloor called Thebes Deep," Garner said.

Garner recalled Scott Krail's insistence that the canyon would be a waste of their time. Krail's brash claim had struck an uneasy chord then, but Garner had ignored it. Now, looking at the mark he had just drawn on the map, Garner's concern began to build in earnest.

Aboard *B-82*, Lucas Stimson jumped back when the hatch leading to the riser shaft popped open from the other side just as he was about to open it himself. He was even more startled to see that it was Charon coming the other way.

"Oh! Hey, boss," Stimson said.

"Lucas." Charon nodded once, then started to close the hatch again in front of his second-in-command.

"What are you doing way down here? Slumming?" Stimson meant it as a joke, though the question was a valid one. The riser shaft housed the pipes of the OLS—the offshore loading system that carried the rig's oil from the fuel reservoirs to the docking station for the transfer tankers. The shaft was packed with pipes and conduits with hardly room for a service ladder between them; Stimson could think of no reason for Charon to be wasting his time down there.

"Last time I checked, I didn't need your permission to inspect my own rig," Charon said, hostility brimming in his voice. "Who made you the fucking hall monitor? I told Krail that I would supervise the off-loading to the *Voyager,* and that's what I'm doing." The Global *Voyager* was one of two shuttle tankers built especially for *B-82*. At full capacity, the OLS could off-load nearly five thousand barrels of oil an hour to the *Voyager*'s carrying capacity of 850,000 barrels.

The deck supervisor seemed stung. "Okay, Matt, but it's my job—"

Charon wheeled on Stimson, his face flushed. *"I said I'll handle it,"* he spat. "We've all got a shitload of work to do before the *Voyager* gets here and then it's gonna take eighteen mother-humping hours to drain *this* pig into *that* pig."

"I know—" Stimson began.

"Do you?" Charon's face was only inches away from his own. "I don't think you do. Because if you did, you'd know we haven't got time for you following along behind me. This platform is gonna get crowded enough without you standing on my head in the goddamn riser shaft."

Stimson took a step back from the unfounded assault. "Whatever you say, Matt. I was just going to save you some work."

"I didn't ask you to do that."

"And you didn't tell me you were gonna come down here and—"

Charon's entire body seemed to clench. "Is there an echo in here?" he asked. "I thought I just told you I'm handling the oil transfer. And it's handled. Go play air hockey or watch the tube or, better yet, get some sleep. You're gonna need it and I'm gonna need you."

The sudden shift in direction broke the tension between the two men. Stimson, at least, managed to exhale. "Good night then, Matt. I'll see you in the morning."

"Oh-five-hundred," Charon agreed. He watched his deck supervisor make his way back to the service ladder, then climb back up to the topsides.

When the sound of Stimson's steps had receded into the general din of the rig's machinery, Charon turned back the other way and headed for the utility shaft.

There *was* a shitload of work to do. That much was the truth.

15

With Junko's departure, Susan Conant reluctantly reclaimed her role as the *Phoenix*'s first-aid technician and principal medical officer. The duties were intimidating for her to accept at any level; after all, she had joined the expedition as a whale biologist with an academic interest in Carol's work on acoustics. Now she was the best thing they had for a doctor, though she still could not imagine how a two-month community college course in industrial first aid could have prepared her for such responsibility. Carol and Byrnes also had IFA training, not to mention a lot more political clout aboard the *Phoenix,* but she was the one who'd been volunteered to be the crew's nursemaid.

It wasn't the responsibility that unnerved her as much as the fact she felt woefully unprepared to take proper action if anything really did go wrong. She could handle burns and scrapes. She could tape an ankle, splint a leg, or perform CPR—anyone on board could handle those things. She could even handle the crew's daily exams. But no one left aboard really knew how to handle radioactivity if it breached their fragile cocoon. In the meantime, she was in charge of maintaining the *Phoenix*'s internal environment. And for her, the only thing more unnerving than the dry, mechanical *criiick*-ing of the dosimeters was the *dit-dit-dit* when they detected nothing. For all she knew, the damn things probably didn't even work.

The only way to stave off disaster was to take the proper precautions, and Junko had written out all of these in detailed longhand before she and Garner left for Halifax. The procedures seemed to be a study in contradiction: rinse well but conserve water, give nasal swabs regularly but don't exhaust the supply of cotton swabs, bag anything that had been exposed but keep finding equipment with which to work, watch what you're doing but watch what everyone else is doing too. No one knew how much of anything would be enough; no one knew how much longer it would be before they could just go home. That was the most disheartening feeling of all.

So far they had been lucky, but the threat of contamination was a constant, silent danger. Radioactive water soaked the hull, drifting over all the external structures and cooking major pieces of equipment. It was only a matter of time before it leached through the hull to the inside. The slightest kiss from a radionuclide and an object could be contaminated for centuries or hundreds of centuries. Any one of them incidentally exposed could die quickly, or worse, die very, very slowly. The isotopes Junko had described had among the longest known half-lives, so long that any effect on living systems had to be estimated from known natural sources. Anything presently alive would be long dead by the time an isotope with a half-life of thirty thousand years decayed to a "low enough" level.

Despite her placid bedside manner, Susan felt

trapped and scared. She really did want to leave the ship, to put the nightmare of the pervasive, invisible killer behind her and return home. Every time they had taken a vote on the matter, her hand was poised, ready to shoot up as soon as someone else raised his or her hand first. But the others only looked at each other, waiting to see who would be the first to admit a weakness, abandon the expedition, and probably jeopardize their reputation for future Nolan Group field studies. Good-paying field-tech jobs were rare enough without volunteering to go back to Seattle and sit in a cubicle.

She missed her parents back in Maryland and at night she had to resist the urge to radio her sometime boyfriend at Woods Hole. Frisch had orders too: Carol had determined that the radio be used for essential communication only—which currently meant only the Coast Guard, Brock Garner, or the Canadian NERTs. So Susan did the only thing she thought would be of any value in assuaging her own fears: she prayed, simply and resolutely, not to screw up.

She tried not to think about the dwindling number of crew members aboard the *Phoenix*. The attrition was surreal, destined only for the same foolish end as the men aboard the *Sverdrup Explorer*. Whenever she allowed herself to sleep, she was haunted by the memory of Ramsey and Dexter and how the men had looked only hours after leaving the water. The fact that she had been the first to suspect radiation poisoning was little comfort to her now. At best, she had managed to extend the men's survival by a few days; at worst, she had illuminated the discovery that involved all of them in this entire mess. In trying to save two lives, they might eventually kill two dozen, including herself.

Outside, Byrnes, Zubov, and a half-dozen others checked the deck equipment for exposure. The dosimeters' readings told them when to change the exposure tags from green to some other color indicating the equipment's relative degree of contamination. By now, practically all the regularly used outside equipment had received a red HIGH-LEVEL CONTAMINATION tag. None of this had apparently been transmitted to the film badges worn by the crew inside the ship—they looked the same every day. Still, they provided a constant reminder, like some kind of foreboding mood ring, that anyone could be contaminated at any moment. If that happened— *once* that happened, as it surely would, eventually—the victim would have to be spirited away, stripped naked, vigorously scrubbed, then carted off to the infirmary to wait and see just how bad the exposure had been.

Not one badge had actually changed color since they were first given out. Susan had become so preoccupied with monitoring the tiny squares of film, so distracted by the color that never changed, she wondered whether they did anything at all. They were probably ineffectual placebos that provided only peace of mind, like the "shark repellent" carried by wartime aviators over the South Pacific.

She made the midday check of the laboratory technicians, running a dosimeter over their clothing and bench spaces. They, like the hot plankton cultures in the freezer containment boxes, tested negative for leaks or residual contamination. Once they had stripped off their gloves and lab coats, she reminded them to check themselves at the wall-mounted dosimeters set just inside the hatchway to the main corridor. The internal dosimeters had also been silent since they had been installed and Susan wondered if she should check their respective power supplies.

Bored, frustrated, and a borderline nervous wreck, Susan entered one of the airlocks, stripped out of her inside clothes, and pulled on one of the external suits, tucking her film badge into one of the suit's shielded pockets. *Screw the quarantine,* she thought; she needed some air, even if it was contained air. She needed to soak up some natural light. She walked the deck for a while, gazing dreamily out at the icescape drifting past them, and eventually made her way to the foredeck. She pulled the badge from her pocket, set it on top of a spool of cooked winch cable, then waited. Within a few minutes, the badge began to fog with a dull haze. The film changed from yellow to gray, then red, brown, and finally, black. The metamorphosis took less than thirty seconds.

Okay, so the badges were working. As long as she saw only cheerful yellow films clipped to the lapels and belt loops of the others, she was doing her job. That did little to assure her that she was any more prepared for the tasks at hand, or those to come. They were a professional crew even at the slackest of times, and in the past few days everyone had come to be extra vigilant in watching each other's backs and procedures, but no one could be completely careful all the time. Eventually, someone would mess up.

A few minutes later, she stepped back into the airlock, peeled away her suit and respirator, then wriggled out of the cold-weather clothing inside that. She showered in the second-stage enclosure, re-dressed in her inside clothes, and pulled her wet hair into a ponytail. She grimaced at the feel of her dry, tight skin—the constant scrubbing was proving hell on it—and made a mental note to borrow someone's moisturizer. Then she stepped out of the airlock, crossed the empty lab, and headed for the galley for a bite of lunch. At the corridor entrance, she stopped and waved her hands in front of the flat metal plate of the sentry dosimeter.

The sentry's red light suddenly winked on, followed by a shrill electronic alarm.

Susan jumped back, unsure for a split second what was going on. Then the realization slammed into her and her entire body prickled with paralyzing fear. She had been exposed. She had no idea exactly *how* exposed, only that she was contaminated. Contaminated. Contaminated.

Omigod, omigod, omigod. Panic rattled in her head. *I've been exposed. I've been exposed and brought it inside. Now what?*

The *Phoenix*, moored to a suitably large piece of ice, dutifully awaited the return of the Canadian Forces helicopter. As before, a fluorescent "X" had been marked on the ice to indicate the landing point, but strangely, no one from the ship was outside to greet their arrival. The built-in anxiety of Garner's acrophobia was amplified further still by the sight of the apparently deserted vessel far below: another ghost ship on the Arctic Ocean.

"They're not answering our hail, sir," the pilot called back.

"Just land. Now." A thousand possibilities clawed at Garner's imagination.

Even as the helicopter set down on the ice, there was no confirmation from the *Phoenix*. The daylight was beginning to fade and Garner sent the helicopter off with a wave of gratitude. He and Junko were halfway back to the ship from the landing pad when a single crewman—a weatherbeaten winch operator by the name of Oliphant—appeared on the foredeck. He lowered a ramp down to the new arrivals.

"Don't bother to roll out the red carpet on our account," Garner said, angry sarcasm masking his concern. "Where the hell is everybody?"

"Crew meeting," Oliphant grumbled, jerking a thumb toward the ship then helping with their packs. "Carol wanted to give all of us a refresher course in rad safety." Oliphant looked guiltily at Junko. "We, uh, had an exposure."

The doctor's eyes grew wide. "An exposure! Who?"

"Susan Conant," Oliphant said. "She just stuck her hand out in front of the dosimeter in the lab—the sentry doodad, like we're supposed to—and it set off the alarm."

"What about her badge, didn't it show?"

"She wasn't wearing it, I guess," Oliphant admitted. "Like I said, Carol figured we could all use a reminder."

"My God," Junko said. She wasn't certain whether she was more concerned that there had been an exposure or that Oliphant seemed to be so lackadaisical about it. "Where is she?"

"The infirmary," Oliphant said. "It's been a pretty hectic day," he added, but by then Junko and Garner had passed him, headed for the ship.

The first two hatches they came to were newly sealed off. Oliphant showed them a third entrance, which had a battery of additional handwritten instructions posted inside the airlock. Garner and Junko stripped away their external gear, rinsed, and pulled on lighter Tyvek suits for use inside the ship. The crew meeting was just breaking up in the officers' mess as the two travelers arrived.

"What's the news?" Carol asked.

"We were about to ask you the same thing," Garner said. "How's Susan?"

"She's shaken up, but from what we can tell it was a minor exposure."

"How minor?" Junko pressed.

Carol provided the details as they followed her down two decks to the infirmary. "One of her suit cuffs wasn't properly sealed. She had mild burns on her skin but we've treated them. The second-stage dosimeters kept the contamination from getting farther into the ship but we're still checking the lab for traces."

Susan was sitting up in bed when the three of them entered. Her skin was still a pinkish color from the scrubbing, but the area around her hand and wrist showed little in the way of external welts or swelling. It could have been much worse.

"How are you feeling?" Junko asked Susan.

"Stupid," Susan replied. "Very stupid. And I've never been so well scrubbed in my life."

"Did you take blood?" Junko asked Carol, who nodded. "We should keep an eye out for leukopenia over the next couple of weeks. Even one gray is enough to damage organs or the circulatory system."

The disappointment weighed heavily on Susan's face. "I'm so sorry. We didn't need this." She had been expecting the worst of Carol's wrath, but her boss was surprisingly compassionate.

"We're all sorry this had to happen to anyone," Carol said. "But at least it wasn't a serious exposure. You've been doing a great job watching out for the rest of us. I hope my little pep talk just reminded everyone we're not out of the soup yet."

"You'd think they'd know better by now," Garner mused.

"They *do* know better," Carol said sharply. "Everyone's been doing great, all things considered. They're not trained for this kind of stuff—hiding from something that's invisible, watching everything they touch. They're not used to all these procedures and scrubbing and—"

"We understand," Junko said, placing a comforting hand on Carol's arm. "But this kind of thing is exactly why we can't afford to relax our guard."

Carol hesitated before replying. "I think we'll all breathe a little easier once we know what we're dealing with." Carol turned to the two arrivals again. "*Do* we know what we're dealing with?"

As Junko examined Susan further, Garner briefly relayed their findings from Alvarez's lab and the latest predictions of the PATRIC program.

"I think we've found an alga capable of taking up the hot bacteria from the water," Garner said.

"Then what do we do with the algae?" Carol pressed.

"I don't know yet," Garner admitted. "But at least the sponge idea works."

"In theory. In the lab."

"Carol, we're trying. We're making progress. Trust me, remember?"

"Based on bathymetry alone, PATRIC gave us a number of possible sources," Junko said. "Brock wants to curtail the search of all candidates and start with one, the Thebes Deep."

"I've never heard of it," Carol said.

"That's exactly why I think we should start there," Garner said. "There's a reason no one's heard of it, and I think that reason may have sprung a radioactive leak."

"You're sure about this?"

"No," Garner said. "But it's the best educated guess we've got."

Zubov poked his head into the infirmary, relieved to see that his friends had returned. "Educated guessing, huh? I hope you're not looking to matriculate using Medusa."

"No luck?" Garner asked.

"Short of stripping off all the metal and rebuilding her from scratch, no way. She can still sample what she was designed to, but forget about getting any more rad levels from the water."

"She's done her duty," Garner said. "Medusa's already given us enough data to suggest some possible sources using PATRIC. We can start using the model as our nose, and see where it takes us. Looks like we head on through Fury and Hecla Strait into the Gulf of Boothia—the model says it's our best bet."

"And if the model is wrong?"

"We make a better model," Garner shrugged.

"That's what I was afraid of," Zubov grunted.

"What do we have to do next?" Carol asked.

"We head for Thebes Deep," Garner said. "I'll go up to the bridge and tell them to head west. Depending on the ice cover, we should be through the strait by tomorrow at the latest."

As Junko remained in the infirmary, Zubov returned to assist Byrnes on deck. Momentarily alone in the corridor, Carol turned to Garner.

"I don't like this," she said. "The closer we get to the source . . ."

"I know."

"I can't allow what happened to Susan—and Jeff and Tony—to happen to anyone else."

"I know that too."

"So please tell me that you're really, really sure this will all work out fine."

"I can't do that. Not yet."

"Brock—"

There it was again, the pleading in her eyes, the trust that stirred so many emotions not quite forgotten. She was looking for a promise he could not yet provide, but maybe her faith was enough to push him through to a solution.

He took her shoulders in his hands and looked deeply into her eyes.

"Everything will work out fine," he said. "I promise."

It was what they both wanted to hear, at least. Now it was up to him to make that promise a reality.

The *Phoenix* cruised almost directly west throughout the night, passing easily through the fields of broken ice that drifted across its path as it rounded the northern fringe of Melville Peninsula. Garner and Zubov spent most of this time working on Medusa, stripping off the burned-out gamma spectrometers and restoring the device's original hardware. After midnight, they deployed the sampler from the *Phoenix*'s A-frame and collected some updated data on the plankton populations in the narrow conduit of Fury and Hecla Strait. At last, exhausted, the men retired to their cabins.

By the time they were roused, the sun had risen high above the horizon and the Gulf of Boothia stretched before the ship. To the west, the landform of Boothia Peninsula rose out of the water, an abrupt profile cutting through the surface of the sea.

They were ten nautical miles from the southeastern end of Thebes Deep when Garner spotted something moving above the horizon directly in front of them. It was not approaching or retreating, but apparently engaged in some kind of search-and-traverse flight plan parallel to the track of the *Phoenix*.

Zubov and Junko joined him at the rail. "It's too small to be an airplane," Zubov mused, studying the object through a pair of binoculars. "At least, too small to be a *piloted* airplane."

Junko took the binoculars from Zubov and followed his gaze. "It's a flying dosimeter," she said finally. "Remote controlled. Used to track the dispersal of radionuclides through the atmosphere. In fact, they are often used in parallel with programs like PATRIC for modeling purposes."

"Cool," Zubov whistled. "Why don't we have one of those?"

"I doubt even the Nolan Group could afford it," Junko said.

"How about Global Oil?" Garner asked. He had spotted the Global emblem on the mechanical silhouette of an oil rig dead ahead. "Big enough budget there?"

"Maybe bigger than theirs too," Junko replied. "I'm thinking Pentagon proportions."

"Interesting." It was Garner's turn with the binoculars. "But they're operating it for a reason. They've got to be looking for the same thing we are."

"Why would something like an oil rig even be equipped for this?" Junko asked. "It doesn't make sense."

"No, it doesn't. Unless it isn't really Global doing the surveying." Garner trained the field glasses on the massive platform. Below the rig and barely visible against the massive bulk of the GBS, he focused on the low profile of a nuclear submarine.

"Six-sixty-six," Garner said as he read the sub's hull number. "The *Hawkbill*."

"Should we know that?" Zubov asked.

"She's a U.S. nuclear attack sub," Garner explained. "Refitted with the latest in cartographic equipment and used to carry civilian researchers up here."

"To do what?" Junko asked.

"Ordinarily, to draw the best maps of the Arctic seafloor ever created and collect reams of data on the ice. In this case, I have no idea. They could just be stopping in for coffee, or they could be assisting the rig's crew with some surveying."

"Using a flying dosimeter?" Zubov sounded unconvinced.

"Something's up, all right," Garner agreed. "If the Canadian Coast Guard knows about this, I'm wondering why they didn't tell us."

"And if they *don't* know about this, then somone's got some explaining to do," Zubov remarked.

"We should let them know we're here," Junko suggested.

"I'm surprised they haven't already done that very thing," Garner replied. "The *Hawkbill* should have heard us coming before we even came over the horizon."

"If the Global rig didn't want us to identify ourselves, the *Hawkbill* certainly would," Zubov suggested.

"Unless they're already expecting us," Garner countered. "We could have just stumbled into our own welcome party."

As if in response, the walkie-talkie on Garner's hip crackled. It was Frisch, patching through a call from the *Phoenix*'s radio room.

A clipped voice, immediately recognizable as Scott Krail, greeted him through the tiny speaker. Garner and Zubov exchanged looks of stunned surprise.

"Good morning, Commander," Krail said cheerfully. "I'm glad you could join us. We've got ourselves a little situation here and I hope you're just the man who can help."

16

The *Phoenix* approached to within half a mile of Global *B-82,* where it was met by a motorized launch dispatched by the oil rig. The most obvious feature about the two men who picked up Garner, Carol, and Junko was that neither of them was wearing a protective suit. As the boat turned in a wide arc back toward *B-82,* its wake broke the mirror-calm surface of the dark blue sea.

"We're having a little problem with environmental radiation," Garner shouted to the launch's pilot over the roar of the outboard motor. "Maybe you've heard something about it."

"They say we're fine here," the helmsman replied curtly. He was an ensign, young and rigid and focused only on the task at hand. He was only in as much danger as his commanding officer had told him, something Garner still found unnerving even after his own experience in the Navy.

"Not anymore." Garner cocked his head back

toward the *Phoenix*. "That's a twelve-thousand-ton radioactive sink. Every inch of her outside surface is hot from the water we've just passed through."

"Commander Krail didn't see that as an issue," the other escort said.

"Krail doesn't know what we know," Garner countered.

"You'll have to take that up with Commander Krail."

Company men following orders. But whose orders, exactly? Perhaps even more disconcerting, the advice they were following appeared to be sound. Why had the radioactive slick suddenly disappeared? According to the PATRIC plot, B-82 should be right on top of one of the most likely places for the leak, yet apparently, no radiation had been detected here—at least not enough to warrant protective measures. That made things all the more puzzling. If the *Phoenix* was only chasing a mirage, as everyone from the Nuclear Regulatory Commission to the Navy had suggested, then what was Krail suddenly doing here with the *Hawkbill*? He had practically laughed Garner out of his office in Arlington, yet he had surreptitiously taken Carol's concerns seriously enough to commandeer the *Hawkbill*, and do so fast enough to beat the *Phoenix* to the scene. That kind of mobilization suggested a tremendous amount of panic and enough political clout to grease the keels of naval mobilization, if there ever was such a thing.

Now here they were, one happy group, ostensibly united in the exploration of this mysterious leak, but the radiation was the only thing that was now absent.

Yes, Garner had several questions for Scott Krail.

With his tanned skin and crisp, pressed uniform, Krail looked more like the social director of a cruise ship than the commander of a military operation. This appearance was all the more pronounced by the greasy surroundings of the rig and the obvious disparity between Krail's men and *B-82*'s working crew.

"What are you doing here, Scott?" Garner demanded before he was even off the launch.

"Just rolling out the welcome mat for an old friend." Krail smiled. "What's your pleasure?"

"My pleasure is to know—"

"Tell you what: Let's talk about it upstairs," Krail said, cutting Garner off. He briefly introduced Charon and Stimson, then turned and led the contingent up to the topsides. They were ushered into a claustrophobic conference room someone referred to as the tank.

"We're soundproofed here," Krail explained, "so we can stop pretending you're just a research ship that happened to be in the neighborhood. Good to see you, Brock. Sooner than expected, but still, reassuring."

"Then answer my question," Garner said tersely. "What are you doing here? You could have told us something about this before and saved us all a lot of work."

"Not true, buddy. Most of the NRO satellite data we've been tracking began to come in only after you came through Arlington."

"You said there wasn't a chance in hell of anything up here being military-related," Garner snapped.

"I lied, Brock," Krail said matter-of-factly. "Sometimes it's part of my job. And to be honest, at the time we spoke, I didn't have confirmation of the size and nature of the problem, so I couldn't know what Carol's group had found. Since then we've been comparing the satellite data to your results and compiling a plot of possible scenarios."

"Then you've been monitoring our communications," Carol said.

Krail nodded without a trace of embarrassment.

"Echelon has been tracking all your communications and data transmissions. We've had our own nuclear specialists looking them over. But we're missing the most essential part—the data from Medusa and your on board radiometers."

There was nothing especially cryptic or covert about Medusa's treatment of data, but they were transmitted from beneath the sea's surface through a fiber-optic cable. The rest was simply stored on board the device and downloaded directly to a computer. Echelon, the global-surveillance satellite network for monitoring electronic communications signals, was most adept at capturing messages sent via satellites or regular telephone lines. The system had been developed under the purview that it be used only on international communications, but in the corridors of Nav Intell, everyone knew the attraction of monitoring "potential domestic threats" was far too great to be ignored; it simply had yet to be properly legislated.

"What do you mean, 'pretending' we're a research ship?" Junko asked. "Doesn't everyone on the platform *know* why we're here? Haven't you briefed them?"

"In addition to its specified drilling operations, *B-82* is a surveillance and listening post for the Central Arctic," Krail explained. "That's confidential information, and to give you an idea *how* confidential, only about a quarter of the men on this rig know anything about its military association, much less its specific activities. They're rotated in on three-week tours and the crew foremen make certain they keep to the task at hand, which is exactly what it appears to be: drilling oil."

Zubov shook his head in amazement. "What in the hell could a listening post on top of an oil rig hope to hear? Except the drillhead, that is."

"That's not the half of it," Krail explained. "The hydrophones are laid out across the seafloor from the hub, the rig's GBS. Then we have a communications hub that uses shielded cables and satellite relays."

"And it's all paid for by the profits from the oil," Garner surmised.

"We're justifying our existence," Krail said with a slight smirk. "Exactly as Congress mandated. If the CIA can operate brothels and the FBI can run casinos, we can do this. Even in peacetime, the military has to provide a service to the public in order to keep the ax off its budget. For the sake of high technology, most of these men—"

"—Most of my men don't mind being seen as gas jockeys," Charon finished. He was tired of having to sit through another of Krail's open-door discussions about his (formerly) top-secret facility.

"All in the name of God and country," Krail smiled back.

"No, all in the name of *me*," Charon corrected him with a fiery glint in his eyes. "God and the President are just my VPs in charge of production." If the visitors to the tank were mildly taken aback by Charon's arrogance, Stimson took the remark in stride. He knew that his boss, in his own mind, meant every word of it.

Krail was less accommodating. "Then I'll let you all get back to your business just as soon as my situational authority here is complete," he said to Charon.

Like the rest of the newcomers, Junko was impressed with Krail's revelation but could not yet make sense of it. "Hydrophones, caches of oil, the Cold War. James Bond stuff. I don't see how this relates to Thebes Deep, much less a leak of nuclear weapons waste."

"Me either," Carol admitted. "You seem proud of your toys, but I don't see how it includes us."

Garner watched Krail as he smugly related B-82's capabilities and secret history in tantalizing bits and pieces. But there was something insincere about Krail's confidence. If Krail's team was missing Medusa's data, then they had little or no information about the composition or concentration of radionuclides in the slick—but this didn't explain their apparent lack of concern for contamination in the vicinity of *B-82*. Even the *Phoenix*'s handheld radiometers had shown a remarkable decline in the radiation levels around the ship since they left the bottleneck of Fury and Hecla Strait. According to Krail, the radio-controlled dosimeter, flown in increasingly wider circles, was also showing little atmospheric radiation and virtually nothing above normal background levels. Krail was nervous, and with good reason: an atomic genie was out of its bottle and no one knew exactly where it was.

It had been days since they were last able to use Medusa to directly monitor the radioactivity of the water column, and it was possible that they had completely lost track of the leak. Then again, if they were very close to the source, the leaking isotopes could still be trapped in the bottom water, next to the sediment and out of reach of their surface instruments in any regard. Dredging the sediment was an option they had previously not needed to consider, since the radiation had been confined to the water column. Here, the bottom was too deep and too hard to contemplate dredging any significant amounts of sediment. This uncertainty was, in part, what led PATRIC to produce multiple, indeterminate sources for the leak.

So far, their most reliable method had been to follow the scent upstream. Medusa's short but valiant survey was what had brought the *Phoenix* here; Krail's group was using satellite data. Neither method gave any clue as to what the source of the radioactivity could be or precisely where it was.

"Answer the question, Scott," Garner said again. Krail's cagey attitude was beginning to wear on him as well. "What's with this 'tank,' what's with the *Hawkbill*, and what *exactly* is down there?"

Krail did not flinch. Charon and Stimson were clearly apprehensive about what he would say, but they knew that time had run out on keeping *B-82*'s mission a secret.

"Three hundred feet below us is the lip of Thebes Deep," Krail began. "Another six hundred feet below that, give or take, is the bottom of the trench, which branches extensively into an elongated canyon running northwest to southeast. About two nautical miles in that direction"—he pointed approximately northwest— "is where *Scorpion* went down."

"*Scorpion* was a Soviet nuclear submarine that sank here in the mid-1980s," Zubov explained to Junko.

"And you think that's the source of the radiation?" Junko looked doubtful. "I'd be very surprised if that's true. The amount and composition of the isotopes we've seen would suggest otherwise. Not to mention the passage of time—it doesn't jibe at all with the timeline we've been developing."

"We know that," Krail said patiently. "In some ways, *Scorpion* is very much responsible for us being here—all of us, including *B-82*. But no, it is not her reactors or weapons that are the problem." He looked at Garner. "Remember I told you one of her compact transmutation reactors had been salvaged? The other was never found and was assumed destroyed or buried by landslides. Even if that reactor was undamaged and kept chugging away on the seafloor for the past two decades, it wouldn't produce a slick the size of what you've found."

"You mean there's a *second* rad source down there?" Carol asked.

Krail shook his head and paused as he drew from his coffee cup. "Not exactly. *Scorpion*'s sinking wasn't the real problem for us. In fact, the salvage operation provided us with more intelligence about the Soviets' sub-building capabilities than we ever had before. The problem was that she could penetrate Thebes Deep without our knowing it and begin snooping. Check the charts—even a magnetic compass is useless for navigation out there."

"Were you worried the Soviets could station hidden submarines here within striking distance of the U.S.?" Junko offered.

Krail almost chuckled. "With the advent of ICBMs, the Soviet subs were practically within striking distance of the U.S. while still in their slips."

"Then why?" Carol asked. "Besides the proximity to North American landfall, who'd care about protecting a hole in the ground?"

"Unless it's part of our defense system," Garner suddenly proposed.

"There you go," Krail said. "No shitting you, Brock."

"*B-82* was set up as some kind of gatekeeper, but a gatekeeper for what? Not the wreck of *Scorpion,* this far away. And not as a passive listening post—you have SOSUS for that." The others could almost see the tumblers in Garner's mind turning over. "There *is* something else down there, and it's leaking. Something man-made, but not a sub. Judging by the isotope signatures Junko has developed, that means it's either a silo or a waste dump. Stop me when I'm getting warm, Scott."

"You're red hot," Krail admitted.

"Since a silo or a weapons arsenal wouldn't be built inside a weak-kneed canyon, let alone allowed to leak, I'm guessing nuclear waste. Weapons waste."

"Like I said," Krail nodded. "There's no shitting you." He looked over at Charon and Stimson. "See that? For the record, I didn't have to tell him anything. The smart bastard figured it out all on his own."

Krail cleared his throat and continued. He had relayed this information before, to far more sensitive and powerful audiences. Now, it seemed, what once had been a matter of the highest national security was little more than a dusty embarrassment.

"With the development of the A-bomb during World War II, the world—okay, the United States—began to search for high-grade deposits of uranium. As you probably know, virtually all rock and soil on earth have at least some amount of natural uranium. But the really good stuff—the kind needed for making pure compounds for plutonium development—was believed to exist only in the Congo, in Czechoslovakia, and in northern Canada. Czechoslovakia was obviously out, and the Congo was too far from home. That left the Eldorado mine at Great Bear Lake and other sites like it here in the Arctic.

"Now it all seems trite, but in the heat of the moment, the whole damn-the-torpedoes mentality to get the bomb built, anything seemed possible. Hell, even the things that didn't seem possible were given gambling money. Radium was going for twenty-five thousand dollars per *gram*. The United States knew there were sizable deposits of pitchblende in the Arctic, and pitchblende means uranium. They also knew the Arctic was a little too close to the Soviet Union to leave it entirely unchecked. Everyone knows about the Manhattan Project now, but back then, it was only one branch of America's nuclear advancement program. The Naval Ordnance Laboratory operated several speculative ventures of its own, and at least one of those was operated as a joint effort with the Russians. The Manhattan Project had fuel reclamation sites at Hanford and Oak Ridge—today they also have South Carolina and Idaho, but back then there were only two approved military dump sites. Hanford alone took on ten thousand tons of radioactive waste—the question became, how could we hide just as much waste generated from other secret projects, many of which were going on outside the continental United States?"

"You find a remote trench and hope it's deep enough to contain the evidence," Garner said.

"Exactly," Krail said. "Eventually, Los Alamos won the race to the bomb and the NOL projects were halted. They picked the Thebes Deep from a list of possible dump sites and rolled barrel after barrel of atomic waste into it until all the evidence was gone."

"Were they *nuts*?" Carol said. She couldn't believe what Krail was admitting. "What about undersea earthquakes? What about leaks?"

"Yes, it was a risk," Krail admitted. "A massive geological survey of the site was carried out and it was determined that the benefits outweighed the risks. Depth, low bottom-water circulation, natural caverns and clay deposits, and—most important—a whole bunch of nothing in every direction. The military conducted seismic tests on the seafloor, then drilled a laundry chute into bedrock an eighth of a mile deep *years* before industry technology caught up to them. The geologists told them that if the seabed moved, or slumped, or collapsed, it would only bury the waste cribs further.

"To answer your next question," Krail continued, "I don't know the number or position of the barrels, the size of each barrel, or what was in the damn things: Whoever filled that hole wasn't taking stock for Tiffany's. They built a concrete plug over the opening, brushed off their hands, and waited for eternity to arrive."

"But there wasn't anything like B-82 here," Carol said. "What did they use for a sentry?"

"There wasn't a perceived need for one," Krail answered. "With the coming of the space race and satellite technology, the U.S. didn't want anything to mark this area. There was kind of an unspoken trust with the

Russians, even during the height of the Cold War—anything to do with the NOL nuclear projects was off-limits."

"They didn't need it," Garner speculated. "The development work with the Naval Ordnance Laboratory was probably enough to get Russia's own nuclear development programs moving long before that."

"They still need uranium," Krail countered. "Or plutonium. And there's plenty of both down there. Even if *Scorpion* was only in the area by coincidence, it was enough of a message that the waste site needed a full-time guardian. You have to run the numbers a couple of times, and squint, but *B-82* really is cheaper than a long-term defense operation with submarines, ships, or satellites. No alternate arrangements, short of an Adopt-an-Iceberg program, generate their own revenue."

"Even if it is in Canadian waters," Carol muttered to Junko. "A nuclear-free zone. Which, as far as they know, it is."

"Would you rather see this material dumped in international waters?" Krail challenged.

"I'd rather see it not dumped at all!" Carol shot back.

"At three hundred meters, it's too shallow to be a long-residence dump site in anyone's backyard," Junko said. "The current specifications say twelve hundred meters."

"The current specifications didn't exist in the forties," Krail said tightly. The last thing he wanted to get into was the rationale of a fifty-year-old decision. "Christ, they sat people out on *lawn chairs* to watch the Trinity testing. They thought they could block it with sunscreen—that's how much they knew about the danger. This godforsaken hole in the ground was as high tech as it got in those days—the specifications called for four levels of containment and geological stability for one thousand years."

"*Four* levels of containment?" Junko interjected. "I count three: the pit itself, the barrels, and possibly a stabilizing compound like cement or glass inside the barrels—assuming they thought of that. So what's the fourth level?"

"Beats me," Krail said. "I wasn't even born when all this went on. All I have are some classified government memos to go by, and those aren't noted for meticulous detail."

"The reports mentioned a bug that was supposed to be a natural barrier to leaks," Charon offered, in the first hint of cooperation Krail had witnessed. "Some kind of bacteria." Garner and Junko exchanged an excited look and asked Charon if the name *Thiobacillus* was familiar; he said it wasn't. "But I do remember a couple of reports I was shown that mentioned bacteria as a containment layer."

"They might have inoculated the barrels, or simply poured the *Thiobacillus* on top of them," Junko speculated. "At least that explains how the bacterium got into the slick."

"And our search ends here," Carol said. "There's no way anything but the pit is responsible for the leak."

"Do you still have those reports?" Garner asked Charon.

"Hell no," Charon replied. "That was fifteen years ago at least, when *B-82* was still on the drawing board and we were doing the site survey. The reports were older than I am. They probably wound up in the attic of some long-dead admiral."

"I still can't see the need for all this paranoia," Carol said, waving her arm around her. "A multibillion-dollar facility just to guard some second-rate bomb waste? These days, who would even want it?"

"No one, we hope. But fissionable products are never a safe bet," Krail replied. "The nuclear age in the eighties was not what it was in the forties. Today is different again. Because of the terrorist threat, waste sites no longer reprocess nuclear fuel to separate plutonium, but the pit below us has reprocessed waste in abundance. It was always assumed that stealing plutonium, or producing it from uranium milled on land, was far easier, cheaper, and likelier than any attempt to break into an unguarded waste dump. Only the U.S. knew about the Thebes facility, and we believed only we had the technology to attempt any kind of recovery."

"Do they?" Carol asked. "Do the Russians even have any submarines left?"

"It's not a two-player game anymore," Krail said. "These days we don't know who the enemy is. There are all these little high-tech factions springing up around the globe. Forget James Bond stuff—the Chinese took half our technology from Los Alamos and posted it on the Internet! Waste sites aren't regulated or inventoried nearly as much as live weapons. Sellafield is missing some plutonium. The Marshall Islands are missing some too. And the rest of our potential enemies have money to bribe whoever has the right technology. Sure, they're still more apt to use traditional means, but the reasoning on B-82 has always been, If it isn't broken, don't fix it."

"But now it's broken," Garner finished.

"It seems it is," Krail said, showing his first trace of discomfort. "And we don't know where, or why. We're still sorting through the seismic records taken by the rig crew. It could be a landslide, or even an earthquake. The canyon is extremely branched, and locating a given epicenter is not an easy task."

"You say you've checked the opening to the pit—the 'plug'?" Garner asked.

"Of course," Krail answered. "First thing. It was intact. Then we moved up the main trench to *Scorpion*'s location. Nothing."

Nothing. The word hung in the silent room.
Eventually, everyone's gaze turned to Garner.

They gathered in another of *B-82*'s secured areas, the
communications van, which included a mainframe
computer for the resident Echelon routers and recording devices for practically anything that moved on, under, or above *B-82*. This extensive database included
detailed seismic charts of any movement along Thebes
Deep, its time, intensity, and, as closely as could be determined amid the convoluted folds of compressed
basalt, its precise location.

"We'll need charts too," Garner said to Krail and
Charon. "Coast Guard, Navy, USGS, NRO, DFO,
SASS—*all* of them. If it describes anything about the
bathymetry down there, I want to see it. The time for
secrets has passed."

"The time for national security hasn't, Commander
Garner," Charon countered.

"We can't keep the right hand unaware of what the
left hand knows," Garner said. "It seems to me that's
what started this problem in the first place."

The rig's surveillance officers complied with Garner's
request while Krail retrieved his charts from the
Hawkbill. The resulting morass of chart paper buried
the room's conference table, but Garner was convinced
that a solution resided within the geological, hydrographic, and atmospheric data laid out before them.

Garner and Krail began with the latest NRO satellite
data, which described the radioactive disturbance as
originating roughly north of *Scorpion*'s location,
then trailing out to the east and passing south of Baffin
Island. The information from NOAA's high-latitude
weather satellite confirmed that the prevailing winds were
pushing the slick along with the surface currents. The
swath described by the infrared projection showed that

the highest levels of radiation passed in almost a direct line through Victor Tablinivik's coastal hunting grounds on Melville Peninsula and the cruise track of the *Sverdrup Explorer*. Then, as Garner had predicted, the slick continued east, dangerously close to the south-flowing currents that would carry the radiation into the northwest Atlantic.

With this information, Garner had Krail send the radio-controlled dosimeter up over the westernmost point of radiation noted by the satellites. The data from the flying instrument were downloaded to Junko's PATRIC projection, and, within hours, they had narrowed the most likely source of the radiation to an area of less than ten square miles. Even better, they now had a finite set of coordinates to compare with Krail's enhanced charts of Thebes Deep.

The charts' resolution diminished farther away from the locations of *B-82* or *Scorpion,* but between the submarine salvage operation and the construction of the oil rig, a remarkably detailed map of deep-water currents had been derived. This information was now used to trace the path of the leaked radioactivity through the canyon, then over the lip of Thebes Deep and into the bottom circulation of the Arctic Ocean.

The *Hawkbill* continued its survey of the north end of the canyon to locate the highest levels of radiation. At the same time, the submarine's electronics rendered a detailed, up-to-the-minute plot of the fault's dimensions in the vicinity of the leak. The survey was expected to take most of the following twenty-four hours, so Carol and Junko returned to the *Phoenix* for some much-needed sleep. Garner and Zubov bunked in one of the rig's guest rooms, then returned to Charon and Krail to begin discussing the best ways to seal the leak.

"I still don't understand it," Krail said, regarding the map of the canyon for the hundredth time. "How the hell can the waste crib—here—be emitting radiation into the current *here*?" He slid his finger along the chart. "There must be five miles between them."

"Second-guessing seafloor slumps and subsea quakes is about as reliable as predicting the weather," Garner said. "If the military was able to find one natural cavern for their dump site, there's probably an entire network of them down there. The collapse of any large spaces would cause new fissures to open up. Between the masses of denser rock, the radiation seeps along the point of least resistance until it breaches the seafloor."

"But *miles*? Through the basin itself?" Krail asked.

"Unlikely, all right," Garner agreed. "But unless there's a *third* rad source down there you're not telling us about, that's exactly what happened. The plug is intact and there's no leakage here, because the waste seeped north and into a bottom current drawing it out to the east."

Charon was even more impressed by Garner's conclusions. "It slipped out the back door." He looked at the chart once more and the distance between the expected source and the actual source. "I'll be goddamned. Who would have thought to look there?" He was visibly pissed off.

Krail smiled in spite of his fatigue and cocked his head at Garner. "He did. Just now. Weren't you paying attention?"

"So we've really got two problems," Charon continued. "First, we have to collapse the canyon wherever it's leaking and hope the demolition does its job."

"I can get us anything we need," Krail said. "Enough explosives to backfill the Grand Canyon, if need be."

"Then, with the source of the radiation cut off, we have to pick up the slick and try to contain it," Charon continued.

"That's where the *Ulva* sponge comes in," Garner said. "We can draw the radioactive bacteria into the algae attached to the ice, then corral the ice in a safe location until we figure out what to do with it."

"Assuming *that* works, then all we have to do is collect the contaminated algae," Krail concluded

"Yeah," Garner muttered. "Somehow." As long as the menace was still in the water, it had the potential to kill. Removing it from the water would be the most challenging step of all.

The discussion lasted until midnight. Charon focused on every word like a bird of prey watching a prospective meal. Satisfied with his own evaluation of the proposed plan, he retired to his cabin. There he stripped to his underwear and T-shirt, dropped his hands to the deck, lifted his feet onto the edge of his desk, and began doing inclined push-ups. He continued in this way, his arms steadily pistoning up and down at exactly twenty reps per minute until sweat beaded his forehead and his face turned an angry red.

His every thought was focused on the plan proposed by Krail and revised by Garner. It was more than audacious, it was dangerous. Even if the charges were placed meticulously, with full knowledge of the geological foundation, there were a million chances for things to go wrong. In burying this supposed "back door," a dozen more openings might be created. If a single charge was placed wrong or haphazardly, nothing might happen, or the entire wall of the canyon could be brought down, taking *B-82* with it.

That *B-82* could be damaged must be a constant consideration in their plan.

That the destruction must be complete was Charon's consideration alone.

Charon finished his push-ups and stood up. Toweling himself dry, his eyes flicked to the angry scar that curled up the inside of his thigh, terminating at the base of his penis where his testicles had once been. His only war wound. Charon well remembered his own cautious optimism when his troops had returned from their unquestionable victory (just ask CNN) in the Persian Gulf. Though they had bombed the enemy into oblivion and ferreted out every bunker and weapons nest, Charon still had nightmares about what the victory might really have cost his men. Nightmares about exactly what invisible biological or chemical horrors they might have brought back to the States on the soles of their dusty boots.

Even before the term "Gulf War syndrome" was bandied about, something had begun slowly killing Charon and his men, and whatever it was had likely been administered by their own military. Independent medical consultants first suspected the anthrax vaccines and insect repellents that had been dispensed by the truckload. Then they suspected the depleted uranium used to harden ordnance and armor. The culprit turned out to be the most benevolent source of all: squalene, an extract of shark liver oil, with which U.S. Special Forces troops were inoculated to help promote blood clotting of large wounds.

By the time Charon felt the first discomfort in his loins, his wife was already pregnant with twins, their first and only children, though the horribly twisted and malformed beasts she had birthed could hardly be called children. The biological monsters lived less than a month, casting a dark pall over his marriage. Succumbing to overwhelming depression, his wife took her own life with a single shot from Charon's service revolver. Had he known what was yet to come, Charon would have hardly believed that his personal horrors were just beginning. The ravenous cancer that devoured his testicles came the following summer. Then came the late-night phone calls from his men, or their widows, and the unanswerable question: why had their own military done this to them?

Charon was hardly a sentimental man, but the nightmares still came. Certainly his unblemished service career in covert operations had moved him to the top of the selection list of commanders for *B-82,* even if he wanted nothing more to do with the military. He had expertise in demolition, petroleum geology, and even deep-sea salvage that brought him to the top of a very short list. Besides that, the military had learned to work extra hard to buy the support or the forgiveness of its most afflicted veterans. To take the post on *B-82,* Charon retired from "active" duty and took on the guise of a Global crew chief—one who knew how to keep a secret, particularly where orders were concerned. Orders he liked were followed to the letter; orders he didn't like were subject to interpretation. When the latter category began to outweigh the former, Charon found himself increasingly in the position of a mercenary, using his wits and experience to benefit whoever could pay him. Who was right or wrong never seemed to enter into his consideration anymore.

Charon had dedicated his life to the performance of duty with no fixed address. He liked to keep it that way. He had signed onto *B-82* because he had been asked and remained because it gave him leverage. He still had a mission and he had a country to protect, and it was no one's goddamn business which country that was.

After many long seasons in charge of the floating marvel of exploration that was *B-82,* Charon had discovered only that he was incapable of forgiveness.

17

The warmth of the sun made the snow increasingly dis-
agreeable beneath Victor's boots. His *komatik* jerked
on the end of its rope harness across the large soft spots
between the patches of wind-polished snow. The slush
only added to his fatigue and lessened his sporadic
progress. His stubborn support of the traditional way
had never seemed more foolish. His back ached. His
hands were worn raw. The thick calluses on his feet
burned. And he had lost yet another tooth. It was all he
could do to keep his sled, half filled with a disappoint-
ing catch, moving generally northwest toward his village. It was hardly unusual for a day or two of warmer
springtime weather to make the snow melt, but these
prolonged, elevated temperatures were another thing al-
together. Growing up, Victor had experienced maybe
two spring seasons this warm, but now they were becoming commonplace.

The sea ice usually provided the shortest distance to
anywhere, but now Victor found he had to double back

dozens of times and stay closer to land. Ice he had crossed only days before was now faulted and weak with great chunks calved from the shore and drifting freely on the black ocean. Even the strongest snow bridges—the perennial migratory paths of the Inuit hunters—had grown dangerously fragile. Thoughts of drowning were never far from Victor's mind. One ill-placed step and he could plunge into the icy sea—*komatik*, dog, and all. Janey was an adroit swimmer, when she had to be, but the sled and its paltry load of fish would sink straight to the bottom. Victor would be not far behind it as his heavy garments filled with bitter cold water and the salvation of the surrounding ice pack merely broke away under his weight. They said the sensation of drowning was a surprisingly pleasant one, but surely not as pleasant as surviving.

Victor had walked nearly continuously for six days after leaving the *Phoenix*, the residue from the *qablunaq* food sitting heavily in his gut. Yet even had he known his route paralleled that of the ship, he would not have asked for a ride. They had their hunt and he had his. But he secretly prized the rock from Elephant Island given to him by the *qablunaq* named Garner. Yes, it was just a stone and the true distance to Elephant Island meant little to Victor. But a gift from a stranger, especially a *qablunaq*, was rare indeed. Victor had kept the souvenir in his pocket, as cherished as any talisman.

The hunter and his dog reached their destination just after dawn on the seventh day. Victor topped the final ridge of ice with a grunt and squinted ahead with grim satisfaction. Home. Quiet and still—strangely still even at this hour—the buildings slept against the snow without even a trace of smoke or a warm glow from the indoor lamps. Unfailingly located after two hundred miles through this limitless bleak splendor with nothing but the sky and the land to guide him.

Victor stopped to catch his breath, but only for a

moment. The longer he stood, the more firmly the wet snow would soak his boots and freeze to the runners of his sled. Too much pride would make him heavy. It had been difficult, it had been unprofitable, but *Kannakapfaluk* had guided Victor back to his home and that was all that ever mattered. He had been allowed to hunt among the polar bears, to visit the *qablunaq* as an ambassador, to have this little adventure, then to return home to share his fantastic tales with the others. In that instant Victor realized how much he missed this desolate oasis and he found the strength to push his legs through the final yards. He thanked the spirits, then he thanked both his ancestors and his descendants, for nothing happened without their combined efforts.

The settlement was little more than a cluster of two dozen prefabricated shelters in the drifted snow. Victor's house was plain, a two-room particle-board box hung on aluminum studs and stocked with second-hand furniture, but it would seem like a palace compared to the tents and snowhouses he had built for himself over the past weeks. Even among the settlement's humble inhabitants, the buildings were considered to be more of an outpost—a construction of little meaning beyond reliable shelter from the wind providing enough commerce to be taxed by the government. A ridiculous excuse for quelling the nomadic lifestyle of the Inuit and teasing them with the trappings of the *qablunaq* world of which they wanted nothing.

The coastline here was ideal for kayaks and nearby was a river that had once spilled over with fish. Now Victor's settlement was a familiar place for Anika and the other wives to sew and for the men between jobs to drink and to listen to the CBC's *Hockey Night in Canada* on Saturdays. A campsite close enough to chase the caribou herds with snowmobiles or hunt seals on the shore with rifles. A sturdy place for the women to raise the children—at least, until they were old enough to see the need to leave—then the colleges in Manitoba or Saskatchewan lured them away, never to return. Some of the younger Inuit called that the age of common sense.

Far from the age of common sense herself, Janey sank up to her belly in a nearby drift, then bounded from spot to spot until she extricated herself, her up-curled tail waggling like a sprung coil. Had the other dogs in the village seen this display of indignity, they might have teased her mercilessly.

In that moment, Victor realized he probably knew more about animal behavior than that of his own son. Worse, he probably would have reprimanded Annu for exhibiting the same kind of undignified behavior—the unpardonable sin of a child being childish, for which Victor's own father had scolded him several times. Certainly, though the sensation was strange in its sudden prominence, Victor missed his family. He always missed them on the hunt, but, as he grew older, he appreciated them a little more with each return. He thought of Anika and wondered whether the spirits had taken her *lewkeemeeah* back into the sea. Like a hunter, sometimes it could go away and sometimes it did not come back. Sometimes *Kannakapfaluk* took away the pain and to any Inuk that was a blessing.

Victor trudged forward, his attention more on the rope harness he had fastened around his torso than on the path ahead of him. He had approached to within a quarter mile of his village before he saw the *qablunaq* vehicles parked beyond the darkened and lifeless structures. He saw the four-wheel-drive trucks of the Canadian Armed Forces and a large snow tractor—vehicles for *qablunaq* war. Moments later he saw the *qablunaq* troops in their insulated fatigues and furry caps moving from building to building, putting padlocks on the doors. Approaching closer still, Victor saw their guns. He saw them smoking cigarettes as they spoke to one another but he recognized none of them. As an experienced and practiced Inuit hunter with an unfailing knowledge of the land, Victor's skills were highly valued by the *qablunaq* law enforcers. From time to time Victor served proudly with the Canadian Rangers, a paramilitary group that garnered the respect of even the most jaundiced Inuk. Maybe the soldiers were here looking for men to help with a poacher or a rescue.

Then Victor saw a row of gray flannel blankets flapping listlessly in the cold, dry wind. Without looking further he knew those blankets covered the bodies of his family and neighbors. The hunter knew too well how any animal, even such an awkward one as man, adopted a certain innate reverence when faced with the death of its own kind.

By tradition, the Inuit would lay their dead beneath piles of stones, since burial in the permafrost was so difficult. The deceased would have their possessions set around them for use in the afterlife, and would sometimes be surrounded by a circle of ceremonial stones known as an *ilovgak*. As Victor approached closer still, he could see that the bodies were not set in intended graves but merely placed here temporarily like drying fish.

He dropped his ropes and continued forward without his sled, the realization of what he witnessed making his legs feel like lead. An Inuk is not afraid of death, but he is afraid of the dead. Mistreated in death, the spirits of the dead could return to exact revenge. So Victor kept walking, dreading the thought of what lay beneath those blankets, if only because he could not imagine anything more vengeful than this.

Standing among the soldiers was a lone woman with

a small child clutching the hem of her snowsuit. Victor knew the woman as Marie, a government social worker from Iqaluit. She looked as though she had been crying the entire way. Then he saw the DIAND doctor who came to the village every two months to take their blood—the one who had told them of Anika's *lewkeemeeah*. Marie and the doctor were talking to a uniformed *qablunaq* who seemed to be in charge of the standing around.

From the west, a snowmobile approached. The driver was his neighbor, Eddie, a broken Inuk who no longer hunted anything but government checks and alcohol. As Eddie altered his course and drove over to Victor, he looked like he had been recently successful at both. Victor had never liked Eddie. Even in a culture that once encouraged spousal exchange and came to accept alcoholism and suicide as practical and inevitable, Eddie stood out as a sad example. It was not Annu but Eddie's son, Victor realized, who now clung to Marie.

"*Qanueppit*?" Victor called out. What's happening?

"Holy shit, eh?" Eddie shouted to Victor, nodding his head toward the village. "Fuckin' army shut us down." He gunned the snowmobile's engine with one last twist of the throttle, then switched it off.

"What happened?" Victor asked. The snowmobile's engine died with a cloud of blue smoke in the silent air. He spoke in Inuktitut, giving them some privacy and challenging Eddie to be an Inuk. Dignified. It didn't work.

"They tol' me there's radiation in the water," Eddie replied. "And the food. And the goddamn houses, eh?" Eddie coughed an ugly cough and spat a bolus of yellow phlegm into the snow.

"But what *happened*?" Victor pressed. There had always been some sort of bacteria. Mercury. PCBs.

Toxins ten to a hundred times the levels the government called "healthy" and none of it originating within a thousand miles of this place. Sickness fell here within the snow, poisoned mothers' milk, and clung to the surface of the ice. But even this had never produced a line of gray blankets in the middle of the road.

"Out there." Eddie nodded to the nearby coastline. "They're tryin' to keep it quiet in front of us 'stupid Eskimos'—like we're gonna hire a lawyer or somethin'—but I heard 'em talkin' about a spill out there, drifting by us. They're gonna quarantine the whole fuckin' coast."

Victor thought about this. The *qablunaq* on the big red ship had been talking about spilled radiation and their planned route would have taken them north of the peninsula in the past few days. They told him he was sick from it too, but not sick enough for a blanket in the road.

"You're lucky then, huh?" Eddie challenged him. "The radiation killed them all while you were out playing Nanook." Victor didn't know if it was the anger of envy or disdain for his stupid luck, his convenient absence when the deadly water washed over their land, but he had seen the sneer on Eddie's flat face before.

"What about you?" Victor asked the flat face who had survived to spit and grin at him.

"I was over in Pelly Bay with my kid until last night," Eddie said. Eddie's wife had died several years earlier and Marie had taken a motherly interest in the boy since then. "Marie was already here an' the soldier boys came by helicopter a coupla hours later. The three of us is all that's left," he added, meaning the two Inuit men and the boy. "Holy shit, eh? Not much screwin' to be had this weekend."

Victor said nothing. He stepped around Eddie's machine and continued trudging toward his house. Marie and the uniformed *qablunaq* saw him and walked out to meet him, Marie hugging her arms. Seeing Victor, she began to cry again.

Marie and the soldiers told Victor not to worry. They escorted him into town, past his dark house to one of the other shacks that had been converted to a field hospital. Two other men from the village, they explained, were still missing. It was assumed they had gone hunting. Victor thought that was a bad assumption but he said nothing.

Marie, the doctor, and all the *qablunaq* who looked at Victor wore hoods, gloves, and breathing masks. Victor had to find humanness in their faces by studying only their eyes. They asked him to strip to the waist and the DIAND doctor listened to him breathe. They took his blood and told him to piss in a cup. They stuck a sticky plastic swab up his nose, just like Dr. Junko had done. He turned to the head soldier and started to relay the story of the scientists on the big ship, but the soldier cut him off and said "we know." The soldier sounded annoyed that he might need more blankets. He had no interest in what Victor knew, even as a Ranger. That was the most deflating of all.

They wanted him to wear a respirator but Victor refused. They wanted him to sign a medical release, but he refused that too. They confiscated his meager catch of fish and told him it was probably contaminated. They took blood from Janey, then tied her up outside. Then they gave him some cold tea and iodine and some tablets that tasted like chalk, but denied his request for *muktuk,* the flavorful skin of the beluga whale. Only when they had finished poking and probing did they take him to see his dead wife and son and then told him he was lucky: while he was out walking, those who had stayed had grown sick from a sudden flood of radiation and died from the exposure. Walking, they called it.

Not hunting—*walking*. Even Marie, born and raised on the peninsula, didn't see the purpose in Victor's travels. He felt like a ghost already.

They told him a helicopter was coming in the morning to take him, Eddie, and Eddie's son down to Churchill. They said there was no more outpost here and that the army would be dismantling the buildings. Then they left him alone in his shack and told him to get some sleep.

Victor sat there for a long time, ignoring the lifetime of family mementos all around him, his clothing half removed as he prepared for bed. Across the road, he heard the *qablunaq*—those who had not taken the snow machine back to wherever they were stationed—retiring for the night. He heard Eddie yelling in the next shack and the sound of Eddie's son crying and thought what a miserable trip it would be on that helicopter to Churchill.

Then there was nothing but silence and darkness. Victor dressed again and sat quietly by the door as he might by a seal hole. He waited until he was sure of the silence, then he gathered up his belongings and stepped out into the night.

A single floodlight had been erected by the *qablunaq* to illuminate the central part of the village but there was no sentry. The twenty-seven gray blankets lay unattended in the road, out of the wind. Victor approached them, peeling back the corner to reveal six dogs, several of his friends—all of his friends—and, eventually, Anika and Annu. He knelt close to them, studied their faces. Their skin was very dry, and reddish in places, but they looked peaceful enough to be sleeping. Their spirits had gone and Victor believed that was a good thing. He kissed them good-bye.

It is said that an Inuit hunter never cries. It is, at worst, a sign of weakness and, at best, pointless self-pity. Suddenly Victor felt as though he had been crying his entire life, but no one had ever seen or heard him. He had cried when his sister died, cried when his parents died. Now he cried for Anika and Annu and for all his past losses as well. He cried until his well of tears had run dry and all that remained of his pain was a tight, angry ball in the pit of his stomach.

Then he stood and gathered his tools, an Inuk once again. He retrieved Janey from behind the hospital. The dog looked up, nuzzled Victor as he untied her, but she did not bark. She trotted at his heels as he passed the sheds of snoring *qablunaq* and retrieved his sled, now abandoned and empty after the soldiers' inspection. Finally, he headed north, out of the village and past the reach of the floodlight and beyond the sound of the generators. In the night sky he located a trio of stars, part of a familiar constellation. The white man called them the Belt of Orion, but the Inuit believed the stars represented three lost seal hunters. They followed only each other, but at least they did so in a straight line.

Victor walked, ignoring the stiffness and fatigue in his limbs and the dampness in his clothes. The snow was still weak but partially refrozen, firm enough under his boots and far less treacherous than the southern route. He and Janey would travel nonstop until dawn, then see where that left them.

There was time enough for one last trip onto the ice. One last foolish hunt. With *Kannakapfaluk* guiding him, Victor, too, would soon find a better place.

18

Garner stood on *B-82*'s helideck, looking out over the water and watching the sun struggle into another Arctic spring day. Despite the persistent chill of the wind, it felt good to be outside without a radiation suit. On the deck of the *Phoenix,* still moored a half mile away, he could see a handful of Carol's crew clambering over the deck, wearing their leaded protection against the cooked external surfaces of the ship. Beyond the *Phoenix,* what the radioactive slick was doing was anyone's guess. Garner hoped, against any common sense, for the spill to display some kind of predictable behavior.

He, Zubov, Krail, and Charon had huddled in the communications van long into the night, weighing their options and studying the latest data coming in from the *Hawkbill*'s radiometers. By midnight, they finally narrowed the most likely location of the seafloor leak to three possible positions within a mile and a half of each other.

Later, Garner tried to snatch a few hours of shut-eye. Sleep eventually came, though only after he fended off a flurry of calculations and contingencies that swirled in his mind. By dawn the first details of a plausible containment operation were beginning to come together. Properly prepared or not, the plan was in motion and now it was their collective task to keep the machinery moving forward.

The same could not be said for *B-82* itself. Below, Charon had the wellhead stopped and called an all-hands meeting of the Global crew. The result was an unnatural silence throughout the structure as it squatted on its steel haunches in the weak daylight. What Charon could possibly be telling his men that would make sense of all this was anyone's guess.

Zubov stepped up onto the helideck. "Contemplating Sophocles by sunrise, Commander?" he asked.

"With all due respect to Albert the geologist, tell me we haven't found the 'Plague of Thebes' down there," Garner mused. "A plague of plutonium—itself named after Pluto, Roman god of the underworld, as you may know. Patron of the earth and all its dead."

Zubov shook his head. "Where do you get the time to do all this reading?"

"Clean living," Garner replied with a wry smile.

"Pretty quiet around here without the dynamic duo trading shots, huh?" he mused, meaning Krail and Charon.

"You don't trust them either?"

"Are you kidding? They're like a couple of rabid weasels thrown together in a shoebox," Zubov snorted, then dropped his voice as if their conversation was being overheard, which it most likely was. "So what's the deal here? If Krail is representing the long arm of the law and they're really freaked about this, then why isn't half the Arctic fleet up here, not to mention the Canadian Coast Guard? Why are they willing to let the *Phoenix* into the game at all?"

"You heard Krail. We've got the data."

"We're willing guinea pigs, more like it," Zubov muttered.

"Would you rather have them take what we know and use it without our supervision?"

"Of course not."

"Me neither, so just hold on for the ride. Like it or not, they still need us. They need the information that Medusa collected and they want to know exactly what we know. We're worth more to them than any two dozen support ships the Navy could provide, and we're a lot less conspicuous."

"A ship of opportunity? A decoy?"

"Probably both," Garner admitted. "But you might have guessed that when we were plucked from the *Lansing*."

"Doesn't mean I have to like it. My patsy suit is still at the cleaners from our last 'favor.' "

From the south, a dull thudding could be heard, growing louder in the quiet air. Garner raised his binoculars and identified a U.S. Navy Sikorsky slowly approaching. The helicopter dangled a harness from its broad underbelly, from which hung a pallet of stout yellow canisters—containers packed with explosive, probably C-4. Farther away the *Rushmore,* a big, hulking Navy landing ship even larger than the *Phoenix,* could be seen making its way toward them through the fractured surface ice. Stowed beneath a thick tarpaulin and strapped to the deck of the *Rushmore* was a large package about the size of a small bus—or a sub. Garner correctly guessed that this was the advanced-prototype ASDS—Advanced SEAL Delivery System—Krail had requested to assist the Sea Sprite. A platoon from SEAL Team Two, experts in cold-water operations, was also on its way. Clearly, Krail was increasingly comfortable exercising his "situational authority."

"There's your answer." Garner nodded toward the *Rushmore*. "We're not the only patsies anymore. It looks like we're finally going to get some help."

"I wish I could believe that," Zubov said. "It just means more chiefs to screw us out of moderation and into some kind of commando mission. The dedicated scientists find the problem, then get stampeded by the warhawks once again."

"Not necessarily," Garner mused. "As long as we keep that in mind, it's less likely to happen. Not much reassurance, but it's all we can control."

Demolition supplies continued to arrive aboard Navy ships for the rest of the day and well into the evening. Near dusk, the Global *Voyager* arrived to begin offloading the oil stored in *B-82*'s 1.2-million-barrel fuel reservoir. As Charon continued to debrief his crew, Krail, Garner, and Zubov compared notes in the communications van. The latest sonar plots and bathymetric charts from the *Hawkbill* were truly astounding. The location immediately around the leak, or leaks—a craggy, hanging valley at the north end of a fault system they had come to call the Devil's Finger—was defined and rendered in increasingly striking detail with each passing hour. Significantly, the thinner and weaker areas of the ocean floor were illustrated with enough resolution to suggest the best locations to plant the C-4 canisters. As the helicopter returned to its ship for pallet after pallet of explosives, Krail gave the pilot the best position to deposit the canisters as the SEAL platoon went to work in the submersibles.

"Global has given us the use of their icebreaker, the Global *Vagabond*, sister ship of the *Voyager*," Krail explained to Garner. "I've also got the Canadians' *North Sea*, the largest icebreaker I could get on short notice.

The *Rushmore*'s got the new ASDS, which we'll use with the Sea Sprite and *B-82*'s JIM suits to place the explosive."

"What's in those canisters?" Garner asked.

"C-4, mostly, according to Charon," Krail said. "Packaged by the SEALs on the trip up. They prefer to work with the same explosives across the board, but I think under the circumstances they had to scrounge some TNT and HBX as well." Developed by the British during World War I, HBX explosive was still used in modern weapons, notably torpedoes. "The divers will set up two different arrays of charges," Krail continued. "The first set—the C-4—will be used to fracture the rock on the canyon wall. The second—an array of ammonium-nitrate cratering charges—will be set to move around the debris that's left."

Garner let out a low whistle. "How long will it take to place all that?"

"The charge delivery shouldn't take more than twelve hours, then we can wire the arrays together with primacord and hook them up to an electronic trigger."

"Not acoustical detonation, or a timer?"

Krail shrugged. "Charon says he doesn't like them, especially with so many charges so close together. The bastard's got a high enough potential for short-circuiting without my questioning his area of expertise."

"I've got to hand it to you, Scott," Garner said. "When you get mobilized, you do it in a big way."

"I could say the same thing about you. It's easier for me—I've got the toys and the authority to use them." *Authority,* Garner noted, continued to be Krail's word of choice.

Charon entered the van just then, shaking the cold out of his limbs. Zubov was a step behind, closing the door as they entered.

"The crew's been briefed," he said. "They'll have the shop closed no later than oh-nine-hundred tomorrow."

"What's the script?" Krail asked.

"Two-week shutdown for structural inspection. Mandatory R and R for all nonessential personnel," Charon said, meaning the Global workers. The shutdown in production would end up costing Global Oil Corporation about three million dollars a day in lost revenue. "I'm supervising the loading of the *Voyager* from the fuel cells in the GBS myself—should be done by morning. Then Global will supervise the transfer of the oil from here back to port."

"We're going to need your ice-wrangling equipment," Garner said. He was referring to the myriad of devices that the rigs had available to deflect the ice from possibly destructive collision with the GBS—everything from water cannons to reinforced seines, Kevlar rigging, and kegs of dynamite.

"No way," Charon said. "If this activity sends some of the pack our way, I'll need it to protect the GBS."

"Then how about some of Global's other wrangling equipment?"

"Maybe. The *Vagabond* will have some on board and I can ask the boatswain on the *Voyager.*"

"I'll need three ships' worth."

Charon thought this was funny. "Who the fuck are you? Christopher Columbus?"

Garner showed Charon the diagrams he had made of the proposed *Ulva* sponge. "We'll use three ships with icebreaking potential—the *Phoenix,* the *Vagabond,* and the *North Sea.* The *Phoenix* is already cooked, so she'll mark a course down the inside of the slick with the *Vagabond* and the *North Sea* flanking her. Stretched out from the *Phoenix* on either side I'll want a set of nets and ice slings. The ice will be scooped into the nets and the *Ulva* seeded onto the ice by bombing and spraying. The three

ships will then move along the length of the slick, several
times if necessary, until the radionuclides are stripped from
the water."

"You're joking," Charon said, looking at Garner's
diagram.

"I wish he was, Commander," Zubov replied. "This
is just the easy part."

"Oh really?" Charon asked. "The wrangling equipment is designed for use by rig support ships, not the
full-sized vessels you'll be using."

"I know." Garner nodded. "We'll be depending
heavily on the ships' captains and Sergei's skills with
winches and rigging. But first we need the SEAL team to
stop the leak."

Charon turned to Krail. "How's that coming?"

"We have the *Hawkbill* guarding the C-4 canisters as
they're brought in. The *North Sea* will dispatch the rest
of the team ahead to meet the *Phoenix*. The men are all
yours at that point. We'll pull back and you can drop
the curtain on the Devil's Finger."

"What's the tonnage?" Charon asked. Krail grabbed
a pocket calculator off the chart table and calculated
the total combined explosive force of both the C-4 and
the cratering charges. Charon glanced at the result and
nodded. "Enough."

"I hope so," Krail said. "As it is, we're gonna trip
every seismometer between here and Tokyo."

There was a knock at the door of the van. Stimson
poked his head inside. "The *Voyager*'s captain wants a
word with you," he nodded at Charon.

"Good to go?" Charon asked Krail.

"Whenever you say so, Commander," Krail agreed.
"Unless there's anything else we'll need from them."

"Wranglers," Zubov suggested. "The human kind."

"Can we take a couple of your ice wranglers?"
Garner asked Charon, referring to the specially trained

crewmen on the rig whose job was to fend the ice from the GBS.

"I've only got five and one's a civilian," Charon said. "You take two and I'm left with only three."

"Three more than us," Zubov said.

"Sergei and Byrnes are good, but they'll need some expertise in setting the apparatus," Garner explained to Charon.

"All right," Charon grumbled. "But I don't want them more than a quick helo ride away from the rig, in case I need them." They agreed to keep the helicopter on *B-82*'s deck for shuttling personnel back and forth over the operations area, then Zubov and Stimson left to arrange the transfer of equipment and personnel to the *Phoenix*.

"Thanks, Matt," Krail said to Charon. "We appreciate your cooperation."

The masked condescension in Krail's comment sparked Charon's anger. "Like I've got a fuckin' choice here, Krail. I'm just trying to protect my charge and get alla you off my deck ASAP." He picked up an armload of SASS plots and left the van.

"What the hell was that about?" Krail muttered, then went back to his charts. " 'Like I got a choice here,' " he said in a fair imitation of Charon. "Like any of us do, asshole."

Garner opened a secured line to the *Phoenix* and radioed the latest information to Carol.

"Charon is giving us some rigging and ice wranglers," he explained. "When the *Vagabond* gets here, she'll follow you and the latest PATRIC plot to the easternmost location of the slick at the surface. The *North Sea* will meet you there, then you can find a suitable floe and yoke up. Once the ships are rigged to the ice, we'll bring in the *Ulva* by water bomber."

"How long is that going to take?"

"Long enough for us to finish plugging the leak."

"Are we going to be able to get enough of the *Ulva*?" she asked.

"Alvarez figures we've got the season on our side. With the breakup of the sea ice, there should be plenty of *Ulva* spores in the surface waters south of Greenland. Once the bombers transplant the *Ulva* to us, it's just a matter of towing the ice through it—mowing the lawn until all the *Thio-uni* is absorbed."

"There's a lot of room for something to go wrong," Carol grumbled. "Even without Murphy's Law."

"Murphy? Never heard of the guy. Use as much ice as you need," Garner continued. "Just as long as it's corralled in some stable location. The buildup of ice leading into Fury and Hecla is ideal, but we'll still need more containment."

"Oil spillage booms, something like that?"

They worked out the approximate latitude and longitude for a potential holding pen for the contaminated ice. It would be difficult getting the booms through the narrow Fury and Hecla Strait, but the land itself provided a natural holding pen too ideal to ignore. "I'll get back to you with details as soon as we have them." Garner smiled as he heard Carol transcribing the information and barking orders to Byrnes and the others aboard the *Phoenix*. "Give 'em hell," he said.

"Dammit, Brock, I hope—"

"Me too," he said. "*B-82* out."

"Whatever," Carol muttered and the call was ended.

"A little slack for a military operation," Krail commented with sudden disdain. With Charon out of earshot, Krail seemed to want to irritate someone else.

Garner retained the calm grin on his face but his eyes flashed at Krail's remark. "Let's keep one thing straight," he said. "We're not here for the military."

"Oh, Christ," Krail said. "Not you too. What is this, Pick on the CO Day?"

"Scott, we're not here to help NOL sweep its mistakes back under the rug. We're here to try to cork the bottle before it starts a chain of events no one will be able to stop."

"Easy, buddy. This isn't a competition. We're all on the same side."

"Really?" Garner said, the tension in his voice rising. "Does Charon know that? Does the Navy? Now the *Phoenix* is involved, a platoon of SEALs, and the Canadian Coast Guard. All in some sort of loose-knit force with no definite leader, despite what you think. That's how miscommunications happen. That's how people get killed."

The smile ebbed from Krail's face as he listened to Garner's accusations. Keeping his voice low, Krail stared directly back at his friend. "I appreciate your concern for Carol's safety, Brock. We're all a little freaked out by this situation, and I believe that's a good thing. It'll keep us sharp. But make no mistake about it, I *am* in charge here. These men have to get my approval to wipe their asses, and each and every single one of them is dedicated to the success of this mission. You are involved because you possess a unique scientific knowledge critical to the success of this mission. Critical, but not irreplaceable. If you have a problem with that, I can make certain that you, Medusa, and the *Phoenix* are commandeered or removed entirely from this operation. Do I make myself clear?"

"For once, yes," Garner replied. There was no point in challenging Krail's assertion. On the contrary, Garner had successfully reminded him that the highly volatile chain of command on *B-82* was being questioned. It might even inspire Krail to keep Charon on a little shorter leash.

Now, with Carol, Zubov, and Junko leading the convoy of icebreakers back toward Baffin Island, Garner wished someone was watching his own back.

At the end of the third watch and another night without sleep, Charon retired to his cabin and pushed himself through another intense regimen of calisthenics. Sweat glistened on his forehead and the veins stood out on the lean, bulging muscles of his arms, legs, and chest. Though his heart rate barely elevated above normal, his anticipation of the events scheduled to unfold over the next few days made him feel like a bull moose awaiting the rut.

The loading of the *Voyager* had nothing to do with it: Stimson had called Charon out of the van expressly so that they could monitor the conversation between Krail and Garner. Garner was right, of course. No single officer could oversee the entirety of the growing operation, which left Charon free to conduct the demolition exactly as he wanted.

The collapse of the canyon had to be successful, but Charon had his own reasons for that. His personal experience gave him reason enough to loathe a venture like *B-82*. Then, as some kind of ironic bonus, an acquaintance in the NSA had introduced him to military interests in India. Advance payments began coming in to a numbered bank account, enough money given with enough sincerity to convince him the foreign concerns were legitimate and they were willing to pay generously for his attention. To reward his pain. With a battery of spy satellites monitoring their land-based nuclear-production activities, the Indians' interest in *B-82*'s destruction was twofold: first, to eliminate the sentry the facility represented over a large cache of uranium and plutonium reserves, and second, to smash a significant hole in the Americans' satellite surveillance capabilities.

The Indian Navy had already purchased several nuclear submarines from the aged Russian arsenal and was actually beginning to think the pit at the bottom of Thebes Deep was a viable location to scavenge bomb ingredients. Let them dream. They didn't have the hardware to do it, they didn't have the divers to do it, but enough time, money, and hatred had a way of changing that. Realistically or not, they also perceived Commander Matt Charon as the one best capable of compromising *B-82*'s activities. As their generous investment in him continued, they had little other choice. Decommissioning the waste facility was as effective as destroying it, but that would never occur as long as *B-82* was generating profits and the fuel deposits below it showed no immediate signs of running out. Charon needed a catastrophic failure of the structure and biding his time wasn't making that need any smaller. By now he had taken far too much money to change his mind. He needed to find a plausible excuse to permanently compromise *B-82* and to find one before the Indians ran out of money or patience or both.

Then, like a reprieve from God Himself, Krail contacted him and started talking about the possible leak. When Krail first announced the news in the tank, he could have picked up the little pissant and kissed him right there in front of everybody. Suddenly, Charon had the absolute best of plausible excuses, and now the Navy was bringing in boatloads of SEALs and equipment to assist him.

No amount of planning could have played more perfectly into Charon's strategic needs. As the walls of the fault folded in from the north—collapsing the Devil's Finger, then progressing southward—the concussion would be amplified by charges Charon himself would place along the length of Thebes Deep. *Scorpion*'s demise had shown such a result was possible, and Charon retained an exhaustive knowledge of the canyon's weak geological foundation from the earliest surveys leading to *B-82*'s construction. A second set of charges at the GBS itself would do the rest of the job, toppling the rig into the new eastern depression in the canyon system.

Stimson and the others would follow Charon's commands to the letter. The rest of the operation would be removed from the area or focused on the Devil's Finger. That left only Krail or Garner in any position to question the movements of the demolition operation. If either of them tried to challenge him, Charon might have to bury him in Thebes Deep as well. Come to think of it, that wasn't such an unattractive option.

I am become Death, destroyer of worlds. Quoting the Upanishad, Robert Oppenheimer had reputedly spoken those words on the eve of the first successful A-bomb tests. The phrase occurred to Charon now as he finished exercising and ran a towel over his close-cropped hair. His body quivered with the strain of his workout and the newfound power he believed he possessed.

"I am become Death, destroyer of worlds," Charon repeated to his reflection in the small mirror above the sink. He smirked. "Cool."

19

The U.S. Navy Sikorsky S-61 lifted off the deck of the *Rushmore* and deposited the platoon of sixteen SEALs Charon had requested on *B-82*'s topsides. As Garner watched, the blunt, humorless special operations men spilled forth from the helicopter and went into the briefing Charon had arranged. As they had done with the contingent from the *Phoenix*, Charon, Stimson, and Krail led their visitors directly to the tank for an in camera debriefing. While there were no longer any civilian employees on the rig, Charon still insisted on taking every precaution against intercepted communications.

Forty-five minutes later, the SEALs exited the tank and divided into three groups. The platoon commander and one diver would follow Krail's command on the *Hawkbill*, eight divers would join Charon on *B-82*, and the remaining six divers would return to the *Rushmore* to prepare the ASDS for deployment. As Krail explained the operation, the smaller, more maneuverable ASDS and Sea Sprite submersibles would use the data generated from the *Hawkbill* to place the C-4 canisters and cratering charges at the bottom of the Devil's Finger. Charon's crew would then take over the wiring of the charge arrays to a central trigger located on the stable platform of *B-82*. Finally, when the all-clear was given, the C-4 would be detonated, followed quickly by the slower-acting cratering charges that would bring the walls of the canyon down on top of the radiation leak and reseal the seafloor.

That afternoon, Charon confirmed that the oil reservoir in *B-82*'s GBS had been offloaded. The gate valves of the offshore loading system were shut down and the platform was secured. Charon assured the rest of the group that there was no possibility of damage due to concussion from the explosives, or the loss of oil from the GBS if the charges produced any pressure effects in the fossil-fuel lenses below. With a measure of chagrin, Garner realized that Global *B-82* was about the only thing within twenty nautical miles of the detonation that was even estimated to be secure when the Devil's Finger was collapsed. Even if all went as planned, the ships and broken floe ice could be tossed around as easily as floating corks. As the seafloor buckled and collapsed there might be any number of catastrophic aftereffects. Large ice floes might break into thousands of uncontrollable pieces as the sea surface heaved up, creating massive wave disturbances.

Garner continually raised these concerns to Krail as the SEAL squads began setting the canisters into place. What worried Garner even more was Krail's focus on the actions of the SEAL platoon to the exclusion of all else—including, perhaps, common sense. Contrary to Garner's more cautious evaluation, Krail apparently wanted the plan to proceed with military expediency and about as much subtlety.

"The C-4 packages are being set into the bottom at an angle," Krail explained. To illustrate, he held up two pencils with their bottom ends angled toward each other like a distended V. "Once they're wired together, they'll be detonated in pairs along the fault, moving north to south. The effect will be like knocking snow off a roof—the seafloor will collapse onto itself. The cratering charges will then backfill the canyon below and bury the fissure where the radiation is entering the bottom current."

"Assuming the charges are buried deep enough to fracture the bedrock in the first place," Garner countered.

"Always *assuming*," Krail said, slightly annoyed. "But it's quicker and more decisive than attempting any kind of dredging or backfilling, even if we had enough sediment to work with."

The most difficult part of setting the charges was pushing them far enough into the sediment that the concussion worked directly upon the bedrock, not sideways into the sediment layer or upward into the water column. Then, once the walls of the canyon were collapsed, the veneer of natural sediment would act as filler around the larger pieces of fractured bedrock. The chances that the radiation would migrate through the sediment—especially the clay-based elements—were practically zero. The radiation seeping in through the bottom of the fault would effectively be cut off from the water flowing over it.

"And you're certain you want to start the chain reaction from north to south? *Toward* the rig?" Garner asked.

"Charon called it, and convinced me to agree. We need the momentum from the shallower end of the canyon to drag the deeper portions with it. Besides, we've got a five-mile distance and a few hundred meters' depth between the blast and the rig."

"Not much for a surface wave to traverse, or a fissure in a fault line, for that matter."

Garner's rational persistence began to irritate Krail. "So what do you suggest? Moving the rig to the south, or tunneling the leak farther north?"

"I'm only suggesting we do this in stages, a few charges at a time."

Krail shook his head. "It'd never work. We might not generate enough force. You know as well as I do, we have to absolutely pulverize the rock or we're just creating a temporary stopgap."

"You can't possibly know exactly how the fault is going to react to that much explosive power."

"That's right. In fact, the only thing I do know is how much C-4 I'm able to set down for this operation. No cement. No trenching. Just a pile of canisters and a few tough bastards to put them in place. I know that if this isn't enough, there ain't any more for us to use on short notice. That being the case, I'm not inclined to be poppin' off charges onesy-twosy until we're all out of ordnance and that wall of rock isn't even dented. This is Charon's area of expertise, and for once, I'm inclined to agree with him."

"I understand, Scott," Garner said. "I just need to know we won't be creating a bigger problem."

"We won't be."

Krail's certainty was as much of a guarantee as Garner could expect under the circumstances. "How long until the last of the charges is in place?" Garner asked.

"Two hours, twenty minutes," Krail said without the need to consult his watch. "After that Charon's men can primacord the detonators together using the JIM suits and the Sea Sprite. The whole array should be in place by the end of today."

"And you're sure you'll have enough force down there?"

"Yes I am."

"All at once?"

"We'll get it, buddy. We'll do whatever it takes to cut off the flow by dusk tomorrow and then you can handle the slick. If you ask me, that's the real problem."

The deadline Krail alluded to had been defined only that morning. The NOAA weather satellites showed a late spring blizzard passing through the area within the next thirty-six to forty-eight hours. In addition to reducing visibility and making the surface operation uncomfortable, the weather would in all likelihood wreak havoc with the wrangling nets deployed by the icebreakers. The current plan was to cut off the source of the leak before the storm hit and move the surface vessels far enough east that they would miss the worst effects of the weather. With the majority of the C-4 canisters already in place, the success of the operation hinged on Charon's group linking the charges for sequential detonation on time.

"What's the estimate from Charon's group?" Garner asked.

"Exactly on time and precisely on budget, of course," Krail said. "He knows what needs to be done, and he also knows we'll be cutting things pretty damn tight, even if he saves us time by walking on water."

"So, given the choice between two unpredictable forces?"

"Between Charon and the storm? My money's on Charon. It has to be."

Convinced that things were as much under control on the oil rig as could be expected, Garner had one of Krail's men take him back over to the *Phoenix*. He wanted to double-check the arrangements Carol's team was making. The Global *Vagabond* was now within two hours of their location. The *North Sea* was making good progress through Fury and Hecla Strait, and agreed to meet the other two vessels north of

Committee Bay, where the radioactive slick merged with the ocean's surface.

Typically, rig crews used towropes or water cannons to deflect the course of surface ice away from the platform. A preferable method used wake wash to push the ice a few degrees in one direction or another to avoid collision. Each of these methods depended upon small, maneuverable boats specially designed for the task, and never was such an exhaustive relocation of the ice required. Given the resources at hand, Zubov and Byrnes tried to achieve the desired results from a fourth method: Kevlar-coated ice nets, which could be stretched around the floating ice like a hammock. On the *Phoenix*'s afterdeck, the two men tried to rig some sort of arrangement that would allow two massive ice seines to be attached to the A-frame on the ship's stern. The winches would not have to reel the nets in—the slack could be taken up by either of the flanking vessels—but the rigging had to prevent undue stress from tearing the lines or pulling them off their spools.

As Garner arrived at the *Phoenix* on the Navy launch, Zubov glanced up. "Don't even ask," he said, raising a large wrench in Garner's direction.

Garner kept walking, entering the *Phoenix*'s superstructure through the last airlock remaining open. He scrubbed down, changed into his indoor clothes, and met with Carol and Junko in the ship's ward room.

"We've got good news and we've got bad news," Carol began. "And the bad is worse than the good is good."

"Let's start with the bad," Garner said.

"There's a Canadian Forces report out of Igloolik that an entire Inuit settlement was exposed to a sudden, severe influx of radiation," Junko said. "A DIAND doctor found them on her regular two-week rounds." She looked as though she was still having difficulty digest-

ing the news, which she was. "There were no survivors."

Garner winced. "Where?"

"Melville Peninsula," Carol said. "Northwest of
where we found the *Balaenoptera*."

"We still haven't been able to determine what they
mean by *sudden* or even *severe*," Junko continued. "So
far it looks to be equal to the worst we found in Foxe
Basin."

"That means the slick has reached at least one popu-
lated area." Garner had studied enough charts by now
to picture the area clearly in his mind's eye. "With luck,
it will keep moving east, offshore and away from anyone else."

Junko looked skeptical. "There are dozens of settlements along that coast," she said. "Scattered, low population, but human lives nonetheless."

"I'm only saying it could be a lot worse," Garner
replied.

Junko retreated. "You're right," she admitted. "It's a
far better scenario than it could be, at least until the
contamination approaches Hudson Bay or the North
Atlantic." She paused, uncertain whether to continue.
"It's just that Melville Peninsula was—is—"

"—Where Victor said his family lived," Garner finished.

"That's right."

"Junko," Carol said. "We all feel bad about Victor's
case."

"But I told him I would *help* him," the doctor explained. "That I would come by the village to look at
his wife and child as soon as possible."

Carol wrapped a sympathetic arm around the petite
doctor. She could identify all too readily with Junko's
frustration.

"'As soon as possible' isn't possible yet," Garner

assured her. "For any of us. Chances are they were already dead by the time Victor stumbled on us. Even if we went directly there, with the correct medical supplies, we might still have found just what the DIAND doctor did."

"There are survivors," Junko said. "Other settlements where it isn't too late."

"We'll get back to them as soon as the slick is contained. All right?"

Junko nodded, accepting the comfort of Garner and Carol.

"At least it gets better," Carol explained. "When the Canadian Forces tried to clean up the incident, they needed the help of the Canadian Coast Guard. Parsons briefed them on our little junket here and the two of them managed to convince Don Szilard in Ottawa that we're not just following some mirage. Szilard agreed to their terms and the upshot of all their bureaucratic tongue wagging is that we now have two additional icebreakers at our disposal: the Canadian Coast Guard vessel *Des Groseilliers* and the CIS *Sovietsky Soyuz*. They're on their way up Foxe Basin right now."

"That is good news," Garner agreed.

"Um-hmm." Carol chewed her lip. "Though it's a bit ironic that we left home with the intent of studying the effect of shipping noise on whales and now we're practically putting on a demolition derby.

"I told them to wait outside Fury and Hecla Strait for further instructions," she went on. "Once we see how, or if, the *Ulva* sponge idea works on a large scale, we can brief them on how to begin cleaning up the front end of the slick and meet us somewhere in the middle."

"Exactly what I'd have said," Garner said with a wink. "Damn, you're efficient. You remind me of my first wife."

"That doesn't surprise me at all," Carol said archly. "You seem to have excellent taste in women."

Zubov tramped into the ward room, Byrnes close behind. "How goes things astern?" Garner asked.

"I think we'll just be able to swing it," Zubov grumbled. "But don't expect it to make the cover of *Better Homes and Rigging*."

"If the setup works, it looks like you'll get the chance to explain it to a CIS icebreaker. The captain's a guy named Kistiakowsky. How's your Russian?"

"About as rusty as most of their navy."

"That's still better than the rest of us."

"Rigging the seines isn't the hard part," Byrnes chimed in. "The hard part will be finding pieces of ice small enough to wrangle but large enough to have some influence on the slick."

"Scott's got all the latest ice cover and movement data from the weather satellites," Garner said. "I'll have him relay it to you and the others, then you can round up the most suitable pieces."

"Maybe a collection of smaller pieces?" Carol offered.

"Yes," Garner agreed. "Easier to manage and a greater surface area for the *Ulva*."

"What are you going to use for seeding the algae?" Zubov asked.

"Martin Mars water bombers," Garner said. "Once you're under way, they'll be skimming the Atlantic south of Greenland to fill their tanks. Alvarez figures that we'll get enough *Ulva* by happenstance to provide a large enough culture."

"The bombers will dump the water, then we'll tow the ice over the slick and hope it takes up the *Ulva* and the *Thio-uni* on the way to the containment area," Carol continued. "Whatever escapes the sponge can be siphoned off the surface and pumped back over the ice."

Garner caught Junko's look of concern. "You look a little dubious of our primitive methods, Doctor."

"Quite the opposite," Junko admitted. "What I've seen in the past forty-eight hours rivals the most fantastic technology I've ever seen."

"A hole in the seafloor is 'fantastic technology'?" Carol asked.

"Considering when it was built, yes," Junko replied. "This supposed arsenal was built in the forties. But subseafloor disposal of nuclear waste wasn't proposed—not seriously, anyway—until the early 1970s."

"And we've been fighting it ever since," Carol said.

"No, that's *seafloor* disposal," Junko corrected her. "Barrels dumped onto the bottom. Or what they did after the tests in the Marshall Islands—forty totally cooked U.S. warships towed back to the States and sunk off the western seaboard close enough to keep an eye on. The worst of the waste is still stored aboveground until it cools enough to allow burial. But with *sub*seafloor disposal, all you need is a pit and as little as ten meters of good clay sediment to provide a natural barrier to the isotopes and prevent corrosion of the barrels. A pity the idea had to be dismissed so quickly."

"Why was it?"

"Well, to hear the stories at the Department of Energy, a calculated effort was made to disregard every potential candidate for a new high-level waste site except the one in Yucca Mountain, Nevada. There, despite an active fault system, a recently vented volcano, and rapidly percolating groundwater, they've spent over fourteen billion dollars planning a waste storage facility tunneled a thousand meters into the rock."

"Sounds like a conspiracy to me," Zubov said. "Congress is using its black project money to build an underground facility for UFOs or faking more moon landings and billing it to the taxpayers as a nuclear waste dump."

"Those may be more laudable purposes than anything they're proposing now," Junko admitted. "Uranium 235 has a half-life of seven hundred million years! What man-made structure can compare to that? Look at the Hanford site: 40 percent of the waste tanks leaked, drip-ping a million gallons of waste into the watershed. Today's containment technology—if you can call it that—isn't much more advanced. Burying waste might work someday, but you'd have to drill down about a mile. The heat of the waste—we're talking about tem-peratures exceeding eight hundred degrees Celsius—would, in theory, melt the surrounding rock and seal the waste away, far below any groundwater. Obviously that isn't an option here, so we're back to burial in the seafloor."

"If the seafloor is such a good disposal site, then why is this one leaking?" Carol asked.

"That's what's got me worried," Junko said. "Not only *that* it's leaking, but *why* it's leaking. No one seems to know what form the waste was in when it was deposited. Let's assume the standard, fifty-five-gallon galvanized barrels, since today's steel-lined concrete tanks weren't available and would be too difficult to de-posit. Let's further assume that the waste wasn't treated—it contains long-lived, highly radioactive fis-sion products and small amounts of plutonium iso-topes. Plutonium is the stuff bombs are made of. If there's plutonium down there and it's leaking in some soluble form, as it clearly is, then we can assume the waste wasn't stabilized by drying and mixing with con-crete, as is done today."

"Unlikely they'd bother hauling that much cement way up here," Zubov agreed.

"So at most they would have added an alkaline base

to the liquid waste, plating out the dissolved residue, but keeping the remainder of the fissionable materials intact." She turned back to the PATRIC plotter, typed in some hypothetical data. "Even Scott doesn't seem to really know how much waste was originally there, but we can reasonably guess how much has leaked by looking at the effluent from the Devil's Finger. An academic exercise, really, because whether it's one barrel or a hundred, there's the same opportunity for rearranging fissionable materials into a critical mass when we add this much energy to whatever's down there. It's all generating heat; that's why high-level wastes need to be stored aboveground, so they can cool."

"You're talking about an uncontrolled nuclear explosion," Garner said.

"Yes, possibly," Junko agreed. "At the very least, corrosion of the drums may have led to a buildup of hydrogen, ammonia, and methane in the repository—a potentially explosive mixture."

Zubov looked at them. "And here I thought all we had to risk was starting a new ice age. Man, Palau is looking better every day."

As with many modern submarines, the sonar room of the *Hawkbill* was positioned forward of the sail, just below the weapons-loading hatch. It was a position very close to the ship's center of balance and far from the noise generated by the engine room and the single seven-bladed propeller. The space was cramped in most standard Sturgeon-class vessels; the *Hawkbill* was even worse, as several additional racks of electronics had been installed to accommodate the enhanced sonar array and other instrumentation.

With funding from the Department of Defense and the National Science Foundation, the forty-two-hundred–ton vessel had been modified to carry researchers into the

Arctic Ocean, which remained among the world's most complex and least understood ocean basins. The most extensive of the *Hawkbill's* modifications was the addition to the outer hull of two SCAMPs—Seafloor Characterization and Mapping Pods. Distinct from the bulbous sonar dome on the bow of the ship and its spherical sonar array, the SCAMP profilers added two additional systems to the *Hawkbill's* sensing array: one that generated a fifty-kilometer swath of bathymetric information about the seafloor, and a second that performed subseafloor profiling of the sediment. The SCAMP arrays had been the most instrumental in detailing the bathymetry of the Devil's Finger and now provided the best locations for the placement of the C-4 charges. A second system, the acoustic Doppler current profiler or ADCP, was used to determine the effect of wind and ocean currents on moving floe ice; these data, in conjunction with the satellite information, would be instrumental to guiding the ships forming the *Ulva* sponge.

Krail conferred with the submarine's sonar operators as the latest bottom profiles were developed by the ship's computers. *Conferred* was a generous term—in fact, Krail nearly snatched the data from the operators as soon as they were acquired and forwarded the information to Charon.

On the seafloor, Charon's men continued placing the C-4 canisters along the lip of the canyon, moving slowly but steadily toward the oil rig in two squads. The first squad consisted of the SEALs, including the crew of the ASDS, who were in charge of taking the canisters from the surface to various strategic positions deep within the Devil's Finger. The second squad was Charon's men from *B-82*, who wired the charges together into a demolition array. The original plan had called for Charon and Stimson to quarterback both units from the communications van on *B-82*, five nautical miles away, but Charon apparently grew frustrated with that arrangement and donned a JIM suit himself. That had been two hours ago. Krail had been so absorbed with the charts, so intent on controlling his own team members, that he had lost track of Charon's exact whereabouts.

Krail got on the radio to both the ASDS and Sea Sprite, asking both submersibles whether they had seen Charon. They hadn't. According to Stimson, back in the communications van, Charon was still down in one of the JIM suits.

"Who is he using for surface support?"

"Commander, the last time I tried to watch Matt's back, I nearly ended up facedown on the deck with a three-day headache."

"I assume the last time he wasn't in charge of wiring a trainload of C-4," Krail snapped back. This motivated Stimson to cycle through the comm links, asking the SEALs who were still submerged where Charon might be. The various answers that came back offered no conclusions.

"Two billion dollars' worth of listening equipment and you can't locate a loudmouth like Charon?" Krail spat. He suspected Charon was listening in on the exchange, had heard every word, but was too absorbed in his work or too resentful of playing by the rules to respond. "Find him. And if you can't find him, get him on the comm link with an update on his status and position."

"Will do, Commander," Stimson said. From his tone, it wouldn't surprise Krail if Stimson chose to forget that pledge before the microphone clicked off.

20

At thirty degrees Fahrenheit and ten atmospheres of pressure, the water column along the lip of the Devil's Finger was desolate but clear and utterly black except for the high-intensity lamps of the demolition team. To the amazement of the youngest and fittest SEALs, encased in the relative luxury of the ASDS and the Sea Sprite, Matt Charon's ceaseless activity and immutable vigilance seemed driven by strength of will alone.

The high-capacity tanks on Charon's pressurized JIM suit had allowed him to stay at depth for nearly the past six hours straight and ten of the previous twelve. In the same amount of time, five different men, including Stimson, had taken a shift in the second JIM suit before it was taken back to *B-82* with a damaged regulator. Before allowing the second suit to be taken away, Charon had insisted its air tanks be scavenged, refilled and removed, then left where he could commandeer them if necessary. He resolved he would not surface again until the task was finished, even if it meant having someone lower another set of air tanks down to him.

Inside the bulbous suit, Charon was insulated from the cold, detached from the fatigue that penetrated every pore of his sweat-soaked skin. He was dimly aware of the suit's bulky resistance to movement as he clambered along the fringe of the Devil's Finger. The slow, steady bottom current tugged at his body, threatening to topple him over, but his mental focus negated any sense of distance traveled. He had by now traversed enough seafloor to equal three crossings of the five-mile distance between *B-82* and the leak. This was an incidental consideration to Charon; it was merely what needed to be done to achieve his objective. If he needed more adrenaline he need only think of the sinister ache in his scrotum that never ceased, and his rage gave him all the energy he needed.

As the underwater operation progressed, Charon positioned himself as the leader of the unit in charge of burying the canisters as well as the one wiring the primacord. Because of the depth involved and the limited availability of practical dive equipment, the SEAL pairs had necessarily taken to working in shifts. There was no question that fatigue came quickly on the long, uneventful trips from the surface, or in wrestling the disagreeably tight joints in the ungainly pressurized suit, yet one mistake while planting the C-4 canisters could also mean immediate death for someone. Several of the younger men tried to mimic Charon's bravado and endurance, offering to stay longer in the ASDS or the Sea Sprite, but Charon warded them off. What they interpreted as concern for their individual safety was merely another aspect of his need for control—as long as no single unit stayed down for too long, the chances that anyone would deduce what he was really up to would be considerably reduced.

As each pallet of canisters was lowered to the bottom, it was Charon's task to designate their placement along the fault line. He could carry no maps with him, only the image of the seismic profiles he had committed to memory. Each time he moved along the lengthwise axis of the trench he had to mentally place himself relative to the bathymetry he knew would help him most. As his lamp passed over each feature on the seafloor, the compass and positioning sensors in his helmet immediately translated his tracks to chart coordinates. Krail noted the progress of the planned array from aboard the *Hawkbill,* relying principally on the information Charon relayed (or did not relay) to him, while Charon himself needed to keep the actual array carefully laid out in his mind's eye.

Once the manipulator arms of the submersibles had burrowed the canisters into position, Charon coordinated the SEAL divers who wired them together. Since the wiring was completed in stages, Charon was the only person who could fully know how the entire array would detonate once the trigger circuit was connected. As far as Krail or any of the men in the submarines could know, the array was being assembled exactly as it had been planned in the communications van. Charon alone knew that when the trigger was activated, the array would produce the expected unexpected result with scientific precision. At a burn rate of twenty-one-thousand feet per second, the shit was going to go down very fast.

What Krail and the others could not possibly know on their piecemeal shifts was that Charon had placed nearly twice the agreed-upon explosive force along the south ridge of the Devil's Finger, the end closest to B-82. The canister teams also had no idea that these southernmost charges were wired to detonate first. The canyon walls would come down as planned, but as only Charon knew, the overload of charges at the south end of the array would generate a domino effect along the

fault line that would course straight through the footprint of *B-82*'s GBS. By the time anyone realized the
detonation had gone awry, the rig would be lost and
Matt Charon would be a wealthy man.

With a little luck, they might even plug the damn
leak too.

"One pallet left," a voice came over his headset. It
was the pilot of the ASDS, which, like the Sea Sprite,
had been fitted with special manipulator arms to guide
the charges to the seafloor. "It's Miller Time,
Commander. Why don't you take a break and let us finish up?" It was at least the sixth time, spurred by similar sentiments from both Krail and Stimson, that the
pilot had reiterated the request.

"One pallet left," Charon echoed, as if that were explanation enough. He had been counting down for fifteen pallets, or seventy-five canisters, each carrying the
destruction potential of twenty HBX torpedoes. He
could wait as long as it took for "one" to become "two-
thirds," "one-third," then "done." It would then remain only for the wiring unit to connect the canisters
into an array that would unite all this brutal explosive
force into a single, massive detonation that would fell
the trench.

"Suit yourself," the pilot's voice came back, just
cheerfully enough to crawl under Charon's skin. "We're
dropping this off and heading for the bar."

"Fine with me. The nearest one's about seven hundred miles to your rear."

The last of the canisters was set into place and activated nearly three hours ahead of schedule, in part because of the SEALs' unparalleled endurance, in part
because of Charon's bullish restrictions on shift
changes. The ASDS crew quickly added the final
charges to the rest of the array, following the wiring
scheme that Charon relayed to them. With the array
set, all that remained was to run the primacord trigger

the length of the fault line, back to the rig, where the
detonation would be dispatched.

"We were gonna stick around and help you with the
spool," the pilot of the ASDS called over to Charon.
"But you probably want to carry it back to the rig yourself." Loaded with primacord, the spool weighed nearly
eight hundred pounds in air, one-sixth of that underwater.

"Why? Don't you ladies think I could?" Charon
said, his relief allowing a trace of humor to slip into his
familiar growl.

"Any doubts of that vanished about four hours ago,
sir," came the pilot's amused reply. "Climb on and we'll
give you a lift."

Charon checked the wrap of the primacord around
the package of mixed explosive, then slowly maneuvered
up and onto the ASDS and checked the primacord's release mechanism on the spool. The three-quarter-inch
line played out smoothly, and Charon tapped his metal
hand on the vessel's hull to indicate the set. The sub's impellers whined to life, easily lifting both the spool and
Charon off the bottom, then glided south toward *B-82*.

The realization that the array was finally set sent a
wave of relief though Charon's body. He closed his
eyes, listening to the chatter coming through the headset: Sea Sprite to Stimson, Stimson to *Rushmore*, the
ASDS to *B-82*, Krail's high-strung baby-sitting from his
sonar-laden nest aboard the *Hawkbill*.

"Chief?" Krail was saying. "Chief? How's it looking?"

Charon awoke from his reverie, if only to prevent
Krail from calling him "Chief" one more time—another
disregard for proper rank. "Give us another hour on
B-82 to complete the trigger. Assuming we get all green
lights on the trigger panel, we'll be ready to blow."

"Excellent, Matt. Excellent." If "Chief" was bad,
"Matt" was worse. Krail seemed to think that as long

as Charon was technically retired from military service, as long as Krail held "situational authority," he could call Charon anything that came to mind.

"Save it for the blow," Charon said. "We're not at the whorehouse yet."

"Yeah, but the neon sign's in view."

Charon closed his eyes again, aware only of the gentle vibration of the hull beneath him and the wire unraveling behind, back into the blackness shrouding his extremely generous gift to his friends in Delhi.

"We haven't had much need for ice wrangling around here because the pack is either frozen year-round, or the current carries it past us, to the north," Stimson explained to Garner as he returned from the *Phoenix*. The two men were now in the communications van, examining the latest ice-cover data from the NOAA satellites. "We still practice it, of course, same as lifeboat and fire drills. But it's a lot easier to do with tugboats and water cannons than what you're proposing with those big-assed ships. Don't they have anything smaller they could use to retrieve some more manageable pieces?"

"They have a hovercraft aboard the *Phoenix*," Garner mused. "I doubt Byrnes would be fond of intentionally running it over the hot ice, but it's worth a shot."

Stimson looked dubious. "What's the horsepower?"

"Beats me, but it's a good-sized vehicle."

"Too bad we can't get a couple of the Navy's hovercrafts up here on short notice," Stimson said.

"I'll talk to Scott and see what he can do."

Garner once again reviewed the uncomfortably narrow margin for error between the position of the C-4 array, the cratering charges, and the footprint of the rig itself. Krail was right. There was no way to physically enlarge this distance for greater safety, so the ripple effects produced within five miles of the detonation site were unavoidable no matter how much explosive force was used.

"It's your house," Garner said, meaning *B-82*. "I just hope we don't huff and puff and blow it all down."

"The GBS itself is designed to withstand six million tons of ice, which the engineers say we'd only get around here once in ten thousand years," Stimson said with pride.

"Well, let's hope this isn't the year," Garner cautioned. "I'd say what we're planning to do in the next few hours throws any engineering specs out the window."

"Agreed. We'll be ready for it. Matt has checked in with Krail on the *Hawkbill*. He's nearly ready, and they expect to get the fireworks started a little early."

This was good news. The weather—more blowing snow than a true blizzard—was still forecast to pass directly over their location before continuing more or less eastward toward the ships performing the containment operation. The key meteorological ingredient was not visibility or wind chill—though these would certainly affect the comfort and safety of the containment crews—but the wind's speed. Sudden strong gusts or erratic whirls could damage or destroy the nets, or, worse, send the slick spinning in a direction radically different than what was anticipated.

The slick, its volume, direction, and degree of radioactivity, was constantly on Garner's mind. A new color-enhanced image from the NRO polar orbit satellite showed the radioactivity as it stretched across the surface to the east of their location. The angry red swath was now nearly thirty miles long and half a mile wide, gliding steadily through the western terminus of Fury and Hecla Strait. Once the leak at the bottom of the Devil's Finger was plugged and the radioactive source cut off, the overall length of the slick would gradually diminish from tail to head, but it would continue to follow the current toward Foxe Basin and, beyond, the North Atlantic. No longer an ice age in the making, but still potentially devastating to the Grand Banks and the eastern seaboard, not to mention the entire fresh water supply for the top of the world. As the *Des Groseilliers* and the *Sovietsky Soyuz* started to control the slick with containment booms, the shape of the menace would change once again, pooling into a rounder, deeper formation that might easily sink below or flood over the booms, especially in rough seas. Once the slick was captured and the *Ulva* and *Thio-uni*-saturated ice pieces were securely corralled, the ice would still have to be neutralized and disposed of as quickly as possible. Garner still hadn't thought of a way they could do this, and it nagged at the back of his mind, a migraine in the making.

Garner picked up the radio and placed a call to the *Phoenix* over a secure channel. Frisch patched him through to Byrnes, and Garner relayed their thoughts on using the hovercraft to help wrangle the ice.

"Dammit. Not my best toy," Byrnes whined. "She's practically still in the box. The last thing I want to do is get her cooked like everything else on this ship."

"We haven't got another choice," Garner said. "There's only so much ice you'll be able to corral between the larger boats. After that, you'll need to push or pull as many smaller pieces as you can into the nets." Unlike the wake pushing employed by tugboats and rig support vessels, the hovercraft rode atop the water on a cushion of air. It would have to push much smaller pieces of ice with its rounded nose, and even then, the craft might simply pop up and over the calf it was trying to wrangle. The pieces selected would have to be very small to be manageable, and that meant collecting a daunting number of them, or dynamiting larger pieces into a more cooperative scale.

"Sergei isn't going to like it," Byrnes warned. "We just got the A-frame rigged, now we'll have to pull it all off to remove the hovercraft from the aft hangar."

"Serg doesn't like anything," Garner assured him. "Besides, it'll be good practice for when he tries to explain the setup to the Soviets. In the meantime, we'll work on getting some Navy hovercrafts up here."

Garner heard Byrnes chuckle. "Sure, why not? Let's haul even more floating iron up here."

Garner agreed. "Either this operation will end up cooking half the U.S. fleet or—"

"Or the polar bears can walk from deck to deck and forget about how contaminated the water is."

"How are your provisions holding out?"

Byrnes quickly checked with Carol, who conferred with Halford in the galley. "Water's fine. Food's a little low."

"Don't tell me—you're down to filet mignon and coq au vin?"

"Those are C-rations in Halford's book." Byrnes laughed. "He says we're practically down to crackers and we may have to start eating Jell-O powder right out of the box."

"Maybe we can scrounge something from *B-82* or the *Rushmore*," Garner said. "They should have something to spare."

"Anything. At least some fruit slices to go with the Jell-O. We can do Jell-O, but *just* Jell-O really sucks."

"I'll see what I can do," Garner promised. He signed off and relayed the latest updates to Krail and Stimson. The next-to-last group of Charon's crew was removed from *B-82*'s topsides and Garner caught a launch with them over to the *Rushmore*.

As the small boat bucked the icy chop, the bracing wind in his face, Garner smiled as he recalled Byrnes's bellyaching about their lack of inspired sustenance.

Just Jell-O really sucks.

Then an idea began to gel.

21

After twenty-five years as a polymer chemist, David MacAdam thought he understood the industrial invention process. As a research-and-development scientist for an international firm, he knew there were always projects under development and few of them ever survived to justify their ravenous appetite for human capital. For those ideas that did take wing, MacAdam was well acquainted with the typical progress to be expected of any intellectual property: anything that he or his colleagues dreamed up, researched, or published was automatically considered the property of the corporation. This was industry standard practice, though it had never sat well with MacAdam. Eventually he admitted aloud what he knew all along: that if he ever wanted to stretch his wings, he would have to become an entrepreneur. There was certainly no chance that Pegasus Chemicals would satisfy his craving for more in his professional life.

That was why—only a dozen years ago, though it

now seemed like a lifetime—MacAdam left Pegasus for the sake of a "prolonged personal sabbatical." His one-car garage was an inadequate replacement for his company lab bench, but he did have full-time effort and enough creative vigor to begin developing a kernel of an idea.

MacAdam called it Plasroc, a high-density, synthetic glaze that might someday be used to contain toxic materials, which were currently processed by sealing them in glass or porcelain inside stainless steel–lined drums or tanks. MacAdam knew the containers were more for the convenience of moving the material than for containment; it was the slurry that actually kept the toxins in check, defined the form of the barrels or ingots poured, and determined whether or not the disintegrating particles—enduring little bastards that they were—would ever get out.

What MacAdam envisioned was a polymer that, when hardened with a specially modified resin, would be thousands of times more effective than existing containment slurries at a fraction of the cost. It would also be much easier to use. Whereas most alternatives required decanting the toxin into a liquid containment that later hardened, Plasroc could be sprayed over any open or enclosed surface before being sealed. In this way, the compound could be used to bond toxins "on the shelf" in barrels or waste tanks or render wastes inert while they remained in the ground, as was necessary for many of the abandoned chemical weapons dumps. There were dozens of alternative containment compounds, of course, but Plasroc had its innate plasticity as its trump card. MacAdam's compound had the ability to immobilize toxic elements where they lay, whether that was in the water column, the ground, or in a proper waste facility. He was certain of this, on paper at least. He only needed to synthesize a trial-sized sample.

Over the next two years, MacAdam's equations became tabletop distillation experiments, then migrated to gigantic vats the size of furnace boilers. When space restrictions and citations from the Adelaide public health office closed him down, he moved his wife and daughter to a farmhouse a hundred miles out into the country where a ramshackle barn served as his Plasroc brewery for the next eighteen months. To MacAdam's delight, Plasroc performed precisely the way he had speculated it would the first time he scribbled some rough calculations on the back of a paper napkin.

Six months later, it seemed as though his timing could not have been better. The perceived threat of chemical or biological terrorism had never been greater and abandoned dump sites of former weapons arsenals were turning up all the time. Nuclear reactors from the former Soviet arsenal were simply dumped into the ocean or were necessarily sent two thousand miles by train for reprocessing at the Mayak Chemical Combine, a tedious, dangerous, and costly enterprise. Then the arrogance of the modern atomic tests by India and Pakistan had rekindled the debate about nuclear weapons development and what to do about their high-level wastes. In one especially absurd proposal, Australia had been asked by the nuclear community to consider being the sole repository of the world's high-level atomic wastes. As a kind of backhanded compliment, it was reasoned that the island continent was one of the few areas on earth that possessed "both the geological and political stability" to confidently locate a massive, enduring waste-processing facility. To anyone who sought to find applied technology as a remedy to these waste disposal problems, Plasroc could easily be heralded as the wisest containment method for the new millennium. And David MacAdam alone held the patent.

Inspired by world events in the daily newspaper to

aggressively market his invention to the highest bidder, MacAdam was decidedly nonplussed by the underwhelming response to his proposal. His wife, Anne, continually assured him that he was simply ahead of his time, though their credit-card agencies and banking representatives could hardly continue to agree. Reluctantly, MacAdam came to realize that when he left Pegasus—which never would have afforded him the latitude to develop Plasroc in-house—he left behind the credibility of an industry association. The three-thousand-square-foot laboratory he had built in his barn, complete with all the steaming vats and wheezing pipes of any mad scientist's abode, did little to promote the potential of what was inside.

Eventually he had to give up his dream, and returned to Pegasus with hat in hand to ask for his job—or any job—back. With Plasroc gobbling up a second, then a third mortgage on their farm, he would have to keep the commute out to the country, much to his teenaged daughter's chagrin. In an especially benevolent gesture, MacAdam even offered Pegasus the Plasroc patent outright, in the hopes that they could use their formidable resources to bring the material to its full potential. It was that promise that kept MacAdam from going utterly out of his mind during the daily three-hour round trip to his new, entry-level job.

Pegasus sat on the patent. And sat. And sat. When a brief economic recession hit Adelaide, MacAdam's job was among the first to be downsized. At the age of fifty-eight, MacAdam agreed to take an early retirement and the return of the undeveloped Plasroc patent as part of his severance package.

Now nearly sixty, MacAdam had all but forgotten about Plasroc. These days, the inventor preferred to spend his time helping to tend his wife's garden. He endured the evil glares of his daughter, who matured slowly, married badly, and continued to consider Plasroc responsible for all the family's misfortunes. He drank as much beer as his ulcerated stomach and his meager pension afforded him and he stewed in his bitterness with full appreciation of the word.

With winter now on the way, there was much work to be done in the garden to harvest whatever they could for canning or sale at the local farmers' market. The massive vats of Plasroc sitting in the barn were still viable—the solutions could be stored for decades, even centuries in separated, inert form—but the brewery was otherwise abandoned. In another week, maybe two, MacAdam thought he would begin calling the scrap dealers to come and make him an offer for the metal. Then again, he'd had that thought every few weeks for the past two years. Anne told him to forget about it—after all, they didn't need the barn for anything else.

As he raked and pulled shoots in the garden, MacAdam's back ached and his head buzzed with a pain threaded by frustration and stitched in granite. All told, Plasroc had cost him twelve years of his life, his stable if uneventful career, his home, his credibility, his daughter's respect, forty pounds on his already bony frame, and 750,000 perfectly good Australian dollars. The only thing it hadn't cost him, it seemed, was the affection and respect of his wife. Some days that was almost enough to balance the ledger. Almost.

From the fifth row of vegetables, MacAdam heard the telephone ring inside the house. A moment later Anne pushed open the screen door and stepped out onto the porch. MacAdam stood and smiled at her. He couldn't help it, for she was always smiling at him first. Despite their rocky path, she had aged gracefully, the sweet, upturned lines at the corner of her mouth forever hopeful that all things would work out for the best.

"Telephone's for you," she called.

"Who's it?"

"A Yank. Says he's calling from the North Pole." With all the frustration and adversity they had endured in the past decade, Anne seemed unwilling to find any surprise in this. A telegram from Father Christmas himself was just another day in the life of David MacAdam, madcap inventor and retired rock builder.

"What's it?"

"He says he needs your magic brew. A lot of it."

"What d'ya mean, 'a lot'?"

"Twelve thousand yards, he says." The corners of Anne's mouth lifted even further, breaking into a full smile.

"Serious?"

"Um-hum. He says he needs it in three days so he can save the world."

MacAdam dropped the rake and began to run.

The odd simplicity of Byrnes's comment stayed with Garner the entire trip back to the *Rushmore*. By the time he had boarded the vessel, he remembered an article he had read about a kind of synthetic rock someone had developed in Australia, a plastic compound that could seal toxic wastes and render them inert for long-term disposal. A chemical slurry that, when properly prepared, could contain environmental menaces like nuclear wastes just like fruit slices suspended in Jell-O.

Garner relayed the sparse information to Carol, who in turn radioed a request back to the librarian at Nolan Group headquarters. Twenty minutes later, Garner had David MacAdam's home telephone number. Half an hour after that, both Garner and MacAdam had a great start on the information they would need to permanently contain the radioactive water.

Talking to MacAdam, Garner quickly realized that the Plasroc was exactly what was needed to complete the cleanup of the contaminated ice. Once the hot ice—with its load of *Thio-uni*–laden algae—was captured in the containment booms, it had nowhere to go. The contamination might be taken out of the water, but as the ice melted, as the algae and bacterial cells died, the harmful isotopes would only seep back into solution. This was the problem of containment that had been bothering Garner since they had left Halifax. Now it seemed like the only possible answer.

As Garner understood it, the main containment solution was a gluey, environmentally inert mass that could be sprayed through industrial-scale fire equipment. A second organic chemical, a sealing resin, was then sprayed onto the first solution and the combination bonded into a high-density compound. So tight was the crystalline structure of the Plasroc that the toxic elements—whether they were bacteria, chemical weapons, or radionuclides—were trapped forever, at least in human terms.

Garner then contacted both the *Hawkbill* and the *Phoenix*. A three-way radio conference was quickly established and he quickly relayed the details of his plan.

"You are out of your freaking mind," Carol said.

"Can you give me a better solution?" Garner asked, grinning at the pun. "Once the leak is stopped, the slick will continue along its present course, to the east-southeast. Then the water bombers will splash the track with the *Ulva* and the *Ulva* can go to work soaking up the contaminated *Thio-uni*."

"Then the *Phoenix, Vagabond,* and *North Sea*, with some help from Byrnes's little runabout, will start mowing the lawn," Zubov added from aboard the *Phoenix*.

"While the *Des Groseilliers* and the *Sovietsky Soyuz* bring the containment booms up from behind," Garner continued. "Meeting MacAdam and his magic gelatin at the western end of Fury and Hecla Strait."

"Like I said: out of your mind," Carol repeated.

"Not at all. The only two things we don't know yet is how much of a delay the storm will cause us, and where the best place to draw the containment booms will be."

"Then we'll need a dredging ship," Krail noted, listening in from the *Hawkbill*.

"We will," Garner agreed.

"It's going to be hard enough to *find* a dredger, much less one we can get up here and operate around all this goddamn ice," Krail muttered.

"I'd also like you and the guys from the U.S. Geological Survey to review the latest sediment profiles you have for the areas east of here."

"What are we looking for?"

"Clay-based sediment, ideally. A hundred tons' worth at a depth where excavation is reasonably possible. That'll be our target. That's where we'll tell the cleanup crews to plan on catching the contaminated ice."

Krail wasn't as confident in this arrangement. "I'll have a look at our profiles for Committee Bay." Lying immediately east of the Gulf of Boothia, Committee Bay bounded Melville Peninsula and would be the last position to capture the slick west of Fury and Hecla Strait. "It's a tall order—the bottom is pretty much solid bedrock in there—but I'll relay the coordinates of any areas that look promising. We may have to go into the strait itself."

"That's getting a little close to Igloolik, don't you think?" Junko quickly pointed out. Igloolik was the largest settlement on the peninsula. After what had happened at Victor's outpost, the doctor's immediate reaction was to quickly avert any further risk of human exposure.

"Once the waste is bound into the Plasroc, it should

be stable enough to bury almost anywhere," Garner tried to assure her.

"And *before* it's stabilized, I say we arrange an evacuation," Junko countered. Even as she voiced this concern, they all realized that any attempt at evacuation at this point would probably be incidental to the radiation already inflicted on the unsuspecting population. She quickly thought of the other settlements on Melville Peninsula—perhaps twenty-five hundred Inuit in total—and added them to the evacuation list.

"Looks like I'll get on that too," Krail said, resignation mixed with sarcasm in his voice. "There goes my lunch break."

"I'll get on the horn to Parsons and the Coast Guard," Carol offered. "Between the Canadian Forces and the RCMP, we should be able to clear a path."

Junko was yet to be convinced. "Will we have enough time for all this?" she asked.

"We'll make time," Garner replied. "The radioactivity won't leave the containment booms until MacAdam says it's inert."

"When can we expect our Aussie friend to arrive?" Zubov asked.

"He asked for a couple of days, plus the travel time to get here."

"There's one more thing we don't know yet," Zubov said. "Whether or not the demolition team will actually stop the leak."

"It'll be tight," Garner admitted. "We can't wait to find out if Charon's demolition works."

"Then let's get MacAdam on his way," Krail said, "regardless of what's waiting for him when he gets here."

"Have Charon's men done their job?" Junko asked. Her concern was less with Charon's competence than with the potential explosive reaction from the waste dump itself.

"They have," Krail said confidently. "We'll be ready to plug the leak within twenty-four hours."

"Then let's focus on that," Garner said. "Because if it doesn't work, finding mud banks will be the least of our worries."

22

As placement of the demolition charges was completed, an eerie calm descended over the corridor between the Devil's Finger and *B-82*. The almost continuous exchange of encrypted human information—bearings, timing, logistic concerns, and good-natured jibes— passing between the divers, the *Hawkbill*, and the *Rushmore* now gave way to the sound of automated machines. As each C-4 canister was activated in the trench, an electronic chirp was sent back to the trigger console on *B-82* to verify the charge was working. The console then sent back an automated timing signal that activated the canister, verified its frequency, and checked its connection to the rest of the detonation array. Finally, an electrical signal was sent along each wire connecting the array, confirming that the trigger signal would be passed through the array in the proper sequence and that there were no power lapses or short circuits.

As each arm of the array was activated, the

corresponding situation lights would illuminate on the trigger console, with a duplicate signal relaying this information to a status board on the *Rushmore*. The lights verified only the status of the canisters, not their actual position on the seafloor. Ordinarily, the precise position of any single canister could be confirmed by triangulation on the device's built-in transmitter, but this exercise was not done, given the large numbers of canisters in close proximity to each other and the limited time available.

Once again clad in the JIM suit, Charon confirmed the subsurface wiring of the trigger console, then rendezvoused with Stimson topside. Charon's crew would set off the detonation from *B-82* while Garner and the rest of the group monitored the status console on the *Rushmore*. Krail agreed to remain on the *Hawkbill* as it was removed from the detonation zone, ready to return to the area as soon as the landslides had subsided. Within hours, the *Hawkbill*'s sensors could tell the others whether the leak had successfully been plugged; what followed from there would be Garner's headache to address.

"How long now?" Krail asked Charon over the headset. "I've got a couple of geologists here ready to wet their pants with anticipation."

"Give me twenty minutes. I'll give the all-clear in fifteen—five minutes to detonation."

Krail signed off and glanced at the two scientists sitting near the sonar console. "Hear that?"

"Sure did," said one of the geologists. He seemed a little irked by Krail's comment about their impatient anticipation. "Though geologists *are* used to dealing with a longer time scale than hours or minutes. We can wait."

"No we can't," the other geologist interjected with a wide grin. "This is going to be freakin' *great*." The sonar operators and geologists on a typical SCICEX cruise had little in the way of excitement to look forward to, save for the regular tedium of their mapping protocol and occasional visits by ringed seals, which apparently mistook active sonar pings for mating calls.

"We've got twenty minutes until all hell breaks loose," Krail said. "Just make sure our ears are ready."

The single most important aspect of Stimson's personality—the thing that earned him the respect of a man like Charon and allowed him to hold a second-in-command position at a post like B-82—was his calm but meticulous attention to detail. Like the best vice presidents, Stimson was an excellent mop-and-bucket man, passing diplomatically behind his boss to ensure that all the crap fell exactly where it was supposed to and, if not, to tactfully deal with the situation as though it had all been in the original plan. After Charon had directed the transfer of more than eight hundred thousand barrels of oil stored in B-82's GBS into the Global *Voyager*, Stimson's main duties had been to make certain the rig was secure and that all but the six men designated as essential personnel were airlifted from the platform. For the most part this had been easy; the Global workers didn't need to be asked twice to take two weeks' leave with pay. Those directly under Charon's surreptitious military command, however, needed a little more persuading. Despite their remote location, these were men trained in the dogged pursuit of the hunt, even if that pursuit involved radio transmissions and satellite relays more often than guns or grenades. They earned their post by volunteering for the missions no one else wanted. The backfilling of Devil's Finger was the biggest thing to come near B-82 since its inauguration, and every single crewman wanted to be a part of the proceedings. The news was not well received when Charon announced that only a half dozen men, including himself and Stimson, would be allowed to stay on the rig. In truth, even that was overstaffing—it only took two men to monitor the trigger console and perhaps two more to briefly oversee the rig's essential functions, especially with the wellhead shut down and the GBS drained of its valuable contents.

In the hours immediately before the detonation, while Charon was wrapping up another marathon shift in the JIM suit, Stimson repeated his systems check of the topsides. He checked the hydraulic systems in triplicate. He checked the safety and emergency equipment. He checked the bleeder valves, the riser shafts, and the status of the OLS pipes snaking across the seafloor. He was about to check the capacity gauges for the three fuel cells in the GBS's reservoir when Charon called him back to the trigger console to check the wiring contacts. Now, with only twenty minutes remaining until the detonation, Stimson suddenly remembered he had never made it back to look at the fuel cells.

The GBS weighed nearly thirteen million tons when empty and perhaps twice that amount with the reservoir filled. The reservoir itself was partitioned into three fuel cells, which in turn surrounded four maintenance shafts, each seventeen meters in diameter and extending from the topsides to the base of the GBS. The trio of fuel cells was monitored from a central control room, and it was from this location that Charon's crew had overseen the transfer of oil from the rig into *Voyager*'s massive storage tanks via the OLS. As Stimson now checked them, all three cells showed secured status and the corresponding capacity gauges showed less than five hundred barrels in each. Ordinarily, Stimson would have been satisfied with this, except one of the gauges seemed to be reading less than zero gallons. He tapped the gauge with his finger, frowning. The tap failed to create even a responsive waver from the needle, suggesting that the gauge itself may have shorted out. A broken gauge should have produced a warning light on the control console, but when Stimson investigated this, he found that the warning circuit's fuse had also apparently shorted out.

Annoyed at the growing runaround, Stimson retrieved a backup fuse and got the warning light to come on, but this only verified that the gauge wasn't working. He quickly unscrewed the gauge from the panel and temporarily replaced it with one from another cell.

As the replacement gauge was attached, its needle came alive, jerking once, then slowly sliding over to the right.

It came to rest at three hundred thousand barrels.

Stimson felt his skin crawl. Three hundred thousand barrels was roughly what each cell contained before the reservoir was bled into the tanker. But it was impossible for the off-loading procedure to overlook one cell, since the design of the system mandated that oil was siphoned from all three cells in concert. This prevented the possibility of an unbalanced load in the GBS that might cause the platform to list or even pivot, despite its massive weight. For a single cell to retain its oil, someone had to go down in the riser shaft and physically isolate it from the OLS—no small task in itself—then cover his actions from the rest of the bleed crew by disabling both the gauge and its backup system. Under regular crew conditions such an act would be impossible, but the past few days had been anything but regular.

Stimson didn't have to speculate any further. That someone had to be Charon.

There were now ten minutes until the detonation.

Stimson caught up to Charon in B-82's dive room. Charon had just climbed out of a JIM suit and was still soaked in sweat. As Stimson entered, Charon was helping one of the remaining four crew to repair the damaged breathing apparatus and regulator of the second suit. The task seemed incredulous to Stimson; surely there were more important duties to be performed at the moment.

Or maybe Charon was planning some kind of escape.

"I just came from the reservoir control room," Stimson said, his heart pounding. "What's going on, Matt? You told me the GBS was dry and sealed before you went down."

Seeing the look in his commander's eyes, Stimson knew immediately that he should have reported the problem with the reservoir to Krail or Garner—anyone—before challenging Charon directly. Stimson's trust in his commander had always been absolute. A part of him wanted to believe that it was just an oversight. That they could delay the detonation, call back the *Voyager,* and drain the overlooked oil. Or perhaps Charon felt the rig was in no danger at all, so an imbalance in the GBS was thought to be within acceptable risk. Stimson wanted to believe these things as he searched for an explanation, but Charon's suddenly murderous expression stopped such speculation cold.

Stimson glanced at the second man, a junior-grade lieutenant. "We've still got oil in the GBS—cell three still has a quarter million barrels in it."

"Oh, Christ." The lieutenant's face paled. "Who dropped the ball on *that*?" The news was clearly a surprise to the man, and for a moment Stimson was relieved to know that any two-against-one confrontation was in his favor.

Stimson returned his eyes to Charon and kept them there. "Do you have your sidearm, Lieutenant? I need you to help me place Commander Charon under arrest." He squared himself in the hatchway, the only exit from the room except for the JIM deployment portal in the deck.

The lieutenant looked down, where a small gear bag evidently contained his pistol. A radio also jutted from the bag and Stimson silently wished he could somehow *will* it into his hand.

Then the standoff was broken. Even Stimson could not believe the speed with which Charon moved. One moment he was standing there, fifteen feet from Stimson and half as many from the lieutenant, the next he was a whirlwind. Charon grabbed the ungainly JIM helmet on its support chain and pushed it into the lieutenant, driving him against the rear wall. Then Charon was down, rolling, grabbing the gear bag as he careened across the deck. Almost before Stimson registered movement, Charon drew the pistol and fired, hitting the lieutenant in the face before he could recover from the swinging helmet. Then Stimson felt a wrenching pain in his leg as Charon's heavy boot lashed out, snapping the knee joint.

Stimson fell to the deck with a yelp, banging his head heavily on the steel plating. Eyes closed, he could feel Charon's legs crushing down on his throat and chest. Then he felt the barrel of the gun, still hot from firing the first round, pressed against his temple.

He opened his eyes, pain flooding up from his lower body. Across the room, the lieutenant lay dead, the heavy JIM helmet still swayed awkwardly on its hoist. The radio lay on the deck several feet away, taunting him.

Still pinned to the deck, Stimson moved his eyes to meet Charon's.

"Why, Matt?" Stimson whispered. *"Why?"*

"Trust me, you wouldn't understand," Charon said.

Then he pulled the trigger.

"Five minutes at my mark," Charon's dispassionate voice came to the *Hawkbill* and the *Rushmore* exactly on time. "Mark."

"Five minutes," Krail relayed to the scientists.

"Not a moment too soon," the *Hawkbill*'s officer of

the boat remarked. "The bad weather's almost on top of us—gusts to fifty knots and cold as a witch's tit."

Krail could easily decipher the severity of the growing storm on the basis of the weather data scrolling through the *Hawkbill*'s computers. Below the surface, however, the atmosphere was as silent and motionless as it was in any weather. They might as easily have been sitting in drydock in San Diego.

"Don't worry about it," Krail said. "Thanks to Macho Man Matt, we're exactly on schedule. It'll all be over before you know it."

Throughout his military career, Scott Krail had cherished these moments—the moments after the forces have been assembled and before the tactical strike, when infinite unlikely possibilities gelled into a unified force, poised to vanquish the enemy. It was a moment of adrenaline and pride, before anything happened, for better or worse, to shatter the silence.

Krail loved this sensation, which he never thought he'd feel again from behind his desk in Arlington. Now, with less than five minutes before the strike was activated, he realized one more thing: he hated that desk.

As the storm arrived over the Gulf of Boothia, a growing fog blanketed the *Rushmore*'s superstructure while curtains of sleet coated the windows with a thin veneer of ice. Inside, the ship was warm and comfortable. Garner watched as each arm of the detonation array was lit up and confirmed, hovering around the demolition array's status console like an expectant father. He was constantly in and out of the ship's radio room, either listening to the communication between the various dive teams or relaying his own instructions to the *Phoenix*. According to Carol, the water bombers were en route and the *Sovietsky Soyuz* and *Des Groseilliers* were ready to deploy the containment booms. Zubov and Byrnes were out in the hovercraft, directing the captains of the *Phoenix, North Sea,* and *Vagabond* as the side-by-side chain of linked vessels scooped mountains of ice into the wrangling nets with a cautious eye toward the storm that would soon pass over their location.

Garner tried to envision the entirety of the massive operation. By day's end, the leak would be stopped and the ice collecting could begin in earnest. With a little more luck, David MacAdam and his Plasroc would arrive in time to continue the containment without any delays in the process that might free the slick from their tenuous grasp. Garner mentally checked and rechecked each of these arrangements, then he tried to speculate on the most likely problems to disrupt the plan.

Electronics failure was as good as any place to start and there were a lot of lights on the status board. What the SEALs seemed to consider routine was unquestionably the largest concentration of raw explosive C-4 Garner had ever seen. Both Krail and Charon had shrugged off the potential for an uncontrolled nuclear reaction as the canisters along the canyon were detonated. Their assurances, however, were based less on safety concerns than on a reluctance to adjust the plan that had already been set in motion. Garner thought again of Krail's enthusiasm for detonating the entire site at once and hoped, were these men to err, that it would be on the side of moderation. However the detonation proceeded, Charon's efforts had been exceptional, and with each passing hour Garner believed the man deserving of some new medal or distinction. He was hard to deal with, cantankerous to the point of being dysfunctional, but they all knew the success of the demolition operation fell directly on his broad shoulders. So far, he had responded to perfection.

The radio was alive again, with Charon prompting status confirmation from the *Hawkbill* and the *Rushmore.*

"*Rushmore* good to go and standing by," Garner relayed to the others.

"*Hawkbill* good to go and standing by," Krail confirmed. "Godspeed, Matt."

"God has nothing to do with this," Charon said. "Detonation in fifteen seconds on my mark . . . Mark."

At exactly 4:20 P.M., Charon pressed the trigger aboard B-82. A single chirp indicated that the signal had been sent in sequence to each C-4 canister.

For the first few seconds, Charon could hear only the sound of his own breathing.

Aboard the *Rushmore,* each light on the status board switched from ACTIVE to FIRED as each C-4 canister was detonated along the canyon. A moment later, the lights corresponding to the array of cratering charges showed that these, too, had fired completely and successfully.

Aboard the *Hawkbill,* Krail and the others could only listen to the proceedings outside. The sonar operators put the sound of the detonation on the sub's intercom system. A muffled *whump* echoed through the ship as each charge was fired, gradually fading away as the detonations moved farther away from the submarine. It was far too soon to know if the detonations had done any good; for now, the awesome power they were listening to was enough to warrant celebration. The *Hawkbill*'s officers shared a knowing wink, as did the geologists and sonar operators—it beat the hell out of listening to the advances of an amorous seal.

The officer of the boat shook Krail's hand. "Congratulations, sir," he said. "The captain wants to know if you also do abandoned buildings and bar mitz-vahs."

Krail smiled but said nothing, his ear cocked to the small speaker in the ceiling. The C-4 explosions had all but ceased; now there came the sound of the landslides created by the collapsed fault—the implosion itself. The seafloor was stirring all along Thebes Deep, not in punctuated explosions, but a slow, grumbling release of energy that suggested something far more powerful than man could ever create.

For the briefest moment, Krail thought of the captain of the ill-fated *Scorpion*. Was this the same sound he and his men had heard before sinking to their deaths? Then his reverie was broken as Garner hailed him from the *Rushmore*. "What the hell is going on, Scott? I thought we were going to take it in stages."

"We are," Krail said.

"Not from here, you're not," Garner replied. "I show all charges fired."

Krail moved quickly forward and confirmed this information with the sonar crew. All the canisters had been fired, leaving them nothing for a second attempt if the first failed.

"Dammit!" Krail yelled, slamming his fist against a bulkhead. *"What the hell is going on out there?"*

Confusion ricocheted between the various segments of the submarine's crew, then Krail barked at them to be quiet. As the crew complied, the room was again filled with the sound of earthquakes, rippling along the length of the Devil's Finger and into Thebes Deep.

"Can we get some kind of trajectory on these aftershocks?" he asked the sonar crew. "A vector on the seismic wave? Something? Anything?"

A moment later, the crew had acquired the data. "Bearing one-zero-three. South-southeast, sir. Toward the *B-82*."

Krail wheeled and ordered the boat brought to periscope depth. "Where's Charon? Get him on the line now!"

It was Garner's voice that answered the call.

"Scott—the rig is blown!" Garner yelled. "One entire side of *B-82* just went up in flames!"

Then came the sound of another muffled explosion, followed by the sound of shredding metal. Krail could only assume this was the collapse of the drilling platform.

"Where the hell is Charon? Did he clear the platform?"

"Negative. Christ, Scott—the whole thing just went up!"

Now Krail had a periscope view of the rig, blazing furiously in the middle of the fog-soaked blizzard.

"You're closest," Krail said. "Move! Do whatever it takes to get someone on that rig."

"On my way," Garner replied. Below his voice came the sound of pandemonium on the *Rushmore* before the connection went dead.

In the dive room of *B-82*, Charon knew he had accomplished his mission just as surely as he knew he was about to die. First the detonation, then the rumbling aftershocks, had shaken the entire structure on its footing. Then came the explosion of the GBS, tearing away at least a third of the structure and throwing the platform into a precarious tilt. Inside the topsides, the concussion from the blast was like a grenade inside a trash can; Charon was thrown to the deck and came up with his ears bleeding.

The communications van, where the trigger console and the bodies of the last three of Charon's men were located, was showered with debris and flaming crude oil. Among the rig's emergency systems was an automated forced-water supply designed to extinguish accidental flare-ups, but, left unattended, it would have little impact on a blaze of this size. As more and more of the topsides was drawn into the inferno, Charon knew he would have to abandon the rig. It had been his plan to leave the rig before the first tremors could travel along the canyon, but he had grossly miscalculated the effect of the C-4. The charges had done their job exactly as planned; Charon had underestimated the recoil effect of the bedrock and the effect of the explosive release of gases trapped in the oil deposits below.

The metal of the disintegrating superstructure screamed and yawned open. Newly molten materials waged war with the blowing snow, releasing sizzling geysers of steam all around him. There was another explosion as he stepped out onto the topsides, and burning oil rained down onto his parka. Rather than beating down the flames, he stripped off his burning clothing and kept moving, down through the structure.

Now it seemed he lacked the luxury of waiting for Krail or the others to arrive. Charon had never intended to use the JIM suit for an escape, but with the safety capsules instantly destroyed, it would serve adequately as a lifeboat. His revised plan was to contain himself inside the thick carbon-fiber carcass until help arrived. He could then claim ignorance of whatever had gone wrong on the rig and blame Stimson and the others, whose bodies would never be found.

It ordinarily took two men and a chain hoist to prepare and deploy a JIM diver. Out of water, the suit alone weighed nearly four hundred pounds. Charon climbed down into the dive room and wrestled the suit from its wall rack, letting it drop onto the deck, then swiveled the crane holding the helmet into position. The tanks for both suits were fully pressurized—

he would *walk* to the *Rushmore* if he had to, then begin lying his ass off until his unemployment insurance kicked in.

He climbed into the fallen suit, then tugged on the massive, dome-shaped helmet. Through its portholes Charon could see the room beginning to flood. Moments ago the room had stood fifty feet above the ocean's surface; now the platform had been so radically bent by the explosion that the deck would soon be underwater. Icy, grease-filled water began to pour into the suit as Charon's fingers struggled to find the collar locks. Within seconds the suit would become a fluid-filled casket.

Paralyzing fatigue began to claim him. His arms seemed to be moving slower, losing ground against the coming flood. Worse, his brain began to fog from the effects of hypothermia as he lay immersed in the water, only a few feet from the sanctuary of the deployment portal. He tried to crawl over to the hole in the deck in his ungainly, four-hundred-pound carapace.

The lights went out around him and the room was plunged into darkness.

Charon wondered if it was all in his imagination.

"No goddamn way am I going up in this weather." Roger Tibbits, the designated pilot for the *Rushmore*'s helicopter, stood before Garner with his arms crossed. His eyes narrowed beneath a boyish shock of unruly red hair. "I'm just not that keen on dying today, Commander."

"Neither am I," Garner assured him. "But I have to get a team onto the rig to stabilize it and check for any leaking oil. We can't take a launch over there while the whole thing could topple over onto us."

"And you think flying over it is any safer?" Tibbits scoffed.

"I don't think flying over *anything* is safe but we

don't have a choice," Garner insisted. "Meet you on deck in five minutes. That's an order." However accurate under the circumstances, the words *that's an order* felt alien to Garner even as he uttered them.

"Thanks for acknowledging my concerns, *sir,*" Tibbits called back to Garner as he turned and headed off down the corridor.

The Sikorsky was in the air less than fifteen minutes later with Tibbits, his copilot Brian Dunlop, Garner, and a squad of eight SEALs equipped to locate and treat the rig's survivors. The helicopter rocked and whined as it rose into the snowstorm, but the hands of the pilots were steady on the controls.

From an altitude of two hundred feet, sliding out of the greatly reduced visibility, the burning oil rig cast a surreal profile. One entire corner of the platform had been blown away, sending a geyser of flaming crude onto the topsides as it twisted and hung suspended ever lower over the water. Explosions continued to rock the structure as oil-covered surfaces ignited and melted away, dropping pieces of the platform into the sea. Thick black smoke boiled into the air, mixing briefly with the snow flurries and the steam created by the fire-fighting equipment before being carried away by the wind.

"Here you go," Tibbits shouted above the thudding of the rotors. "Don't say I didn't warn you." Far below, the platform's helipad was nearly cleaved in half by the collapsed swing boom.

Garner's stomach was churning as much as the sea below as he unbuckled himself from his seat and was clipped into the sling harness suspended from the helicopter's hoist. He exchanged a thumbs-up with the operator, then the line was away, lowering him quickly toward the burning platform.

The helicopter swung around in the westward wind, dropping Garner through a swirling cloud of oily smoke and setting him heavily on the deck. He quickly scrambled out of the harness as the SEALs descended behind him. The structure continued its catastrophic groaning as the men made their way across the topsides, looking for any sign of Charon and his men.

Below the helideck, the crew quarters were destroyed. The rescue team could now see that one of the fuel cells below was filled with burning crude oil, though the GBS had apparently contained most of its inflammable contents. Leakage of oil into the sea appeared to be minimal, with most of the immediate hazard coming from the blackened shards of the rig itself. The utility shed and control room were completely missing, while the communications van had been torn from its foundation, taking the trigger console, and possibly Charon's team, along with it.

"Where do you want to look?" one of the SEALs shouted over the tortured sounds of the dying rig.

"Deck to deck until we find six bodies," Garner said grimly.

They managed to climb down to the bottom deck of the topsides, which was now nearly half submerged in the water. Garner was the first into the dive room, where he found the bodies of Stimson and one of Charon's lieutenants sloshing in the icy water, both dead, apparently from gunshot wounds to the head.

The string of bizarre events was becoming clear to Garner. "Looks like we've got a sabotage on our hands."

"Charon?" someone asked.

"Or one of the others," Garner said, though he doubted anyone but Charon was in a position to orchestrate this disaster. "We know Charon was alive to push the button, but not if he knew about the oil in the GBS."

"We're still missing four bodies," another SEAL remarked.

Garner surveyed the rest of the room, tilted precariously on its end and angled into the sea. "And one JIM suit," he observed.

In the remnants of the rig's control room, Garner's team could find no way to see what was going on below. None of the closed-circuit cameras around the GBS or the plug were showing images. Either the connections to the monitors had been severed by the blast or the cameras themselves had been destroyed. Until the cameras on the submarines could be redeployed, the JIM suit was the only way to determine whether the rig was leaking oil beneath the surface. It was also the only way to find out whether the saboteur had escaped in the other suit. With the help of the SEALs, Garner climbed into the second JIM suit and asked for thirty minutes on the bottom before they reeled him back up.

"Any longer than that and we may be joining you down there," someone joked tersely. "Keep your head up, sir."

With the helmet closed securely over him, Garner allowed the others to heave the suit into position and gently slide him into the water. A moment later, the suit lost its out-of-water awkwardness and Garner was sinking to the bottom on the end of his umbilical and safety tether. On the way, he activated the suit's lights and comm link, then reconfirmed that all the suit's life-support systems were up to full power. He had been in a JIM suit only once, years before during a Navy deep-sea rescue course. The design of this suit was more refined, but it didn't take him long to figure out how to manipulate the legs and the twin-fingered pincers on the end of the arms. He hoped he wouldn't be down long enough for the amount of air in his tanks to become a concern, but the suit's regulator didn't seem to be providing a proper flow of air.

He angled his lights onto the reinforced concrete ice-wall of the GBS as he descended—it appeared to be intact all the way to the bottom. Even if the blast had ruptured one or more of the fuel cells, he hoped the external integrity of the GBS would keep the oil from escaping the reservoir.

He landed on the bottom directly beside the GBS. His helmet lights illuminated fresh piles of twisted and charred debris raining down from the rig above. Most of it had fallen straight down, while the rest was carried sideways over the lip of Thebes Deep. Garner walked slowly along the base pad for a few more minutes as he inspected the GBS, then retraced his steps so that the umbilical did not become wrapped around some new obstruction.

He was about to continue his inspection in the opposite direction when something heavy crashed onto the back of the suit, making him stumble. He craned his neck around to peer out the top portal of the helmet, expecting to see a piece of fallen debris. A flicker of light from a second helmet lamp told him it was the other JIM diver.

Garner clumsily turned around to face his attacker, straining to identify him through the suit's portholes. The other diver lunged again, knocking Garner backward. He stumbled over the edge of the GBS and fell heavily on his back.

As Garner struggled to right himself, the other diver attacked, pushing him sideways toward the lip of the canyon. Garner clung to an extrusion of bedrock and used this to slowly pull himself upright before the next collision came. This time as he turned to face his assailant, he could clearly see Charon's face inside the other helmet.

The problem with the suit's regulator was growing worse. While Garner had the air inside the pressurized suit to rebreathe, the carbon dioxide would build up quickly without proper scrubbing and recirculation. He thumbed the comm link inside the helmet, not knowing if the umbilical would still carry his message to the surface, much less to the *Hawkbill* or the *Rushmore*. "Is anybody there?" he called, struggling to keep his balance. "It's Charon. Charon is down here and I think he's trying to cover his tracks."

"Repeat that, Brock?" Krail's voice came back a moment later.

"I said Charon sabotaged the rig and now he's trying to kill me," Garner said, grunting as he dodged another one of Charon's blows. "I could really use a lift here, fellas. I could be out of air before I can get back to the surface."

"Matt? What the hell are you doing?" Krail demanded.

"He can't hear you," Garner replied, his breath coming in gasps. "His suit doesn't have an umbilical or a safety tether."

Krail couldn't believe what he was hearing. "Then how did he expect to get back up?"

Charon came down heavily on Garner's back. The bulky suit, awkward and stiff from its internal pressurization, was difficult to control and Garner felt himself going over forward, toward the edge of the canyon.

"I don't think he plans on coming back up," Garner grunted. The temperature inside his suit had begun to climb. "Unless it's on my back." If Charon had somehow managed to don his own suit, there was no way he could have attached the umbilical or its comm link. He was running the suit on its air tanks only, improperly pressurized with nothing connecting him to the surface. With Garner's own regulator malfunctioning, either one of them could collapse from oxygen starvation, if fatigue or Thebes Deep didn't claim them first.

Charon continued to step around Garner, lunging at him with his mechanical claws. Like a pair of sparring crabs, the two divers circled each other less than twenty feet from the edge of the dropoff. Charon swung again, his clawed hand banging noisily on the porthole of Garner's helmet. Garner sidestepped the next blow and wheeled around. Then another blow hit him from above: debris. Garner recognized it as the swing boom that had fallen across the helideck. The massive, elongated structure was falling to the seafloor on top of them. Garner was jerked sideways as the debris wrenched at his umbilical, then released it as it sank past.

Realization came too late for Charon. The metal scaffolding slammed into him, then continued to career over the edge of the canyon. He was trapped inside the framework as its inertia carried him backward into the black depths beyond.

Garner stepped forward and saw the light from Charon's helmet as he tumbled into the deep. A hundred feet down, two hundred, the illumination from Charon's suit vanished from sight. A moment later, a silvery cloud of bubbles clawed past his light on their way to the surface.

Garner staggered back, breathing heavily and still stunned by the spectacle he had just witnessed.

The rock beneath him began to shudder. A moment later, the fractured lip of the canyon suddenly gave way. He instinctively moved back but the collapse was happening too quickly. Only the suit's safety tether prevented him from falling after the edge of the fault as it fell into Thebes Deep. A moment later he hung suspended by only two thin lines over a newly formed canyon. An aftershock had dropped the seafloor, block-faulting a five-mile trough along the edge of Thebes Deep. Garner realized he had just felt the perfect stimulus for generating a tsunami, once incorrectly known as a "tidal wave"—a sudden, massive displacement of the ocean's surface. In his madness, Charon had created a disturbance as great as any earthquake or volcano.

Garner's vision began to fog as he started to black out.

"Fellas? Anybody up there?" he called again into the comm link.

There was no reply from anyone at the surface. Garner waited, still breathing hard, collecting his thoughts. The blackness crushed in from all around him, broken only by the rumbling of the rig, far above.

"Hello?" he called again, hoping for any reply.

Only silence. A deathlike chill crept over Garner on the bottom of the sea.

Then Krail's voice came back. The connection crackled and broke several times. "We'll get you up right now, Brock. Sorry, we've been a little busy."

Garner could feel the slack being taken out of the umbilical. A moment later he began his painfully slow rise to the surface.

Krail sounded hesitant, uncertain how to continue. "Brock, we've got some bad news. It looks like that last series of aftershocks generated a large surface disturbance."

Garner winced as his fears were confirmed. "Have you warned the *Phoenix*?"

"Negative. We've still got too much interference from the storm."

"What do you mean, *interference*?" Garner snapped. "With all the equipment you've got?"

"We're trying our damnedest, buddy. I'll talk to you on the surface. Over and out."

Garner switched off the comm link, realizing the futility of his anger. If a rogue wave had been generated, it could travel between the detonation site and the *Phoenix* in a matter of minutes, if not seconds. If that was the case, then a possible source of the "interference" was that the ships themselves had been capsized or damaged.

Garner reached the surface and the JIM suit was removed. He quickly transferred to a launch that brought him back to the *Rushmore*. There he contacted the *Hawkbill* again and relayed to Krail the details of his encounter with Charon. The two commanders sketched out a plan for stabilizing what remained of *B-82*.

"What's the status of the leak?" Garner asked. "Did we plug it?"

"It'll be an hour or two before we can even see it in all this stirred-up sediment," Krail said. "But that's our job. You're the one with all the work to do now. I'll find someone to get your ass out to the slick ASAP."

"Any luck getting through to the *Phoenix* yet?"

"Still working on it," Krail said.

Garner ran his fingers through his hair in frustration. "Let me know the *second* you hear anything," he said, then signed off.

Just then Tibbits stepped into the corridor from the helideck. His eyes met Garner's and he immediately regretted it.

"Come on," Garner said to the pilot before he could protest. "You're taking me back up."

"It's called murking," Tibbits yelled back to Garner over the pounding of the rotors. He was referring to the helicopter's painfully slow progress to the east. "Fifty knots at fifty to a hundred feet until we get some kind of visibility."

The pilot wasn't being facetious. Since the *Phoenix* could not be located using instrument flight rules alone and flying by visual flight rules in the blowing snow was almost impossible, the pilots resorted to a combination of both. While Dunlop, the copilot, monitored the GPS and checked that the Sikorsky remained over water,

Tibbits gripped the collective, looking for sudden obstacles and keeping his eye on the radar altimeter.

Garner was strapped into a jump seat behind the cockpit, facing aft, an orientation where, as Tibbits pointed out with a fierce grin, "All the statistics show that you're a helluva lot safer in a crash." The pilot had evidently heard of Garner's acrophobia and wasn't above using any tactic to remain on the deck.

"Then I guess we shouldn't crash," Garner hollered back.

"No promises, sir," Tibbits said, only half joking. "On a day like this, it's like flying inside a glass of milk."

The fog was pale gray outside the cockpit windows, cut irregularly by swirling snow and glimpses of the cold, black sea one hundred feet below. Garner's uneasy imagination was fueled by a host of disturbing mechanical noises, from the whine of the transmissions to the blaring of the inverters. While Tibbits set a course for the *Phoenix*'s estimated position, Garner occupied himself by monitoring a comm channel kept open for any word from the ship. The farther they moved to the east, the more the helicopter was buffeted between the corridors of blasting wind. He took careful note of the emergency locator beacon and the evacuation procedures stenciled on the door beside him, just in case.

Thirty minutes later, passing over Committee Bay, they should have arrived at Tibbits's estimated position of the *Phoenix,* but there was no sign of the ship or its two companion vessels. Given the vastness of the area traversed, it was more likely that Tibbits had simply strayed off course or miscalculated the vessels' track. Rechecking the map and their instruments, Dunlop confirmed that the landfall below them was indeed Melville Peninsula, which meant they had somehow flown south of the *Phoenix*'s location. As the helicopter turned back in a wide arc, Garner couldn't help but look more closely at the sea surface for any sign of debris or wreckage. The floe looked as if it had been fractured into hundreds of smaller pieces and Garner once again worried about the aftereffects of the detonation.

A true tsunami was unlikely in the confined and relatively deep basin of the Gulf of Boothia. But small solitons, a related phenomenon occurring as an isolated rogue wave, were often generated in narrow canals or in the wake of fast-moving ships. Given the depth of the gulf, the force of the detonation, and the lack of obstructions in its path, a soliton of gigantic proportions could have originated over Thebes Deep. A soliton could travel for miles as a wave only a few inches high, then, upon reaching shallower water, could grow without warning into a massive wall of water. As a single, towering wave crest without a corresponding trough behind it, water exploded forward with nowhere else to go. Once the subject of maritime folklore, solitons had been proven to exist via calculations and scale-model reproductions only after they had demonstrated themselves with devastating and deadly results.

Another half hour passed without any sign of the icebreakers. Contact with the *Rushmore* was still possible, though fading the farther east the helicopter progressed, but the support ship had been no more successful in contacting the *Phoenix*.

"I dunno, sir," Tibbits said, a shade less confidence in his voice. "We should be right on top of them."

"Keep looking." In Garner's mind there could be no other alternative. They had just half an hour of fuel left to expand their search area before they would have to head back to the *Rushmore*.

Garner sent one more hail over the radio, then squeezed his eyes shut against a passing wave of vertigo. He blinked it away, then tried to discern the surface once again. Sea and sky blended into a single, vague shade of gray. One moment they looked to be two hundred feet above the ice, the next it could have been fifty. Or less. It wasn't hard to imagine a low-slung island or an iceberg the size of a building flashing out of the fog at them.

The helicopter bucked roughly and Garner snapped his eyes open. He turned to look forward at Tibbits. "What is it?"

Through the cockpit door, the pilot appeared to be struggling with the controls. "Nothing, sir," he panted. "Just a little *fata morgana*."

"Say again?"

"A little snow blindness, is all."

"It's a real bad time to say you told me so, Roger," Garner cautioned.

"Don't worry, it'll pass," Tibbits said. "Always does. I'll just revert to instruments—"

"Get it up!" Dunlop shouted and Tibbits cursed again.

In the blinding whiteness, the helicopter had slowed its forward speed too much while descending too quickly. Tibbits pulled the collective back to the very top, to no avail. Garner felt the bottom drop out of his gut as the helicopter plunged toward a ragged plateau of sea ice.

"Oh shit," Tibbits said. There was no anger in his voice, only quiet resignation. "I'm sorry, sir."

Garner's throat constricted in sudden terror. "*Sorry about what?!*"

"Mayday mayday mayday! *Rushmore,* this is Sierra two-two-niner," Tibbits shouted into his headset. "We are ditching at this position."

Garner heard Dunlop yell at Tibbits, whose reply was lost below the scream of the engines. Through clenched teeth the copilot began to read the helicopter's coordinates as the violent spin continued. It all happened so quickly there was no way to know if the *Rushmore* even heard them.

A split second later, the altimeter reached zero and the helicopter smashed into the ice.

23

For the third time in the past hour, Byrnes grappled with the hovercraft's steering controls to prevent the seafaring hot rod from flipping over on its inflatable cushion. After a gut-wrenching bounce, the craft landed heavily, right-side up, sending a cascading spray of water up and over the windows.

"*Damn*, this thing is fun!" Byrnes hollered, quickly steering back in the opposite direction.

Sitting next to him, Zubov grabbed for the safety handle beside him and cursed under his breath. "Slow down!" he growled, uncomfortable with Byrnes's recklessness.

"Yeah, yeah," Byrnes replied. "Do you want to get done with this before that storm hits or not?" The hovercraft nosed over a partially submerged floe and both men felt the air forced from their lungs as the vehicle smacked the water once again. Byrnes jockeyed the controls, swinging the stern around and once again attacked the mass of ice bobbing in the wash. Byrnes's "reckless" piloting was doing more to keep them upright than risking unnecessary danger.

The squad of SEALs assigned to the *North Sea* ably assisted the Canadian Forces personnel in dynamiting the edges of the larger pieces of floe, calving several large but manageable pieces into the water. Using sonar, ice radar, and the Global wrangling equipment, the three icebreakers had managed to collect nearly a quarter million tons of ice. The hovercraft was now relegated to scurrying between the thick lumbering hulls packing small pieces of ice between the larger chunks. Despite the hovercraft's limited size, it seemed they were actually making some progress. By midday they had greatly supplemented the larger ice floes scooped up by the string of icebreakers. The man-made, composite iceberg was beginning to take shape.

They spent most of the day within two miles of the *Phoenix,* attempting to wrangle the smaller pieces of ice into a large seine Zubov had rigged behind the craft. The thick radiation suits that protected Byrnes and Zubov were clearly not designed for this kind of work; movement was awkward, and as the day warmed to twenty degrees Fahrenheit, the interior climate of the suits became stifling. Zubov actually welcomed the chance to uncoil himself from the low cockpit and climb out onto the cushion to maneuver the ice into the seine using a long piece of steel rebar.

Even under comparatively calm conditions, the sea surface was a problem: huge chunks of ice floated everywhere in fractured assemblages rising from the water a few inches to ten feet. In addition to navigating the tight and treacherous confines, both men in the hovercraft had to keep constant watch that they didn't back over the seine itself—at one point Byrnes compared the process to trying to spread a picnic blanket from the basket of a Tilt-A-Whirl. Worst of all were the heavier, overturned "blue" bergs that lurked just under the surface. They were as hazardous as a submerged log, or "deadhead," to an ordinary boat. A deadhead could tear the keel off a boat, or worse, suddenly upend it and toss its occupants into the water.

As if the driving process wasn't demanding enough, the ice itself seemed determined to mock their efforts, allowing itself to be wrangled only in infrequent and patronizing intervals. The largest pieces were far too heavy to tow, even for the craft's ample horsepower. The smallest pieces hardly seemed worth the effort, but following Zubov's direction and profanity-laced encouragement, they repeatedly packed the seine. When filled, it would be towed back to the larger nets strung between the *Phoenix*, the *North Sea*, and the *Vagabond*, where its meager but essential load was deposited. The smaller pieces not only increased the total surface area available to receive the *Ulva*, but also kept the larger pieces from rolling against each other and destabilizing the load in the nets.

"Nice work, fellas," someone called down from the *North Sea*. "At this rate you should have a hundred square yards collected by the year 3000."

"Great idea, Brock," Byrnes muttered under his breath as he reversed the craft and pulled around for another load. "Really glad we listened to you."

"Now you understand my pain," Zubov said as he stepped through the hatch to attend to the next herd of ice.

On the bridge of the *Phoenix*, Carol had regained a regimented command that would be the envy of any field general. The skeleton crew that remained aboard continued to work in round-the-clock shifts to control all the ship's main functions and, under Junko's watchful direction, monitor everyone's overall health and analyze the data coming in from the gamma spectrometers. Despite their grumbling, Byrnes and Zubov were working minor miracles with the hovercraft, chasing down the smaller fragments of floating ice as effectively as any sheepdog. The captains of the *North Sea* and the *Vagabond* maintained their flanking positions with an expert hand, confidently steering the ungainly, forty-five-thousand-ton wagon train in a direct path along the slick.

Roland Alvarez called from Dalhousie and described to Carol what he believed would be the most likely place to find surface concentrations of *Ulva morina*. His first and second suggestions were off the southern and eastern coasts of Iceland, respectively, but there was no way the water bombers would have that kind of range. His third choice was off the southern tip of Greenland, not quite half the distance, but they would be gambling that the area would have enough *Ulva* for their needs. To confirm or refute this, Alvarez needed to consult the regional mean water temperatures over the preceding winter, and he had yet to find the data he needed. If anything, he suggested hopefully, the spring conditions and the breakup of the pack ice greatly improved their chances of finding *Ulva* spores floating freely in the surface waters of the Atlantic. Averaging just twenty-nine degrees Fahrenheit, the area south of Greenland typically had the coldest surface temperatures of any ocean in the world, conditions in which the microscopic *Ulva* apparently thrived.

Armed with this news, Carol elected to gamble. Within hours, the Canadian government had commandeered the only flight of Martin Mars bombers east of the Rocky Mountains and Carol relayed the flight plan to the bomber crews. Three bombers would collect the *Ulva* from the waters offshore of Nuuk, then head almost directly west some seven hundred miles to the corridor of ocean containing the slick. Together, the three planes could douse nearly twelve acres of the surface with the *Ulva* solution, dropping more than twenty-one thousand gallons of the displaced seawater onto the site in less than a minute.

Once the surface water had been seeded with the algae, the three icebreakers would continue their journey east, toward the containment booms moving up Fury and Hecla Strait. After much discussion with the ships' crews and the biologists among them, it was clear that the ice would have to be towed slowly enough to allow the *Ulva* to take up the hot *Thio-uni* and adhere itself to the ice, yet quickly enough to collect all the algae in this manner before it began to settle from the surface waters. The phytoplankton cells were too small to be killed by the two-hundred-foot drop from the belly of the bombers, but no one was willing to bet that the *Ulva* would not be destroyed by sudden changes in salinity, temperature, or air pressure. In Halifax, Alvarez and his students were trying to find out.

To the east, now just forty miles off and closing slowly, the *Des Groseilliers* and the *Sovietsky Soyuz* had received their containment booms and were attempting to define the best place to position them. First they needed to isolate the slick between the five vessels—three to the west and two to the east. As a containment pen was rigged around the condensed slick and the coordinates confirmed, the team would begin dredging the sediment and open a pit in the seafloor big enough to bury the solid mass of Plasroc.

All this only if Garner was right. This time Carol knew he was really pushing it.

She had been keeping a constant eye on the weather reports and was anticipating the thick gray bank of clouds that appeared hours later on the western horizon. For once, unfortunately, the forecasts of the meteorologists had been correct. With the front came low-level fog mixed with snow flurries, and soon after that, all communication with Garner and Krail faded out. Frisch assured her it was only a temporary condition.

Communicating with Garner directly did not seem to be an option at the moment. The bulk of the bad weather now sat squarely between B-82 and the *Phoenix* and was slowly whirling and churning its way in their direction. While messages could be relayed from the *Rushmore* to the *Des Groseilliers,* then back to the *Phoenix,* direct communication with the *Rushmore* seemed to be temporarily interrupted. Frisch said it was because of the atmospheric disturbance created by the storm and launched into some long-winded discussion about how radio waves could bounce off the ionosphere at certain angles, spanning hundreds of miles over one arc, but completely missing another.

"So much for all our high-tech toys," Carol muttered. "Can we work around it?"

"Well, no," Frisch admitted. "Either we have to move or the storm does."

"The way we're all strung together, I guess we'll have to wait for the storm."

"I can still send any message you want over to the *Des Groseilliers,*" Frisch offered. "Maybe they'll have better luck."

Carol considered it, then shook her head. "No, it can wait. Assuming the detonation worked, Brock is probably on his way over here already. And if it didn't, they'll all be too busy to worry about us."

"I heard Patrick and a couple of the techs talking in the galley," Frisch said. "They figure the wind might even help push the slick our way a little quicker."

"It'd be nice to have something go our way, wouldn't it?"

"I'll keep working on a direct connection for you," Frisch said.

"Thanks," Carol replied, without half the appreciation

she should have conveyed. What was one lousy radio connection in this whole operation? The rest of it was, well, progressing. At least the parts of it that could be controlled. Yet Carol remained troubled by the realization that she couldn't talk directly to Garner. Once again she found herself needing her ex-husband, and admonished herself for even admitting it. She needed to see him or hear his voice over the radio and glean some comfort from his assessment. She needed to hear him say everything would be all right.

She was interrupted by the clumping of Zubov's heavy boots coming up the steps to the bridge.

"Finished?" she asked with a weary smile.

"For the moment," Zubov said. "The Navy boys want to dynamite some more of the fast ice and see if they can free up some more debris. I figure it's best to let a SEAL with a bunch of dynamite do whatever he wants." He pulled out a well-worn bandanna and wiped it across his broad, sweat-slickened face. "Any news from Brock?"

"Nothing yet," Carol said. "It seems we're 'experiencing technical difficulties'—something to do with the storm."

"How long have we got?"

"An hour or two before it's on top of us. It seems to be a pretty slow-moving front."

"Did it mess up the detonation?"

Carol shrugged. "I imagine it did. But I assume everything went well. Either that or it hasn't gone yet and they'll let us know when we can get moving."

"Great. More time for Patrick and me to play bumper buggies out there."

"You've done a heck of a job, considering what you've got for a Zamboni."

"I think you'll need to buy Byrnes a new hovercraft if you ever want to see him smile again. What we don't cook, we'll probably end up puncturing or burning out. Don't ask me what's keeping that engine together."

"You can call it a day as soon as the bombers arrive."

"When will that be?"

"At worst, about the same time as the blizzard arrives. They're already on their way, so we're keeping our fingers crossed that the weather will hold a little longer. With any luck, the bombers will be able to do the drop before the wind or visibility gets any worse."

Zubov gave her a dubious look. "Since when have you known us to have any luck?"

The three water bombers filled up with fuel in Newfoundland, then again at Nuuk, Greenland, before beginning their daunting mission, an elongated, triangular flight path across Iceberg Alley: Davis Strait and the North Atlantic.

With a two-hundred-foot wingspan and a displacement of eighty-one tons, the aircraft were large by any standard. Originally designed to be long-range bombers and troop transports in the South Pacific campaign of World War II, the Martin Mars aircraft were later refitted for large-scale drenching of forest fires along Canada's west coast. A seventy-two-hundred-gallon water tank, filled by scoops lowered from the belly of the plane, allowed the Mars to drop sixty thousand gallons per hour over a fire, or a quarter of a million gallons in a typical six-hour bombing shift.

Slowing such an aircraft to seventy knots and dipping its belly into the water for a touch-and-go approach was far different in the North Atlantic than on a serene mountain lake. Here the pilots' main concern was not in clearing the trees lining the oncoming shoreline but to outguess the rolling water itself—none of the crews had ever attempted it. The slightest misjudgment of the sea's surface or the height of an oncoming wave and the bomber, slow and growing heavier as it gulped in its liquid payload, could easily be washed into the sea.

As the Mars dropped through the final few hundred feet, the captain gave his first officer control of the throttle, which would have to be steadily increased as the tank was filled. During the thirty-second intake scoop, the weight of water in the plane increased by more than a ton per second, requiring proportionally greater lift. Finally, with the belly of the beast fully loaded, the Mars could return to the sky and begin to lumber another eleven hundred miles west to where the drop zone had been determined. For the present flight, they would only have enough fuel for one approach— perhaps two—with no margin for error.

As the Mars approached the drop site, a thick overcast negated any advantage afforded by the weak springtime sun. Westerly winds buffeted the heavy planes, which protested in response and doubtless lost a little more fuel efficiency.

Every member of each four-man crew—captain, first officer, and two flight engineers—split his attention between his assigned instrumentation and the sea below, trying to catch a glimpse of the surface. The captain of the lead plane cursed under his breath. "A landmark or two would be nice," he grumbled. "Otherwise we'll end up blowing our wad with no backup supply."

Finally, the bombers made radio contact with the *Des Groseilliers* in Fury and Hecla Strait. The Canadian icebreaker assured them they were on target and the bombing path was indeed directly west. At 160,000 pounds loaded weight, any miscue on the aircrafts' approach meant a long, circling return—or in this case, no return at all.

In the lead plane, the first officer continued to hail the *Phoenix,* and sighed in relief when the ship finally answered. The *Phoenix*'s mate gave them the coordinates and the first approach on the bombing run was begun.

"Okay, one time." The captain radioed to the other planes. "Let's one-time this baby and get our asses home."

The clouds parted at an altitude of two hundred feet and the black surface of the Arctic Ocean came into view. Before them stretched the long corridor of water opened by the vessels, flanked on either side by fractured pieces of floating ice. Below them, sliding quickly past, was the tethered trio of vessels—the *Phoenix,* the *North Sea,* and the *Vagabond*—and the small mountain of ice carefully cradled between them. This was a planned overshoot—the *Ulva* was to be dropped west of the vessels so that the current could carry it back over the slick and past the collected ice.

They were two minutes from the drop zone and exactly on the correct approach.

"Engineers to stations," the first officer announced. Suddenly the big aircraft was alive with noise as the water tank was prepared for purging.

"Ninety seconds," the captain announced. Over the radio, the pilots of the other two bombers confirmed this information.

"What the hell is *that*?" one of the flight engineers suddenly said. He crawled forward into the cockpit and pointed toward the sea roughly half the distance to the horizon.

Then the others saw it: a distortion in the surface. Seconds later, the sea itself rose up, flicking along its length like a carpet being shaken. The ocean rolled and exploded upward, flinging huge chunks of ice aside. For a moment, the water seemed suddenly to be speeding up at them, then just as suddenly it passed below, streaking to the east and falling away behind the bombers.

The captain thought he knew what he had seen, but could not fully comprehend it. Then he thought of the ships below them and wondered if they could see the massive wall of water rising up from the ocean. They had to. It was impossible to miss.

In the time it took him to reach for his radio, the damage was already done.

Although the radio message from the bombers was sent too late, the planes themselves were responsible for lessening the wave's damage to the containment operation. As the three Herculean aircraft roared overhead at low altitude, every eye aboard the three icebreakers turned skyward to watch. Then, as the planes moved overhead, those below turned to the west to watch the bombing run. That was when they saw the wave rising suddenly out of the ocean.

The wall of water reached sixty feet. Those who were close enough to a hatchway quickly ducked inside; the rest found some object bolted to the deck and hung on for their lives. The wave struck within seconds, heaving the three ships upward at the stern and smashing into the ice strung between them. The sea momentarily washed over the afterdecks, then cascaded over the rear of the superstructure before rejoining the wave as it rolled past.

Only the orientation of the vessels—directly east and perpendicular to the wave front—kept them from capsizing against the monstrous force. A dozen bodies were thrown into the water and cries of "Man overboard!" began to ring out even before the wave had finished passing. The ice nets twisted and buckled against their rigging and the booms holding them screamed in protest.

All available hands moved to the railings to begin pulling people from the water. On the *Phoenix*, Zubov began barking orders to have everyone exposed to the water taken to see Junko in the infirmary. Then he learned that Junko herself was one of those exposed. He ran the length of the vessel just as the petite woman was pulled from the water. She looked like a child in her oversized cold-weather suit and smiled weakly when she saw him.

"Oops," she said. "That first step was a doozy."

Zubov kneeled beside her as she tried to regain her faculties. "What happened? What were you doing on deck?"

"I was bored," she admitted. "I came out to watch my man work. One minute the boat was under me, the next it wasn't."

Through his concern, only two of Junko's words stood out to Zubov: *my man.*

"Get her inside," Zubov said to the two crewmen who had retrieved Junko. "Move!"

"It's all right, Sergei," she assured him. "I'm fine. I'm sure I wasn't in the water long enough for anything to happen. Besides, I think there's going to be a few other cuts and bruises for Susan and me to look at."

Unconvinced, Zubov started to follow her back inside. The two crewmen returned to the afterdeck and suddenly the two confidants were left alone in the airlock.

"It's okay, Sergei," Junko repeated. "I'm *fine,* really." Even as she said this, her teeth began chattering from the frigidity of her saturated clothing. She nodded over toward the *Vagabond,* where at least a dozen hands were trying to keep the ice nets from tearing away completely. "You're needed out there," she said. "I'll still be here when you get back. Promise."

At that moment, nothing mattered more to Zubov than to press his lips against hers. He drew her close and kissed her deeply. "I'm sorry," he said.

"Don't be. Go now. You've got more important work to do."

On the bridge of the *Phoenix,* Carol picked herself up from the deck and looked through the large windows at the carnage around the ship. She knew that the icebreaker was designed to be able to roll almost completely on its side without capsizing, but that design had just been well tested. The mate reported that everyone swept overboard had been accounted for and was being treated. Her second-worst fears seemed to be equally unfounded: all three vessels were still afloat and upright. Most of the collected ice had been pushed out of the nets, scattered forcibly to the east, but had remained in an extended line between the hulls. Assuming the nets could still be used, it would be an easy matter to gather up the pieces.

As the shock subsided, she tried to piece together exactly what had happened. The wind had been strong and erratic, but certainly not enough to generate a rogue wave.

But that soliton meant something had happened to get an awful lot of water moving very fast. Like an earthquake. Or a detonation gone wrong.

She was suddenly very afraid about what might have happened. If a wave this size had traveled a hundred miles, what was left of *B-82*?

"The bombers are on the radio," the mate said. "They're ready to come around on final approach." It seemed absurd to Carol that with all the sudden destruction on the water, she still had to confirm the release of the *Ulva*, a highly suspect operation itself.

The mate read the look on her face. "They know," he said. "But it's now or never. They have to off-load or head back to base and try it another day."

Carol looked out at the operations area, at the ships and machinery that now looked about as capable and coordinated as toys in a child's bathtub. Their best hope to stop the slick was circling above them, and it wouldn't be coming back anytime soon.

"Do it," she finally told the mate. "Tell them to start the bombing." *There's got to be something we need more urgently than another twenty thousand gallons of seawater,* she thought. Outside, the ocean continued to surge around the bobbing vessels and splintered ice.

Carol felt numb. Then the word came up that Junko had been one of those washed overboard and Carol started to head down to the infirmary. As she passed the communications room, she heard the radio crackle.

"Who is it?" Carol automatically asked Frisch. She expected it to be the *North Sea* or the *Vagabond* checking in, or perhaps a final confirmation from the water bombers. Incredibly, it was the *Hawkbill,* for the first time in nearly four hours. Carol was disappointed it wasn't Garner's voice but Krail's.

"Scott, it's Carol," she said, taking a headset from Frisch.

"Thank God. Better late than never."

"Hey, solitons are like horseshoes and hand grenades, right? Close is good enough."

There was a palpable strain in Krail's voice. "How bad was it?"

"I don't know yet," she said. "Sergei and Patrick are outside with the others, checking the nets. A few folks got wet, and exposed, and we're looking at them. The *Ulva* is being dumped right now."

"Otherwise you're okay?" Krail was trying to reassure her with understatement.

"For the time being, but we've likely lost all track of the slick and will have to move this little circus back into Foxe Basin. What the hell happened?"

"There was an accident—an *incident*—with the charges. We're still examining the wreckage—"

"Wreckage!"

"Yes. *B-82* is gone—at least, it's burning. The platform was badly damaged, possibly destroyed, but we've got the fire under control and there doesn't appear to be any oil leakage."

Carol's mind was reeling. "Slow down, Scott. What happened?"

"It looks like sabotage. Charon did it and we don't know yet how successful he was."

"What does Charon say about it?"

"He's dead, Carol." Krail's voice wavered. "A lot of men are dead."

Carol's heart thudded heavily in her chest. "Where's Brock?" More silence. "Scott—*where's Brock?*"

"We don't know," Krail admitted. "Tibbits and Dunlop were taking him to your location. They radioed back that they couldn't find you, then we lost track of them. They may have gone down en route but we haven't picked up any locator beacons."

"Are you *looking* for them?" Now anger was rising in Carol's voice.

"Carol, we've got other situations on our hands," Krail said. "If we send anyone else up in this weather they'll likely come down as hard. We're trying—"

"Then try harder!" she screamed into the microphone, then tossed it at Frisch as she stormed out of the radio room.

Carol headed directly to the airlock and dressed in an exposure suit. She found Zubov and Byrnes tending to the wrangling nets strung between the *Phoenix* and the *North Sea*. About a mile to the west, the third Mars bomber finished releasing its load into the ocean—from there, the surface currents would allow the *Ulva* to mix with the contaminated *Thio-uni*. They had less than an hour to get the rigging rebuilt and return to pushing the ice together.

"How bad is it?" she asked them.

"Twisted to shit, but we'll live to bitch another day," Byrnes said.

Carol nodded at the team of SEALs clambering onto the net from the other end. "Can those guys handle it alone?"

"If they have to. Why?"

"Get the hovercraft fueled up. Brock was on his way

to warn us about the soliton and his helicopter may have gone down."

Zubov paled. "Where?"

"That's what Patrick and I are going to find out," she said. "They've got to be closer to us than them."

She sensed Zubov's immediate reservations with this idea. "Serg, we need you here. And Patrick is the only one checked out to pilot the hovercraft."

"That's debatable," Zubov muttered, still rattled from Byrnes's bump-and-grind driving style.

"No arguments," Carol said. She looked at Byrnes. "Let's go. Now." She turned on her heel, then grabbed a passing technician by the arm of his suit. "Looking for something to do?" she asked the young man.

"Uh, actually I was gonna—"

"Good. Get someone out there in a Zodiac. Get a water sample and have it analyzed. See if we've even got any *Ulva* here, then find out the cell concentration." She turned back to Zubov. "Get up to the bridge and see if there's anything—*anything*—those bombers can do to help Scott. Got it?"

"Got it," Zubov said, then moved off at a trot.

Carol and Byrnes were mobile ten minutes later. Byrnes jettisoned the seine from the hovercraft, checked the fuel tanks, then took them along Melville Peninsula and across the sea ice on the eastern shore of Committee Bay on a beeline back toward *B-82*.

Over level ground or water, the hovercraft could reach twenty-five knots, and for nearly an hour, Byrnes pushed the throttle forward for optimum speed. Visibility was still bad—they could probably drive over a downed helicopter without seeing it—but the winds appeared to be subsiding.

"I hope you can see better than me," Byrnes said.

Carol held the safety rail against the rapid vibrating and jostling of the craft. "I'm trying," she said. "Keep the radio on for any news. From anyone."

Just as Byrnes reached for the radio, there came a massive jolt to the craft's port-side bow. They had hit something—either a rock or a hummock of ice. There was a tremendous *crack* as the fiberglass hull split open from the impact. Both Carol and Byrnes were thrown roughly against their seat belts, then the cockpit tilted over at a crazy angle.

Carol braced herself and realized that the hovercraft was bouncing along on its right-side cushion. The ice streaked by only inches outside her window; Byrnes was suspended above her, wrestling the controls.

"Hold on!" Byrnes shouted. "We're gonna flip!"

Carol heard the pitch of the hovercraft's engine change, then felt her entire weight fall against the seat belt. Ice scraped along the roof of the craft, now its bottom.

There was a second impact and the sound of tearing fiberglass was overwhelming. The cockpit seemed to be disintegrating all around them. The craft bounced again, then rolled over onto the sea. A bolt of pain shot through Carol's legs, making her scream. Stunned by the impact, she could only watch as the hovercraft lurched to a stop and began to fill with water.

As she started to lose consciousness, she wondered how close they were to the slick, and whether the liquid death rising toward her was radioactive or not. Either way, the cold would probably kill her first.

24

Astrong, *remarkably warm breeze straight down the Strait of Juan de Fuca, caressing the San Juan Islands. The sound of a new nylon sheet gliding through its eyelets and the wind and the snap of canvas as the* Albatross's *mainsail billowed full against the wind. Not just sailing, floating. Flying—*

Garner regained consciousness with a start. All around him was the sound of wind, not breathing life into the sails of the *Albatross* after all, but ravaging the torn fuselage of the helicopter. His body was still strapped into his seat, which was tipped over on its side. His lips tasted of copper and salt: blood. His face was apparently covered by it, growing thickest near a savage pain that crossed his forehead. Then he remembered the Sikorsky going down—this time for real, as opposed to a hundred illusory instances of the same event. For all his fears and white-knuckled worrying, he had still been utterly unprepared for the reality.

Cold. Twilight faded into night.

Garner closed his eyes again and focused on moving each of his limbs and their respective digits. Aside from the gash in his forehead, he was apparently intact and unbroken. His chest hurt like hell from the harness, probably bruised black, but the seat itself had been torn out of the fuselage and lay on the ice next to the rest of the wreckage. Intended or not, Tibbits had been correct about the "safety" of facing the rear. Garner owed him his life.

Tibbits . . .

Garner struggled to his feet and stepped over to what was left of the helicopter. It looked as though the cockpit had torn away from the other pieces and rolled to its present position. The rest of the wreckage was hurled in all directions during the spiraling fall from the sky. The main cabin, where Garner had been seated, was nowhere to be seen. The instrument panel, too, appeared to have sheared away, leaving only a tangle of wires and the hollow ribs of the airframe in its place. The areas housing the radio and the helicopter's emergency beacon were smashed almost beyond recognition. All the windows were punched out, and the rear of the helicopter, including the rotors and the engines, was entirely torn off. The wind gusted freely though the shredded remains of the fuselage, fluttering the remaining shards of torn aluminum.

The metal around the pilots had been stripped away, replaced by a gouged and ice-encrusted swath of snow littered with blood and shards of metal. Tibbits had an ugly gash below his helmet and, from the disjointed angle of his head, his neck was probably broken. Garner checked Dunlop's broken body for a pulse, to no avail.

The sensation of guilt, of grief, struck Garner as painfully as the fresh gouge in his skull. The knowledge that he had dragged the pilots out in this weather chilled him more than any arctic wind ever could.

The heavy smell of fuel was everywhere, coating the wreckage and soaking into the ice, but there was no indication of burning or fire. Garner surveyed his surroundings. Between the darkness and the fog, the visibility was still less than a hundred feet. There wasn't a known landmark in sight—except for the tail section of the fuselage, which lay upside-down in the water about twenty yards away—and no way of telling which direction they had come from or which way Tibbits was going at the time of the crash.

Garner's watch read 9:30 P.M.—the same day, he assumed. As nearly as he could recollect, the helicopter had been closer to the *Phoenix* than B-82 when it went down. The *Phoenix*, along with the other two icebreakers, should have been ninety miles almost due east of the oil rig, but in the subsequent search, Tibbits had gone farther south, over the coastline of Melville Peninsula. Location and distance could only be guessed at until the storm and the darkness broke, and without proper shelter, Garner knew he couldn't simply sit down and await rescue. There was no way of knowing whether the *Phoenix* even knew about the Sikorsky, or whether they had survived the soliton, but the *Rushmore* was undoubtedly aware of the missing helicopter and, assuming the situation at B-82 was under control, Krail would be sending out a search party.

Whatever else was going on, the *Phoenix* likely needed him more. Zubov's words came flooding back to him: *We need you here, man.*

Garner stepped around the site, scavenging any useful provisions he could find. In his parka were a pocketknife, a disposable lighter, and some fishing line—pieces of Medusa's repair kit. From the wreckage, he gathered two warm blankets, the charts, several tufts of insulation, and a small first-aid kit. He scrubbed the blood from around his eyes with melted snow, then daubed alcohol on his wound and wrapped his head with gauze as best he could. He completed the dressing with goggles and a knit cap, but this did little to ease the throbbing ache. For whatever reason, the manufacturer of the kit found it more essential to include a grease pencil for its first-aid potential than a packet of aspirin. Using the pencil, Garner scrawled the message GONE TO PHOENIX on the side of the cockpit in thick black letters. He couldn't help but laugh at such a message in the middle of so much icy desolation.

Finally, he piled his meager assortment of survival tools onto the blankets and tied them together around a shaft of aluminum. The makeshift hobo's sack could be dragged along, relieving him of any load to carry. Peering across the ice at what he believed to be the shore of Melville Peninsula, he chose the direction that felt the most sensible and began walking.

Carol didn't know how long she remained unconscious. From the sound of trickling water and the orientation of the hovercraft, she guessed it was only a few seconds.

Like her, Byrnes was still strapped into his seat in an upside-down position. Just out of Carol's reach, his face was turned away from her, slumped down to the port side. He didn't respond to her shouts and she didn't want to contemplate the possibility he was dead.

The cockpit of the craft was pointed down at a cockeyed angle and she could only hope that the ice holding up the stern was strong enough to hold them a little longer. If the cushion had torn away from the underside, the fractured body of the hovercraft would sink like a stone; if it hadn't, the cushion would hold the cockpit underwater like a kayak that refused to be righted. With the very real possibility that the water was highly radioactive in addition to being lethally frigid, the prospect of floating seemed to be a worse fate. Assuming it was still attached and not blown halfway to Newfoundland by now, the cushion's bright orange color would provide a good marker for the rescue craft to find. When daylight came. And if anyone was searching for them yet. Between the apparent calamity at *B-82* and the industrial-sized untangling going on around the *Phoenix*, it could be hours longer before anyone even noticed they were gone.

As Carol tried to release herself from her seat, a bolt of pain shot upward from her left leg, causing her to scream. From the inflamed but strangely dead sensation, she concluded that a bone—the tibia or the fibula, but probably not both—had been broken when the impact sent her into the dashboard. There was blood on her boot below the cuff of her snowsuit, which might even mean the break was severe enough to puncture the skin. First she needed a splint of some kind, and a tourniquet. And no one was going to hand them to her.

Any movement of her legs sent another wave of pain washing over her and she fought to stay alert. She focused instead on her arms, extricating one, then the other from her seat harness. Around her, the shell of the cockpit groaned from her gingerly movements. The craft had come to rest tilted at about thirty degrees, and as this pitch increased the vehicle threatened to nose over and release its grip on the ice. A single error in judgment and she would fall headfirst into the water only a few feet below her.

A simple solution, then: don't slip. She released her seat belt and took up her own weight by holding on to the safety handle beside her seat. To pull her legs out from under the dash, she climbed at an angle toward the stern, stretching her body between the twin seats.

She was now only inches away from Byrnes. She rolled over against his right shoulder and gently shook him.

"Patrick?" she whispered. Then, louder, "Pat?" She touched his cheek. His flesh was cold, though it was impossible to tell if the condition was from internal or external circumstances. Byrnes's arm came up without resistance as she peeled away his glove and checked for a pulse, finding none there or in his neck. Finally, she turned his head to face her. His pale blue eyes stared blankly back at her.

Carol closed Byrnes's eyes, then her own.

She wept.

Then, with a sudden jolt, the hovercraft dropped lower in the water, breaking her reverie. The water was now less than two feet below her boots, rising steadily higher with each passing moment. The nose of the craft was filling up and the additional weight would soon pull the rest of the wreckage after it. She pulled back her right foot and struggled to sit up, ready to fight once again.

Carol continued crawling into the rear compartment of the hovercraft, a low, open space used for transporting passengers or small payloads. Finding single footholds along the hovercraft's roof, she tried to fashion a staircase to move herself farther astern, toward the engine and the main hatch. Each time her left foot even grazed an obstruction, pain shot through her hips and spine. Each time her right foot pushed her up, the hovercraft seemed to step down into the water a little more, negating her progress.

She clenched her teeth and continued upward. She blinked the anguished tears from her eyes and began to sing a song from her childhood: *The itsy-bitsy spider went up the waterspout.* The words seeped from her lips in a light, innocent pitch, barely louder than a whisper. *Down came the hovercraft and washed the spider out . . .*

The hovercraft responded accordingly, angling over farther still and dropping another two feet. The seat where Carol had dangled only moments before was now half underwater. The remainder of the instrument panel slid under the water with a wet gurgle. The lack of any burning or protest to the flooding by the electronics told Carol the vessel was entirely without power, even if she could reach the radio.

Out came the sun and dried up all the rain . . .

Although the roof was now nearly vertical, she slithered across the surface in search of provisions. Any loose debris that hadn't been tossed forward into the water was piled in small drifts against the rear seats. Except for the modest gear they had packed for the possible rescue of Garner, there was little more than the usual assortment of junk that accumulated in any vessel. The haversack they had filled with food, water, and warm clothing was, of course, nowhere to be found. There was a pair of exposure suits, but she doubted she was flexible enough to crawl inside one. They would provide little more warmth than an ineffectual blanket, but they were orange and that, at least, meant being seen amid all this white. A flashlight with a lantern battery, which might penetrate eighteen inches into the fog. A Danielle Steel novel, which would make good kindling if Carol could find some matches. A rifle and enough shells to ward off any curious polar bears. A five-gallon gas can, filled with the fuel mix for which Byrnes had adapted all the *Phoenix*'s motorized machinery. Some rope—just enough to hang herself—and two paddles that gave her just enough wood to fashion a splint.

Then, last, a kit containing a flare gun and six emergency flares. She couldn't imagine a better situation to declare an emergency, but she couldn't fire off a flare from inside the cabin.

She could hear the wind howling outside and knew she would lose most of her shelter once the hatch was opened. If she crawled outside she might never get back in, or the hovercraft would simply leave her behind as it completed its halting fall to the bottom.

She also knew she didn't have a choice in the matter.

Then the itsy-bitsy spider went up the spout again.

With three long, desperate steps, she reached the release handle on the outside hatch. Were the hovercraft still upright, she would have lacked the leverage to open it, but in the cabin's inverted position, the released hatch pulled open under its own weight.

Carol gasped as the cold wind struck her. Although the overcast persisted in the night sky, it had stopped snowing and the fog had lifted. She pulled on her hood and goggles, then tossed her supplies onto the ice one piece at a time. Even with her body weight helping to hold down the rear of the craft, the ground was at least four feet away. She would have to pull herself over the lip of the hatchway headfirst, then grip the top of the opening and lower herself to the ground.

She almost succeeded. As she angled her legs outside, straightened her back, and began reaching for the ground with her one good leg, she lost her grip and fell heavily to the ice, landing on her rump. Her leg raged in protest and for a moment all Carol could do was close her eyes and wait for the blinding pain to pass.

Tears came again; she fought them back. Eventually she struggled to her feet and looked around. A continuous plateau of fast ice extended from the wreckage to the shore. Even if she knew which shore it was, even if the distance were only a hundred yards, she couldn't imagine making the trek. Until the hovercraft sank from sight, she would have to remain with it.

She took up one of the paddles and wedged it in the hatchway. Balanced on one foot, she grabbed the open hatch and slammed it closed against the shaft of wood, snapping it in half. She placed the two pieces on either side of her broken shin and, as a temporary measure, bound them together with the rope. The effort left her too exhausted to even contemplate whether she should somehow stabilize the fragile wreckage and climb back inside the shelter of the cabin. Instead, she loaded the gun and fired one flare. The bright red projectile streaked into the sky and exploded somewhere in the fog layer above. Still, she hoped someone, somewhere, had seen its muted red glow.

"One down, five to go," she muttered, then, exhausted, sat down heavily to rest.

Relieved of Carol's awkward and sporadic motion, the hovercraft stopped complaining. It dangled on the edge of the floe, nose in the water, and provided partial shelter against the wind. The cushion provided a large, orange marker that would be easy to spot, once the weather allowed anyone to go aloft.

Carol gathered up the rifle, the remaining paddle, the suits, and the novel, then pulled herself to the downward end of the wreck. Crawling into the crook formed between the hovercraft's roof and the edge of the floe, she sat down and waited for help to arrive.

The weather cleared as the storm moved off to the east. The visibility improved but it was still several hours until dawn. As he walked, Garner could see a little farther ahead on the ice and landforms along the horizon. For the previous three hours, he had progressed in what he could only hope was a straight line; he could only estimate how far he had walked from the helicopter. He knew only that he had vastly underestimated how far north the helicopter had been when it went down. Several times the fast ice he was traversing ended abruptly, forcing him to backtrack as much as half a mile to find a continuous path. He also had to be alert for thin spots and soft, breakaway pieces of ice underfoot; thankfully, most had been recently refrozen by the blizzard.

Garner guessed he was somewhere on Melville Peninsula, but still nowhere near the entrance to Fury and Hecla Strait. That meant that, to the west, there was nothing but water between himself and *B-82,* almost a hundred miles away. To the east was the peninsula, with nothing but the occasional Inuit settlement. North, somewhere, was the *Phoenix,* and so he followed the coastline, keeping the frozen surface of

Committee Bay to his left. If the *Phoenix* and the other vessels had progressed past that point, into the strait, there was no way he could hope to reach them. Garner ignored such speculation and trudged onward.

Hunger had raged in Garner's stomach for hours. Now, as he walked, he saw something round and pink pressing against a translucent window in the sea ice. It was a single *Cyanea arctica,* a species of jellyfish indigenous to the Arctic that could grow up to six feet in diameter. This one was small, it was probably contaminated, and as a cnidarian it possessed nests of stinging cells for self-defense. But to Garner it was a long-over-due meal. He knelt down, chipped through the ice, and pulled the jellyfish through. Garner cut the top off the jellyfish's bell, which was apt to have fewer stinging cells, and cooked it over a small fire. The soft, shapeless form could not have looked less appealing and was more than 95 percent water, but the remaining flesh left a warm, satisfying sensation in his belly.

Soon Garner forced himself to resume walking. The crunching of his boots and the sound of his own breathing soon fell into a steady cadence. While he remained acutely aware of his surroundings, the utter lack of reference points lulled his mind into a contemplative state. Foremost among his thoughts was the welfare of those aboard the *Phoenix,* and what he might find whenever he reached them. If the soliton had been generated but produced little damage, he was confident that Carol, Zubov, and the others could shrug it off and regroup. If, however, the soliton was a large one and hit them directly, he doubted even the formidable bulk of the three icebreakers could have stayed unaffected.

His thoughts, as they always did, progressed to the minute details. He wondered if the *Ulva* bombers had reached their mark, and whether MacAdam had managed to scrounge up enough Plasroc and make the interminable trip north, at least as far as Cape Dorset, where his ground support was waiting. There were still too many pieces left to fit in the logistic jigsaw puzzle, too many intangibles. With or without him, the containment operation would proceed as it had to; if the operation failed, it would not be for lack of gallant effort, but the consequences would be much more horrifying than anything they had witnessed so far. Murphy's Law or not, Garner couldn't do a thing to help until he got where he was going.

Ultimately, he thought of Carol. In an ongoing series of poor decisions and unexamined failures in Garner's memory, Dr. Carol Harmon was an enduring reminder of The One That Got Away. As the divorce and the day-to-day reasons for it faded from memory, Garner found he could never forget the desire and affection of those years. Certainly nothing about either of their lifestyles had changed enough to suggest another attempt would yield a different result. If anything, their careers had only accelerated and further diverged.

He still loved her. It was the logistics that forever got in the way.

Dawn would be coming soon. Garner stopped to rest and looked to the east for any hopeful trace of light. As he retied his bundle of provisions, various parts of his body forced him to choose between continuing without rest and stopping to seek shelter. Clouds still obscured the stars, but the moon gave him enough light to see and, finally, a point of reference by which to guide his trek.

Then suddenly, perhaps three miles to the north, a startlingly bright flash of light rose into the night sky and burst over the desolate landscape: a flare.

For the first time in six hours, Garner altered his course.

With a definitive snap, the ledge of ice below the hover-craft finally gave way. The vehicle flipped completely vertical, then it wheeled over on its side, smashing onto the surface. The hatch snapped off at its hinges but remained gouged into the ice while the rest of the hovercraft disappeared from sight, pulling the tattered remains of the orange cushion with it to the bottom.

The entire spectacle took less than a minute, though Carol had received ample warning. She gathered up her pitiful camp and crawled away from the edge of the fractured ice.

She was too exhausted, too cold, and too hungry to fret over this latest setback and its implications. The wind had died down, but the darkness and the cold remained. She was now completely exposed on the ice with no practical way of making a shelter or getting to the ship and no obvious way for the ship to find her.

As her strength continued to ebb, she believed she could feel unconsciousness coming on, perhaps forever. With the numb, helpless feeling that permeated her entire body came a host of regrets, of words never spoken and deeds left undone. In that moment she realized that she wanted more than her research was giving her, more than the Nolan Group could ever provide her. Most of all, she wanted to *live*, but that possibility had never seemed more remote.

There was no sight of any approaching lights, either by air or on the surface, in any direction. For all she knew, she was the last person alive for a thousand miles.

She loaded the pistol and fired another flare. She had three left.

Then she closed her eyes.

At first Carol thought it was some kind of mirage, a hallucination. A single light bobbing toward her across the ice, as if a passing stranger out for a stroll just happened to see the flare. But this was no illusion. Carol quickly grabbed her own pathetic lamp and waved it in return.

"Over here!" she tried to shout, though what remained of her voice was little more than a croak.

The jouncing of the light increased; the stranger was running. She could now see that it was a single figure, wrapped head to toe in goggles, gloves—and one of the exposure suits from the *Phoenix*.

"*Here!*" She strained again.

"Hold on, I've got you," came the reply from across the ice. She knew in an instant who it was and her tears began to flow freely, whether from relief, astonishment, or collapse, it didn't matter. The one person who could find her *had* found her and that feeling was incredible.

"Brock!" she cried, trembling, still not wholly convinced this was not a dream.

Then he was there, next to her. She felt his arms close around her and nothing else seemed to matter.

"My leg," she cautioned, as if the ungainly, primitive splint didn't speak for itself.

"Okay, okay," he said, urging her to keep still. "We'll take care of it as soon as we can." She felt like a child in his arms, and began relating the story of Byrnes and the hovercraft wreck as best she could.

"We have to get you some shelter," Garner said. "How far is it back to the *Phoenix*?"

"I don't know," she admitted. "Fifteen, twenty miles. More. There's no way you can—"

"Rest," he said, pressing a finger to her lips.

Garner wrestled the broken hatch back from the edge of the ice and turned it over. The smooth, rounded outer surface would serve as a sled, and the second paddle, threaded through the broken hinges, made an adequate handle. He lifted Carol onto the hatch and wrapped her with the blankets and pieces of insulation. Last, he tied the rest of their provisions and the jerry can of fuel onto the hatch and tested the weight of the makeshift yoke across his shoulders.

"Let's go," he said to her, then kissed her on the forehead as she drifted off to sleep.

25

Hours after Garner and Krail confirmed the travel arrangements for David MacAdam, Global Oil arranged to send its utility ship, the *Villager*, to a rendezvous with the containment operation taking shape in Foxe Basin. Though lacking any aesthetic appeal, the *Villager* was the only vessel of its kind in the world. The blunt bow of the six-thousand-ton vessel was reinforced with steel plating eight inches thick, capable of navigating almost any obstructions the sea could toss in its path. Mounted on its stern was one of the sturdiest deep-water dredging apparatuses ever engineered, an invaluable asset for contouring the shifted sediment above depleted oil sands or clearing obstructions for the placement of a new platform. Amidships was an equally formidable pump-and-nozzle system, which could be used for purposes ranging from washing down pipes and derricks to filling new GBS structures with hundreds of tons of molten ballast. Booms, tanks, and sediment buckets lined every available surface on the *Villager*'s decks and crowded around her relatively small superstructure, which was necessarily moved forward. Someone once remarked that the *Villager* resembled a "real" ship that had been exploded from somewhere inside the hull, leaving a garish collage of rusted, tangled piping and winches that somehow still managed to earn a living. And earn she did: though the ship had been built specifically to assist in the construction of *B-82,* Global now recovered its expenses by loaning the vessel to other companies' platforms in the North Atlantic and the North Sea. As new rigs sought to plumb increasingly hostile environs and older platforms sought to extend their original production cycles, the *Villager* had become a profitable nursemaid.

MacAdam arrived at Cape Dorset after a thirty-eight-hour flight in a McDonnell-Douglas C-17 Globemaster, its 160,000-pound payload bay loaded to capacity. In the rear of the aircraft the sealing compound and its stabilizing resin filled a pair of sixty-five-hundred-gallon brewer's tanks that had been taken directly out of MacAdam's barn and loaded onto a convoy of Army flatbed trucks. Now the tanks would be emptied into the hold of the *Villager* for the rest of the journey to Fury and Hecla Strait.

MacAdam slept little during the trip. Instead he requested regular updates on the weather they would be facing, then attempted to factor this information into his calculations for the mix and disbursement of the Plasroc.

Grateful to be on stable ground, however temporarily, the chemist accepted a warmer change of clothes from one of the Canadian Forces officers, who then relayed word of his arrival to those aboard the *Phoenix.* They, like practically everyone who had helped MacAdam wrestle the Plasroc the ten thousand miles from Adelaide, seemed genuinely excited—hopeful with a touch of admiration—that he was able to come along with his marvelous invention. After so many years of denial, MacAdam had to admit he liked the attention.

The *Villager* arrived in the afternoon. MacAdam and the Canadian Forces officer traveled down to the harbor and were waiting as the ugly vessel emerged from the fog and found a berth along the government dock. To MacAdam, the main deck of the bizarre ship looked as though it had sustained several *kamikaze* attacks, and he cringed at the thought of his refined compound being pumped into her squalid hold.

"Is she supposed to look like that?" he asked the officer timidly.

"Gad, I hope not," replied the officer.

The landing plank was lowered and the captain himself was the first one to disembark. He was a tall, sturdy man with an ample belly, broad shoulders, and a half-hearted attempt at a beard. He looked as though, in a pinch, he could simply pick up the boilers full of Plasroc and place them on the ship himself. The captain moved quickly and MacAdam found himself taking a half step backward as he stopped in front of them. Not knowing exactly what to do, MacAdam saluted. He had saluted a lot of people in the past two days, just in case.

"No need to salute me, Mr. MacAdam," the captain said. "I'm no civil servant." He glanced at the officer. "No offense."

They began with a quick tour of the ship and its storage tanks, piping, and dredges. Given this insight, some sense of intended function began to emerge from the apparently disjointed mountains of iron, pulleys, and pumps.

The captain recited a seemingly unending list of the *Villager*'s specifications. "At full capacity we can dredge up to five thousand yards of soft sediment—or fifteen hundred of hard—at depths to three hundred feet. We can load at a rate of sixty thousand barrels an hour, with a fluid capacity in the hull of two hundred thousand barrels—"

"Barrels?" MacAdam asked.

"Fifty-five gallons each, ten million gallons or more

overall. What you actually get out of the tanks and the pumps, mind you, will depend on the viscosity of your chemicals. We've also got two auxiliary pump systems if you need 'em." The captain turned back to MacAdam. "Any questions?"

The chemist was still staring around at the ship, his eyes unblinking.

"Just one," he said, a nervous smile on his lips. "Is all this for me?"

The Plasroc was transferred to the *Villager,* then the unsightly vessel and its voluminous cargo rendezvoused with the icebreakers at the containment area the next morning. Following directions from the *Phoenix,* the ship drew alongside the containment pen strung between the *Des Groseilliers* and the *Sovietsky Soyuz.* A few minutes later, a motorized launch arrived carrying Zubov. He welcomed them to the effort and suggested he was "not exactly the boss around here, but as close as you're gonna get at the moment."

Seeing the haggard, exhausted look on the big man's face, MacAdam got his first real sense of the battle that had recently been waged across the breadth of the Arctic. His own efforts, in comparison, seemed as banal as those of a delivery boy.

Once the *Villager*'s dredging crew had been briefed on the size, type, and location of the area to be dredged, Zubov turned his attention to MacAdam and the tanks of Plasroc.

"How will the Plasroc respond to cold weather?" Zubov wanted to know. *Cold* was a relative term. The average temperature of the slick was thirty-eight degrees—insufferable for humans, balmy for the *Thio-uni,* and murderous for the ice—while the air fluctuated between eighteen and minus ten degrees Fahrenheit, depending on the wind.

"I've done the calculations a dozen times," MacAdam replied, "and I think we'll be fine."

"What about dilution of the compound itself?" the captain asked.

"Dilution shouldn't affect its viscosity or its integrity," MacAdam said. "It was designed with liquid wastes in mind, and a number of those are stored in containment reservoirs. I've mixed a more dilute solution to resist clogging your sprayers, and it should bond easily without losing much strength. We should be able to get a stable concretion without compromising the time required for the resin to harden."

"That's a lot of 'shoulds,'" Zubov said. "What would it take to use a full concentration?"

"Warmer water, I suppose."

Zubov turned to the *Villager*'s captain. "Is there any way you can pump heated water over the slick first, then follow it with the Plasroc?"

The captain scratched at his beard. "We can try it. The main system is full of the plastic crap—no offense, Professor—but the auxiliary systems are still free."

"You'd need to pump clean water from outside the slick, then spray it out over the containment area," Zubov recommended.

"Then it'd depend on the distance between the draw and the slick, between the good water and the bad."

"Until we can get the ice down here and get the slick contained, we have to consider it all bad," Zubov said.

The captain shook his head. "If the *Villager* wasn't already filled to the gills, I'd say screw all this fucking plastic—again, no offense, Professor. For the same effort, we could melt the hot ice and pump the slick straight into our hold."

Zubov shook his head. "Too dangerous, even discounting the fact that you would cook the guts of your lovely boat here. There's no way you'd have enough capacity to take on the entire slick, and even if you were willing to make a dozen trips, I doubt anyone would open their doors to let you offload the waste-water."

The captain evaluated Zubov's analysis of the situation, finally nodding in agreement. "This is one shitty pickle you've got here."

"Hopefully not for long," Zubov said and clapped MacAdam on the back. They stepped into the *Villager*'s chart room and Zubov unrolled a map showing the most recent sediment profile of the region. His finger came to rest over a large shaded area marked SILT/CLAY MIX just outside the eastern terminus of Fury and Hecla Strait.

"The soliton threw our original plans all out of whack," Zubov explained. "We lost hold of the slick before it entered the strait, so catching it coming out is our next option." On the chart it was evident how the comparatively narrow channel of Fury and Hecla Strait—little more than ten miles across—would help direct the slick into a limited number of possible areas at the top of Foxe Basin.

"Until the ice arrives, this is where you can start dredging a deposit site for the bonded Plasroc," Zubov said. "The geologists tell me that the clay will act as a natural sarcophagus."

"It won't really be needed," MacAdam said confidently, "but it's always nice to have a second layer of containment." He pulled out his calculator and derived an estimate for the final size of the sealed mass. The captain extrapolated this figure to the volume of sediment they would need to dredge and suggested the pit could be dug in another three days, maybe less.

"Let's shoot for 'less' then," Zubov asked. "Once the hot ice is driven into the containment pen, I don't know how long we'll be able to hold it there." They agreed that, while Zubov returned to oversee the revised plans for containing the slick, the *Villager* could begin dredging a suitable pocket for capturing the Plasroc.

As he returned to the *Phoenix*, Zubov realized he had probably delivered a pretty fair performance of "the man in charge," though he hardly believed it himself. In truth, he was exhausted, he was ready to leave the entire mess to Krail's grunts, and most of all, he was sick with worry about his friends.

They were still lost, thought Garner, but at least they were lost together. It took nearly an hour to backtrack as far as the shore, then they continued north, Carol lying quietly on the concave surface of the hatch, Garner pulling her. He set a consistent pace and rested for fifteen minutes out of every hour.

Victor's words about life in the Arctic came back to Garner. *We get where we are going because of the snow, not in spite of it.* Indeed.

The only sounds were Garner's own labored breathing, the subtle groaning of the pack, and the scrape of the hatch as it slid across the wind-polished crusts of ice. Despite his fatigue, Garner could not help but notice the utter beauty of the sudden calm in the wake of the storm. He had never been a religious man but the serenity of the darkened landscape gave him pause—he and Carol were utterly alone, yet he did not *feel* alone. It was a sensation he had often felt in the Southern Ocean, that there was something innately spiritual about the earth's polar reaches. The unending bleakness somehow filled him with reassurance, providing comfort rather than isolation.

As dusk descended, the sky cleared completely above them and a dazzling array of stars shined down on the fresh drifts of crystalline snow.

"The snow looks so beautiful," Carol murmured as she drifted out of sleep.

"If only there wasn't so damn much of it," Garner grunted in agreement. He stumbled over a small depression in the ice and used this as an excuse to stop and make another temporary camp. He fired off another flare. Two left.

As soon as they stopped moving, the absolute silence descended over them once again. "How are you doing?" Carol asked him.

"We'll get there," he said. "Promise." Garner was breathing hard, sweating under his layers of clothing. Tired but not beaten. He might have been out for a midwinter's jog, not struggling for survival as her protector.

Carol's heart swelled with love for him at that moment. For the strength of will that now carried them across the ice. For the brilliance he had employed to get them this far. For remembering her birthday. Even for the fact that he had come to the Arctic in the first place. All only for her.

"Kiss me," she said quietly. "I need you to kiss me right now."

He did, leaning over her gently. The warmth of his lips, the scent of his skin, pushed aside everything but the moment.

As she gazed into his eyes, a flicker of light glinted across the sky. Looking up, they saw the first curtains rise on a magical display of heavenly light—the aurora borealis had come out to dance for them.

Carol sat up and nestled into Garner's arms. They held each other and watched the pale green and magenta light dance until it faded into the glow of full night.

"Tell me that this wasn't meant to be," Garner said at last.

She had to agree. At that moment, their closeness couldn't have been more right. Garner did what he could to excavate a small shelter in the side of a snowdrift, out of the wind. He carefully lined the makeshift *iglu* with whatever insulation they had, set Carol gently inside, and pulled the hatch over the opening as shelter from the wind. Sleep came quickly to them both.

As morning arrived, they were able to get a clearer look at the surrounding landscape. To the east, along the shore of Committee Bay, some kind of structure was now visible. It looked like a small building, but narrower. As they drew nearer, they could see it was a row of piled stones—three of them, built out on a small tambolo. With a little imagination, they vaguely resembled human figures with their arms stretched out to the sides.

"*Inuksuit,*" Carol said as she craned to look at them. "Inuit scarecrows used to herd caribou, among other purposes. Not this time of year, though—the herds are too skinny after winter."

Garner peered at the piled stones, eerily human in appearance. "I thought they were used as some kind of sacred markers."

"Legends describe them as being seaside guardians, watching for hunters to return from the hunt," Carol replied. "The markers were also considered good luck because if they were followed correctly, they would lead to food where the caribou were trapped and killed. In any event, I think we just found the interstate."

Garner continued his plodding pace, bringing them ever closer to the rock formations. "So what do we do now?" Garner asked. "Wait here for a dog sled?"

"More likely a snowmobile."

Then a sound came drifting though the morning stillness: barking.

"Told you so," Garner said with a wink.

It wasn't a dog team but a single dog. A vigorous Siberian husky with a familiar broad white face and mismatched eyes. "I don't believe it," Carol said as the dog bounded toward them, stopping short and ducking its head to be patted. "It's *Victor's* dog."

"Janey," Garner concurred.

"I might get tired of you being right all the time, you know?" Carol remarked to Garner. "Someday." The delight quickly faded from Carol's face as she craned her neck to look around. "So . . . where's Victor?"

Garner hoisted the hatch once again and followed Janey two hundred yards farther, approaching closer still to the *inuksuit*. The formations, it turned out, were not arranged in a line at all, but in a small, circular grouping. In the middle of the small space, lying on his back with hands folded across his chest, was Victor Tablinivik, his tools and smaller possessions in a neat pile beside him. His *komatik* sled and hunting tools were set inside a small cave eroded into the adjacent shore.

Garner set down the hatch and stooped to examine Victor's body. The hearty Inuk looked to have been dead a few days, judging by the way the recent storm had blown a thin layer of snow and ice around his folded limbs. His flesh was frozen but perfectly preserved. In Victor's folded hands, Garner found the rock from Elephant Island. The Inuk had died holding on to the past, a lasting memory of the frontier that once had been.

Carol was gazing up at the *inuksuit*. "Look at that," she said, pointing up at them. "Two large figures—one slightly larger—and a smaller one. I'd say it's supposed to be Victor, his wife, and his son," she speculated. "He must have heard the news from his settlement," Carol suddenly realized. "He might even have been the only survivor. Do you think—" She hesitated, unsure whether to continue. "Maybe this was the way for him to find his peace."

There seemed to be nothing else to add. Garner and Carol bowed their heads in a moment of respect, then left the circle of stones.

Garner pulled Carol the rest of the way back to the cave on the shore, Janey trotting beside them. Indeed, it looked as though many caribou had been herded into this place over the years, but so efficient was the Inuit use of flesh, bone, hide, and entrails that nothing of use remained for scavengers. On the other hand, Victor's sled contained several blankets, extra clothing, and handmade hunting equipment. For catch, Garner found several fish and a seal carcass, to which Janey had helped herself in Victor's absence.

"Looks like breakfast," Carol said, eyeing the fish.

"Strange that Victor would catch this food and leave leftovers to go to waste," Garner speculated.

"What if he left it for Janey to eat until someone else came along?"

"What if the food is contaminated?" Garner cautioned.

"What if I'm really, really, *really* hungry?"

The fish were frozen solid, but there was enough dried wood on the sled to build a small fire. As Janey went back to her seal, Garner gutted the fish and cooked them over the fire. The flesh may have been radioactive—it certainly was dry, salty, and several pieces were charred on the edges—but both Carol and Garner agreed that it was the most succulent meal they could ever have hoped for.

"Beats the hell out of *Cyanea*," Garner admitted as he chewed the fish.

"I can't believe you ate a jellyfish," Carol said, screwing up her face. "I may never kiss that face again."

"Now what were you doing kissing jellyfish?" Garner teased as he hoisted Carol onto the *komatik* and set her down, he hoped, for the last time. He noted the long, polished runners and the hand-lashed joints that held the pieces of wood and bone together, an intentionally loose arrangement that let the *komatik* bend against the terrain without cracking.

"What do you think?" Garner asked. "Is this an Inuit medevac or what?"

"I say *mush*, driver," Carol replied, stifling a giggle. "Once around the glacier and then home."

"We're not there yet," he said. "But you can enjoy the ride while it lasts."

Carol did. The cold and her injuries had become secondary nuisances. She was in love and one night closer to home.

26

The infirmary was the first place Zubov stopped when he arrived back at the *Phoenix*. Junko had set up a separate area for those who had been contaminated by the monstrous wave, and that area remained filled with patients awaiting treatment. Two of the crew members Junko was monitoring had slipped into critical condition, and while the doctor had managed to stabilize their condition, the men would have to be taken to a proper treatment center as soon as possible.

Frisch stopped in and reported that a helicopter was waiting at Cape Dorset to bring in some more supplies and airlift the patients out.

"You should go with them," Zubov told her. Junko's face appeared flushed, and Zubov wondered if the redness might be some kind of burns from her own exposure to the radioactive water.

"Don't be ridiculous," she said with a wave of her hand. "Besides, I'm needed here. Abandoning ship at this point would be incredibly selfish."

"Not if it means the difference between you getting proper treatment and . . . something else."

"Sergei, I'm *fine*," she insisted, taking his broad face in her tiny hands. "Really. What do I have to do to convince you of that?"

"Promise me you won't go outside anymore."

"Ever?" she asked with a laugh. "I'll miss the spring bloom!"

"Be serious," he said. "Promise me you'll stay inside until all this is over."

She kissed him then, warmly and convincingly. "All right, I promise. Now what about you? Will you get some sleep, or are you just going to keep working until you start to hallucinate?"

"I'm worried about Brock," he admitted. "And there hasn't been any word from the hovercraft."

"What about taking a SnoCat?" she asked. "Have the captain drop one off on the ice. With a full tank of gas, it must have nearly the same range as the hovercraft."

"I thought of that," Zubov said. "But . . ." His words trailed off.

"But you're worried about me," she finished.

"Yes." He looked down at his hands. "Of course I am."

"Then go. You have no reason not to. It'll be hours before anyone is ready to continue the containment. Thanks to you and Carol, things are humming along smoothly here. The icebreakers have rebuilt the containment pen and the slick is being channeled right up the strait. The only thing we don't know is what's happened out there on the ice. Let's hope it's just a weather delay or mechanical breakdown. If it's something bad, I can't imagine a better person to set things right."

"No," he said stubbornly. "I'm needed here."

"You may be needed more out there," she pressed. "Send someone else, if you think he would do a better job of finding them." She knew he wouldn't be able to name a substitute he would feel comfortable putting in charge.

Zubov embraced her again, then went up to the bridge. He designated the *Phoenix*'s mate as a point of contact to relay information to the *Villager,* then he asked the crew to fuel up a SnoCat as soon as they could dig one out of the hold.

The quartz halogen headlights mounted on the machine's engine cowling did little to infiltrate the dense fog that still refused to lift from large areas of Melville Peninsula. Stooped forward behind the blunt Plexiglas windshield, Zubov advanced steadily to the south, one eye on the fractured ground beneath him, the other on the terrain around him, looking for any sign of the helicopter or the hovercraft.

He had long ago come to ignore the discomfort of the wind as it sliced through the chinks in his cold-weather gear, goggles, and facemask. The walkie-talkie unit he had brought with him failed within an hour of leaving the ship as the cold quickly compromised its battery's performance. Zubov's attention was on keeping a sensible search in the vicinity of the hovercraft's last reported position. He could only hope that Byrnes and Carol had backtracked toward the ship on foot after the hovercraft had become disabled—assuming that was what had happened.

This was to say nothing of Garner's whereabouts. At the time Zubov had left the *Phoenix,* there was still no report on what had happened to the helicopter. Zubov knew only that if the helicopter did go down, it was probably beyond the range of the SnoCat's supply of fuel. He would have to remain focused on finding the hovercraft on this trip, then, if still necessary, have the *Phoenix* organize a larger search party and head farther west to find the Sikorsky.

Running against a stiff headwind with its throttle almost fully open, the SnoCat guzzled its initial tank of fuel at an alarming rate. When the fuel gauge showed half a tank, Zubov stopped and topped it up from the jerry cans he had brought along. When the gauge reached half a second time before any sign of the hovercraft—any sign of *anything*—had been located, Zubov cursed loudly and pounded the SnoCat's steering wheel. Too quickly, he had reached his point of no return and would have to abandon his search. Going any farther afield, he would not have enough fuel to get the SnoCat back to the *Phoenix*.

He thought about his predicament for a moment longer, squinting against the bleak visibility that showed signs of clearing as the last vestiges of the storm passed overhead. By dawn they might even be able to mount a proper search-and-rescue mission, but in a few more hours the lives they were looking for could be lost.

He kept going. He could not allow himself to abandon the search.

As the fuel level continued to drop, now past a quarter tank, there was also the risk of the fuel line freezing or the engine stalling completely. Then six of them would be missing in action. Zubov switched off the engine one last time, tried the radio again, unsuccessfully, opened the fuel tank and poured in the dregs of his jerry cans. He barely scrounged half a tank. Zubov knew his desperate foolishness had probably cost him not only his own return to the *Phoenix,* but the lives of his friends as well.

"Smooth move, Sergei," Zubov muttered to himself, then bellowed angrily: "Just brilliant. A real goddamn Saint Bernard you are." In his frustration he banged a jerry can off the fender of the SnoCat and threw the empty container across the ice.

He stooped forward over the silent machine and tried to compose himself. The cold roar of the wind now assaulted his ears, which were still ringing from the clanking rattle of the SnoCat's engine. Resting for a moment longer, he found himself again thinking of Junko and the look of undeniable affection in her eyes as she kissed him good-bye. That he was in love with her—at least, as much as he had ever understood the word *love* to mean—was no longer in question. Certainly his feelings for Junko qualified more than anything he'd felt for any other woman he had ever known. The question was whether he was intellectual enough, mature enough, or sensible enough to tell her how he felt and expect a rewarding response. Sense or not, he resolved to find an answer to that question the moment he returned to the *Phoenix*.

Behind him, a voice called out from the darkness.

"Hey! Want me to get the windows?"

Zubov whirled around. Garner was less than thirty yards away, struggling forward as he pulled a large wooden sledge. Seeing the dog that accompanied his friend, Zubov recognized the contraption as Victor's *komatik*. A single body was strapped to the sled and Zubov assumed it was Victor.

Zubov clapped his arms around Garner in a bear hug, lifting his friend off the ground. Garner looked cold, and worse, he *felt* cold, even through his exposure suit. Garner had given every spare article of clothing to the occupant of the sled.

Now Zubov could see that it was Carol on the sled. She turned her head weakly and smiled at him through her bundled wrapping. "Hi, Serg," she said weakly. "Fancy meeting you here."

Zubov's surprise was replaced with stunned amazement. "Fancy? It's *amazing*." He grinned again and looked back at Garner. "How far?" was all he could ask.

"Thirty miles, give or take," Garner said. "From the

hovercraft. Another fifteen or twenty before that. Feels like I've been walking for a week."

"Amazing," Zubov repeated. "Remind me to call you the next time I lose my car keys. What about Byrnes? Did he stay with the hovercraft?"

"Patrick's dead," Garner confirmed. "His body went down with the hovercraft. We lost Tibbits and Dunlop too. And Victor."

Zubov winced. "Ah, shit."

"I think it was Victor's choice to die." Garner tried to explain what they had found at the *inuksuit*. He didn't want to think about the details of the pilots' deaths. Not now. Their deaths were not by choice.

"I don't believe it," Zubov said. "You tenacious son of a bitch."

"Yeah, we make our own path when we have to," Garner said with a weary grin, his teeth chattering slightly. "Hard to miss you, given all the noise the beast was making—and the SnoCat is pretty loud too."

"Not anymore, smartass. I'm out of gas."

Garner turned and pulled the hovercraft's gas can from the items tied to the sled. "And it just happens we have some of Byrnes's special blend, but no ride. I smell a really good marriage of convenience here."

"Damn right you do," Zubov laughed, taking the fuel and patting Garner on the back again. "Only you would pack an extra forty pounds of fuel, just in case." He topped off the tank once more. "This'll give this gas-sucking thing an extra twenty or thirty miles, but even still, I can't tell you if it's enough to get back."

"It's getting dark," Garner replied. "Let's take our chances."

They attached the sled to the back of the SnoCat, trailer fashion, then Garner set Carol onto the single bench seat beside Zubov. Janey seemed content to continue alongside rather than accept a ride in the back of the noisy machine. For the entire return journey to the *Phoenix*, Zubov could keep his mind on only two things: keeping his bearings in the blowing snow and formulating a contingency plan for when they ran out of gas for good. Too quickly, the fuel gauge again sank to the half-full mark, then continued toward one-quarter without hesitation.

Zubov thought of Junko. He recalled the worry in her eyes the last time they had kissed and promised to resolve those fears as soon as they found the *Phoenix*. He fabricated instead a happier, albeit fictitious, memory. He imagined his love waiting for their safe return, her freshly scrubbed skin smelling of lavender and a small bouquet of flowers clutched in her tiny hands. It was absurdly romantic, but it reminded him of a woman he had seen in an airport once, staring expectantly past everyone else as she anticipated the return of her special someone. Zubov knew no one had ever waited in an airport for him in that way, but he liked the thought of it. He imagined his Junko meeting him at the turnstile, saying she loved him, then being swept up in his arms as she kissed him with the softest of lips.

A large hummock of ice suddenly loomed out of the twilight, snapping Zubov's focus back to the task at hand. Behind them, the *komatik* swayed with the sudden shift in momentum, Garner and Carol were jarred from their exhausted sleep, but the SnoCat retained its lumbering track. Junko would have to hold those flowers a little longer.

As the visibility finally began to improve, the ground revealed itself to be a hundred times more threatening than it had been on the outbound trip. Each time Zubov thought they were making good progress, the floe beneath them would abruptly end, forcing him to circle back to the west and farther down the shore. As night descended, searching for the ships' lights was easier, but watching for breaks or crevasses in the ice became next to impossible. His vision was limited to the narrow cone of illumination projected from the SnoCat's headlights, and most of that was filled with swirling snow.

More unnerving was the noise of the SnoCat's engine, which covered up any audible clues rising from the ice itself. Inside the cab, they could not hear the groans and complaints of freshly rended fissures, or whether a given section of ice was threatening to break, cutting off their only route back to shore. Even far away from the edge of the ice, Zubov had no way of knowing if the ridges they had to cross were strong enough to support the weight of the machine and its occupants. He was following, approximately, the same course he had taken going out and the ice barely held the SnoCat's weight then—for one passenger, without a trailer.

Slow and steady wins the race, Zubov kept repeating to himself, though their measured progress seemed maddeningly slow. As annoying as the constant roar of the engine was, Zubov could only hope that it would remain that way: constant.

Janey appeared to share none of this anxious concern. She bounded along happily panting beside and behind the SnoCat, her curlicued tail waggling in the air. She seemed to enjoy watching these humans struggle, and could apparently tag along all night without fatigue.

Sitting between the two men, Carol endured the trip without making a sound, though she often fidgeted to find a more comfortable position for her leg. Garner looked to be within a whisper of death, and a very quiet whisper at that. He hadn't said ten words since they started back. He claimed to be conserving energy, but his exhaustion was far more obvious. It was all he could do to keep one hand on the handrail, another around

Carol's shoulders. Zubov regarded his friend's appearance with concern—his face was pale, yet tinged with the rosy lace of mild frostbite. Fatigue and several days' growth of beard left his features gaunt and haggard except for the glint of vitality in his penetrating eyes. He was down, but not out—he was never out. No matter what the situation, there was always life in those gray eyes, like a fire burning beneath glacial ice. In all the years they'd known each other, Zubov had never seen that spark diminish.

Then another glint caught Zubov's eye, this one far off through the fog and drawing closer. It was the deck lights of the *Phoenix*—a brilliant, man-made constellation moored to the floe less than a mile away. The ship was straight ahead, moored to the ice itself, and on the far side of her was the man-made berg of *Ulva*-laden ice.

Now Zubov could see ships all around the SnoCat— to the left was the *Sovietsky Soyuz* and to the right was the *North Sea*. By some combination of dead reckoning and blind luck, he had found the one peninsula of fast ice that jutted directly into the very middle of the containment operation. Never before had he been so relieved to see a landing ramp: the steel plates that angled sharply up from the ice to the gunwales of the *Phoenix*.

The SnoCat's engine finally ran out of fuel, sputtered, and died—within fifty yards of its destination.

"Nice driving, Serg," Garner said from the other side of the cab.

"Just like I planned it." Zubov exhaled with relief. "Really."

With the engine silenced, they could now hear the sounds of the other two ships, the generators and winches working tirelessly to draw the ice into the containment booms. The ships were moored all around him, thousands of tons of iron and steel gathered around the floating pen.

A crowd of people was gathered on the *Phoenix*'s deck and they all began streaming down the landing plank to greet the new arrivals. They were wrapped with hoods, scarves, and goggles, and Zubov couldn't identify any of them. He realized it didn't matter who they were, for he didn't really know any of them—Junko wasn't among them, Byrnes was gone, and his only two other confidants were slumped on the seat beside him. Then Zubov felt a twinge of regret: though he was too tired to admit it, he wished there were someone there to welcome him back. Someone important. Someone he loved, who loved him back. Sooner rather than later, he wanted that someone to be Junko.

As he climbed out of the cab, Zubov passed a prayer of thanks to whoever had been looking down on them that day. He wanted to believe it was his family, and all the others who had perished in Pripyat in 1986. They understood hardship. "Thank you," he whispered aloud, but the words were lost to the wind.

Susan was the first to reach them. "Thank goodness you made it!" she said with cautious relief. There was still too much she did not know about the condition of the new arrivals to be unreservedly happy.

Garner was already off the seat and attending to Carol. "Is she—?" Susan began, looking at Carol.

"She's alive," Garner said. "Badly broken leg, maybe some frostbite. Come on, let's get her inside." Garner started to pick Carol up, but instead four of the *Phoenix*'s crew stepped in with a back board to carry her.

"Oh no you don't," Susan scolded Garner as he tried to help. "Not with that head wound of yours. Follow these guys inside and I'll take a look at that too."

Garner followed them back toward the ship. "Cleopatra never had it so good," Carol said as the board was carted along.

"He carried her about thirty miles," Zubov

explained to Susan as the others moved off. "And carried himself twenty more before that, if you can believe it. I doubt I would have found them if he hadn't . . . I mean, I wouldn't have . . ." The emotion of the blessed serendipity silenced him.

"It's okay, Sergei," Susan said, comforting him. "It's gonna be all right now."

Zubov suddenly realized that only he and Susan had lagged behind the others. He glanced expectantly toward the *Phoenix*.

I'll take a look at that too, Susan had said to Garner. Then it hit him—

"Where's Junko?" Zubov asked.

When Susan turned back to him, there were tears in her eyes. "In the infirmary," she said. "She's—" She choked on her words. "Oh, Sergei, I'm so sorry."

Zubov turned on his heel and began galloping toward the ship, Susan close behind him. He sprinted past Garner and the others carrying Carol before they reached the base of the landing ramp, then bounded up the ramp. First into the airlock, he began stripping off his outside clothing. He was now in a frantic hurry and Susan struggled to keep pace with him.

"What happened?" Zubov demanded.

Tears streamed down Susan's cheeks. "She didn't let on how badly she was exposed the first time, because . . ."

"Because *why*?"

"Because she wanted you to get a search organized." Susan turned her eyes toward the floor. "She knew only you could do it."

Dressed in his inside clothes, Zubov stepped out of the airlock into the lab. "She still could have told me. Now she's probably made it worse—"

Susan stopped him at the end of the corridor leading to the infirmary. "Serg, listen to me: Junko's *dead*. She died this morning." Susan struggled to add some words of comfort to the news to make it seem less devastating. Something like *she died in her sleep* or *she died peacefully; she didn't feel a thing*. But Susan had been a witness to Junko's final hours aboard the *Phoenix* and she knew firsthand that none of those platitudes were true. The horrors of Junko's death, how system after system in her body had shut down, how she had slowly burned to death from within, would haunt Susan forever.

Zubov knew none of this. He only knew that he had never felt colder in his entire life.

Carol was taken immediately to the infirmary, where Susan set her broken leg in a cast, treated her surprisingly mild frostbite, and meticulously went through Junko's checklist for radiation poisoning.

Susan was just completing her examination when Garner came in. He had begun to return to life, if only from the warm, familiar confines of the ship.

Carol managed a weak smile. "Hi, honey," she said.

Garner leaned close, kissed her on the forehead. "Safe and sound," he said. "Told you so."

Carol was about to reply when Garner hushed her. "I know," he said.

Carol squeezed his hand once, then drifted into a deep sleep.

Garner looked at Susan. "Where's the big guy?" he asked quietly.

Susan nodded toward the adjoining cabin just as Zubov exited the room. His eyes were rimmed red and sunken with despair. He looked smaller, somehow.

It was the first moment the two had been together since returning to the ship. Garner studied his friend carefully, then embraced him. "I'm sorry, man."

"I could have been here," Zubov said, his voice

strained and fighting back his tears. "If I'd only known."

"You can't look at it like that," Susan said, coming up behind them. "If you'd stayed, Carol and Brock would be dead too. There was nothing we could have done to save her here." In truth, Junko had measured her own exposure at over eight Sieverts—enough to start destroying her central nervous system almost immediately. "She knew she wasn't going to survive more than a few hours and that these two needed you more."

"She wanted to spare the rest of us a lot of pain," Garner said. He could see Zubov was waiting to hear something else. "You can't watch over everyone. No one can."

Zubov choked back his emotions, his glassy eyes gaining a steely resolve. "It's a little hard for me to see that right now, Brock."

"Get some rest," Garner said. "Susan can give you a sedative."

"No, dammit!" Zubov bellowed. "I've got to get back out there."

"Serg, don't push it—"

"Don't push *me*." Zubov's eyes blazed. "We're not out of this yet. You *need* me. And we still need to *set things right* out there. For Junko. For Byrnes and those pilots. For Victor and his family and everyone else. But right now—first, for Junko."

"You got it," Garner replied quietly. "Let's get to work, my friend."

27

May 28
69° 22' N. Lat.; 81° 26' W. Long.
Foxe Basin, Arctic Ocean

As the last vestiges of the slow-moving storm moved off to the northeast, full communication was finally reestablished between the ships involved in the containment effort and those charged with cleaning up the broken remnants of *B-82*. Krail radioed the *Phoenix* from the *Hawkbill* the moment a secure channel could be established.

"Good to hear your voice again, Scott," Garner said, taking the call. He relayed the account of what had happened aboard the helicopter and the likely location of the wreckage. Krail confirmed they had located the downed Sikorsky that morning and shared Garner's despondency about the lost pilots.

"Happens to the best of us," Krail said. "Maybe a few more, unless we can put the lid on this box once and for all. What's the status of the containment?"

The storm front and the severe wave disturbance had diffused the head of the slick, but in the hours that followed, the surface currents continued pulling the radioactive debris east through Fury and Hecla Strait. The ice-wrangling ships regrouped and began moving the *Ulva*-laden chunks through the slick once again. Meanwhile, the icebreakers holding the containment booms waited for further instructions thirty miles to the east, where the *Villager* was now dredging in Foxe Basin. Beyond the most optimistic projections of even a day ago, Garner mused, the combined effort should still come together, but, responding to Krail's question, Garner said, "The *Villager* is still digging and the ice-breakers here are still practicing with positioning the booms on demand."

"That's what you get when you ask a herd of ele-phants to roll a marble around," Krail replied.

"Good analogy," Garner said. "At least they're rolling in the right spot." With a greater depth and more sediment than anywhere in Fury and Hecla Strait, the revised locations were looking even more suitable than the original ones. "So far your sediment profiles are right on the money. The *Villager* has moved a hell of a lot of mud in the past two days."

"That's us: Global Moving and Storage," Krail quipped.

"Don't get cocky," Garner warned. "So far I'd say you're better at moving than storage."

"Ouch—sometimes you know how to hurt a guy, buddy."

Krail confirmed that the *Hawkbill*'s gamma spec-trometers were showing null values all along the Devil's Finger and the corridor leading back to the pit below *B-82*. For all their calamitous aftermath, the detona-tions in the canyon did exactly what they were intended to do: cut off the leak of radioactive waste at its source. Although the water bombers ultimately did not have enough fuel to provide assistance, the fire aboard the oil rig was contained with virtually no spillage from the reservoir in the GBS.

"What about this Plasroc?" Krail asked. "Still think it'll do the job?"

"We don't know yet," Garner admitted. "MacAdam is concerned that the water may be too cold for the compound to gel properly."

"Too cold? In the Arctic? I wish that'd occurred to someone sooner," Krail said sarcastically. "What can we do about it?"

"Cross our fingers and hope he's wrong. The Plasroc berg should be forming by this time tomorrow. Once the polymer is activated, it'll be on its way to the bottom."

"What do you need from us in the meantime?"

"More sounding of the dredge site," Garner suggested. "I want to be absolutely positive the hole we dig is big enough to contain the Plasroc boulder."

"You've got it," Krail added. "Once that's confirmed I guess we'll need to bring in more fireworks to bury the whole shebang."

Garner could almost hear the grin on his friend's face with the word *fireworks*. In Garner's fatigued state, Krail's enduring exuberance for blowing things up seemed less disconcerting than amusing. "*Tomorrow*, Scott," Garner said with a chuckle. "Not until tomorrow."

"You gonna get some rest until then?" Krail asked. "You sound beat."

"Tomorrow," Garner repeated. "Then we can all get some sleep. *Phoenix* out."

In the *Phoenix*'s ward room, the PATRIC plotter continued to receive and translate the latest satellite data. It efficiently rendered an updated, color-enhanced image of the sea surface between Thebes Deep and the eastern terminus of Fury and Hecla Strait. The abbreviated tail of the slick, the last vestiges of radiation leaked from the seafloor, appeared on the surface nearly ten miles away from the canyon before being carried east by the current, through the strait to where the containment pen had been rebuilt. The angry red swath of computer-generated pixels representing the slick showed it was now just twenty miles long and half a mile wide, and even these dimensions would decrease as the icebreakers converged on it. Meanwhile, the *Hawkbill*'s instruments confirmed little if any radioactive debris in the slick's wake. One of the team's two headaches indeed had been solved; the rest was up to Garner and MacAdam.

Garner was still studying the plotter, nearly forgotten since the death of Junko and her expertise. Zubov joined him. "The speed and direction of the slick is almost an exact match with the surface currents," Zubov noted, studying the latest oceanographic data. "No surprise there—the currents have always been our best indication of where the radioactive debris will go."

"The plot shows us where the contamination is," Garner agreed, "but not how the plankton are reacting to it. We need to take a closer look." Anticipating the resistance from his friend, he held up his hand. "Better to find out now than later, right? We'll be busy enough when the *Villager* finishes digging."

"Medusa's still cooked," Zubov pointed out, trying to avoid the inevitable request.

"Not the cameras and the bottle samplers. We've got all the radiation data we can handle now. What we need now is a few plain ol' plankton samples, and Medusa's still the best way to get them."

"I was hoping you wouldn't say that," Zubov said. "That means we'll have to take the ice nets off the A-frame. Again."

"It's only a mile or two of rigging." Garner grinned. "And two thousand feet of net. You make it sound like such a chore."

They suited up and returned outside. As Zubov directed the crew on the A-frame, Garner prepared Medusa for what might well be her final use. He removed the remnants of the gamma spectrometer harnesses, then cocked and calibrated the bottle samplers to collect surface water from the slick. Last, he adjusted the cameras and reprogrammed the sampler's computerized species identification subroutine to look specifically for cells matching the appearance of *Ulva morina*. Once the *Phoenix* released its tether to the other two vessels, Medusa was let out from the A-frame and towed slowly through the slick behind the ship. Minutes later, the device began to dutifully return a stream of data to the computers in the *Phoenix*'s lab. Within an hour, Medusa's computers had returned an analysis that would have taken a team of technicians weeks to derive in the laboratory.

The preliminary results were encouraging. According to the data, *Ulva* was present in the surface waters of the slick in concentrations at least 40 percent higher than the minimum amount Roland Alvarez had recommended. A bioassay showed that the algae had already begun taking up impressive amounts of the contaminated *Thio-uni*, then in turn adhering themselves to the pieces of floating ice. Assuming that the present rate of absorption continued, nearly the entire slick would be absorbed by the time the *Phoenix, North Sea,* and *Vagabond* pulled the last of the captured ice into the containment area. The rest would drift into the algae sponge as the surface currents carried the slick through the area.

Hours later, the *Villager* completed dredging the massive well to contain the solidified Plasroc. The exact position and dimensions of the excavation were relayed to the icebreakers and the *Hawkbill,* then the containment booms were slowly cinched together with agonizing slowness to avoid losing any portion of the trapped surface water. As the final capture of the leak progressed, Garner assigned team after team of technicians to record surface radiation levels upstream, downstream, and within the containment booms. These data were loaded back into the PATRIC plotter and compared to the computer-generated images provided by the satellite. Eventually the plotter confirmed what those who had been watching the slick had long hoped for: virtually all of the radioactive material in solution had been taken up by the *Ulva* and trapped in an area of less than four square miles. While the values inside the pen reached nearly fifteen gray—twenty thousand times the natural background level—readings in the surrounding water were nearly indistinguishable from normal conditions.

"I'll be damned," Garner muttered. "It's working."

For all the fussing that David MacAdam had made over the care and condition of his Plasroc materials, he was even more disconcerted by the notion of being at sea, in the Arctic, after a ten-thousand-mile journey by assorted military transports. As the chemist stood on the *Phoenix* in his oversized exposure suit, borrowed boots, and several mismatched sweaters, Garner couldn't recall the last time he had seen someone so distanced from his natural element—except perhaps when Victor stood in the very same spot.

"You've seen the size of the containment area," Garner said. "Do you have enough resin, or will we need to draw the booms in tighter?" They both knew this was possible only to a certain extent—if too much pressure was placed on the booms, there was the increased risk of bursting the structure, or forcing the water contained within it to slosh over the top, back into the general circulation.

"I think the surface area is fine," MacAdam replied.

"But I'm still concerned about the water temperature inside the pen. Though the temperature anomaly is helping, the net result is much lower than I'd anticipated or calculated." This, Garner noted, silently annoyed, despite the extensive temperature, salinity, and wind data Garner had sent to Adelaide in advance of MacAdam's trip.

Garner reviewed MacAdam's method, his tired brain struggling to step through the complex equations scratched out in MacAdam's nearly unintelligible script.

"Supercooling," Garner finally said. "The smaller the ice pieces get, the greater their surface area. The more surface area, the more cooling you get between the pieces. That's what's driving down the mean temperature." To any athlete who had packed crushed ice on an injury only to receive a surprising introduction to frostbite, the phenomenon of supercooling was painfully familiar.

"Of course," MacAdam said, checking Garner's calculation, then cursing his own oversight. "What can we do about it at this point?"

"Can we get the *Villager* to pump some hot water into the boom area?" Garner asked Zubov.

" 'Hot' water we've got; *heated* water is another story. I'll check with the *Villager*."

"The hotter the better," MacAdam cautioned. "If we use less heat and dilute the compound too much, we'll have a problem getting it to harden."

Zubov gave Garner a frustrated look, then glared at MacAdam. " 'Not too cold and not too hot. Not too dense and not too dilute.' How useful is this 'compound' in the field anyway? We're not baking a fucking Bundt cake out there—"

Garner interrupted before Zubov could finish his tirade. "Anything else, David?"

"Nothing I can think of," replied MacAdam, reluctant to say anything else that might irritate Zubov.

"Then you better get back to the *Villager* and get started," Garner said.

"*Now?*" MacAdam asked, suddenly panicked at being cast center stage. "That's it? We're ready?"

"We're ready," Garner assured him. "Now's your chance."

The difficulty of deploying the Plasroc's base chemical caught the *Villager*'s crew off guard initially; the viscosity of the liquid behaved differently in the ship's hoses than either water, oil, or scrubbing solution. The pumps, too, had to work much harder than expected to maintain their controlled flow. Far too soon after beginning, the *Villager*'s captain began cursing and complaining about possible overheating of his equipment. Only after several attempts and several of MacAdam's conniptions did the solution begin to flow evenly, spraying over the containment area in a fine aerosol. The droplets suspended in the cold air caught the light from the surrounding vessels in a glittering mist as they settled over the remnants of the *Ulva*-laden ice.

On the ocean's surface, the base chemical of the Plasroc resembled thin honey, then began to congeal into thin, disk-shaped formations. The disks, in turn, merged into one another to form a single, wobbly coating that looked exactly like Jell-O.

Moving slowly along the periphery of the enclosure, the *Villager* continued to coat the slick with the liquid polymer. MacAdam dashed from one pump to the next, hovering around the nozzle crews and offering suggestions on the disbursement of the spray. The crew might have listened to MacAdam's advisement about the Plasroc solution, but clearly no one was going to tell them how to work the nozzles, much less how to maneuver around the floating booms. As each section along the perimeter of the pen was sprayed with

Plasroc, the *Des Groseilliers* and the *Sovietsky Soyuz* slowly adjusted their position to retract the slack in the booms and compress the area contained inside. Eventually the gelatinous material around the edge of the containment area was drawn in upon itself, filling the middle expanse as well.

From his position on the *Phoenix,* Garner could see MacAdam step down almost to the edge of the containment booms and look at an instrument dangling into the slick: a thermometer. After much discussion, MacAdam and the captain of the *Villager* had decided not to risk diluting the slick any further with heated water, even if it meant increasing the overall temperature of the slick—the risk of diluting the Plasroc to potentially brittle concentrations was too great.

"How does it look, David?" Garner asked.

MacAdam fumbled with the radio and eventually answered. "Still too cold, I think."

"You *think*?" Garner pressed, becoming annoyed at the inventor's lack of decisiveness. "Yes or no, David?"

MacAdam seemed to weight the question with exceptional consideration. "No," he said nervously. "No, it's fine. Carry on."

They had to work quickly. The sealing resin had to be applied before the base chemical began to sink into the slick. Within minutes they would know if MacAdam's formula was adapted to the conditions; the slightest miscalculation and the plastic rock would remain in its liquid form, unable to bond the radioactive debris.

For a second time, the *Villager*'s crew grappled with the Plasroc's unusual behavior within the ship's pump systems. The first attempt to spray the resin through the ship's water cannons failed. The second attempt failed as well. Several more minutes passed as MacAdam bickered with the pump crew.

On the *Phoenix,* Zubov joined Garner at the rail to

watch the apparent confusion. "Come on, come on," Zubov breathed, clenching his broad jaw. "Better *now* than *later,* boys." His gaze dropped to the surface of the slick. Then finally, "Ah goddammit. I'm going over there." Garner called a launch from the *North Sea* and watched as Zubov was ferried around the containment area to the side of the *Villager*.

Within minutes, Zubov's assistance resulted in one of the *Villager*'s water cannons opening up with a strong flow of resin. As the second chemical joined the first on the surface, it began to form a slurry around the algae and bacteria contained between the booms.

"Looking great, fellas," Garner radioed to the *Villager*.

"Not so fast," came Zubov's reply. "David's back to thinking the temperature inside the booms is still too low."

Garner cursed to himself, then replied to the *Villager*. "Please ask him what, *exactly,* we need to do before we use up all the resin." Across the water, Garner could see Zubov conferring with MacAdam, who took another close look at the Plasroc's performance within the containment area.

"Talk to me, Serg," Garner pressed. "What do we need?"

"More heat," came Zubov's reply. "A *lot* more heat. Fast."

Despite her exhaustion, the painkillers, and the sedatives, Carol couldn't relax enough to sleep. Her leg ached savagely—from the knee down it was purpled from the trauma in a combination of bruising, hemorrhaging, and frostbite. Susan had put a temporary cast on her leg after suturing the tear where the broken tibia had pushed through, but resetting the bone would have to await proper attention. Ironically, as they floated alongside all this radiation, the one thing the *Phoenix* was still not equipped for was taking X rays. As Carol sat up in bed, Susan entered the infirmary. "Where do you think *you're* going?" she challenged her boss.

"I need to see what's happening out there," Carol said, fumbling for the crude but functional crutches Byrnes's men had fashioned for her from plastic tubing and packing foam. "Even if I have to watch it through the windows."

"*Rest,*" Susan urged her. "It's going fine. Brock says the *Ulva* is taking up more than 95 percent of the radiation."

"That's great!" Carol brightened.

"I guess," Susan said, chewing her lip. "But it isn't 100 percent, is it?"

"It'll never be 100," Carol replied. "But 95 is still incredible efficiency. Whatever we can't get will hopefully be diluted by the currents and the levels will fall lower still."

Susan was less enthusiastic. In every spare moment over the past two weeks, she had devoured Junko's field reports on the recommended maximum-exposure levels for various isotopes. Her personal conclusion was that there was no such thing as "safe" exposure. Whatever didn't kill you in this lifetime could very easily manifest itself in the genes of your children. There wasn't a soul on earth who was completely immune from the acute effects of radiation—the ailing Inuit had unwittingly become a harbinger of what might be in store for them all, unless someone started to listen. Junko seemed to know that. She had given her life to it.

Carol saw the fear and disappointment in Susan's face. "What is it?"

"I want to go home," Susan said. "I just want to go *home.*"

"We're almost there. Keep it together. We walking

wounded still need your strength. Come on, help me up to the bridge."

Susan helped Carol up the narrow steps, where Carol plopped herself down in the captain's chair within earshot of the radio communications. Susan helped her prop her leg up, then found her a pair of binoculars through which to watch the final stages of the operation.

Carol quickly located MacAdam and Zubov amidships on the *Villager,* nestled between two of the vessel's water cannons. Listening in, she could hear Zubov saying something about needing a lot more heat and Garner quizzing MacAdam for options.

A split second later, an explosion erupted from the deck of the *Villager.*

28

For those aboard the *Villager,* the explosion came as a complete surprise. Overworked and overheated, then left unattended while Zubov and MacAdam debated what to do, one of the vessel's auxiliary pumps had silently developed an intense amount of back-pressure in one of the tanks containing the Plasroc resin. As the system failed, a thunderous bang shook the sturdy vessel to its keel.

"What the hell?" Zubov had just begun to turn around when the second explosion hit. Instinctively, he dove forward to protect MacAdam, forcing both of them to the deck and dropping the radio.

It was already too late to warn the others. The recoil effect from the released pressure slammed into the second resin tank, tearing open the two-inch steel as easily as an aluminum can. The tank began to bleed the remaining resin onto the deck.

Watching from the *Phoenix,* Garner could not believe his eyes. Zubov wasn't answering the radio and the only thing nearby was Victor's *komatik*. Garner rifled through the sled, drawing out the flare gun from the hovercraft and its two remaining flares—one of these he fired into the night sky on the unlikely chance anyone in the vicinity had not heard the explosion on the *Villager*. Then a glint of metal caught Garner's eye—the worn metal blade of Victor's flaying knife. Taking the knife and climbing up on the fantail, Garner wrapped himself in the tension line from the ice seine apparatus and sawed at it frantically with the knife. As the nylon line parted, the tension in the rigging system hoisted Garner off the deck, rocketing him fifteen feet in the air. The weight of the quarter-mile seine sagged against its pulleys, and the cables on either end of the net were wrenched together. As Garner held tight, the line suspending him was yanked through its pulleys on the *North Sea*. He lunged forward to grab one of the cables as it shot across the water, slinging him nearly a hundred yards out over the radioactive slick. As his momentum carried him past the superstructure of the *Villager,* Garner released the cable and fell to the deck next to David MacAdam.

Zubov and the *Villager*'s crew were frantically trying to regain control of the pump system and only the professor, stunned but visibly impressed, noticed Garner's arrival at all.

Forgotten in the confusion, the resin continued to pour out of the fractured tank.

"Shut off the flow!" Garner yelled to the *Villager*'s crew chief. Now it was time for Zubov and the ship's captain to be surprised at his friend's arrival.

The chief shook his head. "We can't! The entire tank is busted."

"Then shunt it to another pump! We have to get every drop we can over the booms and into the slick."

This could be done. The first nozzle was closed, the gate between the two resin tanks was opened, and resin began flowing though a second nozzle. Though under far less pressure, the nozzle crew was still able to angle the diffuse spray high out over the containment pen. Two additional nozzles were switched over to the tank containing the Plasroc resin and opened full on the jellied surface of the slick. The resin was a darker, less syrupy fluid, and it poured easily over the surface of the large amber pool of foundation, filling in each wrinkle and crack on its surface. As the two chemicals bonded together, the resin was drawn across the base polymer by capillary action, hungrily spreading itself over the entire mass in a uniform layer.

"No!" MacAdam suddenly broke his paralysis. "You're wasting the supply! Unless we can heat up the water, the two chemicals won't bond." The chemist didn't comprehend that the flow was utterly out of control; Zubov and the others were fighting only to determine the least disastrous direction.

They had no time to lose. Even at the reduced rate of flow, the remaining resin would be exhausted within minutes. Garner turned back to the crew chief.

"Do you have fuel in any of these tanks?"

The chief nodded, indicating both the *Villager*'s main fuel supply as well as the scrub tanks from the vessel's oil rig work.

"How fast can you get it connected to another nozzle?" Garner demanded.

"Dunno. But why would you want to—?" the chief began.

"How fast?"

Zubov suddenly realized what Garner was up to. He passed off his line position and worked with the chief to rig the oil jet as quickly as possible. The resin continued to bleed into the containment pen. Each passing second could be one second too long.

"Ready!" Zubov finally shouted. On Garner's order, the oil jet was opened and directed out over the Plasroc.

"What are you doing?" MacAdam shouted, dancing quickly between Zubov and Garner. "Oil is a hydrocarbon! You can't just modify the composition of the liquid Plasroc like that."

Realizing what the inventor's comment implied—chemical destruction of the Plasroc—Garner whirled around and stared at MacAdam. "Why? What will it do?" he shouted, nearly shaking the smaller man.

It was MacAdam's turn to pause. "Actually, I don't know. It just *seems*—"

"Fifteen seconds of flow left!" Zubov shouted over the pump.

With that, Garner turned, drew the flare gun, and fired the last flare into the surface of the fuel slick. Striking the pool of oil, the heat of the flare accelerated into a bluish flame that raced across the surface of the Plasroc. There wasn't enough oil to explode, but there was an ample supply to ignite the slick's surface. Even above the cacophony on the deck of the *Villager,* they could hear the Plasroc sizzling inside the smoldering flame.

"I knew it!" MacAdam sputtered. "The oil was too much—"

Garner silenced MacAdam, then motioned for the crew of the *Villager* to stop full. With the Plasroc flow exhausted, they shut down the pumps. Zubov joined them at the gunwale and they paused, listening.

Though the oil had quickly exhausted itself and covered only a fraction of the entire slick, the dramatic catalyst had been enough to start a chain reaction within the mass of Plasroc. The compound continued to hiss and groan for a moment as it began to change from a liquid to a solid. A chain reaction had been catalyzed by the heat of the oil fire and the entire mass began to harden.

Garner grinned at MacAdam as they both realized what had happened. "Too much? Or too little?"

"Just right, I think," MacAdam said.

"Thank you very fucking much, Goldilocks." Zubov sagged against the hose, breathing hard.

Moments later, the hardened Plasroc began to sink. The Plasroc vanished beneath the surface, a one-hundred-ton man-made boulder sinking directly to the bottom fifty meters below. By the time the material struck the crater dredged in the sediment, the mass of sealed and hardened polymer was virtually indistinguishable from bedrock in appearance or durability.

"Looks like we did it, David," Garner said to MacAdam, finding the obvious allusion too hard to resist. "Another Goliath has been slain."

MacAdam had waited too many years for a proven application of his invention to hide his emotions. The frustration, his long hours in the barn, the enormous debt, they now seemed . . . well, they still amounted to a hill of bitterness, but the hill suddenly seemed a lot smaller.

Krail and his team arrived with the *Hawkbill* early the following day. Krail briefly discussed with Garner and the captain of the *Villager* where the sediment had been redistributed and how the new submarine mountain might best be coaxed into an avalanche, backfilling the crater now containing the Plasroc. They opted for a series of programmable GF-45 mines, the most modern weapons in the *Hawkbill's* reduced but nonetheless formidable array. Paradoxically, the GF-45s had drawn their design inspiration from the stunningly advanced weapons salvaged from the Russian *Scorpion*. However indirectly, the advanced technology of the Soviet submarine had opened the Pandora's box at the bottom of Thebes Deep, and now the descendant of that technology would help to forever entomb that menace.

After the *Hawkbill's* sonar operators confirmed the

position of the Plasroc inside the surrounding mounds of trenched sediment, Krail supervised the placement of the mines. The weapons were detonated one at a time, bringing avalanches of sediment down into the well in stages. Gradually the depressions left around the Plasroc were filled in and the dense clay formed a natural sarcophagus over the waste.

After the congratulations and back-slapping by all aboard the *Phoenix* subsided, Garner and Zubov were struck with the magnitude of what they had just accomplished. Worse was the ominous thought: *Was it really enough? Would it ever be?*

"MacAdam said it would take ten thousand years for an isotope to find its way out of the Plasroc," Garner said.

"And probably another ten thousand years to percolate up through that amount of clay," Zubov added. Then a wide smile spread across his face and he poked his friend in the chest. "Hey, by that time, you might even have your dissertation turned in."

"That's what I like about you, Serg," Garner said. "You're an optimist."

The *Des Groseilliers* was unanimously selected as the vessel to host the operation's victory party—it was the largest ship and, as a Canadian vessel, was the only one legally allowed to carry alcohol. The *Vagabond*, *Villager*, and *Sovietsky Soyuz* opted to leave the site as soon as the all-clear was given, but the remaining crews willingly joined the boisterous festivities.

MacAdam celebrated the success of his invention as though it was the first, and last, victory of his life. He led the conversation and laughter, generously accepting kudos from anyone who crossed his path. He had just realized the reward for ten years of independent research and development. It might even make things up with Anne. "Who knows?" he jabbered to Krail. "Maybe the news of this will be just the publicity I need to bring Plasroc to full-scale production."

Krail seemed to find the remark pleasantly quaint. "I'm afraid there won't be any 'news' of what went on up here," he said. "Not in our lifetime, anyway. It's my job to ensure this incident is kept confidential in the interest of national security."

The grin on MacAdam's face froze, his glass paused halfway to his lips. "Er, I guess I hadn't thought of that," he said.

"Sorry, David. I meant to discuss that with you."

MacAdam took a drink, thought another moment, and shrugged it off. Sure, the security concern made sense, but the military wasn't above funding technology considered confidential. In fact, entire industries survived on it. "Well, at least I'll be able to recover my expenses," he said hopefully.

"We've covered your travel," Krail agreed. "Both ways."

"No, I mean for materials," MacAdam argued. "Consultation. The rip-up of my laboratory, and the Plasroc itself of course."

Krail slung his arm around MacAdam and steered him away from the rest of the revelers. "Sorry again. I meant to discuss that with you too . . ."

The following morning, the stragglers gathered together on the ice floe where the remaining vessels had moored for the night. The latest dosimeter readings showed minimal to negligible radiation levels in the area and the group gratefully walked around without the need for shielded protection. All of them would have to undergo a thorough medical examination the moment they returned home, but for now it felt wonderful simply to breathe. They all owed Junko Kokura their very survival. The nets, cables, and ropes they had used would have to be decommissioned and properly disposed of, but the overall effect of contamination seemed to be negligible. Most of the ships involved in the operation would likely be cleared for duty after a brief dry-docking and chemical scrubbing.

The same could not be said for the *Phoenix* itself. Nearly every single piece of deck equipment was hung with a red tag, indicating the highest levels of measured contamination.

"It looks like a Christmas tree," Carol said, looking wistfully at her investment. "The world's most toxic and expensive Christmas tree." Most of what now lay before them would have to be taken to shore and cut into scrap metal for proper disposal. In some places, the radiation had come within millimeters of leaching through the hull.

"There's one thing I don't understand," Zubov said. "*Scorpion* went down in '85, right? Her reactors weren't the source of the radiation, and neither was the earthquake or explosion that sunk her—if it was, someone would have noticed the leak in the storage well a long time before this. Why now?"

"The pit might not have started leaking then, but as best as we can determine, the disturbance *Scorpion* created was what first cracked it open," Krail said. "That's when the fissure started but it didn't extend through to the seafloor."

"It was likely a chimney fissure that grew laterally over a period of years," Garner speculated. "The crack eventually found its way into the Devil's Finger, more than five miles away from the original waste cribs. The thin crust of the basin floor that helped the explosives do their job so well is what allowed the seep of radionuclides in the first place."

"It had help too," Krail added. "According to the

USGS boys, there was some seafloor shaking last summer that might have finally opened the fissure. That means a slow leak increasing over about eight or nine months, tops. Charon's crew took regular measurements, of course, but the leak was evidently too small to detect."

"Or maybe he knew about it and hoped the leak would ultimately lead to *B-82* being shut down," Garner said. "That's the only reason I can think of for the sabotage."

"You could be right," Krail agreed. "Either way, his own masterwork took care of it. I see no reason to consider rebuilding *B-82*."

Even as he dismissed the notion the others knew it wouldn't be found outside someone's strategic consideration.

Carol shivered. "Doesn't that mean there could be other cracks? Leaks no one has discovered yet?"

"Possibly, but unlikely. It took a hell of a jolt to crack open the pit the first time, and now the waste is buried under an additional hundred feet of rock."

"That's probably what they thought before *Scorpion* came along," Carol said dubiously.

"Yes," Krail agreed. "But billions of dollars in surveillance and two decades of careful monitoring proved them wrong. Add a motherload of C-4 to the argument now. There's no more environmental risk in Thebes Deep. *Scorpion* was a freak accident. Nothing should have breached the storage well the first time and we've just made sure it won't ever happen again."

"That sounds like propaganda lifted from Chernobyl," Zubov said.

"A different time, a different place." Krail shrugged. "Besides, they didn't have Medusa at Chernobyl. Without that fantastic contraption we never would have known where the hell to go."

"Medusa tells us where to go all the time, doesn't she, Serg?" Garner gave his friend a wink. "Maybe next spring, in the Southern Ocean?"

"I've been thinking about that too," Krail said. "The last few weeks have generated reams of data on ice movement, Arctic circulation, and polar geology, not to mention what Medusa managed to find out about the plankton response around here."

"And the proof-of-concept Roland Alvarez suggested for *Thio-uni*," Garner added. The amount of undistilled information the operation had collected was indeed amazing.

"There you go," Krail agreed. "That's got to be ten dissertations' worth of research, just waiting for someone to pull it all together. Unlike MacAdam, you're an American citizen and a decorated defender of the state—at least twice now, if my scoring's correct. I'm sure if you agreed to follow certain, ah, *restrictions* on public disclosure, we could arrange for you to get it all and write it up for publication any way you want."

"And you wouldn't even have to leave home to do it," Carol added. There was a perceptible hopefulness in her use of the word *home*.

The offer was tempting to Garner, but it meant scrapping all his efforts to date and following the convenience of data collected under decidedly uncontrolled conditions. "I'll have to think about that," he said. "This one was messy. This one cost all of us a lot and it might be better to forget than to analyze."

"Without you and Sergei things would have gotten a lot worse," Carol offered.

Krail agreed. "There's no other way to look at it, Brock. We saved countless more from a much worse fate." Krail scowled melodramatically, feigning a painful stiffness in his limbs. "Hard work for a desk jockey like me," he said to Garner. "We could sure use a guy like you full time. You sure you don't want to come back to naval intelligence?"

"Positive, Scott," Garner said. "And I hope you *don't* have a full-time need for this kind of thing or we're all in a lot of trouble." Krail knew exactly what Garner meant—the events of the past few weeks could only have further solidified Garner's decision to leave the intelligence community in the first place. "But I'll admit, the ideal of settling down has a new appeal to it." His arm still around Carol, Garner gave her another squeeze.

"Think about it," Krail persisted. "We won't be leaving the area for a few more days, at least—we're going back to *B-82* to oversee the cleanup. But let's talk again whenever you get to D.C., all right? Swap some war stories at the Old Ebb?"

"It's a date," Garner agreed.

"Meantime, keep that data in mind," Krail added. "Consider it a thank you from Uncle Sam."

Krail bade them all farewell and returned to the *Hawkbill.* Minutes later the submarine eased away and sank smoothly beneath the waters of Foxe Basin, headed back to Thebes Deep.

All around them, the remaining ships were alive with activity as their respective crews disassembled the containment area and bundled the nets, booms, and lines for proper disposal. The first of the support helicopters began to arrive from Cape Dorset to airlift the injured, the dead, and anyone who finally wanted to leave. Seeing Carol leaning on her primitive crutches, two of the search-and-rescue team members approached her with a stretcher, but she waved them off.

"The first to arrive and the last to leave," Carol said to Garner and Zubov. "I figure I might as well enjoy my last few hours of command."

"I always knew you were power-mad," Garner replied.

"You're only half right, sweetheart."

Janey appeared utterly indifferent to all the confusion around her. She ignored the passing personnel and equipment and lay in the middle of the ice floe, gnawing on a large steak someone had given her.

"At least someone has her priorities in order," Garner said with a grin.

"We'll have to get her checked as well," Carol added. "Her fur may have taken up a lot of radiation, and we don't know what else she's been eating."

Finished with her decadent meal, the dog stood and stretched. She responded to Carol's concern by letting out an immense, bored yawn and licking her lips.

"I think she'll be just fine," Garner said, giving the dog a pat. "She comes from pretty tough stock."

Garner's arm lingered around Carol's waist. Zubov gave his friends an appraising look. "You two make a good-looking couple," he observed. "Ever think about hooking up?"

Carol smiled. "Maybe."

"Once or twice." Garner smiled too.

Sadness crept back into Zubov's face. "There's something to be said for second chances, you know," he said softly, thoughtfully. "I'm starting to think that when you meet your soul mate in this world—whoever it is and whatever problems come along—it's worth holding on to them. Savor every moment you have together."

"We know," Carol said. "We know that now." She angled forward on her crutches and the three of them embraced for a long moment. "I think we knew it all along, my friends," she whispered.

The contact seemed to return the color to Zubov's face. He pulled away and zipped up his parka against the chill. "Time to get back to work," he said, jerking a thumb toward the remains of the cleanup operation. "Maybe I'll consider it therapy—there's about a million tons of iron out there that has to be sorted into cooked and uncooked piles."

"Ugh," Carol groaned. "Don't remind me. The loss of the *Phoenix* alone may make the Nolan Group ask for my resignation—not to mention the cost of this little unplanned excursion."

"Relax," Zubov said. "There are costs and then there are *costs*. The financial costs can wait. You two hang out here for a little while. Get caught up on things, you know?" Then he turned and trudged across the ice toward the *North Sea,* leaving Garner and Carol alone with the dog.

As they made their way back to the ship, Garner was haunted by Krail's parting words: Scorpion *was a freak accident. Nothing should have breached the storage well the first time and we've just made sure it won't ever happen again.*

Most of all, Garner wanted to believe his friend was right.

"Were you serious about settling down?" Carol asked him. Janey sat back and angled her snow-white face up at him, apparently also awaiting his response.

"Were *you*?" Garner asked Carol.

"As I recall, I was always serious regarding you, Mr. Garner."

"Yes, you were," he admitted.

"So the question is"—she reached up and kissed him, softly but firmly—"are you ready to make a family?"

"Yes, I am."

"Are you sure? Even with a one-legged woman and a mildly radioactive dog?"

"Unquestionably." He kissed her again, a deep, lingering embrace that removed any doubt. "In fact, I wouldn't want it any other way."

EPILOGUE

It wasn't a Jovian moon, not exactly, but for the time being it would do nicely.

Becky Danielson pulled back her long, fine hair and studied the readouts scrolling across the monitors in front of her. Even after nearly ten straight hours, her pale green eyes still intently tracked the information being produced by the REMUS computers. As a geophysicist and engineer for the U.S. Geological Survey, Becky had long ago learned to work on a different time clock, yet even on a calendar of billions of years, the most mundane of daily reports and status checks still received her undivided attention.

Growing up in the Colorado Rockies, she lived for and amid superlative amounts of snow. Though she was only thirty-four, Becky had now spent nearly a third of her life studying ice. While still an undergraduate student, she toured the Arctic and then the Antarctic; the first time she had visited the Weddell Sea and gone scuba diving inside a floating glacier, she knew she had found her calling. After completing a double major in geology and electrical engineering, she had done her dissertation at M.I.T. on the geophysical similarities between submerged ice formations on Antarctica and the frozen landscapes of Jupiter's moons, particularly Europa. It wasn't surprising, then, that she should be asked to be one of the lead investigators for the Jet Propulsion Lab's REMUS—Remote Environmental Monitoring Units—prototype designed for use in Antarctica as a stepping-stone in the search for life on the outer planets. Water was essential for life and the Antarctic ice cap contained 70 percent of the earth's fresh water.

REMUS was among the latest descendants of remotely operated vehicles, or ROVs, enjoying a renaissance in earth and space research. For years, police and fire departments had been using camera-carrying robots to combat everything from urban terrorism to chemical spills and the sarcophagus at Chernobyl. Mining companies sent reconnaissance samplers into rock crevasses far deeper and tighter than humans could tolerate. The lineage of ocean ROVs had begun with deep-sea search-and-rescue missions for downed submarines and their weapons where time and hazards precluded sending human crews on the sometimes hours-long passage to the bottom. In the 1980s, explorers like Robert Ballard introduced ROV technology to the general public with glamorous expeditions to find the *Titanic* and other noteworthy wrecks. Among researchers, devices like Brock Garner's "Medusa sphere" demonstrated that not only could ROVs go where no one had gone before, but they could go there cheaper, longer, safer, and take better notes. Such forward-thinking scientists called this kind of travel through hostile or unreachable habitats "telepresence." Now, in the barren reaches of Antarctica, telepresence was preparing to go interplanetary.

Becky's latest robot was nicknamed the Bub, a fifty-pound, three-cubic-foot probe designed to sample the icy surface of Europa, Jupiter's second-closest moon and the most likely prospect for other life in the solar system. The latest $150 million prototype included a small nuclear power plant (Jupiter is too far from the sun to permit significant power generation by solar cells) housed in a small, derricklike device that was unfolded on the frozen surface. From there, a fiber-optic umbilical spooled down to the "cryobot"—the main unit—which could tunnel nearly five miles straight down through the ice pack, melting any frozen obstructions to its progress using an extremely high-temperature plasma heater. Entering the liquid cells within the ice, the Bub then dispatched its own satellite, a "hydrobot," to sample the water and analyze its chemical and biological properties. The main problem with the latest design was that, while the device could tunnel marvelously, the rapidly boiled meltwater often cooked the microbes the probe was seeking to collect and made temperature measurements unreliable.

The eventual, mission-approved REMUS would have to be small enough to be packed into the payload bay of a mother probe, strong enough to burrow through miles of solid ice, and sensitive enough to report on the microorganisms it might find at the end of its truly remarkable journey. It also needed to work within the temperature extremes of the Jovian system, which ranged from minus 300 degrees Fahrenheit on the surface of the farthest moons to 54,000 degrees Fahrenheit at the core of Jupiter itself. Working remotely over a distance from earth more than three times that of the Mars Pathfinder, controlling the REMUS in real time would not be possible, so the device would have to operate almost independently of its human controllers—requirements not unlike the administrative protocols in Antarctica, as Becky had come to discover.

Winter is not a desirable time to live in Antarctica. Darkness and wind are constant. The temperature typically ranges between minus twenty and minus 120 degrees Fahrenheit. Between April and September, even the dedicated research population on the continent diminishes to about two dozen from a summertime maximum of about twenty-five hundred. The bite of the weather keeps research ambitions modest, so the potential for large-scale foul-ups is diminished. Survival and pacing are the mantras to follow and work plods along with studious clarity.

Becky *liked* the isolation of Antarctica. In places where most humans would never go, she thrived. In places where humans could never go, her REMUS kicked ass. Becky's current proving ground was Lake Amery, a landlocked water deposit discovered beneath two miles of polar ice. In typical geological underestimation, "water deposit" hardly did the formation justice; with a surface area of 7,400 square miles, Lake Amery was only slightly smaller than Lake Ontario. It was estimated that the water in Lake Amery was between five hundred thousand and one million years old; the water in its basin had not touched the atmosphere in all of human history.

For most of the previous month the Bub had been swimming on the end of its tether, registering the chemical composition of the water and collecting biological samples for laboratory analysis. Twice each day, the hydrobot returned from its journey to inner space and delivered its real treasure: one-hundred-milliliter aliquots of ice containing a dizzying menagerie of microscopic life never before seen. Life from the center of the earth. Most surprising to the geologist and engineer in Becky, she now found her time looking at microbes to be the most rewarding aspect of the entire project.

Jonas, Becky's husband and her senior technician, was in charge of processing the samples. He carefully removed each sample from the hydrobot, decanted it onto a set of microscope slides, then set to work staining and identifying the organic material it contained. Lately it seemed as though the list of previously undescribed organisms siphoned by the Bub was increasing with every trial. Most "new" species they found were only in one or two samples, and then only in trace amounts. The specimens were tagged and preserved or kept frozen for later identification by those more expert and passionate about such things. It was Jonas who first made the discovery—in the hours after midnight and long after everyone else had gone to bed, as was usually the case for the best discoveries. His last aliquot for the night contained a culture material that stained like a bacterium but looked unlike anything he had ever seen. The appearance of the cells was unremarkable, but their abundance could not be ignored. Jonas prepared a dozen slides, each amply coated by the same homogenous culture. He eventually retired to his cot at 4:00 A.M., leaving one of the slides under the fluorescent microscope along with a Post-it note for Becky, asking, semi-rhetorically, *What's this?* Knowing his wife's sardonic sense of humor, he half expected her to replace it with a note of her own, answering, *It's a fluorescent microscope, silly.*

Later that morning, Becky examined the mysterious culture while the coffeemaker percolated through its first pot of the day. Inclement weather had them shedbound for most of the day, so as Jonas slept late, she tried to identify the organism using one of the few but comprehensive reference materials she had on hand. When that proved fruitless, she sent out a dozen e-mails to colleagues from New Zealand to Denmark, briefly describing the find. Those messages were duly forwarded to a dozen more phycologists and microbiologists around the world, several of whom asked her to send the digitized photos of the specimens. Becky responded with a half-dozen high-resolution images of the cells from the microscope's stage camera.

A week later, a phycologist by the name of Roland Alvarez at Dalhousie University sent her a reply, asking if sending him a culture was an option. Alternatively, could Becky send any more pictures? She did.

Two days later, Alvarez responded again, undaunted and with uncharacteristic bravado for a botanist working without a specimen. The species was most likely *Thiobacillus univerra ferrooxidans* or *"Thio-uni,"* a bacterium only known to exist in certain extreme habitats. In a lengthy e-mail, Alvarez prattled on about the marvels of this organism, written up by a student of his and recently discovered again in the Arctic Circle.

Alvarez also seemed concerned about exactly *where* the samples were collected, mentioning somewhat cryptically that it could be "a matter of some significance," though he would not elaborate. He again asked for a sample of the organism, which Becky reiterated she would address as soon as possible. That would be spring, when the weather finally released its grip on mundane human activities like delivering packages.

Until then, survival superseded everything, even scientific curiosity. First Becky and Jonas had to repair one of the radio transmitters and a section of the snow shed that had inconveniently collapsed during the previous night's gale. Then Becky's professional interest would lead her to locate the source of such isotopes, which were confounding the Bub's servo motors and, at the moment, seemed more curious to her than any radiation-gulping organism. Only then would she have time to give Alvarez the information he needed about this *Thio-uni,* and by then it probably would be spring and Alvarez could see the specimens himself.

Biologists could be so impatient—they weren't used to experiments that ran over millions or billions of years, and most curatorial scientists like Alvarez had forgotten the day-to-day distractions of fieldwork, if they ever knew them at all. Still, Alvarez's enthusiasm for the find was enough to bring a wry smile to Becky's lips. Imagine getting so excited about a simple bacterium. And imagine the bacterium itself—an organism that lived beneath two miles of solid ice, subsisting on a diet of concentrated isotopes. And from its abundance in her samples, the little beast must have found a lot to feed on down there.

GLOSSARY

A-FRAME: A-shaped boom on the stern of a ship, from which the largest or heaviest instrumentation and sampling equipment is deployed using a winch.

ALARA: As low as reasonably achievable, in nuclear containment parlance.

ALGAE: Primitive marine and freshwater plants gaining nutrition through photosynthesis. Lacking a true root system or leaves, purists hesitate to call them "plants" at all. The singular form is alga.

ALPHA RADIATION: Relatively high-mass particles consisting of two protons and two neutrons emitted by heavier radioactive isotopes such as uranium.

ARCTIC DISTILLATION: A process by which pollutants put into the atmosphere at temperate or tropical latitudes condense upon contact with colder air and concentrate in the ice, snow, and water of the polar regions.

ASDS: Advanced SEAL Delivery System. General designation for the next-generation U.S. Navy submersibles designed to transport Naval Special Warfare personnel. Unlike previous "wet" SDVs (SEAL Delivery Vehicles), the ASDS keeps its occupants dry in a pressurized capsule.

BALAENOPTERA: Taxonomic genus of Odontoceti or baleen whales. *Balaenoptera musculus* is the species commonly known as the blue whale.

BASALT: Principal, relatively dense rock of the ocean basins.

BETA RADIATION: Low-mass (compared to alpha radiation) electrons or positrons emitted from isotopes that have too many neutrons or protons, respectively.

BIOACCUMULATION: The increased concentration of a trace metal, pollutant, or toxin in higher organisms as a result of feeding on lower organisms tainted with the same agent. Via bioaccumulation, harmless or sublethal doses in lower organisms can collectively become damaging or fatal to consumers higher in the food chain.

CNIDARIAN (COELENTERATE): An organism of the invertebrate phylum Cnidaria, a group of about nine thousand species including jellyfish, corals, and anemones.

DES GROSEILLIERS: Icebreaker operated by Canada's Department of Fisheries and Oceans, known especially for its participation in the $18 million SHEBA (Surface Heat Budget of the Arctic Ocean) study, a modern oceanographic and meteorological analysis of the Arctic. Much like the *Fram,* the *Des Groseilliers* was frozen into the ice to monitor circulation in the Arctic Ocean.

DIAND: Department of Indian Affairs and Northern Development, an agency of the government of Canada.

DOM: Dissolved organic matter. Carbon-based material existing in the environment in solution, below the organism, tissue, or cellular level.

FAST ICE: Ice attached (held *fast*) to the shore.

FLOE: A formation of floating or drifting ice, usually flatter than an iceberg.

***FRAM*:** Norwegian research vessel of the late nineteenth century renowned for its exploration of both the Arctic and the Antarctic.

GAMMA RADIATION: High-energy electromagnetic radiation similar to X rays released by nearly all radionuclides. Gamma rays have no mass and no charge.

GBS: Gravity base structure, the lower, mainly submerged foundation of an oil rig.

GRAY: Unit of measurement quantifying absorbed dose or absolute radiation levels. The gray—equal to about 100 rad—has replaced the rad in general usage.

HALF-LIFE: The time it takes for half the number of atoms in a radionuclide sample to disintegrate. Containment requirements are estimated at five half-lives, until the radiation level drops to 5 percent or less of the original activity. Some examples:

Uranium 235	704,000,000 years
Iodine 129	17,000,000 years
Cesium 135	3,000,000 years
Plutonium 239	24,100 years
Cesium 137	30.17 years
Strontium 90	28.8 years
Iodine 131	8.05 days

HAWKBILL: U.S. Navy Sturgeon-class nuclear attack submarine, hull number 666. In recent years, the *Hawkbill* has been used part-time for civilian research in the Arctic, notably the SCICEX research sponsored by the National Science Foundation in conjunction with several research institutions.

JIM: Bulbous, pressurized, carbon-fiber suit that allows diving to depths of up to eighteen hundred feet or sixty atmospheres of pressure, far beyond the range of ordinary scuba. Named for its originator, Englishman Jim Jarrett.

MEDUSA: Semifictitious sampling device invented and developed by Brock Garner. Towed behind a ship, the spherical device simultaneously records data on water properties, pollutants, and organic content, including plankton abundance and species composition.

NERT: Nuclear emergency response team.

NOAA: National Oceanic and Atmospheric Administration.

NOL: Naval Ordnance Laboratory.

NORAD: North American Aerospace Defense Command.

NRC: Nuclear Regulatory Commission, an agent of the United States government.

NRO: National Reconnaissance Office.

NSA: National Security Agency.

NSF: National Science Foundation.

PATRIC: Semifictitious computer-based modeling software for hindcasting detected sources of environmental radiation and predicting their distribution.

PCB: Polychlorinated biphenyls, a group of organic compounds notorious for their deposition and accumulation in polar environments, as by arctic distillation.

PHYCOLOGY: The study of seaweeds and other aquatic plants.

PLANKTON: Generic term for microscopic plants and tiny animals floating or weakly swimming in the water column. Due to their small size, plankton are transported involuntarily by wind and current action.

PLASROC: Semifictitious polymer resin effective at bonding water-soluble toxic waste.

POLYMER: A chemical compound composed of a repeated number of heavy, complex molecules (e.g., proteins, cellulose, plastics).

PRIMACORD: Pliable, plastic-sheathed cord used to prime or initiate explosives during detonation. Depending on depth (pressure), force may be translated through the cord at up to five miles per second.

QABLUNAQ: Inuit word literally meaning "hairy eyebrows," used to refer to white men. (The *q* is pronounced as a *k*.)

RADIOMETER: Device for measuring radiation emissions (atomic disintegrations per unit time) in the environment, typically in Roentgens-per-hour (R/hr). Specialized kinds of radiometer include the dosimeter, gamma spectrometer, and Geiger counter.

RADIONUCLIDE (RADIOACTIVE NUCLIDE): Radioactive products of nuclear fission.

SAR: Search and rescue.

SEAL: Sea, Air, and Land. Acronym for the elite Special Warfare teams of the United States Navy.

SEA SPRITE: Semifictitious model of pressurized, single-passenger submersible used for undersea structural maintenance and inspection.

SIEVERT: A unit of radiation dose as absorbed by biological tissue (equivalent biological dose). The Sievert differs from the gray by including the damage imposed by alpha particles as well as gamma radiation. The Sievert—equal to about 100 rem—has replaced the rem in general usage.

SOLITON: A solitary wave, related to a tsunami, produced by a sudden influx of energy or displacement of the sea surface. Solitons may cross several miles no more than a few inches high, but amplify rapidly and violently when reaching shallower water.

SVERDRUP: Unit of fluid flow equal to one million cubic meters per second. Named for the Norwegian mariner and explorer Otto Sverdrup.

THIOBACILLUS FERROOXIDANS: Species of bacterium used to mine low-grade deposits of uranium. (*Thiobacillus univerra ferrooxidans*, or "*Thio-uni*," is a fictional construct.)

ULVA MORINA: Fictitious species of fast-growing, chlorophytic ice algae with an affinity for geothermally heated water.

WATER COLUMN: General term for the vertical depth of water between the surface and the bottom.

ACKNOWLEDGMENTS

At some point, every manuscript is like a slick of radioactive debris—an amorphous mixture of suspect and potentially deadly material in need of industrial waste management. *Meltdown* could not have been realized without the thoughtful and patient consideration of a number of friends and colleagues, each expert in their respective fields. The author wishes to thank for their advisement: the U.S. Navy UDT-SEAL Association, L Col. Keith Gathercole of the Canadian National Search and Rescue Secretariat (Ottawa, Ontario), Drs. Alan Lewis and Steve Calvert of the University of British Columbia (Vancouver, British Columbia), Dr. Frank Settle of Washington & Lee University (Lexington, Virginia), Dr. David Morrison of the Canadian Museum of Civilization (Hull, Quebec), Mr. Mark Madryga of the Environment Canada Pacific Weather Office (Vancouver, British Columbia), and certain anonymous acquaintances at the Old Ebbitt Grill (Washington, D.C.). Any errors made or liberties taken with the advice and thoughtful suggestions of these individuals are solely the fault of the author.

Special thanks are also due to my editor extraordinaire, Abby Zidle, for keeping me honest, and to superagent Jimmy Vines for keeping me employed. *Fram!*

ABOUT THE AUTHOR

As a researcher with a Ph.D. in biological oceanography and an advisor to several environmental agencies, JAMES POWLIK has walked many of the same footpaths as Brock Garner in the Arctic Circle, Iceland, and elsewhere. Dr. Powlik has been a consultant on science and education projects for government agencies including the EPA, NASA, the National Science Foundation, and the U.S. Department of Commerce. In addition to numerous articles and research texts, he is the author of the novel *Sea Change,* published by Delacorte Press. He lives in Arlington, Virginia.